Finesilver's Gold

A Jewish Adventure Like No Other

ന

Ruth Shalett Littman

Ruth S Littman

MICAH PUBLICATIONS, INC.

Printed in the United States of America.

Library of Congress Cataloging-in-Publication Data

Littman, Ruth, 1927-
  Finesilver's gold : a Jewish adventure like no other / Ruth Shalett Littman.
    p. cm.
  ISBN 978-0-916288-53-2 (pbk. : alk. paper)
  1. Finesilver, Jacob--Fiction. 2. Jews--Ukraine--Fiction. 3. Jews--Canada--Fiction. 4. Ukrainians--Canada--Fiction. 5. Immigrants--Canada--Fiction. 6. Frontier and pioneer life--Canada--Fiction. 7. Jews--Fiction. I. Title.
  PS3612.I883F54 2007
  813'.6--dc22
                                        2007024852

Micah Publications, Inc.
www.micahbooks.com

Inspired by my grandmother's memoirs,
and to Inuijak, Andrew Red Sky,
and Cannibal Sam, who saved Grandpa's life

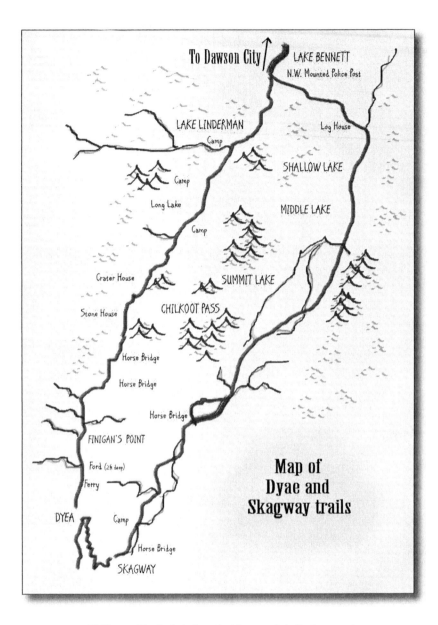

Chilkoot Trail (left-hand side was Malka's route)

"Take the oath again, Daylight," the same voice cried.

"I sure will. I first come over Chilcoot in '83. I went out over the Pass in a fall blizzard, with a rag of a shirt and a cup of raw flour. I got my grub-stake in Juneau that winter, and in the spring I went over the Pass once more. And once more the famine drew me out. Next spring I went in again, and I swore then that I'd never come out till I made my stake. Well, I ain't made it, and here I am. And I ain't going out now. I get the mail and I come right back. I won't stop the night at Dyea. I'll hit up Chilcoot soon as I change the dogs and get the mail and grub. And so I swear once more, by the mill-tails of hell and the head of John the Baptist, I'll never hit for the Outside till I make my pile. And I tell you all, here and now, it's got to be an almighty big pile."

—Jack London, *Burning Daylight* (1910)

PROLOGUE

⌒⊙⊙⌒

Prince of Wales, Alaska, February, 1896

ONLY MINUTES AFTER THE SIGHTING, THE INUIT WAS racing west on the frozen Bering Strait, shouting a stream of commands to his dog team, urging them to run faster, keep straight ahead, hurry, each crack of his whip like a pistol shot in the cold air.

The eager dogs lunged forward, howling and barking, happy to be working again in the high snow. When they reached sea ice, the sled's runners glided easily, frozen water always smoother than frozen land.

Inuijak had been peering through the gloomy arctic light only an hour earlier when his keen eyes had seen the mass, its dark outline barely visible. He smiled now, assuming, as he had then, that the irregular heap lying on the ice-bridge to Russia was either walrus or seal, and his mouth watered at the thought of freshly roasting meat.

Inuijak the Inuit was stocky and square-shouldered, his strong, muscular legs balancing like rooted trees on the back of the rocketing sled. Like his ancestors in this Arctic desolation, he was an expert hunter, patient at ice holes and skilled with the harpoon.

He was twenty years old and took excellent care of his

dogs, resting them often on long sled runs and adding fish oil to their meat. To his wife he was an ardent lover but he did not allow her physical intimacies with male visitors. He bargained shrewdly at the summer barters and sewed fine furskin boots during the long dark months of winter.

During this time he could see nothing but the solid white expanse of ice and snow surrounding him, continuing for all he knew into infinity. The dark mass had been spotted easily lying on the ice-bridge, the Inuit's word for the frozen Bering Strait that stretched for fifty-six miles between his small Alaskan settlement and the land of the treacherous Russian hunters.

Although the animal was at a point almost halfway across the strait, a point beyond which Inuijak and his people never ventured, the risk had to be taken. Either he lived or he starved. His wife, Meqo, had urged him to stay in bed, the soft fur skins cozier and warmer when he lay beside her. With the cruel winds howling outside their snug earthen house and the blinding snow swirling in high, treacherous drifts over the ice, she feared his doubtful chase might continue through the next moon.

"Please, Inuijak, it is so pleasant in our bed," she had entreated, "and the wind howls like a seal in heat. It is so pleasant when we join together as one."

"Ah, my pretty wife," he said gently, already more than half dressed, "the temptation is great, but fresh meat is not to be ignored."

He donned his white bearskin trousers and came to her, affectionately rubbing his nose against hers. His smile revealed strong white teeth. His smooth brown skin, freshly greased with seal blubber against the cold winds, gleamed in the lamplight.

"And if we do not have meat," he went on, "you will grow skinny and spindle-shanked as a runt dog, and the other families will point at you and laugh and, what is worse, think me a poor provider.

"This big lump on the ice may be a great animal, and your pretty face will smile with pride when your husband brings it home. It could be big enough to share with the others, the Great Spirit will be pleased, and that would be a fine gift in this difficult winter."

Before leaving, he nuzzled Meqo on the sweet spot behind her ears. She had fallen asleep, and he knew she would be just as loving and desirable when he returned.

Halfway through the run, Inuijak began puzzling over the dark mound on the ice. It was lying very still for a walrus, unless it was dead. Then this would be an easy hunt, and the small settlement would enjoy a great feast, enough to eat for many full moons.

But the closer the Inuit raced, the less certain he was. Alive or dead, this was no walrus. He thought his eyes were either playing tricks on him, or taking on the dulled glaze of the old ones, for he was seeing the shape as human. This seemed very odd. No one was missing from the settlement; the alarm would have gone out days before. And there had been no Russian hunters in the territory since the deep cold set in.

He pulled hard on the sealskin thongs to slow the dogs, circling the huddled thing until he could be sure. It was a man, deathly still, lying with his arms folded, his head resting at a broken angle on the ice.

Inuijak stepped from the sled and commanded his dogs to sit quietly while he approached the stranger. Squatting, he stared at the man's pale, mottled skin, red beard caked with ice, eyes frozen shut. He guessed the man had been unconscious when he fell, for one leg was bent awkwardly under his body. Otherwise the position would have been intolerable. That leg was undoubtedly broken.

The Inuit's disappointment with the catch began to sit like a stone in his heart. The people of Wales had finished the last of their ptarmigans and caribou, and had only what the men could snare in the fish holes or steal from a distracted mother seal.

Now he had wasted time and energy hunting down this half-dead man. And what was this man doing on the ice-bridge, so poorly clothed and booted? For a moment, Inuijak wondered if this was a sign from the spirits. If so, was it warning or gift?

Carefully, he reached for the man's wrist, moving slowly for fear the man would awake and prove unfriendly. But the human lay inert, although a faint pulse was beating.

The sharp wind, rapidly falling temperature and whirling snow began to hinder the Inuit's movement and vision. He rose to his feet and pulled a thick rope from around his waist. Making a large circle of the rope with a slipknot, he wound it around the stranger's body, pulling tight on the slack.

He then moved to the dogs, loosening the harness of the leader, a large, thick-chested Malamute. With the dog's teeth holding tight to the tow rope, he gave the command to pull, and together they slid the big man over the ice to the sled, laid him gently on the fur skins and pulled the top skin over his wasted body for warmth.

Inuijak rehitched the lead dog to the team and, with the crack of his whip and a shout to the dogs, sped for home.

ONE

꿍꿍

Russia—the Pale of Settlement, December, 1894

A SLIM QUARTER-MOON HANGING LOW IN THE NIGHT SKY
was the only light guiding Jacob Finesilver as he fled his
home in the Russian Pale. He thought the light as capricious
as the fine drizzle of intermittent rain, but the recurrent cloud
cover was an unexpected bit of good fortune.

On this cold, wet December night, Jacob was attempting
to slip unseen from his village and be at least ten miles to the
east by dawn. The enormity of his action would have stopped
him before he started, had he given himself time to reflect.
But concentrating on the ruts in the muddy road leading out
of Khotin, and staying out of the light, took all his attention.

He also listened for the sounds of Russian patrols or
unfriendly peasants who would relish the reward for betraying any wayward Jew. Jacob vowed that he would enrich no
one tonight.

These were his first steps on the road to a new life, and
he walked steadily, thinking of his family left behind, but
anticipating the taste of freedom.

Yet a persistent, nagging guilt insinuated itself between
his memories and the drastic change in his fortunes, goading
his conscience to justify again and again the reasons for

flight. They were compelling reasons, vastly different from each other but of equal importance to Jacob, and his review of them strengthened his resolve to leave Russia forever.

The first was enforced conscription in the Czar's army. He thought about that night, only one in a long string of terrible nights of hiding in the freezing hayloft with his little brother, Velvel, while the Cossacks banged on the door and demanded the boys for army service. The plan to escape was born that night.

He remembered the horses thundering into the yard, the sound of their hooves stamping the snow-packed ground into slick patches of ice. As the Czar's soldiers dismounted, Jacob could sense their anticipation of another victory over these stubborn, maddeningly pious people who lived in a little shtetl. Their contempt for those who refused to fight like real men in the royal forces had quickened their pace and sharpened their scent for the hunt. This was the kind of military exercise that made good use of the Cossack's strength and unrivaled brutality.

"They don't want Mama, and they don't want girls. At least for soldiers. So stop worrying. It's boys they want, even little boys like you. Now hold on to me, they'll be gone soon." But he feared for his sisters, two pretty little girls of ten and thirteen, hiding in the wood stove to avoid being made the butt of their jokes and fondled with their big, dirty hands, or raped.

Holy One, Holiest of Holies, Jacob had prayed, let them go away and leave my family in peace.

"Jacob," Velvel whispered, "why do they keep coming back? How can the Czar take all the boys away and make them be soldiers?"

"Because," Jacob whispered, "he's the ruler."

"Are we really . . . cowards, Jacob?"

"No, little one, we would make splendid soldiers. But not on the side of our enemies."

There was a sudden shout of command and the barn door was thrown open. Heavy boots kicked at the stacks of hay, and the soldiers cursed at not finding a Jew hiding inside.

The boys trembled, waiting for the men to climb up to the loft, Velvel so frightened his cries would have been heard but for Jacob's hand over his mouth. The older brother rocked him to calm him, his own blood pounding in thunderous beats. They waited, sweat-drenched, eyes closed.

"And what is up in the loft?" the commandant shouted.

"Only hay, Sir," a soldier replied, anxious not to climb the rickety ladder.

"And if you are wrong, you cringing weasel, you will spend the rest of your days wishing you were dead," the commandant said. "Shit on these Jews! They're more trouble than they're worth. Out!"

When Jacob heard the horses galloping out of the yard, he hugged Velvel with relief. It was over, but he knew the pogroms, the unjust taxes, the regular sacking of their homes and possessions would go on. He also knew the Cossacks would be back for him, and that conscripted Jewish boys were rarely seen again, alive or dead.

The crescent moon appeared unexpectedly between the dark clouds, and Jacob dove into some heavy brush. Concentrate, he told himself, or you will be picked like a rose in the snow. He lay there and waited for darkness, then resumed his steady pace through the bare thicket. He tried collecting his wayward thoughts, but they were insistent, dwelling on the poverty and unrelenting bigotry he had known. He shook his head to rid himself of these dismal constants in his life, and gave free rein to the second reason he was leaving.

His evening prayers had been said when Uncle Aaron had brought them the amazing news. Uncle Aaron, the simpleminded man with the brain of a child.

"Gittel! Jacob! Children! Listen to me! Have I got something to tell you!"

Uncle Aaron had burst into his sister's house, coat misbuttoned, hat askew, his two long black curls flopping around his face. He stood triumphantly in the open doorway and shouted to the household. Spittle flew as the words tumbled out of his mouth.

"Gold! Do you hear me? Gold! More gold than in the houses of the Pharaohs! More gold than King Midas ever dreamed of! Gold that will pave the streets and . . . and . . ."

"Where, Uncle Aaron? Where is the gold?" Jacob asked, leading his agitated uncle to a chair. "Sit here, tell us, we're all ears."

"Yes. I must tell you, Jacob, for it is you, our youth, who must go and find it. It is you who will save us." Aaron licked his dry lips. "They have found gold in Alaska. Men have struck gold in Alaska. Alaska! Do you realize what that means?"

Jacob's mother threw up her hands, turning impatiently from her brother. "Alaska," she said in disgust. "Why don't you just say the Square of Times in New York City and be done with it."

His mother knew by the set of Jacob's jaw that her son had already decided to go and that neither argument or love would stop him.

Jacob was startled out of his reverie by a rustling in the dead leaves. He stiffened, alert and wary. His right hand gripped the heavy piece of wood he carried for protection.

At that moment, the clouds scurried away from the moon's face and an animal's furry snout was visible as it poked through his tangled enclosure.

Jacob laughed. "Welcome to my sylvan glade," he whispered, reaching out to touch the frightened deer, but it turned, eyes wild, bounding away and out of sight.

He was wet and clammy in spite of the cold, and perspiration trickled down into his eyes from under his cap. "Pull yourself together," he scolded himself, "you're only a few miles into a long journey and already you're as frightened as a baby." The sound of his own voice steadied him, and he prayed silently for longer stretches of darkness. He must be far from his village by daylight or the risk of discovery was too great.

As if answering his prayer, the moon disappeared behind a cluster of swollen thunderheads, and in the sudden blackness he paused and listened. Satisfied that all was well, he adjusted his knapsack, which held a few clothes, toothbrush, maps, and his siddur, tallis and tefillin. Without his three religious effects necessary for morning and evening prayers, he was not Jacob Finesilver, eldest son of the pious Avram the carpenter, and might as well stay home.

Moving through the tall grass, he kept to the shadows at the edge of the open field until he had crossed the vast expanse into the deep forest. There was no sound, no bird singing, no laughter. Ever since Jacob could remember, this forest had been his playground, his familiar and well-learned arbor where every tree, path, and bushy clump was known and recognized. Tonight, it was a trail of chance, a dark, hostile adversary to his flight, and he picked his way cautiously through the inky thickets.

This was the first time Jacob had left his home and family, and the sudden realization intensified his fear and sense of isolation. This pilgrimage could last for years, lonely, uncertain years that stretched blind and obscure as the land he would be roaming. With the vast unknown looming before him, he had the momentary wish to be a little boy again, safe in the bosom of his loved ones. But the wish was self-indulgent, useless, and he shook it off impatiently, concentrating on moving through the intricate maze of brambles catching at his clothing.

Suddenly, the harsh, unexpected sound of voices, punctuated with bursts of obscenities and curses, cut through the deep silence. He dropped to the ground, listening, trying to get his bearings, puzzling out the direction of the voices and what they were saying. If he had gone the distance figured on the map, the meadow was to the north just beyond the grove of pines in which he huddled. The voices were speaking in Ukrainian and he recognized the curse words, the words all children learn first and then mischievously use to pepper their own language. His family spoke Yiddish at home. They also read and conversed in Russian and Polish as well as many of the dialects, for which he was now profoundly grateful.

He quickly weighed his options: to boldly walk into the meadow was risky, for he guessed the voices to be a local night patrol. A simple excuse like taking a midnight stroll was unthinkable; he was too far from home. But if he tried to skirt the meadow, there might be guards along the perimeter, his position then even more questionable.

Knowing that furtive action was too suspect, Jacob decided to bluff his way through. He got to his feet and walked out of the brush.

"Halt!" the voice cried. "Stop or I shoot!"

"Shoot? You would shoot me, an unarmed peasant?" Jacob said in Russian. "Would they give you a medal for that?"

The soldier was young, smooth-cheeked, shorter than Jacob and painfully thin, his uniform voluminous and ill-fitting. No older than seventeen, this boy who acted so grown-up should be pitied, he thought. The uniform conferred status, the big rifle, courage. But the sobering thought that the rifle held real bullets, and those bullets could kill, dispelled Jacob's pity.

The guard peered at Jacob through the gloomy night,

steady and unafraid, the gleaming rifle poised in his hands and ready to fire.

"State your name."

"Please, if you don't mind," Jacob said, keeping his voice light and innocent, "put up your gun. It makes me nervous to see it aimed at my poor head. And my name is of no consequence, for I'm afraid I'm only a poor peasant on a fool's errand. My wife is pregnant, and woke up in a fever of desire for fresh milk. You know how that is," he said, confidential, man-to-man.

The young guard lowered the rifle and smiled. "Indeed I do," he said, anxious now to sound grown-up. "A fat wife with child is worse than a sick horse, is that not so?"

"Without a doubt," Jacob laughed. "So you do understand. And where am I to get milk at this time of night?"

Before the soldier could answer, a second guard approached, his rifle slung loosely in his hands. Jacob recognized him immediately. As a small child, he had played with a group of children from the town, before the first pogrom of his life had rolled over his home and family. Since that event, friends outside the shtetl were not welcome, and the Russian children were not permitted to play with the Jews.

In spite of the years gone by, Jacob recognized Stepan, the boy with the blue glass marbles. A bully even then, fat-faced with little piggy eyes set close together, a cruel, selfish child who delighted in capturing little field animals and holding his large hands over their mouths and noses until the twitching stopped. He was older now, but Jacob knew he had not changed.

"Why, by all the Saints, if it isn't Stepan!" he cried.

"And who is this who knows me?"

"It is I, Anton Antonevsky," drawing the name quickly from his memory of Dostoyevsky, "one of your childhood pals from town. Do you not know me?" Jacob knew this lout would never have read good literature. He doubted the man could read at all.

"Anton? I remember no Anton," the soldier grumbled. "Come on now, the truth. And don't give me that Anton shit!"

Jacob laughed. "You haven't changed, I see. Still the same lovable, friendly fellow you were when we played our games together." Jacob winked at the other guard. "Is he not?"

"Lovable? Friendly? You're not talking about Stepan," the younger man said. "His face is fixed permanently in that scowl. And he probably has no friends. Not even his mother!"

Stepan nodded. "That's right." He walked closer to Jacob and stared into his face, studying the features in the dim light.

Jacob had begun growing his full beard over two months ago, anticipating the long trip. A practical move, for soap and water would be difficult to find. The beard was now an unexpected bonus in disguising him.

"Anton, eh?" Stepan said, still skeptical. "Well, I did not know any Anton then, and I don't know you."

His face turned menacing, and he spat out the next words as if they had a foul taste.

"As a matter of fact, you look like a Jew. Yes, the more I look at you, the uglier you become." He laughed, a coarse and unamused sound that squeezed Jacob's gut. "There is one way to prove it, you know. Drop your pants!"

The younger guard grew uncomfortable with his comrade. "Come now, Stepan, enough. The man is only seeking milk for his pregnant wife."

"Oh, now, that is a different story," Stepan said, "and how did that happen? Surely *you* didn't make her pregnant. I have heard that a Jewish prick has no hat on it. And you Jews never do anything without a hat, eh?"

"I have heard that, too," Jacob said evenly, "but I

wouldn't know firsthand. What do you say, Stepan, a game of marbles? I can remember you winning every game."

"Yes, I won every game. Because I was better than you."

"Aha!" Jacob cried. "So you admit you know me!"

Stepan gestured in impatience and spat on the ground. "To hell with you," he said sharply, "and to hell with your pregnant wife. Get yourself out of my sight before I lose patience and shoot you."

Jacob grinned and poked Stepan with an elbow. "Ah, old friend, thank you for being here, and for guarding our countryside with such diligence and patriotism. We're all better off because of soldiers like you and your young comrade. And don't get into trouble or I personally will come looking for you." Stepan turned abruptly on his heel and walked away.

"You heard what he said," the younger guard warned Jacob, adding in a whisper, "and if I were you, I would vanish into thin air. Now!"

"Right. Well, good night," Jacob said, moving away. When the guards were out of sight, he broke into a run, stumbling over clumps of sodden mud and rocks in the open field. His heart beat erratically from the exertion and the unexpected confrontation, but the more he thought about it, the more astonished he was at how easily the soldiers had been outwitted.

Was it just good luck? He wasted no time on the question, remembering instead how simple the plan had seemed. "The boat from Sevastopol, isn't that right, Jacob?" Uncle Aaron had said, looking over his nephew's shoulder at the map. "You see, right there you . . ."

"No, Uncle, to go that way I would need a passport and papers. Running from army conscription hardly entitles me to either one."

"Ah, yes, I see. Odessa, then?"

"No. I can't take a boat. I'll have to walk."

"Walk? On your feet, walk? How can you walk to the ends of Russia? And what will you do, then, here, at the water between Russia and Alaska . . . *walk* across? Like . . ."

Jacob laughed. "I don't plan to walk on the water, Uncle, I'll cross it when it's frozen solid."

"Ah!" Uncle Aaron tapped his head in appreciation of his nephew's brilliance, then reached into his pants pocket and brought out one kopek. Handing it to Jacob, he said, "Here, my boy, take this to give away in Alaska."

"Why?"

"Chances are greater for a safe journey if you have *tzedakah* to give at your destination. A little charity goes a long way.

Jacob smiled at the memory of Aaron and his superstition, but his uncle was only following the old wives' tales against the evil eye. Like the great rabbis since the days of the Talmud, he saw no harm in the popular stories, and promised to give the coin to charity.

"So, Jacob, across the steppes to Omsk, here, and then into Siberia. Oy, but it's cold there."

"I know, but if my planning is right, I'll arrive in summer. I don't know much about it except what little I've read or heard, like their prisons, and labor camps."

"Mm-hmm. And what kind of weather is it when you cross the Siberian Lowlands?"

"Winter, I'm afraid, and probably the hardest part. No picnic, Uncle, but I think I can do it. Unless I'm living in a fool's paradise."

"If only He would provide . . . !"

The maps Jacob now carried, treasures from his father's old books and papers, made the journey look plausible. The Ural Mountains posed no problem if he kept to the foothills, and he was confident of help from Jewish families along the way. He knew of several houses located in cities of the northern Pale, established for poor Jewish travelers, or runaways, that required no payment. Once in the Siberian taiga, the timber forests and rocky, mountainous area east of the Trans-Baikal, he would be on his own.

But could he, a student of the Talmud and a poor carpenter's apprentice, really live on his wits and ingenuity as hunter and trapper? His answer was one of Uncle Aaron's favorite sayings: "If there is any room for question, something is wrong."

Hours later, Jacob's steps slowed with fatigue as dawn streaked across the eastern sky. He had been walking since leaving Khotin. The aching in his leg muscles warned of the onset of cramps. Anxiety to put miles between home and the next town had resulted in a careless lack of pacing. He was cold as well as exhausted. The next village was still a few miles away, its outskirts most likely quiet and unpopulated, a perfect area for shelter. A grove of birch trees between two low and barren hills looked promising, and Jacob settled himself into a nest of leaves. A sharp wind came up and stirred the leaves around him into little golden whirlpools that rose and fell with the currents, but he was asleep immediately, unaware of a hostile pair of eyes watching from only inches away.

TWO

❦

THE SMALL BIRD PECKED AT THE BERRIES IN THE HAWTHORN tree, battering the clusters against the bare branch, then flitted down in a flash of red wing to catch the plump succulents in its beak. The more the bird ate, the faster he worked, until quickness and inaccuracy sent berries raining down on Jacob sleeping below. He groaned and turned over on the hard ground. When he opened his eyes, he realized where he was and remembered the night before, the soldiers, and this grove where he had fallen asleep. Now his movement startled the bird and he watched it fly off, thinking how smart the bird was to have grown wings. When threatened, it simply flew away. If attacked, Jacob must stand and fight, a sport denied him in the Pale but one he had better learn.

Suddenly, he sensed danger. He shut his eyes, listening, trusting his keener sense of hearing. Then he heard the wheezing and shuffling, the body creaks. Someone moved. Someone close.

Afraid of being caught from behind, and preferring offense to defense, Jacob rolled away quickly and looked back. There, on his haunches like a mouse nibbling at cheese, sat a ragtag old beggar rummaging through Jacob's knapsack.

"Hey, you! Put that down!" Jacob yelled.

The old man turned, stared at Jacob, then resumed his fumbling inside the sack.

"I said . . ."

"I know what you said," the man muttered, "I'm not deaf." He held up Jacob's prayer shawl and shook it in the breeze. "You're a Jew," he said mockingly.

"Correct." Jacob moved quickly to snatch away the shawl and sack. "And you're a thief."

The man sat back on his heels and smiled, baring his decaying teeth. "Worse than that, I'm afraid. Worse than that."

Jacob glared at the man. "Only one day out, and I have to run into the likes of you."

"Ah, and a lucky thing for me it was, too. Where you running from?"

"None of your damn business."

"The law? A girl in trouble? No matter," the man said. "A Jew doesn't need a reason to run, right?"

"See here . . ."

"Aw, don't excite yourself. I have nothing against you. Just wanted to make sure no one is chasing you who might find me."

Jacob studied the old man, and realized he was only a wretched thief from town preying on anyone stupid enough to sleep in unfamiliar surroundings.

"How long have you been sitting here?" he asked.

"Long enough to watch you sleep. Anyone sleeping like that must have come a long way, eh?"

"Where are you from?" Jacob asked.

"Now who's asking the questions?"

"Just curious."

"And if I told you, it would scare you to death." The fellow laughed bitterly and sat down on his rump. "Young Jew, just go on your way and forget this little tête-à-tête of ours. The less you know about me, the better it will go for you."

Jacob nodded and rose to his feet. "Well then, good-bye, thief. I hope your next pickings are more fruitful."

"I did not want your prayer shawl," the old man said querulously "or your books with the funny printing, or your toothbrush. Can't use any of it. Who could I sell it to? The soldiers in town?"

"Then why . . ." Jacob looked at the man in distrust, and the man returned his look with mixture of sadness and anger swimming in his rheumy eyes. "Food, bread, fruit, anything to still the rattling in my empty gut."

"How long since you've eaten?"

"Is it pity you have for the thief, then?"

"Pity? I don't know. Perhaps."

"That's good. Better pity than scorn. But it doesn't fill my stomach."

Jacob took a packet of sandwiches from his knapsack and handed one to the man. "Would this help?"

"A Jew would feed a thief? This they would never believe," the man said, grabbing at the food.

"Who?"

The man winked and chewed ravenously on the bread and cheese. Jacob ate his own share quickly, and was still hungry when his sandwich was gone. He wished now he had kept the other one for himself.

When the old man finished, he wiped his mouth on his grimy sleeve and belched loudly. "Gas," he said, "that's one of the curses of living like this. Gas and hunger, and staying ahead of the Cossacks."

The old fellow's dirty, weathered face, the way his tattered clothes hung on his thin frame and his attitude of surrender and resignation gave Jacob an impression of crumbling decay. The man was dead without knowing it.

"What's your name?" Jacob asked.

"Danilo."

"That's it? Danilo?"

"Just Danilo."

The man's Russian was odd, antique, the phrasing like something out of an old book. "You're not from around here, are you?" Jacob asked.

"No." The man said nothing more.

Repacking his few possessions, Jacob regretted the meeting was over. The old thief had caught his fancy. His inelegant honesty was refreshing, and Jacob had nothing to steal.

"Where will you go from here?" he asked.

"Why does the Jew care?"

"Because this Jew is also a man, a fellow human."

"Ah . . . a fellow human, eh? I never knew Jews were human. I guess that's my failing. But then, prison is never a very good school."

"Prison? Where? What for?"

Danilo smiled again, the weary face betraying the old man's pathetic eagerness to trust the Jew, the stranger, the victim he had intended to rob. In a bitter voice, he said, "I have been in Sibir."

Jacob shuddered. "Siberia?"

"Yes. I escaped. I walked away from hell."

Jacob said nothing. Then, he smiled ruefully and said, "You and I have much in common."

THREE

⊰◈⊱

DANILO AND JACOB TRAVELED TOGETHER FOR THE NEXT few weeks, a course of action accepted by both men. Each needed the other's companionship, though at times Jacob found Danilo odious and contrary. But his advice was invaluable.

The old man had been running and living off the land for almost a year, and he was crafty in the ways of finding food where it seemed none could exist—berries growing as ground cover for sugary sweetness; tubers, identified by top growth, for fiber and bulk; greens that could be eaten raw to keep scurvy away.

But there were days when even the sharp-eyed old man could not find food, especially on the steppe where nothing grew but clods of dry grass. Then the two engaged in philosophical discussions, for it seemed to both that argument was better than gnawing hunger. No subject was sacrosanct, and the debates were often contentious, especially those on religion or morality. The old man had neither, showing his contempt for Jacob's naiveté by calling it "offensive virtue." For Danilo, there was no God, therefore no good or evil. There was only rich or poor, win or lose, getting away with something or getting caught.

Jacob argued these issues at first, but soon learned to

keep quiet. The old reprobate was beyond redemption. They could agree on nothing.

Danilo's lessons in survival had been learned during his lengthy exile in Siberia, and he spoke eloquently of the beauty of the Siberian forests, the lush timber stands and the streams and rivers running with fish. He also described the abundance of game and the kind, trusting natives. This surprised Jacob. He had thought of Siberia as a vast, uninhabitable wilderness.

"Vast, yes, sometimes it will seem endless, as if it's the last outpost of the world. And you will drop to your knees and pray, I suppose, and ask that nebulous God of yours to spare you from seeing still another river, another swamp, another desolate mountain range. But uninhabited? No, people are few and far between, but they're Tartars, kind and generous, their hands never out for money. And they make no pious judgments."

"Judgments? About what?"

The old man sat on a rock and launched into one of his lengthy and picturesque explanations. "Do you think I, Danilo, could go up to a house, knock on the door, ask the buxom peasant woman for food, and be received with charity? Ha! She would take one look at my princely apparel and my honest face and go screaming into her kitchen for a knife!"

Jacob laughed. "Ah, what a picture that paints for me. I can almost see her."

"I *have* seen her," Danilo muttered, "many times. Not a pretty sight, I assure you."

"But you said visitors are welcome."

"Yes, still, be wary. Children playing outside a home often identify a charitable family. But if there is but one single, middle-aged lady, she might seize the opportunity to enjoy a bit of, shall we say, romance with such a handsome young fellow as you."

Jacob frowned. "That's no concern of mine. This journey is all I can think of, so I have no interest in women right now, middle-aged or not."

Danilo laughed. "Sure. And pigs can fly. Well, whether or not you're destined for sainthood, I must still warn you to run from the hungry-eyed widows. It gains you nothing but trouble.

"More importantly," he went on, "you must know how to make a fire and use a slingshot or some kind of weapon. I will teach you, in spite of the fact that you're arrogant and unrealistic."

A quick student, Jacob sharpened his skills with a slingshot on small game. He hated killing, and at night he prayed for forgiveness out of the old man's earshot. But Danilo knew, and lectured him severely one morning after Jacob had downed a snow hare.

"My friend, there's no reason to mourn so for this animal. It isn't a crime when you kill for hunger. If you kill for the thrill of the hunt, that is wrong. Do you believe it's a crime against nature? Is that why you grieve?"

"One of our commandments . . ."

"I know about your commandments," Danilo snapped, "and I don't give a damn for them! More hate and murder has been done in this miserable world in the name of God than all the words in any Bible. And don't," he said, stifling the protest Jacob was about to make, "give me any more sermons!"

That night after their meal, they sat around the dying fire, an uneasy silence between them. Jacob scuffed out the embers with the heel of his shoe and began burying the remnants from the meal.

"Very good," the old man approved, "and now it is time to ask me the question nibbling at your tongue."

Jacob looked up. "Question?"

"Come, come, don't be coy. I'm ready for it."

"All right. I didn't want to pry, but why are you going

backwards with me? You've come this way once, why retrace your steps?"

Danilo picked up a stick and began drawing aimless designs in the dead ashes.

"I wondered how long it would take you to figure that out. The fact is, there's no difference which way I go. I have no home, no family, no friends. My stay in Siberia lasted long enough to lose them all. So what does it matter which route I take? I never had a friend. That's the surest way to lose your independence. And I certainly wouldn't choose one from the unwashed riffraff who were my companions in Tobolsk. My crime was being caught. I did nothing wrong, merely minding my own business, and then I'm arrested for 'revolutionary treason.' Fancy verbiage, eh? And my sentence, innocent or not, was to sit like rotting garbage in that stinking Siberian hole."

He scratched out the ash, drawing with an angry swipe of the stick and tossed it into the darkness.

"The reason is simple, my young friend. You need me. You won't admit it, but it's true. That gives me a kind of power over you, and what more could a lifer hope for!"

The following day, the two men faced a new problem: how to elude the soldiers suddenly appearing in scattered groups along their way. Appropriated from the army as laborers, these men worked on the roads linking one town to another. Since their path lay within the wooded areas, the two men assumed the soldiers posed no threat.

They were wrong.

They chose an enclave of young fir trees just outside Zaitsova as their shelter for the night. It was bitterly cold, and Jacob shivered, hunching himself closer to Danilo. They dared not make a fire.

For the first time since leaving home, Jacob thought of his family, wondering if they were safe, if his escape had caused them more trouble, more punishment than life in Khotin usually offered. He tossed and turned on the hard ground until he fell asleep.

He dreamed of summer. He was a little boy, and the sun warmed his naked body as he splashed in the stream near their home. His sisters had gone to pick berries along the stream's bank while he enjoyed the rare freedom of solitude. The dream turned ugly when boys from town ran alongside, one taunting Jacob by swinging his pants high in the air, another holding a shirt, the third a cap.

"Come on out of the water, Jew-dog, so we can see your ugly body," one yelled.

"Here's your shirt, Jew-dog," another cried, "do you want me to throw it to you?"

Before Jacob could answer, the boys turned into Cossacks, their baby faces gleeful with the abusive sport.

"We will shoot you now," one of them said, his rifle pressed against Jacob's forehead.

The trigger was pulled, and Jacob awoke, trembling. When he looked at Danilo, he had his forefinger to his lips warning Jacob to be silent.

He listened, hearing twigs snapping, footfalls crackling in the underbrush, and then Danilo was on his feet, pulling him quickly into the depths of the wooded grove. The moonlight barely penetrated the thick branches, but Jacob could see out. He froze at the sight of six soldiers standing on the very spot where they had slept.

"Someone has been here. Look, the matted ground gives him away," said the leader.

"It has to be that bastard Danilovitch," a soldier muttered, "Who else would be tramping around on this stinking cold night?"

"He can't be far," the leader said angrily. "Spread out.

You, Khirov, go on for a kilometer or so, and Nikolay, see to the stream below. Baldak, check that grove over there."

With this, Danilo walked out into the center of the startled troop, calmly working the fly buttons on his pants. "You're looking for me, I presume? Well, here I am, minus a pint of pee I just left in the bushes. But never let it be said that old Danilovitch gave up peacefully. It's only because I have lived too long and am tired of running that I appear before you, ready to be taken back. So, get on with it," he snapped irritably, striding quickly away from the grove in which Jacob hid, leading the soldiers in the opposite direction.

Jacob stood like a statue. One against six armed Cossacks was a lost cause. In minutes, the grove was quiet, soldiers and prisoner gone.

Shaken by the narrow escape, Jacob stayed hidden until dawn. Then he walked out of the brush and stirred up the leaves and dirt, leaving behind no hint that anyone had been there.

All the while he was hiding, he wrestled with his conscience for the callous way he had left Danilo to be captured alone. He agonized over the old man's sacrifice and why he had made it—for the act of turning himself in to save Jacob seemed absurd. But after mulling over their quarrels as well as their camaraderie, Jacob finally understood the old fellow's attempts to conceal both his courage and his nobility. He had to concede, unhappily, Danilo's cynical canon of faith: "If you deny yourself friends, there is no loss to mourn when they are gone."

He was alone again, alone to face the perils the two men had faced together. Fear, like bile, rose up in his mouth, and he spat out the sharp, metallic taste. It had been chance that had brought them together, almost like fate taking a hand. But Danilo's knowledge would help Jacob fend for himself.

He was grateful for that. No sense decrying his loss or railing against the cruel force that had taken him away.

He missed the old man. Shalom, Danilovitch, I will see you no more, cap perched backwards on your head, eyes bright with mischief, ready to nag, tease, and dance before me on another day's march. God be with you, Danilo. Try not to push Him away. God be with me, too.

FOUR

ც❀❁ა

THE SLOW, PUNISHING COURSE EAST THROUGH THE UKRAINE
made a mockery of Jacob's plans. Clothing and boots disin-
tegrated during the bleak winter, and heavy snows frustrated
his foraging for food.

He plodded through one town after another, finding an
occasional meal, a night's shelter, and replacements for his
ragged clothing in the few safe houses for Jews along the
way. But most of the time he suffered grinding hunger, the
pains doubling him over for days. The cold was constant
and brutal.

The first safe house had led him to others, but once out
of the Pale, locating Jewish families became awkward. In
towns where Jews were forbidden, he had to promise
absolute secrecy, "not a whisper, not a hint," before they fed
him. Afterwards, they pleaded fear of eviction when he asked
about others.

Hurting him more than his stomach was his discovery of
Jewish families practicing their religion in secret.
Assimilating into Russian life, they called it. He loathed the
idea of denying his religion. "You don't celebrate the
Sabbath?" he asked his host, incredulous. It was Friday, and
sundown had come and gone with no sign of recognition by
the befriending family.

"There can be no reason for ignoring the Sabbath, Sir."

The minute the words were spoken, Jacob regretted them. They sounded sanctimonious and shockingly impolite, even to himself. He deserved the angry retort.

"If you lived in a town that despised you, forbade your very existence, you would not admit your religion either!"

"You have heard of the Marranos, have you not?" The man continued, losing patience with his guest, "Jews who worshipped secretly in their cellars but became Christians during the Inquisition in Spain rather than burn at the stake? You cannot have it both ways!"

"I understand," Jacob said, "but it seems to me . . ."

"That will do!" His host protested. "I do not debate my life's most serious decisions with a youth! Look at you, not much more than a boy. Too young to do anything but rant about truth, unable to see it even if it sticks to the end of your nose."

He composed himself, then spoke as if to a child. "Let me tell you something, my friend. You are very young and don't have enough years under your belt to recognize that it is a raw, simplistic idealism through which you see the world. In this stage of your life, you bumble along, rushing to judgments based on black or white, blind as a bat to the shade of gray. But it exists, oh yes, it exists, and within that gray, life can be more precious than truth! Do you think I can sleep at night, knowing I have not put on a tefillin for years, nor blessed the Sabbath wine, nor presided at the Passover seder since I've lived here? I say my prayers to myself and to the Holy One, but as we all do, with the doors locked and the lights down. And He hears us, and forgives. That is how it is with me and with my fellow Jews in this wretched place."

Jacob thought of this often in the next months, deploring his own arrogance and self-righteousness. The loneliness of the deserted Siberian lowlands gave him time to think about the man's arguments. Too much time, it seemed, the more they piled up in the merchant's favor. But this journey was a lonely exile, and the lowlands an endless emptiness that stretched to the horizon and beyond.

At times he found himself arguing at the top of his lungs with no one around but a stray bird or the insects at his feet. Jacob yearned for the sound of a human voice. Even Danilo's irritable company would have been welcome.

"Live by your wits," the impious and cunning old sinner had counseled Jacob, "you'll be better off. People only get in your way." You were wrong, Danilo. Loneliness is worse.

FIVE

cᘿ☉☉ᘾ

Khotin, Ukraine, Russia, 1895

OPENING THE DOOR TO SAUL MENDELBERG, MALKA said impatiently, "Ah, Saul, coming to call in the middle of my Shabbes baking. I should have known it was you," she scolded. "Your sense of timing is, as usual, impeccable. Well, come in, come in, don't stand there like a tree."

He followed her into the kitchen, watching her trim figure under the long skirt, her characteristic quick steps denying him the more sinuous movement he might have preferred.

"The baking . . . is it really in honor of the Sabbath or my visit?" he asked hopefully.

"I'm not psychic," Malka said sharply, "so you see it must be the Sabbath. Now sit where I can keep my eye on you while I finish this pie crust."

"I would find that most welcome," he said, studying Malka as she worked. He thought she looked beautiful today, her luminous skin reminding him of a sheet of parchment on which the old scribes wrote. Her long hair, as black as midnight, fell to her miraculous waist, the circumference so tiny he imagined that if he circled it with both his big hands, they would overlap. Unfortunately, she had never given him that opportunity. Saul quickly looked down at his shoes. "May I ask . . . where is your father?"

"He's still at the shop. You know how busy a shochet can be on Friday afternoons. Why?" she asked suspiciously. "You have business with him?"

Saul smiled. "You could call it that, I suppose."

Malka looked up from kneading the heavy dough and stared at Saul, puzzled. He was not usually so cryptic. They had been best friends since childhood, his shy, even-tempered disposition a foil for her sharp wit and high spirits. But his devotion, dogging her every step, following her to market, to her pupils' houses, sticking to her like a shadow, was a nuisance. Humor was his saving grace. And laughter was not easy to come by in the miserable village of Khotin.

But never in her wildest dreams could she see that heavy-gaited, ponderous physique as romantic. At the very thought, Malka blushed and returned to her kneading with renewed vigor.

"I suppose you might as well wait for him," she said sharply "but go into the parlor. You'll be more comfortable there, with books to read and last week's paper from Kiev. But don't get the pages out of order, Papa hasn't finished with it yet."

Saul's eyes flickered. "If you wish," he nodded stiffly, and walked out of the room.

How odd he is today, she thought, pinched, thin-skinned, not like himself. Habit would have had him making a joke out of the situation. But she had more urgent concerns. The sun was setting. She flew about the small kitchen, stirred the soup, turned the chicken, washed a plate, a glass, the table top. Everything must shine for the Shabbes dinner.

Malka used the best quality fruits and vegetables, made sure crusts were light, fruits firm, dairy dishes fresh. On no other night was so much attention paid to detail, for Friday's sundown ushered in the Holy Sabbath, the day of rest. To read and sing, to walk among the trees or snow-packed roads, to honor her mother's memory and commune with the Almighty. The week would be dismal without it.

She spread out the lace cloth on the table, part of her mother's dowry. It was delicately patterned in a fine, white thread, the perfect background for the few pieces of old silver she set for herself and her father. And the silver goblet for papa's wine, over which he would chant the blessing.

Malka turned to speak to Saul, only then realizing the parlor was empty. He had left without a word? Was he angry? Had she said something to hurt him? Next time she saw him, she would apologize.

"Good Sabbath, my angel," Nathan Semel said when she opened the door. "Something smells absolutely delicious. Come, greet your papa properly."

Stooping down for her kiss, Semel could barely hide his joy at being home on the Sabbath with his beloved daughter.

He was a strapping man, whose grandiose bearing hid a gentle nature. He reigned supreme in his shop, but at home he could put on slippers and curl up, snoring in his favorite chair. Even a king, like a ball of yarn, has to unwind.

Malka was dismayed by the signs of age and fatigue she saw in her father. His thick black hair was turning gray before her eyes. Still admired by every widow in the synagogue balcony, he had recently lost weight and his shoulders slumped. She bit back the question on her lips, and took his cap and scarf.

"I hope it's delicious, Papa. I had so many interruptions today; it will be a miracle if my dinner is edible. Sit. I'll get your schnapps."

"Oh? What kind of interruptions?"

"Well, Mrs. Perlmutter came by with little David to talk about mathematics lessons, and while we were talking, David cut himself on a bread knife. Of course his mother was hysterical. 'My beautiful baby! My beautiful baby!'"

She giggled. "And you know as well as I that with those big teeth sticking out and crossed eyes, he's no beauty!"

Semel laughed, then downed a glass of schnapps in one swallow and held out the glass for more. But he saw light fading. He picked up the decanter and walked to the dinner table, his eye on Malka as she covered her face with her hands and blessed the Sabbath candles.

She's learned well, he thought, taking over household duties as a motherless child, learning and improving through the years.

Malka removed the linen cover over the braided challah, and together they recited the prayer of thanks. Semel lifted the silver kiddush cup and began to sing, his sweet voice soaring with ease into the high notes and flowery cantillations. He should have been a cantor, Malka had told him once, and he had laughed and said all cantors are fools, but not all fools are cantors.

"And then, Papa," Malka said, continuing as though nothing had interrupted their conversation, "Saul dropped by. He wanted to see you, said you had business together. Do you know what he meant?"

"Saul? The teacher, Saul? Hm-mm." He stroked his beard as though pondering a question of Talmudic significance.

A good performance, but Malka was not fooled. "You *do* know. It was about me, right?"

"Some herring, my angel, if you please."

She passed him the dish. "Is he, Heaven forbid, going to ask you for my hand?"

Semel stopped chewing. It was not easy to be a father, he thought, especially to a girl. Now a boy, that would have been easy, a boy to play chess with and walk arm in arm on the forest paths arguing philosophy, politics, the commentaries. But then he would have missed the pleasure of watching his tiny Malkaleh grow from a cheerful baby to a curious toddler climbing the bookcases or rearranging his desk drawers, to the spirited teen who never hesitated to speak her mind. And what a miracle took place once his daughter reached the age of fifteen. Not the kind of miracle he had encountered in the holy books; for that he would have been prepared. But the kind that grayed his hair and caused him sleepless nights, the kind the old ladies in the village warned him about:

"You will see, Nathan Semel. This lump will become, God have pity, a woman."

"Yes, a female with all the duties of a horse and the rights of a goat!"

"Mark our words well: Your darkest hours are upon you!"

In spite of their warnings, Malka had finally grown up. True, only five feet tall, but with bright blue eyes and perfect teeth and a smile that could melt the winter snows.

But she was also iron-willed, fierce, independent, stubborn and, worst of all, a lovely curvesome woman. This frightened him, and he prayed for wisdom and strength. That she turned out well must have been due to the Holy One, Praised Be He.

"Papa?"

"Yes, my angel, your dinner is fine."

"You were speaking of Saul?"

"Saul. Yes. The teacher. A fine fellow. Good mind, though a bit clumsy and argumentative, but he makes a decent living . . ."

Malka rose from the table, swooped the herring from under her father's nose, and marched into the kitchen. "I know what you are trying to do," she called in a loud voice, "don't think you are fooling me."

Semel heard the kettles banging, lids clanking on the edge of the basin. "But, my angel . . ."

She placed the steaming dish of chicken and dumplings before him, "I understand. I really do. You're afraid I'm going to end up an old maid like Chaya or Yetta. Never! I have too much pride! And even if I did, do you think I would appear on the streets of this town looking like an old beggar woman twice my age?"

She pulled the napkin into a babushka over her head and scrunched her face into a toothless grimace. Then she croaked, "Hello there, handsome fellow, got a kopek for a poor old soul? So alone, so poor, never married. And without one failing!"

Her father chuckled. This was an old game. "No? What about your huge nose? And the lumps and moles on your skin?"

"The better to keep other men away."

"Your foot is shriveled and you hold it so . . ."

"The better to keep me home where I belong."

"You have a mustache and have to shave every day . . ."

"Oh! You have to pick on one little fault!"

Semel roared and slapped his thigh. "Don't do this to an old man! You are much too clever for me, and I think you know it."

Malka laughed too, then removed the napkin and looked her father in the eye. "Papa, I must know, really, it's only fair. Is Saul going to ask for my hand?"

Semel resumed eating, chewing slowly on a morsel of food. "All right, all right," he said finally, "yes, he is going to ask for your hand. His mother was in the shop today, haggling with me over the price of a chicken, dressed like a pauper so that we take pity on her and maybe . . ."

"What did she say?" Malka challenged. "Tell me the truth!"

"All right. You want to know? I'll tell you. She said that you're still unmarried, and if her son wants to throw away his life on a skinny little girl nobody else wants, that is his business. But the dowry had better be handsome, or she'll tell . . ."

"Oh! Oh! The wretch!" Malka cried, furious. She began pacing the room. "Unmarried! I'm only seventeen! Nobody else wants indeed! Who does she . . . ? Oh! This time she's gone too far!"

"Come, come," her father soothed, "she is an old *yenta*, we all know that. Besides, as the saying goes, you are not marrying the mother. . . ."

"And I am not marrying the son, either!"

"Malka . . ." Semel warned.

"Papa, listen to me. I don't want to marry Saul, or anyone else right now. King Arthur himself could ride up on a white horse and I'd turn him down. I think there's a better life out there, somewhere. There has to be. There are children who can't read, girls as well as boys, and they need me to teach them."

She was careful not to go too far. If moved to anger, her father could insist, and her options were already severely limited.

"I hope, Papa, that there's more to life than marriage to a provincial, passionless, unromantic man. I can wait. Please, don't try to make a marriage for me with Saul or anyone else, because I will not honor it."

At the look in her father's eyes, Malka quickly added, "I love you, Papa, and I respect you, but I want to choose my own life. Please, is that so much to ask?"

Nathan Semel would never have admitted it, but he admired his daughter's courage and her flair for words as a wonder and a gift. But go against his will? Never. Impossible. That was not tradition.

That also was not the problem. Semel was not yet convinced that giving his daughter's hand in marriage to Saul Mendelberg *was* his will. So how could he insist on it?

He knew Saul was better off than most of the young men in their village, and with him Malka would never be cold or hungry. But that only sharpened his fear of falling into the old trap: with money in your pocket, you are wise and you are handsome, and you sing well, too. He would like to resign from the whole problem, but that was out of the question. He must put his own head in order.

"So?" she said.

"So," he said, "it will not be Saul?"

"It will not be Saul."

"But it will be someone, yes?"

Malka shrugged. "Who knows? He may live in this town, or Lvov or Timbuktu! But *I* will choose him, not his mother or my father." She paused and softened her voice. "Is that terribly untraditional of me?"

Semel nodded. "Yes."

"Disobedient?"

He hesitated. "Well . . ."

"Acceptable?"

"Perhaps."

Malka leaned back in the chair. "But I must tell you, if I never meet the right man, then I will never marry. You agree to that, too?"

Semel closed his eyes, her last words were almost comical to him. Sure, Malka, he thought, sure, my angel, with no one in the village suitable to your taste, you may end up like Yetta or Chaya. An old maid. With no one waiting to sweep you off your feet, you can feel safe, eh?

"Papa?" Malka said, waiting for his reply.

"Tell me honestly," Semel said, "are you afraid of marriage?"

She thought a moment. "There seem to be so few happy ones. Were you happy with mama?"

"Yes."

"Then yours must be the only one. My married friends speak of it as such a burden."

Semel raised his eyebrows. "Oh? Then they never heard the words of your Grandmother Tsippa, may she rest in peace."

"And what were they?"

Semel's eyes twinkled. "It may be a burden to carry, but a pity to throw away!"

Unable to sleep, that night Malka lay in bed watching two frisky moonbeams playing tag across the bedroom floor. It reminded her of the dialogue at dinner. Her words had been harsh and didactic, she realized that now. Confused, she thought again about marriage, weighing its advantages and disadvantages, wondering if her arguments were as silly then as they sounded. The only answers came from her little voice within, the voice of reason that often challenged her but rarely brought enlightenment or comfort.

She closed her eyes. Help me, she urged silently.

So ask.

What am I, some kind of harpy? What sets me off when marriage is discussed?

I'll tell you what sets you off.

Yes?

No one should make a marriage for anyone.

But the matchmaker . . .

He's the worst!

It's tradition.

Is it engraved in stone?

No.

Did it come down from Mount Sinai?

No.

Then traditions can be ended as well as begun.

Words.

Not necessarily, Malka.
The world is changing. Some day . . .
But not now.
No.
You hurt your father.
I know.
Shame.
Yes. But I feel strongly about it. So strongly that I will
hurt my father before I agree. Is that terrible of me?
Yes.
I love my father very much.
Tell him.
And I will try never to hurt him again.
That's nice.
But I will not let anyone else choose a husband for me.
Fine.
I mean it!
All right. So why are you crying?
I—I may never know a man. I mean . . .
I know what you mean. And it's true.
It's very hard to be a woman.
Yes.
There is no man I know that I would marry.
I have that memorized.
I will not! I will not!
Malka.
Yes?
The girl who cannot dance says the band cannot play.
Go away.
All right. But I will be back.

SIX

✧❦✧

IT WAS THE HEIGHT OF SUMMER WHEN JACOB CROSSED the foothills of the Ural Mountains into Siberia. He saw the flat, weed-cluttered land begin to change shape, gradually swelling into tidy ridges and small hummocks reflecting the careful order of the farmer's plow. Wetlands shimmered in the heat. Golden cultivated fields dotted more and more of the landscape, and young fir trees and birch groves stood green against the azure sky. Cattle grazed peacefully in verdant pastures and fields of corn stood tall, waving in the breeze of summer. With the harrowing winter behind him, Jacob found the vista extraordinary, a welcome relief from the cold, monotonous meadows and unfriendly peasants he had encountered during the past months.

Siberia looked exactly as Danilo had predicted. It was like entering a new country where he could relax with the amiable natives and accept their warm hospitality without fear of police or pogroms. He saw sables running free in the forests bordering the towns. He decided to catch some of them to make a fur vest for the coming winter. By the time he reached Kamishloff he had enough pelts for a whole jacket, complete with hood.

He also found the inhabitants of the pretty town on the banks of the Pyshma River exceedingly friendly and hospitable. Jacob's presence was never questioned. Meals with several different families were always the same: shtshee, a kind of cabbage soup, sharp but delicious, fresh milk, and hot bread. Simple food, as much as he could eat, and never once did any of his kind hosts ask for payment. He learned their customs and adapted to them quickly. The man of the house shook his hand when they met, and Jacob learned to squat on his heels during the meal instead of sitting on a chair. The position was uncomfortable, straining legs still stiff from the day's walk. But he focused his thoughts on the generosity of his new friends.

It was during his stay with one family in Kamishloff that he perfected the bachelor's skill for staying out of trouble. It started when they made him a proposition that was becoming familiar.

"You are a fine, strapping young man, and would be a great asset to our family," his host said one night after dinner. They sat on a log outside the house, the night around them quiet, the only sound the gurgling river just beyond the yard.

"Your kindness is appreciated, my friend," Jacob said, "but I'll be on my way tomorrow."

"This thing you must do," the man said, "why can't you do it from here? This is a nice place, right?"

Jacob nodded. "Very nice. But my business is far, and I can't put off leaving any longer."

The man puffed on his crudely carved pipe, blowing smoke into the night air and watching the plumes curl above their heads before drifting away. "My daughter, Sonya," he said, finally, "she is beautiful, no?"

"She is beautiful," Jacob agreed, and the image of the black-eyed, full-breasted Sonya filled his mind. Her hand had wickedly stroked his upper thigh throughout dinner, and his fantasy had centered on her blatant eroticism in the presence of her family and how wild she might be with him in private.

"And she would make a fine wife, yes?" The man asked.

"Quite a prize for some worthy Tartar fellow," Jacob said carefully. "It's a pity I can't marry until my wanderings are ended. Your daughter can do much better than that." But oh, he thought, one night with Sonya, one night spent unraveling the fabled mysteries of ecstasy with so gifted a teacher, and I would gladly lose my innocence.

The man nodded, rose and tapped the bowl of the pipe on his boot. "You are a clever man. If you come this way on your return, try to stop with us again. You are always welcome."

The third day out of Kamishloff, Jacob entered the town of Tyumen and picked the river bank as a resting place. Sitting at the edge of the Toura river, its waters running with a swift current that gouged out steep inclines to the pastures and fields, he wondered if his luck, all good so far, would hold. The law of averages worried him. Somewhere along the way, he knew it had to balance out. He thought of Khotin and compared that sad, miserable village with this town. Here, instead of dead, rutted lands and scraggly crops, there were flowers everywhere, growing in colorful profusion in window boxes and gardens.

But the blisters on both his feet were full-blown. He limped to the river bank and pulled off what remained of his boots. The soles were worn through, the stitching long rotted and gone. Bits of newspaper and dried leaves stuffed inside his stockings had been pulverized to a powder and floated away on the wind.

Jacob looked at the sorry state of his boots and thought about how homesick he was, how haunted by guilt and worry. Was his family all right? Safe from the Cossacks? Were they being punished for his escape?

He studied the blisters on his feet. They were large, filled with fluid, and so tender he could not bear to touch them.

"Are those your feet?"

Jacob turned. A little boy stood near, sweet-faced and blue-eyed, direct and curious, who looked in that instant like his little brother, Velvel. Jacob caught his breath. Then he smiled and said, "They're my feet, all right."

"They're funny."

"Are they?"

"Uh-huh. I mean, not funny exactly, more like queer." The child laughed.

"Oh. Yes. I guess they are queer. Sore, really, from walking," Jacob explained. "You ever have sore feet?

"No.

"Lucky you." The boy came closer and sat nearby.

"What's your name?" he asked.

"You first," Jacob said.

"Mm-hmm, all right. Gregor."

"That's a nice name."

"Now you," the child insisted.

Jacob pretended to look at his sore feet and wondered if he could trust this child. "Where do you live, Gregor?"

"Not far. In that white house by the garden, see? My mother is baking cookies."

"And your father?"

"He's at work. How can you walk with no shoes?"

"I guess I can't," Jacob admitted. "Perhaps you can lend me yours."

The boy looked down at his little shoes, looked back at Jacob's big feet, and laughed.

"You're fooling me, aren't you?"

"Yes." The child's laughter was infectious.

"But maybe my father has a pair that would fit you."

What if Jacob were a scoundrel eager to gain entrance to the home, harm the parents, take off with a bag full of valuables? Was this child unaware that such people existed?

A woman's voice called out and the child waved and ran home to the white house by the garden.

With the distraction gone, Jacob wriggled down the river bank to dangle his feet in the cool water. He realized this new pain had replaced his hunger pangs, and a wry thought crossed his mind: the way to endure hunger is to hurt in two places. That way you have tolerance for only one pain.

The sun was hotter now, angled just above his head. He felt relaxed and lazy, sleepy, like the bees buzzing around the little boy's garden. In only a minute or two, he was asleep.

"Here, here, we'll have none of that in our town."

Jacob felt something prodding his backside and sat up. "What is it?" he asked.

"No bums allowed. D'you hear me? No bums!"

The man speaking wore a tall hat with medallions marching in stiff military order around the crown. He was bending over as he yelled, and it was his cane Jacob had felt.

"I'm not a bum," Jacob protested, attempting to stand. "I am traveling through your town, that's all. I guess the heat of the noon sun, and the pleasant cool of the . . ."

"No more. Just take your things and move on." The man with the hat stood up, but when Jacob tried to stand, he winced with pain and sat down quickly.

"What have we here?" the man asked. He leaned over and picked up Jacob's foot, examining it closely.

"Nasty, nasty," he said. "You should never have walked on these sores. Look how bad they are. I'm surprised you can walk at all."

"Well, as I said, I'm only passing through. As soon as I can find another pair of shoes, I'll be off again."

"I don't think you'll be walking soon," the man said. "Come with me. I'll see what I can do."

"And why should I do that?" Jacob asked sharply. Better, he thought, to be obnoxious than frightened. The man might be the local constable and start asking too many questions.

Exasperated, the man said, "Because I am Balenkov, the town's doctor. If you want help, I can give it. If you prefer to suffer, by all means, go on."

Jacob went home with him and the doctor lanced, disinfected, and bandaged his blisters. He sat in the doctor's parlor and played checkers with the little boy. Now that his stomach was full and his pain eased, he felt obliged to stay until his feet healed. But he chafed at the delay. Hundreds of miles lay ahead, most in the heart of the coming winter, and his crossing the strait was delicately timed. He must be patient, he must be in perfect health, or he had no chance against the Arctic cold.

"So, Jacob," Dr. Balenkov said, coming in from his waiting room. "How do you feel?"

"Much better, thank you. When can I be on my way?"

"Oh, maybe a week or two. But you must rest those feet. Feet are truly wonderful things. You can stand on them, kick, dance, but they cannot take continuous punishment, especially without shoes, or you see what happens!"

Through the next week, Jacob sat inside the house or in the garden when the weather was balmy. The Balenkov family's kindness was extraordinary and their hospitality and warmth put Jacob at ease. Their peculiar dialect was odd to his ear but not impossible, and he was beginning to think the law of averages had been beaten.

He had forgotten about the local police.

"Jacob Finesilver?" Two officers stood at the foot of his bed. The family had gone on a picnic.

"Yes?" Jacob said, half asleep. As soon as the word passed his lips, he realized his mistake.

One officer threw Jacob's clothes on the bed. "Put these on and let's get going."

"What seems to be the problem? What have I done?"

"We will tell you when we feel like it," the other officer said. His smile was forced and his few remaining teeth were chipped and rotted.

Jacob stumbled on his bandaged feet between the two officers, trying desperately not to cry out in pain as they dragged him along the dusty streets.

"If you would walk faster, we wouldn't have to push you."

As he hurried Jacob along, the officer's eyes moved erratically, as if trying to see everything at once. His companion was a bully but did not frighten Jacob. This one did.

"Cool down, Mitya," the other officer said, "he is more valuable to us alive than dead. Come on, into the police station."

Immediately other officers surrounded him, shoving their rifle butts into his stomach and ribs.

But Jacob disappointed them. He knew their intent: anger him enough to try an escape, and then they would shoot him, nice and legal.

They dragged Jacob to the center of the warm room. With no wall to lean on, he had to stand straight. When he sagged or swayed, one of the men struck him across his bandaged feet with a baton. If he cried out, another slapped his mouth.

"So, Jew, where are your long curls?" Mihail poked Jacob's chest with his finger. "We heard if you cut them, your ass falls off!"

This sent the men into a fit of raucous laughter. One of them moved behind Jacob and pulled down his trousers. "But his ass is still there," the man cried. Then he reached around and attempted to expose him, but Jacob swung and his fist connected with the man's chin.

"You filthy dog," Mitya growled, grabbing Jacob at the neck of his shirt, "we should hang you right now for striking an officer. Permission, Mihail?"

"Shut your mouth, and let go of him," Mihail snapped, but his eyes glittered at the prospect. "That does not mean we won't do it eventually."

Not satisfied, Mitya persisted, "We want to hear you say your prayers. You are the Jew from Khotin? Yes?"

Hands at his sides, teeth clenched, Jacob did not reply.

"Shut up, Mitya," Mihail growled, "your yelling is giving me a headache."

As the light faded in the west window, Jacob sat on the floor and rubbed his bandaged feet to restore circulation. He was waiting for the next move when the two men returned.

The angry officer glared at Jacob. "Damn you . . . you are spoiling my record. Damn you anyway."

"Enough!" Mihail cried. "Take him into the cell and let him rot." He smiled suddenly. "With the other prisoners."

The cell was small. Empty. It had no cot, no toilet, no chair, no window. Forced to lie on the stained, rough-hewn floor, Jacob listened to small animals scurrying in the dark. He had no doubt these were the "other prisoners."

Was this to be the end of his long odyssey? To lie with the rats all night, then be shot in the morning by a couple of demented soldiers?

When the scratching sounds came too near, Jacob rolled away, praying for sleep, loathing the thought of the filthy little beasts crawling over him. But sleep did not come, and he spent the night rolling back and forth to keep them away. At dawn, he heard muted voices from the station and briefly entertained the thought of escape. But how far could he run, on his bandaged feet, and where could he run to? As accommodating as the people of Tyumen were, he had no illusions about loyalty.

There was no breakfast. No lunch. No water or break for toilet needs; without a clock, or meals, or window light, he lost all sense of time.

The cell was stifling, no air coming in through the bars. Dehydrated from lack of water, he felt the heat consuming him. He closed his eyes and tried to imagine the cool stream near his house in Khotin. When he opened them, his father was standing inside the cell.

"Papa?" he said. The vision wavered. "Papa, is that you?" he called. But the vision was gone.

"And who is this calling for his papa?" Mitya stood on the other side of the bars, mocking his prisoner. "He wants his daddy."

Jacob turned his back on the officer and faced the wall again.

"Look at me when I speak to you!" Mitya cried. "I said, look at me!"

In Yiddish, Jacob muttered, "Go to hell."

Strange, the way the vision had fooled him, looking like his father on the day he had died, beaten, just as Jacob now was, but protesting until the last that he would not die at the hands of the Cossacks.

But he had died. The carpenter who had studied the Holy Books and never missed a chance to play with his children or affectionately pat his wife's bottom. David Finesilver had been a fixer, teaching his son how to work with wood, to use glue if nails were scarce, and to use pegs if he had no glue. "Never throw anything away that can be fixed or made into something else. If your hands are clever enough, Jacob, you can fix anything. If your brain is clever enough, you can survive anything. Man was meant to work. And love. That's all a man needs. Work and love."

"But Papa, what about study? Leo says men should study and pray."

"Poor Leo. What can he know of life, sitting like a lump of wet matzo meal every day, reading, arguing, letting his family support him? Someone has to work the fields and milk the cows."

"But Papa, Leo said if we all pulled together, maybe we could be rich and never be hungry again."

"If all men pulled in one direction," his father retorted, "the world would fall over!"

Just before he died, he had taken his wife's hand to comfort her. "Listen, Gittel," he said, "ever since dying came into fashion, life hasn't been safe. I'm not going anywhere without you. I have to see the new baby, don't I?"

He was buried one week before his second son was born.

More days passed, and more nights, each one worse than the last. The rats brought their families with them to dance over the prisoner, some emboldened enough to take a nip here and there.

From time to time Jacob heard loud discussions between the men in the station as they debated the merits of shooting or starving him to death, each voice claiming the "best solution." He knew he was safe as long as they argued.

How could he have been so stupid, admitting to his name like that? He had grown careless, inattentive to danger. The kindness of the Balenkov family had put him off his guard. He would remember that and not let it happen again, if he got out of this.

At noon of the fourth day, he was suddenly released from the cell and dragged into the station. There, speaking amiably to the two arresting officers, was Dr. Balenkov, dressed in his white medical jacket and hat of marching medals. He turned to Jacob, and frowned. "Aha, so there you are," the doctor said. "What a stupid thing to do, getting hauled into the police department when you know you should be resting from surgery. And how terrible you look, so dirty and stinky. Shame on you!"

Balenkov turned to Mihail. "Now, by what right have you arrested this man?"

Mihail tried to stand straight and tall and unafraid, but failed all three. "By the right of authority vested in me by the . . ."

"Bullshit," the doctor said calmly, "the authority vested in you is my approval. And you know it. Now, what is he supposed to have done?"

"He is an escaped Jew, and this message received only last week asks that we pick him up and send him back to . . . to Khotin." Mihail was nervous. His hand holding the paper shook with anger.

"So what?" the doctor said, "are we responsible for some crazy official edict from another district? I will not allow my patient to be treated this way."

"Sir," Mitya interrupted, "I'm sorry to say we must send him back. If we don't, we will be punished. You know that. You also know we will hold you personally responsible for our plight."

He smiled and his eyes did their dance again. Familiar with this trick, and the dim but dangerous wit of the man, the doctor tempered his reply.

"I see. All right. You may have him . . ."

Jacob, stunned, wondered how he could tell a friend from an enemy.

"But only after my treatment is over," the doctor continued. "And not a moment before."

Mitya and Mihail conferred briefly, then nodded. "But just so we know, Doctor, how long will that be?"

"When I say so! Come along, my boy." The doctor took Jacob's arm and walked him to the door. "Don't look back," Balenkov hissed through his teeth, "keep walking, even it's killing you. And don't stop. I won't let you fall."

"You've lost weight," the doctor said, as they talked in

the garden later that day. He had treated the purple bruises, the swollen eyes, and the fresh cuts around Jacob's nose. A large plaster now covered stitches on his forehead.

But more hurtful to Jacob than the bruises was the doctor's casual attitude about his arrest and ordeal in jail. This was Balenkov's town, after all, his regiment, his police. Was he not aware of their cruelty and prejudice? And the rats?

But Jacob bit his tongue. After all, the man had to live here, not Jacob. "How did you secure my release?" He finally asked.

"'You see this hat of mine," the doctor said, grinning like a child with a toy, "covered around with these brass medallions? Each one represents a life I saved, each one for a soldier of this town's regiment. I was honored with these medals, a nice pot of money, and a commission in the regiment higher than anyone here."

He laughed and refilled their wineglasses. "And I love it when I can get the best of those two cretins."

"They'll be back for me," Jacob said grimly. "Don't you want to know why?"

"It doesn't matter why. They are fools. So it stands to reason the error is on their side. And, yes, they'll be back. But you won't be here. In fact, I think I'll kill you off. Then they can close the case."

"Kill me?" Jacob said, startled. "What is this? More bullshit?"

"Oh, my dear fellow, of course," the doctor laughed. "I am very good at that! But I didn't mean it literally. Only medically. I'll fill out the papers myself. In the meantime, you'll be hidden away like a family embarrassment until you are well enough to travel."

Leaning close to Jacob, he said soothingly, "After all, the men were only doing their duty, following orders, nothing more. You people are too sensitive, my boy." He smiled at

Jacob's shocked expression. "Yes, yes, of course I knew. And they had no malice against you personally, I'm sure. You would have done the same were the situation reversed, yes? Of course. So would I. So promise me, Jacob, that you'll remember our little town of Tyumen and its friendly people. And think of us often, with fond memories. And a big smile!"

SEVEN

❧

THE SHORT SIBERIAN SUMMER FLAMED OUT IN A RIOT
of bright fall colors, reminding Jacob that the most arduous
part of his journey now lay directly ahead. He must walk
through the deep winter from eastern Siberia to the Bering
Sea, then cross the frozen strait into Alaska.

Hunger was now as constant as the stars, and Jacob
became much more aggressive in the hunt for small game.
Sometimes he lay in wait two or three days, hiding in brush
piles or behind large boulders, or in deep holes in the rough
ground, hoping that even a chipmunk would dart into view.
Then he could roast it on a stick over a fire, and try to eat it
slowly so it would last longer. But the further north he went,
the less game he found.

He should have seen signs that day of the coming storm.
The air was heavy, dark clouds rolling in quickly, lightning
streaking across the sky. But his thoughts were not on the
weather. He was thinking only of food, searching, digging,
clawing through rough clods of heavy dirt for anything edible, expecting the waters to dwindle at the bottom of a gorge
and hopefully reveal the tender shoots from roots or bulbs or
tubers. Then he would look on higher ground, where fruit
might grow along the slopes.

But hunger and the oppressive heat tired him. He poked

along the bank of a stream and picked a few scattered berries, holding the sweet fruit under his swollen tongue before swallowing. He washed his face in the cool mountain water, then sat down on the silty bottom, bathing his emaciated body and ragged clothes.

When he looked up, he saw black clouds gathering. Before he could find adequate shelter, the clouds dumped their cold, hard rain. As he stumbled through the woods the rain continued, the storm's intensity rising with the wind. Sheets of lightning flashed across the mottled sky and thunder resounded seconds later through the boulder-strewn meadow. He stood amid trees that were straining to hold the ground, their silvery leaves flying from wind-tossed branches and glittering in the lightning like newly minted coins.

Running from under the trees, he found the path suddenly blocked. Tree trunks had snapped and fallen, causing those struck by lightning to burn. Rain hissed inside their thick bark as he groped through the smoke. Gaining the clearing at last, he saw a steady light in the distance. He ran for it and soon reached a small timber house in a grove of pines. He knocked on the door.

"Who is it?" a woman's voice called from within.

"A stranger caught in the storm," Jacob shouted.

A moment later, the door opened only wide enough for the woman inside to see who stood on her threshold.

"What do you want?" she called, struggling to hold the door steady.

"Shelter," Jacob cried. "Only until the storm is over."

There was no answer. He turned to go, then heard her say, "Well, come in then, come in."

He ducked inside and stood awkwardly, dripping water onto the wooden floor. The woman picked up the kerosene lamp and held it closer to inspect her visitor.

"And what are you up to, out on a terrible night like this?"

The light fell on her plump, lined face; wisps of blonde hair strayed out from under a print kerchief tied over her head. She was his mother's age, Jacob guessed, and appeared to have been awakened from sleep. He could see the rumpled bed against the far wall, a fire banked in the grate. The room was comfortable and clean, but the worn furnishings gave away the woman's meager estate.

She replaced the lamp on a table and began scolding her visitor. "Don't stand there making a mess in my house! Out of those wet clothes! Phew!"

Before Jacob could object, the woman was undoing his buttons and hooks, pushing away his hands when he tried to stop her.

"Don't interfere, young man, it's my floor that's swallowing all that water. If you stay, you stay in a change of linen. Or you stay naked. I don't care. As long as you're dry."

She turned and rummaged in an old trunk at the foot of the bed, tossing out blankets, quilts, finally a man's shirt and pants which she handed to him. "My Volya's clothes. Packed away since he died last year. Come now," she urged, "put them on. I'll take the wet rags you're wearing and dry them by the fire."

She watched him standing mute before her, his cheeks scarlet with embarrassment at having to strip in front of her, and she laughed. "I won't look! In the name of all the saints, get undressed before you catch pneumonia. See? I am turning my back."

Jacob peeled away the wet shirt and handed it to the woman. Then his tattered shoes, pants, and the shreds of underwear clinging to his cold, wet body.

Her gaze averted, she took them all, wrung them out over a basin, and hung them on pot hooks above the grate while Jacob dressed in the dead husband's clothes. They were much too small and he sat, uncomfortable, on the trunk.

"Thank you, Madame," he said, "you may turn around now."

"Well, isn't that better?" She laughed at the fit of the trousers ending well above his ankles, the shirt straining at the few snaps he could close. "Volya was a good man, even though he was ill tempered, and beat me when he was drunk," she said. The laughter suddenly died on her lips.

She stirred the embers of the fire and added a log, the dry wood catching and flaming up, allowing Jacob to see her better. Her figure was round and firm, the bosom ample under the flannel nightgown, and her skin glowed with health and vitality. When she laughed, the lined face relaxed and looked younger, and her eyes sparkled coquettishly. "Hungry?" she asked.

"Well . . ."

"Some hot soup, eh? To warm you."

Without waiting for an answer, she stirred a pot over the fire and made a place for Jacob at the table.

"You're very kind . . ." he began.

"Don't be silly." Her voice had become musical, with a girlish inflection. "I don't get much company these days, what with Volya gone and all, and besides my soup is very good. Why not share it with a young traveler, I say."

"It smells delicious." Jacob took the bowl and hungrily spooned the soup into his mouth.

"It's not good to be hungry," the woman said softly, almost to herself. "What is your name?" she asked.

Jacob looked up over the bowl and mumbled, "Ivan."

"A good name. Mine is Elena." As the woman spoke, she absently twisted a curl at her ear. "You like that name?"

"Oh, yes, sure," Jacob said, handing the woman his empty bowl.

"More?" she asked. "It's no imposition when I have a whole kettle full."

But instead of refilling the bowl, she stared at the handsome young man dressed in her dead husband's clothes. A new expression crossed her face. Her dark eyes grew round and over-bright. Jacob heard the ringing clamor of alarm. "So young, so fair," the woman murmured, "and I have been alone so very long."

Her train of thought suddenly clear to Jacob, he blurted, "That's some storm outside . . . it caught me by surprise . . ."

She moved closer, and Jacob was able to catch the scent of strong soap. She looked down at him with a faraway smile, and began to stroke his head.

"Remember our first time, in my uncle's barn, the day so warm we were both like sweaty oxen, remember?"

"Madame," Jacob said quickly, "I think . . . you're mistaken. . . ."

" . . . and I so young, only fourteen, and after you hurt me, then came the good feelings, oh, so good."

Pressing her bosom against Jacob's face, she moaned and held his head fast. His body suddenly responded with a rush of heat and pleasure. Blood pounded in his brain. He reached for her ripe breasts brushing across his lips.

He had never held a woman close or felt her velvety skin on his own, or smelled the pungent fragrance of feminine desire. Jacob's innocence was profound. His eagerness to go further, to finally experience the celebrated rite of passage into manhood, burned in his groin.

"Take my hand," she said softly, pulling him toward her bed. "Let me show you how nice it is to be naughty."

He followed her blindly, falling onto the bed and rolling over until he rested on top. She reached to tear the tight pants from his body, her hand stabbing between his legs, clasping, squeezing, pulling, until, screaming with desire, she spread herself wide to receive him.

It would have been easy for Jacob to surrender to his first

sexual act with this hungry widow. But cool reason betrayed him as effectively as ice water thrown in his face, warning him that after her passion was spent, the woman could just as easily report the sexual encounter as rape. And if a search was still in effect for the Jew from Khotin, what a handsome reward there would be for turning him in.

Added to this were Danilo's words, each one loud and distinct as he had first spoken the exhortation: "You must run from the hungry-eyed widows—it gains you nothing but trouble!" This he did not need. His innocence would have to remain unchanged and his curiosity unsatisfied until he had gained his freedom. If not for fear, he thought with great sadness, sinning would be so sweet.

"Don't mistake me for your husband, Madame," he said sharply, "I am not Volya. I'm married to a wonderful woman and we have five children, and she waits impatiently for my return."

He pushed her aside, rose from the bed, trembling, put on the tight pants, and turned to the warm grate.

The woman stared at him, confused, trying to grasp at reality while still lost in her erotic dream. She shook her head and began to cry. "How can you treat me so badly?"I have been a faithful wife—and even gave you hot soup to warm you."

Her cries diminished suddenly, and she cocked her head and eyed Jacob flirtatiously. "Ah, come to bed. Let us quarrel no more. Here," she said, pulling off her gown, "am I not beautiful?"

Her eyes pleading, she used her hands to show him exactly what she wanted, but Jacob, shaken by the sight, looked the other way.

"No, Madame, you're mistaken if you think I will do as you—as you—my marriage vows . . ."

"They never held you back before," she cried angrily,

"don't you think I know about all the women you've shamed me with? All the whores who have shared your swollen manhood? All the . . ."

"Enough!" Jacob yelled. "Pull yourself together, woman, and see me for who I am! I am not your husband. . . ."

He began to strip the mistaken identity from his body, throwing the clothes at her to make his point. She rose and picked up each piece, holding it to her face, inhaling the smell of her dead Volya.

"Oh," she wailed, "how I have missed you. Why did you have to die?"

Jacob dressed in his damp clothing while listening to her cries, knowing she needed comfort but not daring to offer it.

"Thank you," he said, bowing stiffly, "your hospitality is appreciated but I bid you farewell."

She flung herself at Jacob, tearing at him with clawing hands. "No! Don't go! I can't bear the silence."

"It must be difficult for you to live alone," he said, not unkindly, but easing her away, "and I sympathize with your loneliness, but perhaps if you turned to your faith and your inner strength, you would find peace."

"You are not Volya," she said, her mind suddenly clear. "He would never have said such words to me. He was a beast. A peasant with the body of a king. The body . . ." Her eyes clouded over again and she sank back into fantasy.

Jacob turned toward the door.

"Bastard!" she screamed. "Bastard! When I was young, you wouldn't have left me so. Go to hell!"

She picked up a heavy kettle from the grate, struggling with its bulk, and poised to throw it at Jacob's retreating back.

He ducked out quickly, hearing the kettle smash with a deadly thunk against the door behind him. Her curses still railed at him as he ran out of the grove.

Later, lying under the clearing sky, miles from the woman's house, he thought of the vagaries of female temper, the flimsy stuff of beauty, the powerful and terrifying urge that draws man to woman, even when they are both blinded by self-deceit.

Poor Jacob, he thought miserably, you've never kissed a woman other than your mother and sisters, and that was always a peck on the cheek. You've never even seen a woman undressed until tonight. What good is pious devotion to innocence when desire sits like a hot poker between your legs, stiff and uncomforted?

But he could console himself for now by thinking of the wisdom of his choice. When the woman had offered herself, the fiery heat had cooled instantly. Common sense and Danilo's advice had prevailed. It was lucky for Jacob that the old sinner had shared his wisdom.

"Remember, my boy, shun a billy-goat's front, a horse's behind, and a hungry widow's every side! For when men are scarce, even a herring can serve as a fish!"

EIGHT

ꙮ

J<small>ACOB REACHED</small> L<small>AKE</small> B<small>AIKAL EARLY IN THE WINTER</small>.
His maps had warned him he must cross to the other side of
the lake, but, knowing he could never swim that distance, he
had put it out of his mind.

Now, dressed in the fur jacket he had painstakingly sewn
somewhere on the road between Tyumen and Irkutsk, and
the boots stolen off a derelict's rotting corpse, he sat at the
lake's edge and considered how far he had come and what he
had endured.

It was the hand that had stopped him, with its shreds of
blackened skin hanging from bony fingers. He had been
walking through the bare woods and now stopped short of
the lump in the leaves ahead. He kicked at the leaves and they
blew away, revealing the body underneath in a sickening
state of putrefaction. He turned away, fighting dry heaves
from his empty stomach. Breathing deeply he looked again.
It was an old man, eye sockets empty, maggots feasting in the
gaping mouth. A tramp, he thought, lost and missed by no
one, lying dead for weeks. But he was wearing boots. They
were moldy and cracked but better than the shreds of canvas
tied to Jacob's feet with leather strips. Hesitating only a
moment, he bent to remove the boots. What will God think

of me? But it could not be any worse than what he thought of himself.

He looked around at the edge of the lake, and then studied his maps, the paper as threadbare from use as his rags of clothing. He concluded the country here was near mountain ranges, heavily timbered with tall stands of pine and larch, fir and birch and poplar, their deadfall lying around him in abundance. Perhaps there was no need to swim in the cold current after all.

Waiting until later, when he was certain no one was about, Jacob used one of the dead trunks as a boat. Riding with the current, he crossed the lake unseen and took refuge in a mountain cave whose grassy outcropping blended magically into the landscape. When hours had passed and he was certain there were no roaming peasants or houses within walking distance, he built a fire and huddled close to warm his shivering body.

During the next two months, he begged an occasional kibitka ride across the deep pine forests, knowing he was taking a terrible chance with each wagon and driver. He ate what he caught or scavenged from carcasses abandoned by wolves, afterwards making garments and boots from the remnants. He survived the cold by spending days, sometimes weeks, inside caves, leaving the shelters only to hunt or dig for roots.

But time was getting short, and his only thought was to reach the Bering Sea while the water was still frozen. He took chances, making few mistakes by remembering all that Danilo had taught him, his tenuous existence hanging in the balance by the grace of God and his own stubborn determination.

On the third day of February 1897, he began his trek across the frozen, fifty-six-mile Bering Strait. Painfully familiar with the Arctic cold by now, he guessed the temperature to be close to thirty degrees below zero. The sun was low in the horizon, visible only two or three hours a day, and its position, seeming never to change, was confusing.

There was no sensation in his hands. His feet were chunks of ice that it seemed might break apart with each step. A fierce wind cut through the pieces of woolen blanket given him by a Chukchi native to cover his face, and ice kept forming on his beard, his eyebrows, under his nose and around his mouth. To make matters worse, heavy snow was swirling, blowing with tremendous force one way, then darting back, pushing and pulling him in two directions at once. At more than one point he had trouble determining the direction he had come from and staggered in circles, stumbling over the huge blocks of ice thrown up on the shoreline by the winds and currents.

Jacob's luck was running out. He had traveled over four thousand miles, on foot, wagon, raft and river log, the long journey lasting fourteen months.

Now, helpless in the sweep of the glacial Arctic, clothed in rags, starving, freezing, his eyes blinded by the whiteout and frozen shut, he finally fell to the ice.

"Dear God, Holy One," he whispered, "hear my prayer—help me—for my family—don't let me die here—Sh'ma yisroel . . . adonoi . . . elo . . . he . . . nu . . . ado . . . noi . . ."

The sleep before death came to him as he huddled like an infant on the white wasteland, the bitter winds catching at his whispered prayers and scattering them like crystals of snow into oblivion.

NINE

Prince of Wales, Alaska, February, 1897

JACOB LAY ON A HARD, WARM BED, A MOUND OF FURS covering him from his neck to his feet. Vague, hollow shadows floated lazily behind his closed eyes. Waking and dozing under the furs, only dimly aware of strange sounds and smells, he drifted in and out of consciousness.

Each time he awakened and tried to open his eyes they burned and his vision was clouded. But the pain in his eyes was nothing compared to the pain coming from somewhere below, either in a leg or a foot, he could not be sure.

He lay quietly, hoping it would pass and sleep would come again. But the smell of food bubbling near the bed brought him fully awake.

He attempted to sit up, but failed. His heart was beating, he was alive, and that puzzled him. He remembered the blizzard, and the angel of death hovering before him, beckoning, easing him into a deep, warm sleep. He remembered his confession of faith, the anguished prayer whispered and feared lost in the swirling white hell. Knowing all this, he realized it must have been a miracle that had saved him.

He tried to move and change position, but something bulky and hard clunked against the wall behind the bed.

Then a voice was speaking. He could make nothing out of the words, but the voice was feminine, soft and sweet, as if set to music.

"Come now, brave sir, and open your mouth," Meqo urged, sitting beside the bed. "You must regain your strength. My bird's head soup is tasty and hot, and most nourishing."

She held a cool cloth to his closed eyelids and gently wiped away the tears on his face. "Better?" she asked.

He opened his eyes. The tearing finally subsided, and he was able to see the lovely woman bending over him. She was young, her skin smooth, brown and taut over high cheekbones. In the lamp light her long black hair hung straight and shiny with glints of blue, and was gathered back gracefully with some kind of bone ornament. She was naked except for short fur pants, her full breasts barely brushing against his covers as she spoke. Her dark eyes, lively and amused, watched him studying her.

"You are just as curious about me as I am about you," she said, smiling, "but I do not understand your words when you cry them out in your sleep. They are full of feeling, but the language is too strange." She shrugged her shoulders and laughed softly.

Jacob was weak but lifted his head gamely, trying to reach the spoonful of soup she held in her hand.

"Ah, that is good," Meqo said, "you are hungry. But you must not eat too fast or too much. I will help feed you. I will mother you."

She giggled at this and at the memory of Jacob's long, raw-boned body when she and Inuijak had first undressed him and rubbed warm melted grease over the swollen, frost-bitten skin. The thought of mothering this oversize man whose feet hung over the bed was funny, but she was careful not to hurt his feelings. Wearing her most serious expression, she leaned forward and urged him to drink the soup. The hot liquid warmed him, and he soon slept.

He did not awaken again until the following night when Inuijak returned from hunting. The Inuit went immediately to Jacob's bedside.

"How do you feel?" he asked.

Unable to understand, Jacob could only stare at the young brown-skinned man and shake his head.

"He does not speak our tongue, Inuijak," Meqo said to her husband. "How can we know where he is from?"

"This man came from across the ice-bridge," Inuijak said, puzzling out the problem. "On the other side of the bridge is Russia, where the cruel hunters live. It would be a big joke on Inuijak if he has saved an evil Russian life."

"I do not think he is a bad man," Meqo whispered. "His eyes are kind."

Inuijak nodded. But it did not add up. The Russian hunters dressed correctly for the bitter winters. This man had nothing on but rags. Still, he must be Russian. There was one way to find out.

The Inuit asked, this time in Russian, "How you feel?"

Jacob's eyes widened in surprise. He must be dreaming. How can this be? An Eskimo who speaks Russian? And then the terrible thought struck him; he had not made it after all. He was still in Siberia. The thought was so terrifying, his voice suddenly returned.

"Where am I . . . ?"

"You are in a settlement of Prince of Wales. In Alaska. United States of America," Inuijak said, carefully articulating each word.

"Alaska?" Jacob's voice was a hoarse croak, but the couple had no trouble hearing his excitement. "Then I made it! I made it to Alaska! To America! But how did I get . . . here?"

The Inuit smiled proudly and said, "Inuijak, that is me,

find you on ice-bridge. Thought you were seal or whale, make good meal for whole village. Then I bring you home on sled."

"Then *you* were the miracle." Jacob lay back against the wall. After a moment he opened his sore eyes and looked again, bewildered, at the Eskimo. "But you speak Russian? How . . ."

"Inuijak learn Russian from Russians!" He sat next to Jacob and told him about the intruders who came up from the Aleutian Islands, killing vast numbers of seals and otters for their valuable skins. He told him how they raped the Eskimo women and dealt treacherously with the men, paying low wages for guiding and then stealing pelts from their traps. He paused, then asked his question. "You Russian?"

Jacob nodded slowly, hoping his admission would not make the Inuit angry. "But my work is not hunting," he added quickly. "I kill animals only to eat. I do not believe in killing."

Inuijak turned to his wife, a big smile creasing his face. "You see? *Inua* spirits send us good man, not bad. We should have more faith."

Jacob shifted his position on the bed and again heard the dull clunk against the wall. "What is that?" he asked.

"That is strip of wood to hold bone of leg together. But maybe lose leg."

Shocked, Jacob stared at Inuijak, his throat tight. After a horrified moment, he cried, "Lose my leg? Why? What are you saying? What happened to it?"

"It broke. Bones tear out of skin. Then skin freeze, look bad to Inuijak." He shrugged. "But maybe okay."

Jacob fell back wearily on the bed, too exhausted to understand the Eskimo's words. He would try another time. He hoped it was an exaggeration on the Eskimo's part. Jacob would ask him again when he felt better.

The pain in his leg worsened later that day, and changing position was impossible because of the makeshift splint. He began to be aware of some pain in his left hand. It too was heavily wrapped, and he wondered if it was broken.

The next day, Jacob awoke to find Inuijak tying leather strips to the splint then hanging the strips from a complicated contraption on the ceiling. The Inuit pulled on the strips until Jacob's leg was raised up to a twenty-five-degree angle.

"That better, much better," Inuijak said, a satisfied smile on his smooth, brown face. "Leg go up so swelling go down."

"What is your name?" Jacob asked. "What can I call you?"

"Inuijak. In-oo-ee-jak, yes? Wife Meqo. Mee-ko. And you?"

"Jacob. I don't think I remembered it yesterday, so I must be better."

"Jay-coop. Nice name." The Inuit sat on the end of the bed and spoke gently, struggling to make Jacob understand his limited Russian. "Listen, Jaycoop, leg broke, but not big bone. Little bone next to big bone. I try fix . . . but . . ." He went on to explain that the jagged edge of bone had torn through the frostbitten skin. He had set the bone, which would heal, but the skin was black. A tourniquet tied above the gangrene was loosened a little each day to permit a gradual return of circulation. If Jacob was lucky, the gangrene would slough away and the skin would heal itself. But if infection set in, the leg had to come off.

Tears rolled down Jacob's cheeks. Inuijak had saved his life. His remedies must be proven and therefore accepted, no matter how ancient or homespun, but hope was beginning to fade.

"When?" Jacob asked.

"We know by next moon. You have spirits?"

"Spirits?"

"Spirits to pray to. We pray many times to Inua spirits. Sing songs. Sometimes spirits hear us. Sometimes not."

"Ah, I see. Yes." Jacob closed his eyes.

"It is time to pray, Jaycoop," Inuijak said softly. "We pray, too."

The young couple sang through most of the night. Jacob knew the prayers were for him and he was deeply touched. He tried to pray, but because he and the Holy One had shared the desperate fight for life, he felt he could not ask Him this time for his leg too. But he could hope.

During the following week, the Inuit couple looked under the splint three or four times each day. Inuijak often took a sharp knife to the blackened skin, picking at it with small, delicate strokes. Jacob clenched his teeth during these tedious, painful stretches of time and thought about home and family.

He wondered what good he was to them now. So many questions bedeviled his waking hours. How do you mine for gold on one leg? And what had happened to his left hand? Is there danger of losing that, too? But he did not ask.

When sunlight began to spill down through the holes in the roof and lasted almost the entire day, Jacob knew it was spring. Not spring as he had known it in Khotin; the temperature was still far below zero. Here spring meant only a return of the sun.

But the possibility of losing his leg tormented every waking minute. For the first time in his life Jacob's despair became as black as the rotten, gangrenous skin on his leg, and not even bright sunshine could cheer him.

One morning in late March, Inuijak cut the thongs holding up the splinted leg, lowered it gently and removed the splint and bandages.

"Now we take good look at leg of Jaycoop. Spirits have plenty time to make it better," Inuijak said, smiling.

Meqo stood with her husband by the side of the bed and silently mouthed some words, her body swaying to an inner music. Every once in a while, she would stop and look into Jacob's eyes, as if by sheer will she were sending her prayer straight through him to the spirit in charge. Jacob held his breath and watched her until panic suddenly made him afraid, and he shut his eyes. It seemed a very long time until Inuijak spoke.

"No hide from leg," Inuijak scolded. "You look now. See how fine and straight."

His heart thumping, Jacob got up his courage and opened his eyes.

Inuijak was right. The leg was straight, the bones had knitted as good as new. But the bones had never been the question.

He watched as the Eskimo peered closely at the skin, his nose almost touching the scarred flesh. He turned the leg one way, then another, poking gently with his fingers, testing the skin. Then he raised his head, smiling with satisfaction. "Look, Jaycoop. Look and see what Inuijak and spirits do."

The wound, debrided so painstakingly by Inuijak, had closed. All the careful picking and scraping away of the dead, blackened skin had allowed new tissue to form and take its place. The skin's color was pink and healthy, and aside from deep scarring where the jagged bone had torn through, the mangled leg was healed.

Jacob was whole again. His heart was full of gratitude to the Holy One, Praised Be He, and to his kind and gifted friends and the spirits who watched over them. Songs of joy filled his mouth and tears ran from his eyes. His glance caught the sunlight dancing on the walls, the sudden sparkle as the bright rays grazed the rivulets of water running down from the roof. The world was spinning on its axis, the planets were in place, and everything was as it should be. He would walk again, and he would not be a pitiful wanderer in a new world.

TEN

꙰

JACOB SAT ON THE PILE OF FURS AND WATCHED MEQO
sew, her small brown hands sure and quick as she worked to
attach a hood to a furskin parka. He was able to walk now,
becoming more agile on his healed leg. Sometimes he would
think back to when he had first been brought here, and everything had seemed so new and strange, how frightened he had
been, and how kind his hosts were. They had tried to prepare
him for a disadvantaged life as a cripple, easing him into what
his life might be, and rejoicing when he was healed.

Now in the gloom of the sod house, light from the flickering lamps fell on luxurious furs of fox, seal, wolf, bear and
wolverine, skins of musk, ox and caribou, duck and goose.
Often during his recuperation his gaze lingered over the blubber lamps, or he would admire the handy rig Meqo had built
in the ceiling for cooking pots.

He had the chance to examine the fur clothes they wore
in the deep winter cold, cleverly made to keep in body heat
without causing sweating. Jacob was charmed by Inuijak's
birdskin shirts, worn with the feathers inside for maximum
warmth.

The sod house was small, a warren of niches, cubbyholes,
shelves, and hooks. Against the wall leaned a sealskin basin
for ice, which melted down into drinking water, while sus-

pended from the ceiling was an intricate wooden framework for drying boots and outerwear.

Jacob considered the soapstone lamps works of art, each one carved into a whimsical animal. These burned blubber oil constantly, and he learned that tending the lamps was the wife's honorable duty. The more lamps, the greater the honor. Everything about this Eskimo house was a wonder, he thought, as exotic and rare to him as Chinese spaghetti must have seemed to Marco Polo.

When his host was off hunting for days at a time, Jacob would help Meqo in her various tasks. One day he picked up the needle she used so skillfully.

"This?" he asked.

"Needle," she replied in her own tongue.

He repeated the word and handed her the needle.

"Show me," he said, miming the sewing motion.

Meqo threaded the bird bone needle with narwhal sinew and began to sew with small, almost invisible stitches on the Siberian reindeer skins. She then handed the needle to Jacob, gesturing that he try.

His fingers were stiff. There were only nine; the last one on his left hand was missing, a neat amputation scar in its place. Inuijak, knowing the frozen digit would lead to gangrene, had made the difficult decision during those early hours of his rescue while Jacob lay unconscious.

"Oh, my husband, please do not cut," Meqo had pleaded, "perhaps it will recover."

Inuijak had looked up grimly from his kneeling position beside the bed, his hand poised with the sharp knife.

"Save your nagging for the summer barters, wife, and do not make this job more difficult. You can see the black as well as I. It will consume his whole being if I do not remove it."

Meqo nodded and kneeled with her husband. "It is most clever the way you have spread his poor hand over the wood.

You are surely the best *angakok* in the whole village, and I am but a meddling fool. But, dear husband, could we not wait for the *angakok* from Kozebue? He will be here at the spring melting."

"If we wait for him, this man will already have been consumed by the great bears. I do not wish to do this, Meqo, but I must. Now help me. Bring the lamp closer, and do not let your tears fall into the open wound."

Jacob gazed at that hand now, the sight of it still shocking. But he waved it at the young Inuit woman, showing her by flexing his fingers how well it had healed.

He could find no way, however, to convey his embarrassment about her nudity. Meqo often wore nothing but a pair of short pants made of fox skin inside the house. He had learned by this time that it was custom and not immodesty, but even so, it was difficult not to stare when they were alone.

Even if she had been clothed, watching her work was fascinating. She was fast, sure and uncomplaining. The infinite variety of her chores, the amount of physical labor and detailed work they required, would have intimidated even the strongest Russian peasant woman.

Meqo sewed, her full breasts swaying with each movement. Jacob blushed as he watched her and turned away. He was not made of stone. He had shared their bed, sleeping between husband and wife as Inuijak had prescribed, discouraging Jacob's protests with a fixed stare and explaining that the practice was a proven aid to healing. Even after recovery, when he was no longer in need of their body heat, Jacob had received a lesson in Inuit etiquette.

"I not sleep here," Jacob had said, gesturing, "you— Meqo and Inuijak—this your bed."

Meqo had giggled. "Kind sir, this is the only bed. You

cannot sleep alone. If only I could speak in your funny language, then you would understand."

So he continued to sleep between them, but the couple's intimacies were embarrassing. Inuijak did not, however, offer Meqo to his guest, for which Jacob was grateful.

Now he watched her small fingers fly with the ulo, the sharp curved knife slicing through the skins with each motion.

"Meqo," Jacob said, trying again to make conversation, "when Inuijak home from hunt?"

"Hunt?" she said, repeating his Russian word.

"Yes. That's very good. Hunt. When Inuijak home?"

"Uh—Inuijak go—many moon. You," she said, pointing to Jacob, "stay me. Yes? You—oh—oh—"

Unable to think of the Russian words, Meqo shook her head at her own stupidity. Her husband could talk with the stranger. That was enough.

"Meqo," he said, "I no stay many more moons. You, Inuijak, alone. Jacob go."

She put aside her sewing, her head cocked in puzzlement. "Jaycoop no stay? Jaycoop?"

"There isn't any use, little brown lady," he said, frowning, "Yiddish and Russian and Eskimo just don't mix. I know I owe you all kinds of explanations. But I can't tell you how I left home, or why. I can't tell you where I'm going or how I plan to get there. I wish I could."

He picked out a piece of boiled meat from the steaming pot kept over one of the blubber lamps and chewed thoughtfully, wondering when he could travel again, walk the ice and snow fields to his destination somewhere in this new country. For now, there was nothing to do but wait for Inuijak's return, which was not so unpleasant. He had Meqo's naked beauty for company. But he was thankful when Inuijak returned. "Someone visits!" the voice shouted outside the house. "Hello, hello, someone is visiting!"

Yelling his greeting so as not to surprise the household, Inuijak appeared in the open door with a big smile for Jacob and a hug for Meqo. He had shaken the snow off his clothes outside and now handed them to his wife.

"Good hunt," he said to Jacob in Russian, "we eat meat. Out on rack, two caribou, three seal."

Meqo smiled warmly. "This poor and graceless wife is so happy that great hunter is home. I will serve supper and we will talk about your success."

Inuijak nodded and sat down on the floor. "Jaycoop, you must forgive miserable offering I bring for food, but if you honor me by tasting it, I shall be content."

This pattern of speech was no longer strange, self-deprecation being one of the first customs Jacob had learned. It was almost a game between them, and it was the same with friends as with family. The more significant the act or gift, the more wretched the words.

"I will try my best to fill my stomach," Jacob said, smothering a smile, "but I cannot promise."

"Good. Let us begin. Meqo, we are waiting."

Thus summoned, his wife brought forth a dish with great ceremony, a bird marinating in blubber oil.

"Tell me about the white bear," Jacob said, "did you see him this time out?"

Inuijak made a sad face and hung his head. "Bear lying dead in small hollow of ice. Inuijak feel bad for big old bear. Now, no more bear for Inuijak to fight." In stories both sung and spoken to Jacob, Inuijak had given the bear human qualities, such as dignity and grace for an old age. His sorrow was no act.

"Inuijak," Meqo said, still standing with the pot of marinating ptarmigan, "can you bring yourself to serve our guest this poor offering? If not, I will try in my clumsy way to do it for you."

Inuijak took the plate and smiled broadly at his pretty wife.

"You are too kind, and I am pleased that you honor me, your shabby husband, with this magnificent meal."

Holding the bird by its feet, he brushed off feathers that had loosened after fermenting in the oil, bit around the beak until the skin was pliable, then with his other hand turned the bird inside out. Pulling the skin free, he sucked into his mouth all the fat inside the skin.

"Here, Jaycoop," he said, a grin across his greasy brown face, "now you bite and eat."

Jacob held the bird awkwardly, unable to touch it.

"Bite," Inuijak urged, "bite near bone. Good inside. You see."

He could not offend his hosts and bit down on the bird's innards, his eyes watering, his throat constricting, fighting the rising nausea by conjuring up an image of his mother holding a bowl of chicken, and silently asked God for forgiveness.

But oddly enough, after the first unpleasant moment, the whole bloody, greasy mess was delicious. He sat back, rubbed his stomach, belched, and laughed. When they had all eaten their fill, Meqo crawled onto the bed and fell asleep. Inuijak lay on the floor in front of the dying ashes of the fire, singing happily to himself, the solemn words strung together, no meter, no rhyme, in a high, thin voice.

In the moon when whaling begins,
Maktak is the whaler's food
that comes to those who wait out the storm.
The cover for the umiaq will keep the water out,
And those who help with paddles
And those who make harpoons . . .
Maktak is the whaler's joy . . .
Maktak . . . is . . . the . . .

Inuijak fell asleep, his song trailing in the air like smoke from the lamps. Jacob covered him with a fur skin, climbed on the bed next to Meqo, and slept.

When morning dawned, Jacob dressed in the treasured gifts from the couple—white bearskin pants, a fur parka and a brand new pair of sealskin boots that came to his knees—and ducked out into the cold April day. The polar ice sparkled with blues and purples and greens in the brilliant sunshine. It was time to go, but saying good-bye would not be easy.

"You leave?"

Jacob turned, startled at the sound of Inuijak's voice. The young Inuit stood in the cold, his face crumpling with sorrow, and began to cry.

"My friend Jaycoop," he said, his words tumbling in the flood of emotion, "I know you must leave now, but Inuijak and Meqo we miss Jaycoop."

He tried at first to wipe away his tears, but finally let them flow unchecked. "Take care, my very good friend Jaycoop. Take much care. Watch out for musk ox, and no fear wolf."

Jacob nodded, then hugged the man who had saved him from a certain frozen death, the man he would remember all his life.

"I cannot find words to thank Inuijak," Jacob said, "you saved not only my leg but my life. It is rare when one man has the chance to save another. And I say this to you with all my heart: I promise to show your kindness to others, and that kindness, I hope, will make me as fine a man as Inuijak."

The men embraced, their strong arms about each other, while the low, hollow wail of a dog team drifted out of the rising wind and was carried in the frigid air. Soon the tundra was as silent as the frozen sea. No sound was heard from the little settlement of Wales, and the only movement was a brace of snowbirds flying across the blue sky.

ELEVEN

ᘓᓍᕲᕽᘐ

Khotin, Russia

AN OPPRESSIVE HEAT CAME IN WITH THE ARRIVAL OF summer in Khotin that flared tempers among the best of friends and closest of families. Birds pecked at the dusty weeds drooping in the caked earth, and seedlings turned brown and fell broken among the stunted crops. In spite of the heat, rousing and lengthy discussions took place in Nathan Semel's butcher shop, the kibitzers arguing with each other over the causes of the current weather. Yankel was dogmatic, asserting it was the Czar's revenge on the Jews for their unwillingness to pay higher taxes. Chaim scoffed, declaring the Czar had no such power. What is he? A devil working black magic? (They all spat on their fingers, not daring to utter their answers aloud.) Besides, he added, there's no use shouting "giddap" when the nag is dead. Mendel banged on the counter and yelled for them to stop talking nonsense. The heat is upon us because it is summer. It is common knowledge that in summer, the sun is closer to the earth, the angle of the sun such that more heat . . . Gershon held up a hand and protested the scientific lecture. It is not for us to question or complain, he had said loftily, it is for us to accept and learn from this unfortunate experience. Mendel mumbled something under his breath. Yankel said to spit it out. Mendel yelled that when the head is a fool, the whole body's done for, and Yankel laughed out loud.

Semel listened patiently to all of this at first, even offering a word here and a nod there, but soon realized the discussion was futile and getting on his nerves. The shop was miserably hot. He stopped listening and threw them all out. Most of Malka's pupils wanted to play games and splash in the streams near the shtetl, and she was tired of cramming reading, writing and counting into their reluctant heads. By day's end, she was cranky and frazzled.

One particularly wretched day, she entered the house hoping to relax with a glass of cold tea before starting dinner, only to find her father home. It was unusual. Except on Fridays, he never left the shop before six. He was sitting in the parlor, his feet up on the couch, the paper from Minsk spread across his lap.

"Ah . . . Malka," he said hoarsely, "you startled me."

She knew, by the rumpled look of his clothes and his glazed stare, that he had been asleep. "You? Napping? Papa? Are you all right?" She felt his forehead. It was warm and moist.

"Of course, I'm fine. Fine. Now scoot. I want to finish reading the paper."

Malka picked up his damp jacket and hung it on the hall tree. "I'll make dinner. We're both hungry and we . . ."

"Not now, my angel, not now," he said gruffly. "This heat has stolen my appetite, I'm afraid, although it surely can't hurt me to lose a few pounds."

"I'm not hungry either," Malka said, "but we have to eat something. One should not go to bed hungry."

"Oh? And where did you learn that?" Semel gave a short laugh. "You sound like one of the fools in my shop today, pontificating on the heat wave."

"I am not pontificating," Malka protested, "I am merely stating a point of view. Besides, I know that if we don't eat, you'll be sneaking food all night. A cookie, a piece of cheese, a herring, an egg . . ."

Semel chuckled. "You're right, you're right. But you look tired. Go and rest, I'll make dinner."

"You?"

Semel looked around. "Is there someone else here? Of course, me."

"Thank you, Papa, I only hope there's enough water for a bath."

"There's water, there's water," Semel called as she left the room, "and it's waiting for you."

She turned back into the doorway. "Waiting for me? But how did you know?"

"Am I not human?" Semel asked, putting a hand to his breast. "Am I not melting from this miserable heat? If you cut me, would I not bleed? If you . . ."

"All right, already," Malka laughed, "my merchant of Khotin. You're a wonderful actor. You missed your calling, Papa."

"Well," Semel shrugged, "it's the bard's loss." Before she could answer, Malka watched in horror as her father doubled over and fell to the floor, his face grimacing with pain. She threw her arms around his big shoulders. "What is it?" she cried. "Where does it hurt? Tell me, please, Papa, tell me."

His drawn face was pale, beads of perspiration stood out on the sallow skin. He took his daughter's hand. "It's nothing, Malka, just a pain. It comes and goes. Nothing. Nothing."

"Where? Your heart?"

"No, no. My heart is like an ox's heart."

"Where is the pain?"

"I'm not sure," he said, lying, hoping she could not tell.

"Where is the pain?" she demanded.

He sighed. "My stomach. Here." He pointed to his belly, to a spot just under his belt. "It's nothing. Now go fill the basin."

"I'm not going anywhere until Mrs. Lebedeff comes to look at you."

Nathan frowned, then protested that the thought of that fat, dour midwife in his home, her constant chatter, her icy hands all over him, God forbid, chilled him to the marrow of his bones. "No, thank you," he said, "if we had a doctor, a real doctor in this forsaken town, perhaps I would agree to a visit. But not that old . . ."

"No, Papa, she's the closest thing we have to a doctor, and you know it. She's skilled with herbs and lotions and she has medications that, you have to admit, have helped in the past. Yours will not be the first tummy ache she's seen."

He looked at her with trembling chin. "Ah, but what you do not know is how she has conspired all these years to get her hands on me, how she has pined for me, worked her magic spells to ensnare me. And now you are giving her the chance."

In spite of her worry, Malka had to smile. "You are a terrible liar, Papa, a storyteller, a fabricator of tales more clever and fiendish than any in all the thousand and one nights put together." She kissed his wet brow.

"Then you will forget about Mrs. Lebedeff, eh?" he said.

"Well . . ."

"Good. Just let me rest here a while. You have a bath, and I'll fix dinner later."

Malka decided to do it his way. He looked better. Color was rising in his cheeks, and his foolishness must mean the pain had vanished. But she had misgivings; her father was never sick, and this sudden illness frightened her.

"I'll save my bath until later," she said. "The anticipation is so delicious it deserves to be savored, right? I'll read the paper with you, and maybe later we'll have something cool to eat."

Semel closed his eyes. "Whatever you say, my angel." Then he fell asleep.

But there was no dinner later, and no bath. Semel awoke screaming in pain. Malka, torn between bringing help and leaving her father to suffer alone, finally ran to get Mrs. Lebedeff.

The midwife was not an old and wizened crone, as Semel had complained, but a sturdy, personable widow of fifty-two, who bustled into the house fully in charge. Together, she and Malka helped Semel to his bed, undressed him, and stuffed him, stammering and protesting, into his nightshirt. Malka left the room during the midwife's questions and examination, and returned when Mrs. Lebedeff called.

"Your father has some illness in his belly," she proclaimed with authority.

"Wonderful! I need to suffer these indignities for you tell me that?" Semel cracked.

Ignoring the insult, Mrs. Lebedeff continued, "And I don't have enough specialized knowledge to go any further. However, I do have some powders that should ease the pain. Of course, if you could travel to Kiev or Kharkov to see a real doctor . . ."

"And if the Czar Nicholas were Jewish and my brother-in-law," Semel wheezed out of the side of his mouth, "we could all play pinochle in the palace together

"Your father is a stubborn mule," Mrs. Lebedeff said, "and impossible to deal with. I do not understand how you put up with him."

"I put up with him," Malka snapped, "because I love him. I know he is stubborn, but he is not impossible. The fact that he let me bring you here proves that."

"All right." The woman sniffed. "We shan't argue. Here

are the powders. Mix one with a glass of warm water at bedtime. He will rest and that alone will help."

"Mrs. Lebedeff, what is the matter with my father? Is it . . . serious?"

"I don't know. It could be. Or it could be gas. Or heartburn. Or cramps from too much roughage."

"Or . . . ?" Malka could not bring herself to say it.

The midwife knew what Malka could not say. She shrugged. "Who knows?"

She turned to go but stopped at the door. "I'm sure he'll be better when the heat lets up." Then she strode out of the house like a proud schooner in a keen wind, her bag slapping at her legs.

The heat did not let up that summer. It baked the town dry, warping the barns and browning the fields. No one was spared. Not the Russians, nor the Jews, nor the rodents. Everyone suffered. They talked of nothing else.

In the synagogue the heat rose to the balcony and was trapped under the roof where the women sat and fanned themselves, dabbed at their wet faces, and fainted.

Storms broke almost every week, dumping water and hail on Khotin, after which Semel would stand at the window of his shop and murmur, "Fine, and now come the locusts, and the sickness, and the death of the firstborn. . . ."

Malka worried about her father, but he seemed to improve. The powders worked, and a few nights of undisturbed sleep erased the circles under his eyes. She never brought up the subject of his illness again. Saul Mendelberg, her old suitor, came to dinner once in July and once in August. When he did not invite himself again, Malka decided he had given up. Although she worried about hurting his feelings, she could not discuss it with him or her father. The thought of trapping herself in a loveless marriage based on convenience disgusted her.

She fretted over her father's unwillingness to find a real doctor, at the same time aware how difficult if not impossible that would be. Kiev, as well as Kharkov, was closed to Jews, and it would have taken a miracle to locate a doctor in a nearby city or village.

At night her fears and nightmares tormented her, and she wept at the thought of losing her father. But her tears were not only for him, but for herself.

He would never have a grandchild to bounce on his knee. If it would make him happy, perhaps she should marry Saul. There was only one problem: maybe Saul didn't want her anymore.

On a breathless, sultry Saturday morning, Semel again felt the gnawing pain begin, sat up in bed, and prayed it would stop.

It's not time yet, he thought to himself. Malka will be all alone. She is too young, too unsophisticated, too vulnerable. She knows nothing of the world, only this wretched town and the poor souls who live in it. She has no suitors and does not want any. I cannot let my angel grow into a dried-up old prune. Besides, I have decided I don't like Saul. He has no fire, no vision, no sense of humor, nothing but that miserable mother. You see, Lord, you cannot take me yet. I still have too much to do, right? So am I not worthy of your attention, your blessing? Is not my home also yours where sanctity prevails in all the details of our lives? Is not my knife sharp with no impediment to a swift and painless death for the animals? Is it not enough that I follow all your rules when dispatching meat and chickens? That I am thoroughly acquainted with your rules and regulations governing kosher meat? So please, in your name, can you not bear with me and my daughter and let her eyes fall on some young man worthy of her and all she embodies? Oh Lord, let her find happiness.

By the first snow, Semel was working as hard as ever in

the shop. He had learned to cook a little. That way, explanations were avoided about the new soft foods he had turned to. He was eating less meat because of the pains that came after stew and goulash. He lost weight, but joked with Malka that it made him more desirable, younger, lighter on his feet and able to run faster from the widows. Sometimes, when he could not sleep, Semel fretted about life and its problems, and death and its certainty. He read and reread the books that had belonged to his father and to his father's father—religious books, commentaries, the Apocrypha, and the writings of rabbis and sages of old. They all seemed to share a common wisdom about death and dying, marking the course as natural and desirable. He had read these books many times as he was growing up, and had steeped himself in their facts and philosophy. They were old, yet they still seemed fresh and pertinent. Semel would have preferred a lighter touch, a joke or two to ease his fear. After all, who could be a philosopher in the middle of the night? But from his own conception of the problem and his patient, untiring deliberations, he was finally able to arrive at an answer. It was succinct, comforting, simple, to the point, and gave him a certain measure of peace. No man dies before his time.

TWELVE

⤷◎◎⤶

THE TOWN OF ST. MICHAEL, ALASKA, WAS ENJOYING A
newfound prosperity as the gateway to the Klondike gold
rush. Once perched atop an uninhabited island like a ball on
a seal's nose, its mud flats, now constantly shifting from time
and tides, were sprouting almost overnight with claptrap
warehouses, makeshift piers and the ubiquitous brothel.
Outfitters' shops and shipping offices were open day and
night to accommodate stampeders rushing to the gold fields,
and the smell of fish rotting on the wharves hung over the
town like a stinking cloud.

The gateway led both to and from the Klondike. Men
returning from a winter of dreary isolation and a steady diet
of baked beans thought they had died and gone to heaven
when they saw the fresh fruit, vegetables, eggs, onions and
salad greens in stores and restaurants. These miners, who
were worth millions and had had nothing to spend it on until
now, wolfed down the glorious food with gusto while throwing gold dust at the waiters.

For the eager prospector headed the other way fresh from
a twenty-five-hundred-mile trip from Seattle, all that
remained was to buy his supplies and a ticket on one of two
steamers. Either the *Bella* or the *Portus B. Weare* would take

him on his way to the Klondike's rivers of gold before the Yukon froze.

DON'T LOSE OUT! HURRY! HURRY! HURRY! KLONDIKE OR BUST! HO! FOR THE KLONDIKE! read the signs in store windows. No matter that seventeen hundred difficult and exhausting miles still had to be navigated in anything that floated. They had seen the golden future, and it was theirs. Had they not been witness to the fortunes coming off the sternwheelers from Dawson, men of all ages and backgrounds bringing back millions of dollars in flour gold, placer gold and nuggets packed in jelly jars and duffel bags and shoe boxes and caribou hide pokes?

Newspaper reporters from all over the world screamed questions at the new arrivals: "Where did you find your gold? How long did it take? Is there any left?" Rumors were now fact, and the dramatic proof lay in the headlines of every "Extra" hitting the streets from New York to Shanghai: **"GOLD! GOLD! GOLD!"**

Into this infectious lunacy walked Jacob Finesilver, certain by his own calculations, although the name of the region was not on his maps, that he had reached the famed Klondike at last. He sat on a bench in the town square and watched the crowds run into and out of stores, arms laden, staggering under the weight of their purchases. His frustration grew with the babble of different tongues and the realization that he could not read the signs or the newspapers.

His eye returned to the men and their purchases, and suddenly it all made sense. They were all headed for the same place he was: the gold fields. That's why they were running—to buy supplies in the stores. Obviously that was his next move.

He walked into one of the shops and spoke to the man behind the counter. "Excuse me, are you the owner?"

The man shook his head. "Hey," he called to the other salesmen, "anybody here speak Russian?"

"What can I do for you?"

"Are you the owner of this store?"

"The one and only," Isaac Handleman replied. A trim man in his fifties, he looked dressed and ready for an afternoon stroll down Kiev's main street. Stretched across his velvet vest was a fancy watch and gold chain. His starched white shirt had immaculate French cuffs, and the gold links glinted in the store lights as he straightened his tie. From under the rim of a green eyeshade, a coarse touch compared to the rest of the finery, he looked up at Jacob.

The two men spoke in Russian until Handleman's pithy Yiddish words suggested a switch to the more familiar tongue.

"So, Mr. Handleman, I am Jacob Finesilver, and I want to purchase a complete outfit for mining gold."

"Of course," Handleman said, squinting up at his young friend, "One complete outfit for mining gold. And how, though I hesitate to ask, will you pay for this?"

"Well," Jacob said, "I was hoping you would extend me credit, that is, until my fortune is secured."

"Ah, of course. You will, no doubt, become an instant millionaire and send me what you owe. By dog team?" The man's expression was benign, but his gray eyes seemed suddenly cold and appraising.

"Well, I'll either return it myself or send you the loan by post."

Handleman asked, "Where are you from?"

"From Khotin. In Ukraine."

"Yes. And how did you come to St. Michael?"

"I walked."

"You walked."

"Yes."

"From Russia."

"Yes."

"You walked from Russia to St. Michael."

"Yes."

Isaac Handleman regarded Jacob as if he had dropped from the moon. Oddly enough, the young fellow looked rational. His eyes were clear, his clothes were clean, unlike the usual grime-encrusted veteran stampeders. And there was something about this Jew, indefinable, earnest, perhaps a reminder of himself years before, which touched him.

"So tell me," he said, waving away another customer, "the whole megillah, from beginning to end."

"You really want to hear about it?"

"I'm dying to hear about it."

Jacob drew a deep breath, and said, "Well, I left Khotin in December, over a year ago, and walked east across the steppes and into Siberia, in the summer, of course. The hardest part was crossing the frozen sea at the Bering Strait, but an Eskimo found me when I thought all was lost. I would have died, but he . . ."

Handleman took Jacob's arm and led him into an office at the rear of the store. Pulling up a chair for the younger man, he settled himself behind the desk, lit a cigar, removed his green eyeshade and leaned back in the creaking chair. "Jacob Finesilver, eh? How old are you?"

"Twenty-one. I was nineteen when I left Russia."

Handleman nodded. "And this . . . this walk of yours," he said, blowing smoke, then dissipating it with a wave of his hand, "how did you live?"

"In Russia, between Khotin and Siberia, I looked for Jewish families as I went along. It wasn't easy." Jacob grinned wryly. "And not easy for me to accept charity. We've always worked for what we own."

"Then, in Siberia?" Handleman prompted.

"It was summer, not so bad. It's very beautiful, the lakes and forests make it quite civilized. But the huge land mass is thinly populated. The Tartar people were very kind, and the natives, Indian or Eskimo, I'm not sure, share their food, though sometimes they made me feel a bit like a wolf in the henhouse. But I hunted with them, lived with them, found them clever if not endearing."

Handleman knocked the ash from his cigar and nodded. "Go on."

"In the dead of winter, I tried the crossing to Alaska. I lost that fight, almost froze to death."

"And?"

"Inuijak, from the Alaskan village just across the ice-bridge, found me and saved my life."

"Inu . . . ?"

"In-u-i-jak," Jacob enunciated, "an American Eskimo. He and his wife nursed me back to health." Jacob showed his left hand to Handleman. "They performed surgery, here, and on my broken leg because of gangrene. I owe them my life."

Handleman looked at Jacob's hand, shook his head, and said, "If your story wasn't so incredible, so absolutely outrageous, I wouldn't believe it."

He sat up in the chair and leaned his elbows on the desk. "Even if you're lying, I'd have to admire your ingenuity. Inuijak . . . Eskimos . . . Remarkable. Remarkable! No . . . astonishing!"

Jacob shrugged modestly.

Handleman shook his head. "Tell me," he said, "tell me why."

"Why?"

"Yes. Why? Why did you walk almost five thousand miles to get here? And don't tell me it was for the gold."

Jacob rose, moved to the window of the small office and looked out to the sea. He saw small boats riding at anchor and the waters of the bay sparkling in the sunlight as if handfuls of bright jewels had been strewn across the choppy surface.

"I'll have to trust you, then," he said, his back to Handleman. "I ran from the Czar. His Cossacks kept coming for me and my brother, and I'll be damned if we would have fought or died for such a man."

"But why here? Surely there was another port, another country, without your walking all that way?"

"But no place to go without a passport. You must understand, I wanted to bring my family out, and when I heard about the gold strike, this seemed the best way."

He turned and faced the proprietor. "Don't tell me I'm a fool, Mr. Handleman, or that I won't make it, or that I should count my blessings or any other crap like that. I'll work my ass off but I have to make it. And I will."

Jacob grinned. "I apologize for the outburst. I'm not usually temperamental. But this is my life we're talking about, and the lives of my family, still living, if you can call it that, in Russia with the Cossacks breathing down their necks. So, what do I need for the gold mining here in Alaska?"

"Here?"

"Yes. Alaska, right?"

Handleman squashed his cigar butt in the ash tray, took another from the box, snipped the tip, and lit the smelly thing with a sulphur match.

"My wife objects to these at home, so I get all my real smoking done here. Will you have one?"

Jacob shook his head.

"Well, my young friend, I hate to be the bearer of bad news, but I'm afraid your walking tour is not yet over."

"You won't trust me for the outfit?"

"Oh, I'll trust you, all right," Handleman said, "but you're not in the Klondike yet. You see, there *was* a gold strike in Alaska in '95, but it petered out. The new strike is now in the Klondike. And the Klondike is in Yukon Territory, and the Yukon Territory is in Canada. Which is another country altogether!"

He rose, walked around his desk to a large map on the wall. "Here, look, see there? That's where we are now, in St. Michael, the western coast of Alaska. Now follow my pencil line east, the steamer into the Yukon River, up to Koyukuk, then further north to Fort Yukon, then across the Canadian border into Dawson City and hopefully the gold. That's where it is. Dawson City. Canada."

Handleman could guess what Jacob was thinking: all this time, walking, scrounging for food, living off the land and near death in the savage cold of the Arctic, only to discover his destination was still miles away.

"Don't be disheartened, my friend," the older man said, "and don't forget you have youth and considerable strength on your side. The boat trip can be made in a month or so, and fortunately you're here in early summer and the steamers are running. A few months later, and the rivers would be choked with ice. Then you would have to wait until next year."

Jacob nodded. "All right. Tell me what to buy and where to go. I give you my word that all will be repaid."

"I'm sure it will," Handleman said. "If not, it would be the first time. I'm a very good judge of character."

He put an arm around Jacob and led him back into the busy store, talking continuously as he pulled supplies from shelves and drawers.

Jacob listened closely, piling the goods into a small mountain as Handleman told him he would need a ton of gear, required by the Canadian Mounties at all points of entry. Astounded, Jacob wondered if a pack horse would sit down defiantly and refuse such a load.

He took the four pages of billing from the proprietor, sat
on a box and read them through.

400 pounds of flour
100 pounds of beans
100 pounds of sugar
50 pounds of cornmeal
50 pounds of oatmeal
35 pounds of rice
40 pounds of candles
8 pounds of baking soda
200 pounds of bacon

He looked at the owner, surprised. "Bacon?"
The older man gestured impatiently to continue.

36 pounds of yeast cakes
1 pound of pepper
1/4 pound of ginger
1/2 pound of mustard
25 pounds of evaporated apples
25 pounds of peaches
25 pounds of apricots
25 pounds of fish
10 pounds of pitted plums
50 pounds of potatoes
24 pounds of coffee
5 pounds of tea
15 pounds of soup vegetables
25 pounds of butter
4 dozen cans condensed milk
5 bars laundry soap
60 boxes matches
5 pounds of salt

The list also included a small metal stove, gold pan, granite buckets, cup, plates, utensils, frying pan, coffeepot, a pick, saws, whetstone, a hatchet, shovels, files, drawknife, axes, chisels, nails, sled, rope, pitch, oakum, and canvas tent. There were several changes of clothing for temperatures ranging from one hundred degrees in summer to winters of seventy below, mosquito netting, bedding, medicine kit, blankets, boots, mittens, flannel shirts, heavy wool underwear, wool socks, and snow glasses.

The cost was minimal compared to the staggering effort of hauling the outfit, but Handleman reminded Jacob he would be, for most of the seventeen-hundred-plus miles to Dawson City, a passenger on a shallow draft steamer.

"My new young friend, I couldn't allow you to enter the gold fields without adequate supplies. And this," he said, gesturing from the top of the pile to the bottom, "is only the minimum. You'll be adding to it in Dawson. Bear this in mind, Jacob, for it's as important as these tools of your new trade. One must not enter this milieu with any less than what is here, for if you're unprepared, the other miners will treat you with what they call 'poor grace.' It's their protocol, and has to be respected.

"If, *cholilleh*," he went on, accenting the Yiddish word for "God forbid" with a woebegone expression, "misfortune strikes, the others rally around, but *schnoring* because of poor preparation is not acceptable." Handleman smiled at him, a wistful admission of having missed out. "Ah, *boychik*, you're off to make your fame and fortune. So here, for your idle hours, is a list. Memorize it. Because it just may save that ass you're going to work off!"

As the *Bella* left St. Michael that night, Jacob read the list again in the light from the aft lantern. Halfway through, he shivered with the realization of the magnitude and dangers of his life from now on. When he finished, he read it again.

Do not waste anything. Put it away. It may save your life.
Pile your cache on the ground with heavy rocks over it. Take
  compass bearings and landmarks.
Shoot a dog, if necessary, behind the base of the skull, a horse
  between the ears, ranging down, a deer behind the left
  shoulder. Press the trigger, do not pull it.
Never grab a gun barrel when the temperature is thirty or
  more below.
Do not fire if the barrel is plugged with snow.
A little dry grass inside your mittens will help retain heat.
If caught in blinding snow or fog, camp and do not move
  until weather clears.
Use goggles when walking in snow.
Travel on clear ice as much as possible.
If using a sledge in extreme cold, do not use steel runners.
  Make them of wood and freeze water on them.
Keep furs in good repair.
No man can continuously drag more than his own weight.
Change footgear or wet stockings before they freeze, or you
  may lose a toe or a foot.
Keep the hood of your parka back if it is not too cold so
  moisture may escape from your body.
If toes and heels are cold, wrap a piece of fur over them.
Keep sleeping bag clean; if vermin inhabit bag, freeze them out.
White snow over a crevasse, if hard, is safe.
Do not eat snow or ice. Melt it first.

It was the next line that affected Jacob most. He read it
over and over, shocked at how ignorant he had been of the
dangers ahead. For a moment, he panicked.

That line made everything clear. He would repeat it to
himself over and over during the next few days:

The man who knows little now, will come back knowing
  more than he who knew it all before starting.

THIRTEEN

୧ᢙᢙ୨

Dawson City, Yukon Territory, Canada, May, 1897

ON THE TWENTIETH OF MAY, THE ICE-CHOKED YUKON
River rumbled, heaved and fractured into massive chunks
that were swept away in the swift current, tumbling over one
another like frisky puppies. In the coming days the quicken-
ing thaw would push the ice along the serpentine route of the
great river and finally empty the whole slushy mass into the
delta of the Bering Sea.

Now, with the first day of open waterways, the boats that
had idled impatiently on a dozen shores all winter suddenly
appeared between the beaches of Skagway, Whitehorse, St.
Michael, and Dawson City. From Lake Bennett and Lake
Lindemann came homemade rafts, canoes, barges, scows and
paddle wheelers, puffing and chugging their way up and
down the Yukon River in full dress parade to Dawson. The
race to the gold was on.

Six weeks from now, the river front would be a jumbled
flotilla, with new arrivals finding no room at the shoreline.
Some would have to tie their boats to other boats while the
passengers walked from one boat to the other to reach shore.

On the tenth day of July, one and one-half years since
leaving Khotin, Russia, Jacob Finesilver stood at the rail of

the shallow-draft steamer *Bella* as it docked at Dawson City, Yukon Territory, Canada. Whatever he had feared, doubted, or questioned of himself, whatever injury or illness he had sustained, the hardship and privation and loneliness were now in the past. The long journey had ended.

He stared in disbelief at the sight on the wide beach. There were tents, shacks and cabins everywhere, people milling at the river's edge and beyond to the mountain, and another city rising in the mists of the adjacent Klondike River shore.

As he stepped off the gangplank into the mucky swamp, he was literally hurled into the midst of rabble pushing from all sides looking frantically for kin or friends.

Women from the brothels of Klondike City smiled seductively and dance-hall girls held high their brightly colored layers of can-can skirts and waved them above their heads. All the while, thieves worked the crowd, picking wallets from unguarded pockets. Many on the beach called excitedly to wives or children or sweethearts, while others stood bewildered or overcome at having at last reached their hard-sought goal.

After the passengers came the frightened cattle and frisky pigs lumbering down the gangplank, followed by crates of wildly squawking chickens. Then on a rocketing slide downward came boxes of tools and foodstuffs and medicines, trunks of fancy dresses and woolen work shirts, and all kinds and sizes of shoes and boots.

Jacob caught his first sight of Dawson's Midnight Dome, the mountain rising like a hulking guardian behind Dawson City, its scooped-out center looking to him as if some hungry giant had come along with a spoon.

He turned and twisted, trying to see everything at once, the colors skittereing before his eyes like a sunlit prism. Noise saturated the air, so powerful a force that it would imprint the scene forever in his memory. He wanted to stand and gawk, but the impatient crowd pushed him until he stumbled onto the shore.

It took him more than an hour to check in with the Canadian Mounted Police, then retrieve and store his supplies behind one of the warehouses. He knew he should look for housing, but the scene was seductive; he wanted to be part of it, to join the crowd and laugh and sing and dance and slap someone on the back and say, "Hey! I made it too!"

The noise level grew higher. Newsboys ran along the sand yelling, "Get your *Dawson Nugget* here." Hammers pounded, sawmills screeched and wagon drivers yelled hoarsely as they whipped their animals floundering in the mud. The babble of voices in a dozen languages almost drowned out the din.

Children on the beach were laughing as they chased each other, and strains of music drifted tantalizingly from the dance halls. Jacob heard the hawkers crying on street corners and whistles blowing from arriving or departing boats, while the pretty painted girls preened and beckoned. Pushed with the others like a river current along the wooden sidewalk, he felt as if he had wandered into ancient Babylon.

He had dreamed of the world outside the Pale and during the last seventeen months had seen more curious parts of it than most men see in a lifetime. Yet here in a city of thousands, where he had expected convention and conformity, there was no natural order, nothing commonplace, no precedents to guide him. His instincts warned him to go slowly, try to mix in and adapt to people and circumstance as he had throughout the long walk.

The throng moved Jacob along the main street, past a solid row of shops built on the river side, each one faced with an intricate false wood front. Behind the gingerbread, the buildings were made of logs, stretching back almost to the river's edge.

More stores were being erected across the street, and here and there a tent store stood between in a temporary space. He passed one of these tents, its proprietor sitting on a barrel in front of a huge sign, reading a Jewish newspaper.

Jacob said in Yiddish, "Hello there."

"Hello to you too, my boy."

"You own this store?"

The man pointed to the sign. "See that? It says, 'CLOTHING BY RABINOWITZ + JUST LIKE SEATTLE!' Well, that's me. Rabinowitz. One and the same. Just get in on the *Bella*?"

"I did, yes."

"So, what do you think of Dawson?"

Jacob laughed. "I don't know yet."

"It isn't Kiev," Rabinowitz said, "and that's a fact. But I guess you didn't come here for the opera. Where are you from?"

The question caught Jacob unprepared. "Zaitzova," he lied. "Have you been here long?"

"Just since May. I hope I make enough to get me home, to Seattle. You ever were there?"

"No. This is my first trip. It's nice to meet someone I can talk to."

"Sure. But there will be others. You'd be surprised how many Russians are here." Rabinowitz's eyes narrowed, and he added, "And Ukrainians. You won't be alone for long."

Jacob wondered how the man knew, but let it pass. "I don't mind being alone, as long as I can talk with someone."

"So what am I? The mad monk?" The little man laughed at his joke and caught at the skullcap on his head. "*Nu*, a little tour of the metropolis? Sort of a get-acquainted tour?"

"I don't want to trouble you."

"No trouble, it'll be a pleasure to move around a bit. And business isn't so hotsy-totsy right now. Too warm, I guess. Come, I'll show you."

The two men moved into the mass of people, walking slowly, but were pushed along if they dawdled. They made an odd-looking pair, tall Jacob and short Rabinowitz, the older man jabbering away, hands gesturing, eager to show the city to his new friend.

"This is the town masseuse," Rabinowitz said, "see the sign? It reads, 'Marlene from Boston.' Listen, if she's from Boston, I'm from Japan. But I'll bet she knows how to rub, huh?" The little man poked Jacob with his elbow and winked.

"Now," he continued, "that's the Aurora saloon, but don't be afraid it's the only one in town. We have more saloons than bathtubs! The Bank Saloon, Dell's, Al's, the Red Feather, the Floradora, the Pavilion, and Chisholm's Saloon, which by the way is called the 'Bucket of Blood.' You want to know why? Go on, ask me why."

"Why?" Jacob asked.

"Because, when you get that first drink, it comes with a whisk broom. Why? Go ahead . . . ask me why!"

Jacob laughed. "Why?"

"To brush you off when you come to!" Rabinowitz lost himself in a laughing fit, coughing and choking and wiping his eyes with a linen handkerchief.

"That building next to the Bucket is a mining exchange. A lot of those in town, and a doctor's office, and upstairs is the dentist, Doctor Payne." His eyes rolled up with a smirk at the play on words. "And over there the general store, which isn't really very general, mostly hardware and a few tins of food.

"And that big building on the corner is Diamond Tooth Gertie's, the gambling-house. I needn't warn you about it, eh?"

"And that?" Jacob asked, pointing to a grand-looking store with double mirrored doors.

Rabinowitz made a face. "That? That's the Emporium,

run by a *gonif*, a real thief, who thinks we're all dummies. His prices are too high and his ethics . . . whoo! Oh, it's true you can buy almost anything in that store, patent leather shoes, fresh oysters, even ostrich feathers! I've seen them. This is not a hick town, my friend, even though between you and me and that lamppost over there, I think it's only temporary. Soon as the gold runs out, so will all these crazy people."

"You really think it's going to run out? Soon?" Jacob asked.

"Look, this isn't my first time in a boom town. I've been to Leadville and Juneau and Nome, and I know. The Mounties say there will be eighteen thousand people here this summer, and I'll bet you anything they won't be here next year."

He pointed to a group of men leaning against a store, their shoulders bent as if carrying a great sadness, their faces empty.

"See them?" Rabinowitz said. "Most of them spent their energy just getting here, shooting rapids, crossing the Chilkoot Pass, walking in circles across glaciers because the ice blinded them, doing things no man has ever had to do before in trying to deal with the *haloshes* weather of the Yukon. Now they're too weary even to file a claim. I don't know," he rubbed his chin, "it's like they didn't want anything more out of it than the adventure, the trip. Say, you ever dig for gold before?"

"No. But I'll learn."

Rabinowitz stared at Jacob. "You'll learn, huh?"

"Yes," Jacob declared. "It can't be that hard. Look at all the men doing it."

"Oh-ho! Listen to him. Such a *macher!* It isn't the work, *boychik*, it's finding it!"

"Look, Mr. Rabinowitz, don't make a *tsimmes* for nothing. I'll find the gold . . . you'll see."

"Uh-huh!" the older man said, "I hope I do, my boy. Have you a place to sleep?"

"I have my tent. I'll join the crowd on the beach."

"Take care. It's a rough crowd. Drunks and criminals, and card sharks, lots of no-goodniks among those cheechakos."

"Those . . . what?"

"Cheechakos. You'll hear that word a lot before long. A cheechako is a newcomer. The old timers are sourdoughs, a word for the bread they make. But you'll find all that out before long, too. I'm afraid, my boy, you'll find out more than you want to know."

FOURTEEN

❦

JACOB HAD BEEN CANDID ABOUT HIS LACK OF KNOWLEDGE but cocky when he had said he could learn how to mine for gold. He had no idea how to start, or where. Days of inactivity went by, frustrating days of listening to men talk but not understanding their language. Although he had the motivation and the right tools, he was stymied.

He decided that the only course of action was to follow the miners and hope they would lead him to the gold fields. Some went up the main road to the left, others went down to the right. Some hiked out of town from Front Street, and some disappeared without Jacob seeing which way they had gone.

One day one of the miners, after a mile or so, turned around and glared at him.

"What the hell you doin', boy? Tryin' to horn in on my claim?"

There was no point in angering these men. So Jacob began to hang around outside the Aurora Saloon and again listened to the talk, beginning to hear some words repeated more than others, words like "claim" and "Bonanza" and "Hunker Creek."

He watched the miners up at Moosehide Creek only three miles out of Dawson City squatting by the stream, dipping their gold pans into the water. He hoped to learn by observing others and trying each step in the process when no one was around. He watched the cheechakos wander around, staking claims either up or down from the bigger ones, usually on the bench of land above the creeks. He watched as they wrote on wooden stakes and then banged them into the ground. The movements were uncomplicated, from panning to staking. But Rabinowitz had been right: the hard part was finding the claim itself.

One night, lying outside his tent on the beach hoping to catch a cooling breeze, Jacob willed his thoughts back to that last leg of his journey and the cold, the terrible, insufferable cold of the Russian Arctic that had almost cost him his life.

I was not saved just to sit around and mope, he told himself. Standing and shaking the sand from his clothes, he picked up his shovel and walked back to the gold fields.

The sun climbed higher in the sub-arctic sky, its murderous rays beating down on the men as they toiled in the dust and gravel. Jacob marked time by the number of hours he could work under the eerie light of the midnight sun. He walked miles each day on top of one square patch of hill, digging, testing, cursing the heat and his bad luck.

Where was this gold, this yellow stuff of dreams and fables that made men rich as kings? Surely it was not a cruel hoax perpetrated by reporters' exaggerations on a world still reeling from hard times. He had seen the lucky ones for himself, running red-faced into Dawson, too excited to put down their shovels as they signed their names to claim after claim. Was he too stupid, too unskilled to join their ranks? If so, he would never admit it. He had come here for one reason: to find the gold and reap the rewards of hard work that would eventually buy his family freedom and comfort.

He searched in vain for a free spot on the creeks, finally stumbling by accident on the small twenty-foot site one blistering hot July afternoon. It lay above the big claim at King Solomon's Dome.

The claims office clerk in Dawson was patient, using easy words and pencil diagrams to explain that the big mine was owned by two men, but that small fractions could be staked if the plot was small and not covered by the original owners.

From this same clerk, Jacob learned that the Dome was the source of tributaries running into the Klondike, and each creek up or down from the rich discovery claim was rumored to be spilling over with gold. After checking through the claims book, the clerk told him there were several fractions he could work, some of them abandoned by discouraged miners. His heart pounded with excitement as he returned to the Dome and watched the two men work the site, then stumble into town with huge bags of gold dust each day.

After three days, he walked up to them and in halting English, indicated his intention to claim twenty feet up.

"Sure, go ahead," one said, "old Flannery left it last fall. So you can pick it up, but don't be surprised if there ain't nothin' on it."

"Why you want to go and discourage the greenhorn that way?" the other man said. "He's got his heart set on that scrubby piece, let him have it."

The summer heat was brutal in the gold fields, especially on the high bench, and working in the sun those first days without adequate water almost brought on heat prostration. Jacob learned after his first dizzy spell, when everything around him swayed and jiggled in front of his eyes, that the men carried all those water canteens around their belts for good reason.

But he was digging up nothing but dirt and white gravel. Every day was a disappointment. The work was backbreaking, shoveling into the tough ground, then dragging the piles down to the water and panning small amounts at a time.

After three discouraging weeks, he wondered if Rabinowitz had been right, if all the gold had been taken from these gravelly hills.

His supplies were running low and he had no money and no credit. If this was a wild goose chase, he had spent a lot of time and gone into enormous debt for nothing.

Still, there was never a thought of quitting. He watched the men spread out over the streams and hills, shovels on their shoulders. He saw them returning to town with full pokes. There was gold; his chances of finding it were as good as anyone's.

This day had been the hottest so far, the merciless sun baking the unshaded land above the creek into fields resembling cracked, dry plaster. Panning since dawn, Jacob had hoped to get a head start on the others. He ignored the men watching and snickering from below. So he was a greenhorn. So had they all been once.

First digging with pick and shovel, he carried bucket after bucket of top dirt and gravel down to the creek, his feet sliding in the tailings. The morning went quickly, melting into noon, and still nothing had shown up in his pan. Hurrying in the noonday heat, he forgot to drink, working until he staggered like a drunk and collapsed on a pile of gravel.

He lay still, drinking slowly from his canteen, listening to sounds coming up from the creek, isolated fragments of conversations, a dog barking somewhere in the hills, a crow screaming as it passed overhead. He closed his eyes and within the configurations of hot color flashing behind his lids, he saw the overburden he had been digging out from the side of the hill.

His eyes flew open. He stared at his hands. They were covered with white dust. The gravel in the overburden was white. The same as the gravel in the creek. Where the gold was. Then the creek beds must have flowed higher on the hills, maybe millions of years ago, gradually eroding the land until it reached the lower levels. It stood to reason that if the creeks had once bubbled through the high bench where he was digging, they must have left gold behind.

Jacob picked up his shovel and dug ferociously into the dirt. Time after time he slid down the incline on his rump to wash the dirt in the pan, swirling it the way he had seen others do, tilting most of the dirt and water out the other end.

Jacob had never seen gold after "cleanup." He had no idea what it looked like, its size or shape, or even if his untrained eye could spot it. He knew it was heavier than water, therefore it would be left behind after the water spilled out. He worried that he would miss it, throw it away with the dirty water.

This time, after swirling the water round and round, then tilting it out carefully from the pan, he stared long and hard at the muddy residue. The pan was rusty, caked with dried mud and gravel and for a moment or two he felt numb with ignorance and the fear of defeat. When he tipped the pan sharply and tiny flecks of yellow twinkled in the bright sunlight, he turned the pan back and forth, this way and that. Was this it? Was this what all the shouting was about? Had he really found gold? Were these tiny yellow dots the answer to his dreams?

Yes, Jacob Finesilver! Rich Jacob Finesilver! He whispered a prayer of thanksgiving. On top of his tiny patch of land, he waved his shovel wildly in the air, uttered an exultant cry and shook his fist at the hill. He had beaten it, and beaten the terror of not knowing how to find what he was looking for. And there was more in that hill. There had to be.

He marked two posts, one with his name in full along with the letters "MLP" for mining location post, and placed them at each end of his claim. Standing back, he stared at the posts and slapped his thigh in excitement. He wished he could see his mother's face at this moment, and Velvel's, see their smiles, their acknowledgment of his ability to do what he had said he would. Oh, how sweet this moment.

He made his way jubilantly into Dawson City, paid the recording fee of ten dollars in the claims office, took some jovial pats on the back and a big cigar from the clerk, puffed out his chest and felt like an American millionaire.

For the next month the small claim averaged a half-ounce of gold for each pan. At fifteen dollars an ounce, he figured to dig out one hundred dollars a day. Compared to the ten-cent pan considered rich in this strike, Jacob had dug into a remarkable find.

He moved his tent to the site after the end of July. But not long after that the weather changed dramatically. The days turned cold and short, and Jacob knew mining would soon end for the year. He could do nothing then until next spring.

The trees were now a glorious palette of reds and yellows that flamed for miles over the mountains and foothills. But their brilliant leaves soon fluttered away, leaving the bare wood standing alone against wind and frost.

Knowing each day would be colder and more uncomfortable in the tent, he began building his log house in a clearing behind the stream. By working his claim during the warmer days and building his house each night by lantern light, Jacob kept ahead of his credit at the sawmill. He traded gold for lumber and nails, throwing his poke on the counter as he had seen the others do, taking what he needed until the mill's owner said, "That's it." The merchants in most of the stores and saloons had the knack of eyeballing a poke's worth. Few of the miners cheated, and when one did, he was put on the next steamer to Skagway and told not to return.

Jacob finished the twenty-foot-square house by the first snow, matching the logs so they slanted to drain moisture, and filled the chinks between the logs with moss to keep out cold. He set the door frames into the logs with pegs and piled dirt and moss over the split log roof until it was one foot thick. It was here, on the roof, that he hoped to plant his vegetable garden in the spring.

Most of the work now was not in panning but in digging holes, shoveling up the dirt and gravel and storing the rich piles that would freeze solid over the winter. In spring, he would wash the mixture down a water sluice, hopefully finding gold dust or nuggets left behind. He had made the sluice, a long narrow trough, after the men in town told him it was easier and more productive than using the small pan or rocker.

As winter set in, digging became impossible. The ground was frozen solid four or five feet down from the surface. He had seen the miners down at Indian Creek using bonfires to burn their way into the permafrost, thawing a few inches at a time. To Jacob watching the flames flickering long into the night, it was a scene from hell, and he wanted no part of it.

Time dragged by. He chopped wood for the stove, kept the fire brisk and wrote letters home. None of this, however, was enough to fill the empty hours. He found himself pacing the small cabin, gloomy and short-tempered from confinement. Idleness was anathema to Jacob, the short days and everlasting nights more miserable than hunger or pain.

There was plenty of gaiety and night life in Dawson City, saloons and dance halls and casinos ready and willing to offer the men all forms of companionship, but for Jacob, that kind of fun was hardly worth the effort of the three-mile hike.

Snow was deep that winter; bitter cold hung on for weeks. With no place to go and no one to talk to, Jacob's cabin fever rose higher each day. The closest neighbors were a pleasant family, the man and wife friendly, the two children scrappy and endearing. The woman stopped by the cabin one day with an invitation for dinner. "You can't sit by yourself like this," Mrs. Novak scolded, standing in the doorway and scowling at Jacob. "You're not eating much, I can see that, so come and share our supper."

Jacob smiled. "Please, come in, you are welcome."

"I know I'm welcome, Jacob, but I can't stay. Mr. Novak is fussing just like you, anxious to work and not able to, and the children get on his nerves." She smiled. "So it's really for our sakes that I'm asking you to supper."

He dressed in layers of heavy clothing, strapped snow shoes over his boots, and plodded through thigh-high snow to the Novak's cabin. Not much larger than his own, it was ample shelter for the family of four. Beds were arranged bunk fashion against the walls, and a table set for supper.

"Sit, Jacob, warm yourself," Mrs. Novak urged. She was pleasant and plain, an American from Iowa, looking older than her thirty years. Her pale face reddened with heat as she leaned over the stove and spooned stew onto five plates.

"Why do you have black hair and a red beard?" the four-year-old asked Jacob.

He smiled and unconsciously stroked his hairy chin. "Well," he said, struggling with his new English, "I never not think about it. Maybe Holy One not make up mind."

Her older brother spoke up. "What's a holy one?"

"That's enough," Mrs. Novak scolded, "eat your food and don't bother our guest."

"Is no bothered," Jacob said, "is first time I think on it. Now Jacob wonder about hair, too."

Everyone laughed and Frank Novak brought out a bottle of bourbon and served the three adults.

"This'll warm you up, Jacob, and help yourself, don't wait for an invite."

Jacob matched his host drink for drink, and by midnight, the bourbon bottle was empty. They sat around the stove, laughing and talking in Polish, Novak's mother tongue, Jacob's brain in a whirl trying to juggle Russian, Polish and English.

When they said good night, Mrs. Novak asked Jacob to join them for Christmas dinner.

"Is kind," Jacob said, "but . . . would be wasted for me." He hesitated, "I am Jew."

He watched her face, wondering if this was the last time he would see his new friends, then used the awkward moment to attach the snowshoes. He could weather it. It had happened before.

When he straightened, he saw the couple smiling at him. "So was our Lord," Mrs. Novak said, "so come anyway."

Trudging home, Jacob thought about the Novaks and their friendship for him, a stranger, a man who worshipped differently, whose people had been accused of killing their Savior ever since the crucifixion. All his life he had heard about the priests in Frank Novak's homeland and their unremitting anti-Semitic harangues, the daily homilies eloquent with falsehood and distortion. Yet here were these kind people, offering food and companionship.

At this moment Jacob remembered what Rabinowitz had told him that first day in Dawson, about loneliness in the harsh and bitter winters, terrible stories of men dying alone in their shacks, their bodies found in the spring lying next to a soup kettle in which boiled moccasins had frozen solid. He had warned Jacob of men reduced to skeletons with sunken eyes and rotting teeth, their black and purple skin soft as the sour dough they kept in tins. Mistakenly treated for gangrene, they had died of scurvy.

With the Novaks, Jacob now had friends. And that precious friendship could save him from the horror of isolation. Now he was beginning to understand why some men who had succeeded in living through the Yukon winter alone, had gone mad by spring.

FIFTEEN

❧❧❧

JACOB MOVED CLOSER TO THE KEROSENE LAMP AND studied the matchmaker's florid, finely detailed description of the young girl. The letter was written in a slanted heavy hand, marred here and there by blobs of black ink where the old man's pen had leaked. But it was legible and Jacob scowled at the exaggerated prose.

"Malka," the matchmaker wrote, "is comely but not so much as to entice other men. She is a friendly girl but not flirtatious, and well formed although petite, so she surely cannot eat much."

Jacob's scowl disappeared, and he smiled. It was important that one's wife have a dainty appetite, especially when food was scarce.

"Hardworking," the letter went on, "honest, and from a good family." Did not one's future children, please God, have a right to a proud ancestral line? Her grandfather had been a rabbi, and her great-great-grandfather had sung for forty years like an angel as chief cantor in the great synagogue in Lublin.

"There would, of course, be a small dowry, not much, for the girl's father is only a butcher, though he is a learned man, and one on whom the town can count for wisdom and advice from time to time."

A learned man, to be sure, Jacob thought. To deal with his picky customers was a challenge worthy of King Solomon. He returned to the matchmaker's letter.

Jacob stared at the picture of the perfect Malka, although by now he had committed her features, expression and dress to memory. Her smile was shy, perhaps because of the religious injunction against photographs. Leave it to old Meyer, that arch conniver, who could work his way around Providence when he felt his cause was just.

In the picture, she wore a simple dress with a high lace collar, buttoned cuffs, and no jewelry. A young, pretty girl, petite in a dark dress.

The expression in her eyes made his imagination leap. It was a bold look at the stranger petitioning for her hand. Here I am, the look said, take it or leave it.

He studied the picture and the letter for days, ever since his snowshoe trek for supplies and mail to Dawson City. After his initial inquiry months ago, he had agonized over the wisdom of his decision to send for a bride. Who in her right mind would choose to share the uncertainty and hardship of his life? Should he have offered her money, a dowry of gold, bags of nuggets as a temptation to brave life here, to say nothing of the difficult trail that led to Dawson? But a wife who would accept a bribe was not for him. He had told this to Meyer, leaving nothing out. He trusted that Meyer had read his letter to Malka verbatim, unless the old man had suddenly had cold feet. If she knew all the grim facts, he could lose his fee.

Jacob stirred the embers in the stove. The room had chilled. He added more wood, and the dry logs snapped and hissed into life, filling the cabin with warmth.

So he had been a cheechako, a newcomer, greenhorn they had called him in town. Not such a bad thing to be, and not for very long. He had learned to speak passable English, made new friends, and sent quite a bit of money home to his family. He was certainly a sourdough now. But a lonely one.

It was Cannibal Sam who had made a difference in his life. He remembered his first meeting with the fierce Han Indian trader who had startled everyone when he walked into the Dawson sawmill that day. Almost seven feet tall, wearing tan suede leggings, hip boots and a coat fringed in feathers, Cannibal Sam was an awesome sight.

But Jacob, too, was tall, and met the Indian on an almost equal footing. Each man lived off his own piece of land, asked for no charity and worked hard. Sam respected hard work. Just surviving in the Yukon's Arctic winters was some of the hardest work around.

He took to Jacob, a fearless white man unlike the others in Dawson who crossed the road when they saw Sam coming. Their relationship was business, at first. Cannibal Sam agreed to trade with Jacob, fruits and vegetables and fur pelts stored in the Indian's communal buildings for small gold nuggets, the price to be determined each time they met.

"You also make for Sam wood things Sam not find in store. Wife want shelves, little food boxes, new cradle . . . babies come to Sam's house each year . . . wife pretty, but tired like dead moose."

But it was not their bartering that was valuable, it was the Indian's company. Jacob rarely left home during the very cold months, and sometimes saw no one for weeks on end. Cannibal Sam enjoyed visiting with his friends, like Jacob. "Gets me away from wife and babies. Maybe if Sam gone more, wife not have so many!"

Jacob kept a full tin of tobacco and a deck of cards on hand for these pleasant times he called "shmoozing." Sam took great delight in teaching his new friend the fine art of simultaneously rolling his cigarette with one hand while pouring them each a short whiskey with the other. He would pull the string on the tobacco pouch with his teeth, grin, and say, "Now Jacob and Sam shmooze!"

The one thing they never shmoozed about was how Sam got his name. Jake figured the less he knew, the better.

He thumbed the pages of the letter and thought of old Meyer the matchmaker, laughed at by children for his lameness, the hitch in his gait as he hopped like a drunken hare over the mud-filled streets of Khotin. Meyer, the matchmaker. Since Jacob could remember, the stories about the old eccentric and his life's work had filled his family's house with laughter.

"I don't want to marry Menasha Feldner, Papa! Please don't force me. He's short, and he's losing his hair, and he picks at his skin, and . . ."

"Enough, little girl, you are sixteen and still unmarried, and this is a shame for your parents. Menasha comes from a good family. So his mother is fat as a bowl and needs two chairs to sit on, but his father is a learned scribe and, although poor, his penmanship is superb."

"We don't even know each other, Papa, we've never even been introduced."

"You will meet him at the wedding!"

Throughout the Pale, Jacob mused, strangers married strangers, children were matched up with children before they were old enough to walk.

He laughed as another story jogged his memory.

"So? Nu? How is the bride?"

"Now you ask me, Mama? Now, after a year with Menasha the *meshuggener*? You and Papa should have to live with him, how he gives me pinches when I'm working, bites me when we, well, you know, and that's not all! He whistles in his sleep and grinds his teeth, he's stingy, and he talks with his mouth full. Ugh!"

"Well, I'm glad you two are so happy. Are you pregnant yet?"

Jacob smiled, remembering the remarkably fickle bias of his parents' tales about the matchmaker who had brought them together. He was either a shrewd popinjay or a dedicated Cupid, venal vulture or thoughtful, untiring perpetuator of the faith, depending on Mama's or Papa's affections of the moment.

Uncle Aaron, who made unintentional jokes about serious matters, saw this topic as great material.

"You told me she was young, and she must be forty! You told me she was lovely to look at, and she's ugly as a horned toad! You told me she had a sweet nature, and she has done nothing but curse me and my family! You told me . . ."

"You don't have to whisper," the matchmaker said, "she is also deaf."

There on the table was Meyer's reply, and the perfect Malka smiling at Jacob.

Who are you? he said to the picture. Are you kind? Are you healthy? Do you like to laugh? Will you enjoy lying next to me under the quilt? Or will you only endure it? Can you sew? Are you cheerful? Or will you nag me? Can you read? Can you cook? Will you keep Sabbath even when I have forgotten?

Why could he not be satisfied like the other men, the rough, hard-eyed sourdoughs who never bathed, slept with their boots on and visited the whores in Klondike City?

He turned from the stove and wrote his reply to the matchmaker.

SIXTEEN

❦

Khotin, Ukraine, Russia, 1897

MEYER FINKLE STUMBLED THROUGH THE ICY, SNOW-packed streets of Khotin toward Nathan Semel's house, the letter held fast in his mittened hand. This union was going to be the highlight of his matchmaking life, the zenith of his blessed career: bringing young Jews together in holy matrimony.

Never had Meyer Finkle been so excited by any of his prospective couples, never had he been a party to such an eloquent and intensely dramatic situation as this one with Jacob Finesilver. It was a golden opportunity for Malka, and the play on words delighted him. He had made the pun six times already this day, and would repeat it often before the whole business was over.

Meyer hopped over a ditch running with slush and mud, almost lost his balance but righted himself at the last moment. Don't fall now, *chochem*, he chided himself, that's all you need, dummy, with that ticket to a comfortable old age dancing in your pocket.

Ah, no need to think such things. It is the duty of the matchmaker to bring couples together so they may be fruitful and multiply. That is the reason for this joy.

He rounded the corner of the street and cursed under his breath at the unshoveled snowdrifts and patches of ice. His game left leg, shorter by four inches than his right, kept buckling under the strain of the awkward shoe, its thick sole fitting none of his boots and slipping on the icy surface. A schnapps would certainly take the bite out of this cold night, he thought eagerly, and pulled the bell on Semel's door.

"Meyer! What in the world . . . ?"

"Sh!" Meyer hissed, edging into the house, "is Malka about?"

"No, why? What are you doing here?"

"Good!" Meyer said loudly. "No need for whispering, eh? I'll tell you, I'll tell you, just don't rush me. I'm an old man and I need time to breathe between my words."

"Here, Meyer, sit by the fire. Let me have your coat and scarf, the mittens, the boot, you want to keep the sweater? Fine. So, a glass of tea? A piece of cake? Are you warming?"

"Yes, thank you. No tea. But," he went on, his eyes merry, his manner cozy with Semel, almost conspiratorial, "I have something to tell you that will be astounding!"

"Ah!" Semel sat back from the old man, who tended to spritz his listener as he talked. "So that's why you asked if Malka was home, eh? Another suitor for my daughter? Another wonder still hanging on his mother's apron strings? Another gift from the angels who knows only to bathe after *Havdalah* on Saturday night and at no other time? No, Meyer, thank you, but don't bother."

"Heh-heh. Don't bother, eh? Wait until you hear what I have to say, then tell me don't bother." Meyer reached into his jacket's inner pocket, a smile suddenly replaced the grimace on his face, and he limped to the hall tree. "Such a dummy. Here, my fine friend, listen to this." Meyer read the letter from Jacob, raising his eyes every so often to see Semel's reaction. When he finished, he sat back with a great smile, his potbelly straining at the few buttons remaining on his worn flannel vest.

Semel rose from the sofa and walked about the room, nervously shuffling papers on his desk. He had a foreboding.

"*Nu*? Say something," Meyer prodded.

"It is not for me to say, it is for Malka to say. And what that will be, I cannot guess. As you know," Semel said, his voice beginning to rise, "she is in no great hurry to tie herself down to some pimply-faced *narr* whose mother extracted from you the impossible promise to marry him off. No, Meyer," here the crescendo in full bloom, "it is not for me to say."

The matchmaker was stunned by Semel's response. Until now his thoughts had dwelt only on the beauty of the match and the percentage he could receive. He had been unprepared for such a harangue, and now his bubble burst. "How can you talk like that, after all I have done in your . . . in Malka's behalf? Be offended if you must, but I have to tell you your daughter had better get off her high horse and settle for someone soon, or she will be a bitter old maid."

"My daughter," Semel boomed, "does not have to *settle* for a husband!"

"All right, all right," Meyer said placatingly, "she *is* rather special, but why do you insist on making up her mind for her?"

The fear that grabbed Semel's chest was suffocating him. "Perhaps you're right," he said. "Perhaps I am being too hasty, speaking for her like this. It's just, well, it's just . . ."

"It's a darn good offer, Nathan Semel, and you know it!"

Meyer watched his opponent closely. "You know what, Semel," he declared triumphantly, "you're afraid of this proposal, afraid it's going to be just different enough to appeal to your 'different' daughter."

Semel lowered his head. "Yes."

"But why the gloom? Jacob is from a good family. I know his mother, I knew his father, a fine man and a scholar, as honest and learned as our beloved rabbi. And Jacob, himself, will become a millionaire out there in . . . in . . . *oy*, what a place that must be! I was wondering how anyone could keep kosher in hell-and-gone?"

"Among other things," Semel murmured.

"What's that? What other things?"

"Never mind."

"I know what's bothering you, Semel. It's because it *is* hell-and-gone, isn't it? Because you won't see your daughter any more. Because she'll be in another country, another continent. That's why you're upset."

"Can you blame me?"

"I don't know, I never had children. Which, judging by what I see every day, was one of my better decisions."

"It wasn't one of your decisions at all, you old *bulvon*! No woman would have you!" Semel shouted.

"Forgive me, Meyer. That was cruel. I do not wish to argue with you, but it is impossible for me to answer for Malka. I admit she has the obligation to listen to this proposal, and I will see that she does. But she also has the obligation to do as I wish. I will try, but with Malka, that is not always easy."

"Thank you, Semel, that's all I ask. As for Malka, you should have trained her better when her mother died. She has always been headstrong and stubborn."

"Enough, Meyer," Semel gritted his teeth. "Don't push your luck."

The matchmaker got to his feet. "So, Semel, when will Malka be told?"

"When she returns home. Time enough, Meyer. I will let you know." Semel walked to the side table and poured a brandy for each of them into small crystal glasses.

"Here's to you, Meyer, for fulfilling your duty. And here's to me for fulfilling mine."

The two men nodded and drank down the liquid.

Meyer reached for his coat. "May Malka only have the wisdom to fulfill hers."

It was late when Malka returned. She found her father sprawled asleep in his favorite chair. He had pulled the worn and overstuffed rose velvet eyesore close to the fireplace in the parlor, but the room was cold, the fire had dwindled to a dying glow. She shook him gently, then raised the wick on the lamp.

"Papa? Wake up. It's after midnight, and time for you to be in bed."

"Ah, my angel," Semel said, opening his eyes, "and what about you? So late?"

"That Mendelsohn boy is a slow learner. Besides," Malka said, stirring up the embers, "I'm a big girl now, and able to care for myself."

"And that means?" Semel asked warily.

"That means if I want to go someplace after a tutoring lesson, I should be able to do so without my overprotective father sitting up half the night waiting."

Semel sniffed, his feelings wounded, and squinted at the clock. "Two o'clock? And I must be up at five. That means I bid you good night."

"You're not going to ask me where I've been?"

"You just told me you are a big girl and can take care of herself. Fine. Good night."

"Papa, this isn't you speaking."

"So, who is it?"

Malka sensed this new attitude as a thin deception for her benefit. "I went to a meeting, Papa, at Gershon's house. A meeting for the movement for enlightenment. Do you know what that is?"

Semel's face darkened. A vein swelled above his right eyebrow and began to throb. "The movement for enlightenment, eh? Do you have any idea what this could mean?"

"Well," Malka said, hesitating, caught between truth and something less honorable, blue eyes sparkling with the fervor of a new cause.

"I asked you a question," Semel said.

"Papa, please listen to me. Give me a chance to talk. There are those of us in the village, a small dedicated group involved with new opinions and shared feelings and values, students and Hebrew teachers, merchants, people from the synagogue who believe we can stand up to the Czar, fight his cruel edicts, gain a bit of freedom and dignity for ourselves and . . . and they are starting to defend Jews, starting a collective of sorts to buy guns, small arms, axes, and sticks. . . ."

"And nothing!" he roared. "Do you realize what you're saying? Do you know what the authorities are doing in town? That everywhere there is house-to-house searching going on, police inspections, men and women arrested for the slightest provocation? No? Of course not. How could you? You teach all day, and when you are home, I shield you from it."

Semel released his hold on Malka and patted at her sleeves. "I am sorry, my angel, but your youthful enthusiasm is ill-placed. You can do nothing about the Czar, or his cruelty, or his repression. Neither you nor your young friends, movement for enlightenment or not! And there is no future for us if you continue this madness."

Semel was frightened for his naïve daughter and what her stupidity could evoke from the authorities. How could he have neglected such an important part of her education? He was a fool, and now she would pay for it. The thought made him almost physically ill. Yet maybe this offer of marriage with Jacob Finesilver was a gift, a sign from the Holy One to leave Khotin, escape from the insanity of defending mobs, the police and the Czar. But how does he handle this? How clever must he be to help her see what she must do?

Malka's world was tilting, unsettled by her father's words and the fear in his voice. This was the first time he had spoken so harshly to her since she was a little girl. She would have been grossly offended had she not admitted to herself that maybe he was right. The group she had met with was a ragged one with no logical plan. The young men were hottempered, the women shrill and defiant. They had worried Malka with their intemperate passions, but she had been inspired by a common wish to fight back against the Czar and the hatred and bigotry he represented. If others could take a stand, she had thought at the meeting, why couldn't she? She had hoped her father would counsel her against dropping out. Instead, he now reinforced her desire to do so.

"You are right as always, Papa, it was foolish to think I could fight alongside these people."Semel was surprised at her quick change of heart. "Oh? Now I am really worried. It isn't like you to give up so easily."

"You know I do so only when I'm wrong. Besides, while the thought behind the group is a noble one, they haven't the faintest notion what to do. Perhaps if they ever organize, I may join them again."

Semel took his daughter's hand. "Malka, I know you're lonely. I may be getting old, but I'm not blind. Being with young people is important, but you must pick and choose them carefully."

"I know, I thought I had. And I am not lonely," she added. It was then that she noticed the two glasses, the rims sticky with amber liquor.

She held the glasses up, her eyes questioning.

Semel sat on the freshly plumped sofa and took Jacob Finesilver's letter from his pocket. He paused, then, without a word, handed it to her. Malka read it through slowly, then read it through again. Her face shone with excitement and her expression frightened Semel. Not knowing what to say, and not wishing to blunder into an argument, he kept silent.

Malka spoke first, she cleared her throat.

"I would go if I could, Papa. But I think you know that. Right?"

"I . . . I don't know what to say. . . . I guess so . . . but what do mean, 'would' go?"

"I cannot leave you if you are ill. You never lied to me before, Papa. Why do you lie now?"

"Listen to me, my angel. Sit, and listen. There. Now. I had a stomach upset. Mrs. uh . . . what's-her-name . . . ?"

"Lebedeff."

"Yes. She gave me something and it worked. You know it worked. I'm fine. I haven't had an ache or a pain since then. So don't make a big *megillah* out of nothing. We will discuss *your* life, not mine."

Malka gazed into her father's eyes, looking for telltale signs of his bending the truth, waffling, painting a pretty picture rather than stating the facts.

"Can I believe you?" she asked.

"Yes."

She turned again to Jacob's letter. The color rose in her cheeks. "He writes well, doesn't he? And so much detail. He must be very observant of life around him in this Dawson City, don't you think?"

"Mm, yes. . . ." Semel mumbled, waiting for the other shoe to drop.

"So much beauty in his words . . . about his friends and the animals. . . ."

"Yes, Malka."

"I think I like him, even though I don't know anything about him."

Semel held his breath, afraid of what she would say next.

"He learned how to mine for the gold even though he never knew how, wasn't that clever of him? And he knows how to live in all that cold. And he built his own house out of logs. And he knows how to hunt and find food. And survive."

Malka paused, her brain whirling with the effort of catching at the right words, the right phrases with which to express herself. She was obviously moved by Jacob's letter and wanted to indicate this to her father in the least hurtful way.

"Papa," she said softly, "because there is no life here for me and never will be unless I leave and do not get involved with this new freedom movement, and if you are really well now, I think I will go to this Dawson City and marry Jacob Finesilver."

The statement was made, and assumed the nature of reality, a statement of fact. She had to believe it now. Her heart beat wildly, as if it suddenly was a hiding place for a great secret just given her. The key to her prison had been unlocked.

Her father was shocked by her swift response. Where was this coming from? His, gentle, precious angel deciding suddenly, in a second, to change her whole life. And his. When she spoke again, her words seemed to come through a long tunnel.

"This man, this Jacob, must be very brave. And strong. He says here that he walked from Khotin to Alaska. Imagine! The adventure of it, the pain . . . the glory! And he must be very certain of his future, and his ability to provide, or else he would not have sent for a wife. Do you agree?"

Semel nodded, but said nothing. His world was dissolving in front of his eyes.

"He also makes me think he's a thoughtful man, for he speaks lovingly of his family still here."

Semel nodded again.

"And the way he speaks, his love of the natural world, the beauty around us. The part, here, where he describes the turning of the leaves . . . Papa?"

"I'm listening."

Malka's face glowed with a happiness Semel had not seen before. He was thrilled for her, yet dreaded what this would mean. And he *had* lied about his illness. But more than that, how could she think of embarking on such a dangerous trip, into this uncharted territory across the sea, for God's sake?

Should he not say something, voice his objections? Challenge her impetuous decision?

"Do you approve?" Malka asked. "I would rather go with your blessing than without it."

"I'm not sure," Semel admitted. "As I see it, well, Finesilver *is* a Jew, and obviously a good man. I think I may know his family. But not well. I cannot know everyone in this miserable town. But where is this place he's living? Where is this Klondike? Where in all the holy prophets' names is this?"

His voice grew louder and more agitated. His face turned red, perspiration covered his brow. Malka worried for him, and spoke to lessen his agitation.

"From what I can see in his drawing here, it looks like it's in Alaska . . . no, it's Canada. Right over the border, this line between Alaska and Canada. See? It's very near the Arctic Circle. So it must be very cold. But we are used to cold, aren't we, Papa?"

Semel saw that this Klondike was just across the sea from Russia. So it cannot be that far. But on the same line as Siberia, if Jacob's map could be trusted. He knew that kind of cold neither he nor Malka had ever experienced.

"Let us talk more objectively, let us explore this more carefully. Let us . . ."

"Papa, there isn't anything more to discuss. Jacob needs a wife, I need to be needed. Life holds nothing for me here, we've talked that out already, and there are many things about him to admire. His language is excellent, and he has learned quite a lot of English. He has built his own house, learned to mine enough gold to live comfortably—GOLD, Papa!—and has made many friends in this Dawson City. That all speaks very well for him, wouldn't you agree?"

Semel sighed. "Yes."

"So?"

"So . . . what do you mean, so? How do you expect to keep a kosher home in that crazy wilderness? Where is there a synagogue? A rabbi? Who, in the name of the Holy One, will pronounce you man and wife?"

Malka shook her head. "I don't know. If there is no rabbi, then we will have to have a civil marriage. There must be a judge in the city of Dawson. And when we do find a rabbi, we will again marry. As for a synagogue, well, Papa, that I doubt very much. But prayers can be said at home as well as in the synagogue. Kosher food is asking too much, I think. It must be very difficult to get food there at all, much less insisting it be kosher. Papa, I am a Jewess, now and forever. I won't become anything else just because there will be great hardship in keeping the *mitzvot*. I will do my very best to keep kosher and all the commandments and obligations." She smiled disarmingly. "How could I, as your daughter, do anything else?"

Semel paced the room, wringing his hands. "I do not know what to say. You cannot make up your own mind like this." It is not tradition, he said to himself, but kept silent on that thorny subject. "Then again, this may be the best move for you, the biggest, luckiest thing to happen in your life. But it may also destroy you, hurt you beyond redemption, and that would destroy me. But how can I keep you from it?"

Malka embraced her father, her muffled words thick with tears.

"Don't worry, Papa, and don't be afraid for me. I will be fine. But I shall miss you terribly."

He wept, too. "And I you, my angel," he said, wiping his eyes and nose. "But a nagging thought sticks in my head, let me say it. Then I promise the subject will be closed. What if you don't love him?" His eyes filled again. "What if he does not love you?"

To Semel's surprise, Malka smiled. "Ah, what an interesting thought! Perhaps now, my darling Papa, you can understand better why tradition is not always the answer."

"Yes," Semel countered, "but without the tradition of the matchmaker, you would never be able to leave Khotin, eh?"

Malka wondered if her father had maneuvered the whole situation to this final outcome. At the same time, Semel thought his daughter extremely clever to have worked everything out this way.

Neither would ever know the truth, and it mattered little. Malka and her father were happy, but Malka was happier to leave than her Semel was to have her go. After all the words were spoken, he knew he would never see her again.

SEVENTEEN

୧୨୧୭

THE STORM SLAMMED INTO DAWSON THE DAY AFTER Christmas. High winds poured down through the canyons of the Coast Mountains in the early morning hours, picking up moisture along the way. At the onset, the force of these winds broke thick, ancient trees into kindling wood, lifted cabin roofs from over the heads of sleeping prospectors and ferried the mass of snow back and forth over the Midnight Dome before finally dumping it all on Dawson City.

When Jacob awoke, his crude windows of freshwater ice were strangely dark. Arctic winters were gloomy, the late morning sun visible for only a few hours before sinking into the early afternoon. This was different; the reason, when he figured it out, was unpleasant.

The muddy, opaque light was coming through a barrier of snow, probably driven by the wind into a towering drift piled up against the cabin, covering the window. He had to dig himself out, or eventually suffocate.

The wind was still high, a dismal, muted noise, ebbing and flowing like an ocean tide. The Yukon had taught him that the quiet moments were deceiving, only breathers for the howling beast outside his door.

He dressed quickly, hurrying into two pairs of flannel underwear, two pairs of German wool socks, heavy woolen trousers and furskin pants, and thick-soled snow boots reaching to his knees. But when he pulled on the cabin door, he found it frozen shut. The snow had melted from the warmth inside the house, then refrozen, sealing it tight. He could defrost the frame with hot water, but that took time. He had an idea that seemed faster and more practical.

He removed his outer clothes and started tossing wood into the stove, one log after another. If he made the house hot enough, the snow against the outer walls would melt, freeing up the door. He had cut a fresh supply of logs the night before, and now fed them into the stove's fiery mouth. The action evoked images in his mind of an ancient sacrifice to the monstrous god Baal, but the strategy worked.

By two o'clock, he could open the cabin door and push through the huge drift in time to see the last ray of sunlight slide under the earth. He worked fast to dig out the cabin, then stood up and looked around.

The amount of snow was astonishing. Branches of the tall trees swept the ground under their white burden. The wind, so wild and threatening a few hours before, had died. The glade was silent. Jacob stood in a white and frozen world, a crystal palace as beautiful and bejeweled as that of any of the Czars, and he felt like a child again. Where and how was Velvel, he wondered, who loved to play in snow, to make roly-poly people he named and talked with until they melted.

"Hey, Moishe, come to school with me! Oh, poor Avner! No one to play with until Moishe comes home. Well, you can talk to Esther or Sara. I know they're only girls, but still better than nothing. Oh—oh-oh! There goes your head . . . slipping, slipping . . . gone! Ha! Ha! Ha!"

Jacob could see them all laughing, running through the snow-covered meadow or around the house until Mama called them to come in. Were they still laughing? Or had Velvel been found in the barn at last and thrown into the

Cossack barracks and forgotten? And Mama, and the girls? Had their heads been shaved to make them less attractive to the Cossacks?

Confronting his memories did nothing for Jacob's frustration. If only he could work, he could forget, but neither seemed possible in this bitter, interminable winter. The prospect of marriage with Malka Semel had lifted his spirits, and the pluses were beginning to outweigh the minuses. He was learning a new language, making friends in spite of his shyness, paying off a large debt with hard-earned gold and existing in one of the worlds' most inhospitable climates. Surely all that stood for something.

He looked through the dim light and surveyed his crystal palace. Snow dropped here and there from high branches, and he thought of the one stubborn and unbeatable obstacle in his way: the fetid, airless tunnel beneath his claim and the impenetrable permafrost. It was impossible to dig through the frozen ground without fires every few inches, and even then the smoke and stench ran him out. There was nothing more he could do but live on his dwindling pokes, hope they bought him enough time and food, then begin again next spring.

He started back to the cabin, his arms filled with logs, when a cry stopped him, a keening that shivered the skin of his spine. It came from somewhere in back, or through the trees, or maybe from in front.

He looked around and listened. There it was again, closer. He ruled out dogs. The Novaks, his closest neighbors, had no dogs. And it was not caribou, for they had all migrated in the fall to warmer climes. Wolf, then. Perhaps coyote. Or was it human?

He heard it again, the cry now muffled and pleading, softer, full of pain. Jacob dropped the logs and peered into the deep tangle of woods. He called, "Halloo! Halloo!" but no answer came.

Then he heard branches snap behind him. When he turned, he saw a man tumble with arms outstretched, eyes glazed and sightless. Jacob reached out and caught him before he fell.

He was a big man, terribly emaciated. Jacob held him by his thin, bony arms, and, alternately pushing and dragging, was able to maneuver him into the cabin.

The man's cries rang in his ears, angry and insulting curses spat between lips blackened and thick with blood and frost. But Jacob ignored them and worked quickly to untie the man's heavy clothing. He rolled him over to the warmth of the stove and rubbed his skin gently, as Inuijak and Meqo had done with him. Here, he thought, was his chance to repay their kindness.

The man looked about sixty, with scant gray hair and a deeply lined, sallow face. Around the nose and mouth was a faint blue cast, typical of hypothermia. His hands and feet were frozen, the tips of his chalk-white fingers heavily callused and torn. Throughout most of the night, Jacob rubbed the man's frostbitten skin with warm lard and tried to ease water down his throat. When the man moaned in his sleep, Jacob talked to him to reassure him.

Toward morning, the man cried out again, louder this time, and Jacob shook him gently. "Wake up. . . . is bad dream. See? You here with me . . . Jacob."

The man's eyes fluttered open and he grabbed Jacob's arm, his voice rough and husky when he spoke. "So . . . cold . . ."

Jacob bundled the loosened cover tightly around him and spoke calmly in his ragged English, the soothing tone more effective than words. The man soon relaxed his grip and fell asleep.

Later, Jacob heated water on the stove and made strong tea, lacing both cups with sugar and a drop of condensed milk. His patient drank eagerly and asked for more.

"Good," Jacob said, smiling. "You better now?"

"Hell, yes," the man said thickly, "Where am I?"

"In my house. I find you in snow." Jacob sat on the bed and took away the empty cup. "You cold like ice."

The man stared, his eyes puzzling over Jacob's strange accent. "You sure as hell ain't American," he said. "Slavic? Polish?" The man grimaced, then began to cough and gasp for air, his wracked body shook the bed. Finally he lay back against the wall of the cabin and closed his eyes.

"You try soup," Jacob said, "is good. I make soup to eat. To drink. How you say?"

He brought a steaming cup to the bed and began feeding the man slowly. He could almost hear Meqo's voice saying to him, "Not too much. Not too fast."

"Good," the man whispered.

"Make from potatoes."

After one or two sips, the man pulled away. "Christ, no more. I can't taste it anyway."

"Okay. More later," Jacob said. He tried to pull the quilt up only to be pushed away.

"Scat!" the man snapped. "I can do that myself."

Jacob shrugged.

"Name's Dingo," the man said gruffly, "Dingo Malone. You're Jacob, eh?"

"Yes."

"Okay, Jake. I'll say it this once, and I won't say it again. Thanks for saving my life. Subject closed."

Because Jacob guessed Dingo to be a seasoned veteran miner, he thought he should have known better than to stray outside in a storm. The tin of sour dough in his pack was the real clue. The dough was a common staple for miners. Jacob had never used it. Perhaps now he would learn.

Dingo's curses woke Jacob the next morning. He saw the man standing at the stove with badly shaking hands, attempting to fill the kettle.

"Goddamn!"he cried, dropping the basin of ice.

"Wait," Jacob said, going to his aid, "Jacob help."

"I'm no goddamn child. Just let me be."

"Ice is cold," Jacob protested. "I do it."

"Goddamn it. . . ."

"No swear!" Jacob's voice was suddenly rough, his eyes flashing with anger. "Not in my house."

Dingo threw himself on the bed, one arm over his eyes. "Shit, then, can I say shit?"

"Is okay. But not name of Holy One." Jacob filled the kettle and turned his back to start his morning prayers. But he was too angry to pray. He solved his dilemma by starting the day over again.

Slipping under the blanket on the floor that served as his bed since he had donated his own to Dingo, he tried to sleep. When that was unsuccessful, he rose, dressed, and put on his tallis and prayer shawl. From a small bag he withdrew the tefillin, the straps with small boxes holding the four passages from Exodus and Deuteronomy.

Dingo watched out of the corner of one eye, hearing strange foreign words, seeing Jacob tighten the knot on the strap, then turn the strap seven times over his arm between the elbow and the wrist. "Say, Jacob, why do you . . . ?"

Jacob whirled, silencing Dingo with a look the prospector immediately understood.

"Okay, okay," he said, falling back on his pillow. Jacob placed the other box in the middle of his forehead, looped the strap around his head, and knotted it. When he finished, he removed the phylacteries and put them away.

"Some water, please," Dingo rasped.

Jacob poured from the basin of ice kept in the cabin, holding the cup to Dingo's lips.

"Thanks, Jake. Sorry about messin' up your little sacred churchifying there. I mean, the communion, or whatever, you know, prayers?"

"Yes, prayers."

"You some kind of Russian Baptist, or what? That was sure strange to me."

"I . . . I am a Jew. I say prayers each day. If Dingo not like, Dingo not stay."

"Hey, don't get your nuts in an uproar, young fella, I have nothing against you or your prayers."

The snow began again that night and continued for almost a week, making life at once tense and monotonous for the two men. Dingo recuperated but seemed to suffer now from some chronic lung ailment, coughing most of each night until exhausted.

They had never discussed that day or what had sent Dingo into the worst of blizzards. Jacob, although curious, never asked. Dingo himself brought it up.

Jacob was reading, settled by the stove with his book of poems, when Dingo's voice broke the silence.

"Jake, you married?"

"No. You?"

"Nope. Too mean when I was young, and now too old." He coughed into the wadded muslin Jacob had left by the bed, and lay back. "Sometimes I wished I had."

"Dingo is well soon, then can marry. Maybe girl from Floradora!"

"Ah, don't be a fool. Romantic pap, that's all it is. How old are you, Jake?"

"Twenty-one."

"Just a kid. When I was twenty-one, I was working in a bank as head teller in good old Philadelphia. Made twelve dollars a week and wore a high collar every day. That darn collar near choked me to death. Didn't have a sou to my name. Not even friends."

He ran out of breath. His color was bad, his face pinched, one hand pressed against his chest. But he wanted to talk.

"You're no doubt wondering why I was out strolling in that storm? Damn fool that I was, I thought it was just one of those regular Dawson snowfalls, you know, snows hard for maybe six, seven inches, then quits. Jesus, was I ever wrong."

"Okay. Forget it now."

"Listen, Jake, I gotta tell you. And you gotta sit there and shut up . . . and listen. Cause it's important. See, my claim is way up near Big Skookum Creek, ten above Eldorado, not very big but it's been producing. Some nuggets, lots of flour gold . . . the important thing I gotta tell . . ."

He began coughing, the spasms wracking his thin frame until he could catch his breath. Then he spat into the muslin and leaned his head back.

"Dingo no good. Jacob get soup . . ."

"Jee-sus Chee-rist! No more of that soup!" He looked at Jacob with a sudden impish gleam in his watery eyes. "No offense, but I wouldn't refuse some of your whiskey. What do you say? A tad?"

Jacob nodded, filled a tin cup with a generous shot and handed it to Dingo, saying, "Drink up. To your good health."

Dingo drank in one long swallow, then exhaled slowly. "That's better, thanks." He looked up at Jacob, and continued entreatingly.

"Now, like I was saying, about my claim. I want you to know where it is, just in case I don't make it, well, you know . . . . Naw, don't say anything. I'm no child." He wiped his mouth on his sleeve. "You're not a bad fellow, Jake. But tell me something. Why the hell aren't you working on your tunnel? I know it's gotta be close by. You haven't been near it, and, from what I can see, you're no weak little pansy."

"I cannot work in tunnel. Ice too hard to dig."

"I know that. Permafrost. But you build fires, or you can work through it."

"Maybe next winter. Not now." Offended at the look on Dingo's face, he said sharply, "Jake no pansy! But will not burn and dig . . . burn and dig. . . . Jake once frozen like Dingo."

Figuring Jacob was strong as a horse and unafraid of work, Dingo ventured to ask, "So . . . what happened?"

Jacob hesitated, then told him the story of walking across the frozen strait and his rescue by Inuijak. It was a long story, filled with anecdotes both frightening and funny, and Dingo listened to every word. When Jacob reached the end, Dingo whistled through his teeth and his homely face creased into a broad smile.

"Well, ain't that the limit! Sure beats my tale. You are some punkins, Jake old boy. Yessir, some punkins!"

"But you do not like my soup?"

Dingo smiled crookedly and fell silent. After a while, he turned to Jacob with a serious expression and said, "I got to tell you something important, something that'll help you, why I was coming into Dawson. Now listen up and don't interrupt me. See, I've mined all over, in Colorado, Utah, California and Alaska, but the Klondike here is brutal work, the hardest country there is. You give it all you got, and it gives you a trickle here or a nugget there . . . if you're lucky." He coughed, and rested against the wall. "See, that's why I got this idea for a machine, something that would help thaw the permafrost better than all those fires."

Jacob made a face and laughed. "Sure, Dingo, and I am Czar Nicholas and give you all of Poland."

"Aw, for Chrissakes! Listen to me, you stubborn mule. In my pack is a drawing . . . you can follow directions, right? Well, I . . . I . . . ." He began coughing again, took a deep breath and pushed to finish his thought. "I'll do as much as I can and we'll make it together. You'll see, Jake, you'll . . . be able . . . be . . . able to . . . to work. . . ."

Dingo collapsed. Jacob covered him again and sat by the bed until the exhausted man fell asleep. When the snoring began in earnest, he opened Dingo's knapsack and found the drawing.

It was crude, done in pencil, mostly lines and squiggles, but he made out a six-foot-long, half-inch-round iron pipe with a series of hollow rods. Each rod was sharply pointed and looked about six inches long. The working of the curious contraption was clear to Jacob immediately.

By pouring hot water into a flexible hose at one end of the plugged pipe and setting the rods into the frozen ground, one could, via the steam escaping from the rods, eventually melt the permafrost down to bedrock. If there was a pay streak with gold, it could be dug out and sent to the surface for spring cleanup.

Excited, Jacob saw the machine not only as a challenge to build but a possible solution to the misery of winter. He had nothing to lose by trying it.

"So, you been shuffling around in my sack, have you?" Dingo spoke into the gloom of the cabin and Jacob waved the drawing at him.

"This is real answer, Dingo, I am sure is answer. How you figure this? How you know to use steam in frozen ground? You some smart fellow."

"Aw, I just drew it one day, and studied it some, and actually started to build it myself. But I ran out of steel. There's flexible hose in my pack."

"So, where is machine? I go get it."

"See now, that's the problem . . . follow the gold, yessir, that's my motto. Jesus." His eyes glazed, as if he was looking at some distant scene from his life. "All the places I've been, scratchin' at the earth like a damn dog, looking, always looking . . ."

Although his mind wandered, in between the vague rambling phrases, Dingo was made sense. He coughed again and again, but went on talking, rushing his words as if racing with time. "Jacob, what staggered me so here in the Klondike was the winters, diddling them away while the ground sat there frozen. I knew there had to be a way to beat it."

"So, the machine?"

"I could still do it. With your help. I'm so sure I'm right that I started out from my claim in the damn snow to get supplies in Dawson . . . you know the rest."

Jacob smiled. "I understand. You want Jacob to build it."

"You got it, friend!"

EIGHTEEN

⌒⊚⊚⌒

THE CABIN WAS DARK AND QUIET EXCEPT FOR DINGO'S snoring and occasional whistles in his sleep. Jacob studied the drawing. The more he stared at the melting machine, the less difficult or bizarre it looked. He could probably make it in two or three days and try it out before the new snow iced over. Then, if it blew up or vaporized or just fell apart, he could start over again with very little capital investment.

Jacob settled on the floor for the night, thinking about his new friend, the machine, and the prospect of actually working his tunnel in winter. Although the machine called for iron, he could build it just as well for now with wood.

He grinned, thinking about the difficulties of their conversations, the older man eventually understanding Jacob's polyglot of Russian, Yiddish and terrible English. He would always be grateful to Dingo for coming along as he had. Not only was his debt to his Eskimo friends now paid, but he was forced to speak in English. He was sure he was getting better at it. He could even understand himself.

The project was begun the next morning. Jacob handled the physical labor, Dingo supervised, alternately nagging and cajoling until the melting machine began to take shape. By Friday, a day and a half later, it was almost completed.

"C'mon, Jacob, let's finish it," Dingo urged, sitting up in

bed, his eyes bright and feverish, a deep flush on his weathered face.

Jacob shook his head and began putting away tools and spare bits of wood into the cupboard. "No, Dingo, it is now the Sabbath."

"Sabbath?"

"Yes, Sabbath, day of rest."

"It's nighttime, Jacob. It's gotta be five, six o'clock, at least."

Jacob cleaned away the shavings of wood and began to set the table, the tin plates clanking on the wood surface. He placed two pieces of cloth under the plates and stepped back, pleased.

"Looking good. Should look special for Shabbes meal. I will light candles and then is time to eat."

"Jake, what is this shabbes? Some kind of religious thing?"

"From Friday night to Saturday night is Shabbes. For this time I can read and sleep and pray and talk to you. But I cannot work."

"The Sabbath is Sunday," Dingo protested.

"For you, maybe, not for me." Jacob pulled his chair to the bed and tried to explain.

"Look, we say sunset to sunset starting Friday night. Is called 'Queen of the Week.' My mother sets her table with best linen and cooks special meal. So instead of baked potatoes or turnips, which is dinner most nights, she is saving scraps of chicken or meat and throwing everything else in the pot. Believe me, is fine stew! Of course, memory of stew is lasting all week."

"Yeah, but what about the work part," Dingo said, "no one will know if it's in your own house."

"I know," Jacob said. "My family is close, and we sit and tell stories to each other, and see visions of angels and the sparkling heavens. Not too bad, eh?"

Dingo shook his head. "I'll be a son-of-a-gun. . . . I never knew such things, Jake. A Jew to me was some little guy with a long nose and a hand in everybody's pockets. Aw, now don't get all bent outta shape, but it's not my fault. I never knew one before. At least not as good as I know you."

"So? I change your mind? Good. The more minds change, the better world will be."

"So you keep this Sabbath every week? Never miss?"

"Oh, I miss. Maybe too hungry or too cold, or not sure of day. But I try to keep it. We have saying: 'More than Jews keep Sabbath, Sabbath keep Jews.'"

"Yeah, okay. But you know about Sunday, don't you?"

"I know. No one works here in Dawson on Sunday. Is Sabbath for Christian."

"Right," Dingo said sharply. "So we lose two whole goddamm . . . okay, okay, sorry . . . lousy days."

"So we lose days. But we don't lose with the Holy One. You and me, Dingo, we keep faith."

There was no sense in arguing with Jacob. Dingo had to admire a man who showed respect for another's religious beliefs, but he fussed and crabbed all day Saturday that Jacob was stupid for not working on the machine. Jacob said quarreling was inappropriate for the Sabbath. On Sunday, it was Jacob's turn to fuss, and Dingo repeated the same words, adding, "Both our halos need polishing, my boy!"

During all the weeks of Dingo's stay, and even in the face of his increasing irascibility and mean-tempered words, Jacob fed him, tended him and bathed the poor body that seemed to be shrinking, the bones more prominent with each washing. Dingo's fever remained high, his lungs were congested, and Jacob knew Dingo would soon die.

They worked all day Monday, and by Tuesday morning Jacob had hammered in the last nail of the melting machine.

He and Dingo patted each other on the back and made a toast with whiskey.

"We'll go try it out now, okay, Jake?"

"I don't think so. I mean, Jacob try machine, but bad idea for Dingo to go outside. Very cold."

"The hell you say!" Dingo shouted, bounding out of bed. "That there is MY bloody invention, MY idea to keep you working all winter, MY guts and brains that went into its birth. And you think you're gonna keep me inside while you give it its maiden voyage? Ha! You got another think coming!"

In spite of Jacob's objections, Dingo dressed, sat down on a stump outside, and rattled off instructions with hardly a pause. "No, no, drat it, the other way . . . hold the hose down, aim it, aim it, there . . . the water's too cold . . . pour it into the pan again and build up the fire."

The carved wooden pieces, tubing and hose had fit together after a balky start, but so far nothing was working. Jacob fumbled with the big water barrel, then built up the fire, adding more and more wood. The water steamed in the frigid air but refused to boil. Was it all for nothing? Jacob despaired. Why was everything such a damned challenge? He had long since paid his dues, worked as hard as any of the men. And it was not riches he was after. It was freedom. For that he was willing to labor in the stubborn ground. The reality of his exile and the old bitterness against injustice overwhelmed him. Then he looked at Dingo sitting on the stump, yelling at "Jake," cursing and egging him on. If the man, sick as he was, could still summon the spirit to fight, Jacob had to stop wallowing in self-pity and do the same.

"Hotter!" Dingo yelled, "you call that a fire . . . c'mon, put on more wood . . . more wood! See? There! Now you're really cooking! Pour the water . . . work, you big Jew-boy . . . don't just stand there and suck your thumb! Hotter . . . hotter . . . Ah! Now that's what I call steam! Now dig!"

The water boiled, and steam began seeping from the pipes, at first in little wisps, then in bigger sprays that wet the frozen earth. Jacob's shovel slipped down bit by bit into the melted permafrost. A few inches, then a few more. Excitement built in the men, one shouting encouragement, the other digging in a frenzy of speed and newfound strength.

"We did it, Jake my boy, you and me . . . what a team!" Dingo cried. "I knew it! I just knew it!"

Jacob kept digging, his moment of discouragement lost in the sudden triumph. Down a few inches, then a few more, repeating the process all that day until the cold chased them both inside.

That night, Dingo's coughing was worse. Too keyed up to sleep, Jacob sat by the bed and spooned warm tea into his mouth. They talked of their lives before knowing each other, and the great plans they could now see coming to fruition. They talked of Jacob's mine and how best to work it. Their talk conquered despair. Early in the morning hours, both men, exhausted, finally slept.

By late Wednesday afternoon, Jacob was down sixteen feet in his tunnel below Dingo's stump. The lantern, hooked onto a tree root sticking out of the freshly dug shaft, lighted levels of the new lateral drift.

When the shaft itself looked barren, Jacob dug in another direction at a right angle, looking for gold that should be trapped in the crevices of bedrock. He could hear Dingo's voice, his queries becoming more muffled and distant the lower he dug into the dense blanket of muck and gravel. Loose dirt fell on the newly dug ground, and Jacob shoveled faster to keep ahead of it.

Suddenly, the lamplight fell on a streak meandering along the bedrock. Jacob's shovel had bitten into the grain and opened the rich tomb, revealing it to the light of day forever.

He stared, unable to speak. The shovel fell from his

hands. He ran trembling fingers across the patch of sour black earth. It was as cold as ice to his touch.

He heard Dingo hollering into the tunnel's mouth and the creaking of the windlass as bucket after bucket of dirt was hauled to the surface. The sounds came to him as if in a dream. But the gold streak in front of his eyes and the cold burning in his fingers told him it was no dream. It was real. He and Dingo had stubbornly played their hunches, and won.

He stepped back into the tunnel, took a deep breath, and yelled, "Dingo! Dingo! The gold! I see it! I see the gold!"

"Holy Mother of God," Dingo said softly, "Holy Mother of God . . ."

"I send dirt up . . . you hold windlass line steady?"

"You bet your sweet ass I'll hold it steady, my boy!" Dingo shouted. "Let 'er rip!"

"Okay, Dingo. Here it comes."

There was no answer. The windlass did not move. What was he doing up there? Only a minute ago, the man had been shouting with joy.

Jacob climbed quickly out of the tunnel and almost tripped over Dingo's body. He dropped to his knees in the snow and shook Dingo by the shoulders.

"Hey, you mean son-of-a-gun, speak to me. . . ."

Dingo's words were barely audible. "Jake, a priest . . . get me a priest . . . please. . . ."

Jacob quickly carried him into the house. There was a terrible rattling in his lungs. Every noisy breath was choked with fluid while rasping wheezes rumbled from his sunken chest.

Jacob placed him on the bed and pulled the cover up. "You be fine now, Dingo. Jacob go for Father Judge in Dawson . . . be back before supper. You hear me? Dingo? Dingo? You hear me? DINGO!!!"

His friend was dead. After stumbling into his life a short time ago and giving him back his existence, he had slipped away, leaving Jacob alone. Again.

But Dingo should not leave him like this, with no one to share the excitement of the mining or the great work of their new treasure, the fantastic machine. Tears fell as Jacob raged against the dead man and all the nights he had sat up with him. All the weeks of trying to keep him alive. He tore his shirt at the top button in the traditional act of mourning while confusion and anger and resentment poured out of him. Sitting in the gloom by Dingo's body, Jacob wept for all the frustrations and hardships and pain he and Dingo had suffered. Then he remembered his last words: "Get me a priest."

He should have a decent burial. Jacob knew that bodies sometimes lay outside the Dawson funeral home all winter, the frozen ground denying them their final peace. Jews buried their dead as soon as possible. Jacob wanted desperately to show his respect for Dingo, and having his body sit around until spring would be humiliating.

"I get priest, Dingo," he said, "and you will have finest burial service in Dawson City."

Jacob brought Dingo to Dawson City on a sled and routed the priest from his bed.

"Yes? What is it?" he said, opening the door to Jacob's knock.

"You are the priest?" Jacob asked.

"I am Father Judge, yes."

"My friend on sled . . ."

"Well, bring him in! Don't let him stay out there in the cold. Bring him in."

"No, you don't understand," Jacob said, "he is dead."

The priest had built the hospital on Fifth Avenue in the south end of Dawson with his own hard work and donations from people in the city. It was for this that he was known as the Saint of Dawson. The sobriquet suited his ascetic appearance. High cheekbones emphasized the skull-like face, deep-set eyes glowing with a fervor to serve the poor, his devotion to building a place for the sick, and his immutable belief in miracles. This hospital was all the proof he needed.

Father Judge took Jacob by the arm and led him into the hospital entrance. "Well, freezing ourselves will not help him then, will it?" he said amiably. "But why then do you come to me?"

"Because he wanted a priest before he died."

"Ah."

Jacob apologized. "I could not get you in time, but I say blessing for him anyway."

"Blessing? What kind of blessing?"

Jacob looked into the priest's eyes, hoping not to see there the sullen resentment he always found in the eyes of the priest in Khotin. He did not see it.

"The Kaddish. Our prayer for the dead. Dingo not family, but good friend."

"How very good of you," Father Judge exclaimed, his eyes warm with affection. "And you want to leave him to be buried?"

"No, no," Jacob protested, "I bury him myself if you speak his service. He wanted that."

"But my dear fellow, you cannot bury him now. The ground . . ."

"I have machine. Melting machine. Dingo, my friend, invented it. We make it together, and now I use to bury him."

Father Judge's eyes grew wide with surprise. "A melting machine? Do you know what that means?"

"Yes. I can bury . . ."

"Yes, of course, bodies can be buried in winter. But the mining . . . the whole mining process can change. This is an incredible discovery. You will make millions! More than you would have made in gold! I must tell someone. . . ."

"No," Jacob said quickly. "First we bury Dingo. Then I go back and work claim. Please, let it be."

They trudged up the pack trail to the large open ground above town. In summer it was uncultivated and wild, the tall pines and aspens and birch overgrown with weeds and vines. Now it was barren and covered with snow.

Dingo's body lay in a plain pine casket next to the hole Jacob and Father Judge were digging. Together they had driven the horse-drawn wagon with the casket and the machine up the old road. Now, with the fire going briskly and their digging almost finished, the priest turned to Jacob, his smiling face perspiring.

Father William Judge stood in the snow, his tall, emaciated-looking body clothed in Jesuit missionary garb flowing to his ankles. From a pocket underneath the robe, he took a small Bible and began to intone the prayers in a melodious voice.

"This is surely a fine burial for one to have in Dawson City. I am so indebted to you, my boy, and I know God is smiling on you at this moment."

Jacob nodded and tossed out the last shovel of dirt. He said, "We bury Dingo now."

Wordlessly, they covered the casket and mounded dirt over the top. With the last bit of earth, Jacob began the Kaddish, and when he finished the priest read psalms from his little black book. Then he closed his eyes and turned his face to the sky.

"Hear our prayers, Oh God, hear our prayers for Dingo Malone, Your servant. Hear the words of Jacob, his friend, words only You could have inspired, Oh Lord. We lift our eyes to Thee, and beseech thee, with these prayers on our lips, to bring Dingo, Thy servant, peace."

NINETEEN

ക്കൊ

Malka's Journey

WITH HER TRIP TO JOIN JACOB IN DAWSON CITY TWO
weeks away, it became increasingly difficult for Malka to
find time with her father. She sewed new clothes for herself
and new shirts for Nathan, polished his silver kiddush cup,
and washed and ironed and packed. Dried fruits and vegetables were put up in the pantry for summer, Semel's clothes
were mended, washed and folded away, the house was
cleaned. But evenings were saved for long walks, card games,
or talks by the fire about both trivial and important things:
his shop, her pupils, his widows, her Jacob.

Semel's illness seemed to be gone, to Malka's relief, and
she began hoping it had been only temporary. She watched
him, coddled him, nagged him, always sensitive to his feelings, and, though she was usually cheerful, she now seemed
to have painted on her smile. Nathan Semel was not fooled.
He knew Malka and could sense more than see her emotions
swinging between anticipation and melancholia. She could
not leave him, yet she could hardly wait to go.

Malka had been aware of a restlessness in Khotin, a feeling of rebellion and anger growing in the community. She
was troubled by thoughts of her friends and pupils, fellow

teachers and students rising up, confronting the authorities and being hurt by overzealous soldiers defending the Czar. Where was this going? Was she a coward, leaving them to fight the battle alone? It could not be helped. She had committed herself to life with Jacob Finesilver.

His letters had been arriving almost regularly, although Malka was convinced some were being withheld. The postal officials sneered when she came in for the mail. One pointed to the postmark and said sarcastically, "Oh, look at that, Boris, all the way from Canada. She must be very famous to get a letter all the way from Canada. Maybe too famous to give us a kiss, eh?"

They pushed Malka back and forth, each one catching her by the waist and twirling her around until she was dizzy and begged them to stop. But she was pretty, and to them the game was fun. When she started to yell, Boris snapped, "You and your wretched letters from Canada. Take them and get out! And," he added, his mouth taking on a nasty sneer "if you can't be nice to us, then we can't give you your mail next time. Think it over, Jewish girl, our kisses can't be all that bad!"

She was certain he read her letters, but if she objected to their superiors, her mail might be confiscated altogether. Her anger at this unfairness and her own state of nerves hurried her back to the comfort of home. There she would take a hot glass of tea into the parlor, settle by the fire and read the latest news from Jacob.

The mood of their correspondence was becoming more personal, more revealing, and, as the time approached, more enthusiastic in discussing her trip. Jacob's words seemed softer, with special emphasis on his feelings about life and marriage and the beauty surrounding him.

He described to her the emergence of the spring flowers, their colors and local names, even trying in one letter to draw a picture of the purple pasque flower as its stem came up through the snow. There were many such flowers, he wrote, carpets of them covering the hills, bleeding hearts and geraniums, so many she could gather armfuls without disturbing the scene.

He wrote of the birds returning, robins and sparrows and geese that honked and filled the sky with their homing flights. He wrote of bears coming out of hibernation, wandering "*farblondjet*," stumbling, along the crests of the hills looking for their mates.

He wrote about men who were starving alone in cabins and tents, suffering from scurvy and malnutrition, who had not planned well for the brutal winter and now were close to death. He could not lie to her about conditions; they were very bad in some parts of the gold fields, but many prospectors had known what to bring and had come through the terrible winter in good shape as he had.

Toward the end of this last letter, Jacob recommended that Malka take the same route he had taken to Dawson City, via St. Michael in Alaska. "This would mean going to Montreal, then taking the train west across Canada to St. Michael, where you board the boat for Dawson City. A tedious journey, but by doing this you avoid the dreaded Chilkoot Pass, which is exceedingly dangerous, and has claimed many lives since . . ."

"Lost in thought, my angel?" Semel said. He stood in the doorway, dressed for the synagogue in a new shirt Malka had sewn for his birthday. The worn shoes on his feet had been shined for the service.

"Aren't you the fancy dandy," Malka said, grinning. "You're going to break every old *yenta's* heart tonight."

"And why not? Give them something to look at, I say. But probably a waste of time. With their poor eyesight, they can't see me on the bimah from their balcony seats anyway."

Malka laughed. "Oh, Papa, you're terrible. But you do look grand. I won't be a minute."

Sitting with the women in the balcony of the synagogue, Malka listened to the cantor sing. As he soared to the final note, she felt a deep sadness at leaving home and everything familiar, especially this humble, rickety wooden structure and all it had represented in her life. Her neighbors, friends, all those seated around her were bound together by a common heritage and destiny. When they spoke bitterly of their isolation from the rest of the world, she knew what they meant: poverty exiled them, and exile was the cause of their poverty.

Yet with all they suffered, their faith in God was steadfast, His six hundred and thirteen *mitzvot* helping them uphold their laws. Whether they prayed in Hebrew or in Yiddish, they never doubted God would respond.

Malka had been impatient with orthodoxy as a child, but now with her imminent departure it began to fall into place. She saw through the Jewish mask of laughter and wit, understanding its use to hide despair, but also began to understand her quick acceptance of Jacob's offer. Like people lost at sea drifting hopelessly in a small boat, she felt her only salvation was in jumping free instead of waiting for rescue. Oh Lord, let me know how to swim.

During tonight's service, she felt the gaze of many eyes, an unspoken curiosity, about her intended groom and the crazy ("such *mishigoss!*") journey she was about to make. Her father would not have a moment's peace until he satisfied their curiosity, thundering at anyone daring to question her conduct. Walking home, she gripped Semel's arm and began listing her itinerary.

"So, Papa, you have the schedule, you know where I will be all the time. My tickets are in order, my passport, everything. All that remains is a simple wedding gown, and I will make that tomorrow."

"You have no wish to change your mind?"

"No, Papa, you know how I am. Once I decide on something, that's it. No looking back. No regrets. Jacob is expecting me sometime in June, July at the latest, and if I've figured it all correctly, that is when I will arrive. But Papa . . ."

"Come, come, spit it out, what other instructions do you have for me?"

She hesitated, worried about interfering with his life now that she would have no more say about it.

"I have heard rumors . . ."

"Yes?"

"In the town. . ."

"Yes, I have heard them, too. But do not worry about me. I'm not so brave any more, and I will not challenge the soldiers. I leave that to the young hotheads. If they are spoiling for a fight, I will let them have it. Maybe they can change the way things are, although I have my doubts. Where would another whipping boy be found? But do not give it another thought. So my angel. Good night," Semel said, and went into the house.

The next two days were a scramble of things left to the last minute. Malka cut and sewed the white cotton dress for her wedding and packed the clothes she would wear on the ship and the trains and the boats, whatever awaited her on the long and circuitous trip to the Yukon Territory.

Her wish was to travel light, but this was impossible. The ocean voyage would be cold, the train trip to St. Michael might be warm, and as for the spring weather in Alaska and Canada, she could only make a wild guess.

When finished, she had two large bags, old portmanteaus that had been stored in the cold pantry for years. The locks were broken and the leather peeled and cracked, but they were all she had. With stout belts around them, they would have to do.

The day of her departure was cold and gray, with a stiff March wind blowing her long skirts about her ankles. She wore an old but still presentable blue wool suit for travel. It had a waist-length jacket with a velvet collar, the long skirt reaching to the laces of her high-topped shoes, and a long matching scarf that could serve as a coat in cold weather. She had chosen to braid her hair for the journey. At the sight of her, small, brave, and looking so much like her mother, Semel almost broke down.

Only the ticket agent greeted them at the station. Malka and her father sat on the bench near the potbellied stove and held each other's hands. Semel referred nervously to his pocket watch, announcing to Malka the hour and the minute and how much time they had until the train was due.

Malka was also nervous, chattering about nothing. "Don't forget to plant the garden, Papa. You know how much pleasure flowers will bring you all summer. The seeds . . ."

"Yes, yes, I know." Flowers, seeds, does she think that's the only thing on my mind when she is going out of my life forever? If the train doesn't come soon, I shall lose control and weep in front of her.

The ticket agent dropped the broom with which he had been sweeping the floor and made the expected announcement. They both started at the train's distant whistle. Malka turned wild eyes to her father and hugged him tightly.

"Listen to me, my angel," Semel said, "I want you to know I am proud of you. You're embarking on a great adventure . . . in a strange country . . . with new languages and new people. I pray to the Holy One to watch over you and to bless your union, and . . . and to keep you warm in that cold place."

He wiped at Malka's cheeks, her tears giving him the need for strength. "Never worry about your Papa. You have chosen the right path . . . and for that I shall always be happy.

Now go . . . fly to your Jacob, help him to find his gold wherever, or whatever it may be." Then he walked home to the empty house. "Oh God," he cried, turning and twisting as if the Holy One might be there with him, "don't listen to the ravings of an old man. I do not quarrel with You or with Your scheme of things. But I do have one request, spare us, great Lord of the Universe, spare us what we have to learn in order to endure."

TWENTY

❦

Malka held tightly to the railing of the S.S. *Nicolai* as it moved out of the port of Odessa. She watched everything, trying to memorize the scene. As the sailors threw scraps of garbage overboard for the circling birds, her emotions whirled as scattered as the screaming gulls—heartache, excitement, apprehension each struggling for the upper hand. Live the moment, she cautioned herself, don't fight it, let it be. Sort it all out later. So much is happening now, and so much will happen. If you take it little by little, it won't seem so overwhelming.

The weather was calm when they left port, but the wind grew to gale force a few hundred miles out to sea. Waves rose high above the open deck, and the combination of crashing sea, fierce wind and pelting rain sent passengers scurrying below.

Steerage was crowded and noisy, located near the huge screws of the ship, their rumblings accompanying every moan of the suffering passengers. All night they cried, the sound a rising crescendo with each fall of crockery or baggage. For most, this was their first trip at sea, and nothing prepared them for the alienation and the sickness.

Malka's quarters in steerage were cramped and unpleasant. The bedding, one badly stained muslin sheet on a thin, lumpy mattress, had a foul odor. There was only one small, rusty sink in the corner, and the bathroom was in the hallway. The toilet had no seat and leaked, the floor beneath awash, presenting a challenge to long-skirted females. With no tubs or showers, the sink served as a washbowl for both body and clothing. Scattered about on the unswept floors were scraps of moldering food, a constant source of malignant smells that compounded the passengers' miseries. Lying on her bunk the second day out, dizzy and sick from the violent movements of the ship, she tried to concentrate on something pleasant. She thought of Jacob's generosity in sending her the money for the first-class ticket. He had assured her it was more than enough. But when she had attempted to buy the ticket, the disagreeable agent had shaken his head, pocketed the difference between first and steerage class, and told her she was lucky to be buying a ticket at all.

"First class? Are you crazy? As it is, I will be gracious in allowing you steerage even if there's not enough here to pay for it. Now, little lady, give me a hug and a pinch and that will go far to make up the difference."

Frightened and angry, she grabbed the ticket and ran from his groping hands, wondering if there was a decent official in the whole of Russia who would not steal from her, or worse, ask for that kind of payment.

Then into steerage came two sailors with cold rags and basins. When they came later with food carts, almost no one left the bunk to eat. They were too sick. Even if they had been well, the Jewish passengers could not eat non-kosher food. One old woman who had attempted to dine reported that the food for steerage passengers was vile, mostly bread and water during the day, with a thin soup, cabbage, and potatoes. But it made no difference. At first Malka was too sick, and when she recovered, she had no appetite. Most of the Jewish passengers in steerage ate only the bread and warm water, to which they added sugar or a little brandy.

At the beginning, she tried to help the small children and a few elderly people in her section, but their sickness, plus the violent movements of the boat, eventually drove her to her own bunk. Lying down was not the answer; she was dizzy even when she closed her eyes. And standing up was worse.

But the time spent in bed was not lost. Through most of her life she had learned from every experience, good or bad, and some of these new lessons, though distressing, were valuable, especially listening to the complaints of others.

"Pardon me, Sir," the mother of three said to the steward, "but my youngest child needs her own bed. She is terribly seasick."

"All children have to share the beds," the steward replied, eager to leave the foul-smelling quarters.

"But she is sharing now with three others, not even of her own family."

"That's too bad, but there's nothing to be done." The steward walked away. The mother, not wanting to make a scene, went meekly to her bunk.

"Hey, Mister," shouted a swarthy, fat man, pushing aside the line of passengers trying to speak to the steward. "I want my own bunk and I want it now! If you think I'm sharing this miserable excuse for a bed with anyone else, you're crazy! And if you don't give me what I want, I'll see the captain on this stinking scow and let him know exactly what I can do to . . ."

"Quiet!" the steward said, pulling the man out of earshot, "you'll get your bunk. Now shut up."

The civilized qualities she had been brought up to respect were impractical in this crisis. It was a sorry truth; those pushing others aside for their own ends were successful. In the face of this enigma she began to question her life so far, wondering if this was truly the way of the world.

On the third morning at sea, the captain toured the steerage section with the ship's doctor, taking note of those still sick and trying to cheer the children. He talked with the passengers who were well enough to gather in the main room. His little speech seemed to encourage their recovery as well as their dispositions.

Gold braid gleaming on his sleeves and cap, the captain cut a dashing figure in his navy uniform, but he carried his medium height rigidly, and when he spoke, he looked down his nose as if through the bottom of a lens. His chiseled features, accented by a curled black mustache and gleaming white teeth, won over his audience, who hung on every word.

"I would advise those of you feeling well enough to climb to the open deck and revive yourselves with the fresh air you will find there in great abundance. You may even be lucky enough to spy a sea bird, or a spouting whale. Come now, forget your stomachs for a while. A brisk promenade on the deck will help you put aside the mal de mer."

A lovely speech, Malka thought, but devoid of feeling, more like that of a stern parent addressing a group of unruly children and scolding them with veiled words: Shame on you steerage passengers for being sick. Up now, all of you, and walk the deck to forget your foolish stomachs.

Her own foolish stomach knotted ominously, and Malka hurried from the room.

Later, she walked slowly on deck, holding tightly to the railing for support. Her legs were wobbly, but the brisk, salty air was refreshing. Now and then a wild spray from a wave broke over the side and splashed on deck, wetting her. But it was not unpleasant.

The sea was dark blue, and though she did not see birds or whales, the water seemed to stretch on and on until it ran into the sky. Malka thought, I can understand why so many people before Columbus must have thought the world was flat and feared falling off the edge.

"A ruble for your thoughts," a deep voice said. She turned to see the handsome captain by her side.

"Oh, Captain, you startled me. I was daydreaming, I'm afraid. But nothing worth a ruble."

The captain looked at Malka in a flattering way, his deep brown eyes hardly blinking. "I would never have guessed that," he said gallantly, "for I would expect such a lovely woman to have lovely thoughts."

He was not at all like Saul Mendelberg, the only man Malka knew well enough for comparison. Certainly he was not shy, nor unskilled in the ways of courting, both of these advantages giving him an aura of sophistication and charm.

"Will you allow me to walk with you?" he inquired ever so grandly. Malka nodded. He took her arm and led her along the deck as if they had just been announced at a royal reception.

"My name is Feodor Potemkin," he said in his deep voice, "and I have been the captain of the *Nicolai* for three years. It is a fine ship, my *Nicolai*, although I am afraid sadly in need of paint. We shall put her into port after our return voyage, and she will have a thorough redecoration." His voice was indeed like a large choir of voices.

"Oh," Malka murmured and looked carefully at a deck chair.

"And what is your name? he asked.

"Malka Semel," she replied, and then suspected he had asked her name for less than romantic reasons. Now he would know she was Jewish. Would he stop his strolling, drop her arm, bow stiffly, and fade back into the funnels?

"Pretty name," he said, without missing a step. "From where do you come, Malka Semel?"

Staring at the squareness of his jaw and the deep indentation in his chin, she said, "Khotin in the Ukraine."

"I know it well. I used to have a cousin there by the name

of Profimi. Italian, I think, from the Italian side of the Potemkin family. Very dark and looking like a villain in an opera." He laughed and his teeth sparkled in the sunlight.

Malka's head was pounding. The pitching and tossing of the boat upset her stomach again. She remembered her first walk on deck and how gazing at the horizon had steadied her and chased the miserable queasiness away. She looked quickly out to sea and stared grimly at the line between the sky and the water.

"You are feeling sick again, eh?" he asked solicitously, "and you have found one of the best remedies. Keep looking out there. You will be fine."

"But what does one do at night?" she asked. "That seems to be the worst time. As a matter of fact, if one could stay on deck and never go below, one might never feel this way."

The captain smiled again. "You have learned a truism about the sea, but your sea legs will soon take over. I promise."

A sailor approached the captain with a paper in his hand, and the captain excused himself to read it. Then he dismissed the sailor and bowed to Malka.

"I have enjoyed our chat, Miss Semel, and I hope you will have recovered by the time we meet next. Au revoir," he said and bowed again.

Malka nodded and turned to the railing, just in time.

The winds were constant and surprisingly warm on the sunnier days. April was only a few weeks away and the weather was properly erratic, rainy one day, sunny the next, then snow falling so fast the sailors had to shovel the decks. One week out of home port, the *Nicolai* encountered a serene sea and sunshine, and most of the passengers were able to leave their beds and move about on the pleasant deck. Malka felt wonderful, her seasickness completely gone. She spent most of her time reading or writing in a small diary kept in her purse.

This morning, after a breakfast of warm tea and a piece of a bunkmate's matzo, she took charge of one of the small children from steerage whose mother still languished below, and they played a game of bounce-ball at the stern end of the ship.

"Charming, charming," Captain Potemkin observed as he watched her and the little boy. "And who is this that plays with you? Not yours, surely?"

"No, no," Malka said quickly, "he is one of the Grssel children. He is the smallest, and I took him to let his mother sleep. He's really a very smart child," she added, "and we practice our mathematics tables, too."

"Ah! You are a teacher? Perhaps," he said, his eyes bold, "you will help me with mine?"

Malka stared, puzzled.

"Tonight," he continued, "we are having dinner at eight o'clock, in the dining salon. I would be honored if you would be my partner at *my* table." He smiled. Did she not catch his little pun?

She did. She smiled. "Thank you so much, but I am unable to eat the food aboard ship."

"Surely," he said, his eyes narrowing, "the food is not that bad?"

"Oh, no, it's not the quality of the food at all. It is because I eat only kosher food."

"I see," the captain said, a trifle testily. "My apologies. Had I known this would be a problem on my ship, I would have made other arrangements for serving Jewish passengers."

There followed an awkward silence. Malka bent to tie the little boy's shoelace. The captain helped her rise.

"Well then, perhaps you will join me after the evening meal in the salon for a selection of fresh fruit, and dancing." He took her hand and kissed it. "I would be honored."

"Thank you," she said, again puzzled. If this was a game he was playing, she had no idea of the rules.

She dressed in her freshly brushed traveling suit for the evening and drew sidelong glances from the women at the other tables that said many things and asked many questions: Who is that? Why in the world would the captain invite someone from steerage? That outfit is very wrong for dancing.

But Captain Potemkin was a charming companion, well informed, always attentive, and the gossip around her dissipated in the graceful evening. Games of cards were set up in the salon and an orchestra played light classics and waltzes for dancing. Some of the passengers drifted in and out of the salon to walk on deck, while others dozed in the big chairs or chatted in small, animated groups.

"What a magnificent evening," Captain Potemkin said as he and Malka strode the deck. "On nights such as this, I feel closer to the heavens."

"The sky is very clear, indeed, and look over there." Malka pointed. "That's the Big Dipper."

"Yes. And there is the North Star. Ancient mariners used it to guide their ships, but I am glad we have special instruments with which to work our way through these waters. "So," he said, tipping his cap back on his head, "you are going to America, leaving your Mother Russia for the new world."

"Yes. But America is not my final destination."

"Oh? And what is?"

"Canada."

"Canada! Now there's a wild country. Some of it is as cold as Siberia. I have been there, and I have a friend who went to Alaska for the gold rush. He tells me that . . ."

"Oh! How exciting," Malka exclaimed. "What part of Alaska?"

His expression changed from pleasant to frankly curious. She watched the subtle changes, fascinated.

"Why do you ask?" he said.

"I . . . well . . . I am going to the Yukon Territory, near Alaska, actually, right near the border of Alaska. That's what intrigued me. If your friend described the country to you, then you can tell me what it's like or what to expect, and that will be most helpful."

"And why are you going there? To teach school?"

"No, at least I'm not planning to. I am going to Dawson City to marry a man from my home town. He is there mining gold."

Captain Potemkin smiled bleakly, his eyes flickering the tiniest bit. "What a fortunate man," he said. "Have you known him long?"

"No. Only a few months."

"And he waits for you. So romantic. I admit to feeling a little jealous."

Malka blushed.

"The Yukon, eh? By the pass, I would venture to say, am I right?"

"The pass? Oh, you mean the Chilkoot. No, Jacob, my fiancé, recommends I do not come that way. He says to take the boat from St. Michael to Dawson City."

The captain frowned. "I don't agree. That's another twenty-five hundred miles after you land in Seattle! That is insanity! It is only eight hundred miles to Skagvay from Seattle, and that is where you embark for the real journey. You see, Malka," he said, leaning towards her, his words chilling but sincerely spoken, "the Chilkoot has earned its reputation as a killer only for those who cross it in winter. The steep canyon is treacherous in the ice and snow, yes, but in summer, it is no more than a pleasant hike as through one of the lovely meadows of Khotin."

Jacob had said one thing, and this man was saying the opposite. His manner had changed completely since she had told him the truth. He was down-to-earth now, more believable. And more distanced.

"I'm confused. You must tell me in detail about this pass and then perhaps I can decide."

"I will be happy to. But now I must return to the bridge. I am most grateful for your company this evening, Miss Semel."

He took her hand, kissed it, released it, clicked his heels and bade her goodnight.

As she continued her stroll around the deck, Malka took deep breaths of fresh air and tried not to think of her dismal bunk below. At least the fruit and cheese had filled her empty stomach for a while.

Determined to view the journey so far optimistically, she tried not to see it as the traumatic uprooting it actually was. She smiled grimly at that old proverb extolling the comfort of everyone who was in the same boat. How absurd; the real comfort was in first class.

Her thoughts strayed to the people below, the crowded, dirty quarters, the crying babies and the hollow-eyed women. She saw the men, husbands and fathers who stood by, helpless to feed their families, helpless to make them feel better, able only to hold their heads in the sink or to promise life would be different when they came to America. Hold on, they said, and pray.

She identified with all of them, running from persecution, from the dead ends in which they had lived to a new life in a new world, but so ill-prepared for what they would find. They had so little, their only possessions what they wore or carried. Facing the terrors of a new language and an unfamiliar society, it was no wonder that they and she were frightened.

She looked again at the night sky, the stars so bright and close she wanted to pluck one from its black velvet bed. But it was illusion, and there was no room for that luxury right now. She was on a boat bound for a life she knew nothing about, facing marriage to a stranger.

Turning from the star-filled night, the recollection of her father's words was instant and sobering: "Lord of the universe, You made a fair world, a radiant world—but for whom?"

TWENTY-ONE

❦

THE DAYS WERE COOL THE SECOND WEEK AT SEA, WITH strong breezes to help the *Nicolai* along its charted course. Watching the prow cut through the choppy blue waters with the white foam glistening in the wake to give away its track, Malka sometimes felt it was the wind and not the unremitting engines that pushed the ship.

But she knew the truth. The pounding and clanking of the ship's enormous wheels and screws dominated the steerage quarters. The sound embedded itself in her waking as well as sleeping hours, the rhythm almost replacing her own heartbeat as a sign of life.

She spent most of her daytime hours walking the length of the deck to keep her legs limber and strong. She hated sitting with nothing to do, and used the evening hours to work on squares of embroidery for a quilt. It was to be a wedding present for Jacob, with each of the eighteen squares representing one year of her life. She thought it an excellent way to help Jacob know her better, for to talk of her life in Khotin, exposing the heart of her dreams and thoughts on life and love, was not Malka's way.

They would become acquainted in time. She was certain of that. But she also hoped it would be a result of observation and listening, attention to detail, and a willingness, in pain or pleasure, for one to let the other in. Not from question-and-answer sessions that she felt could only embarrass them both. Thus she imagined her new future.

This morning she worked on the nineteenth square, sketched lightly because her facts about Dawson City and the Yukon were shadowy, gleaned from Jacob's letters. Her father's library had been no help; the shelves and stacks of books held mostly texts on mathematics and language, and commentaries on religious doctrine. There was nothing about the Yukon.

Her embroidery was self-taught, stitches of varying length and form applied to render the design sketched in pencil. Using different-colored threads, she outlined the main figures in a simple chain stitch, then filled in with fancy work that added almost a third dimension.

"That is most beautiful," a familiar voice said, and Malka looked up to see Captain Potemkin standing beside her.

"Thank you."

"And what is that to be? Part of your trousseau, no doubt?"

"Not exactly," Malka said shyly, trying to fold the square into her bag. She had forgotten to secure the needle, and it pricked her fingers.

"Oh, you are bleeding," Captain Potemkin said, taking the injured hand and holding it tightly in his own. "Come with me. I will find you a bandage."

"It's nothing, really. I must do that ten times a day when I'm sewing. Don't give it another thought."

"And what is it that you work on so industriously? Is it to be worn? Hung on a rod? Slept upon?" He smiled wickedly, and raised her hand for a kiss.

"None of those, I'm afraid," Malka replied tartly, pulling her hand away. "Thank you for your interest, but I must be going below."

"But why?" he persisted. "It is so lovely here on the deck. Take advantage of the sun, Miss Semel, for it will soon disappear. We are in for some rough weather ahead."

"Oh? That *is* bad news. I fared so poorly in the last storm."

"I know. Which is why I mention it." He cleared his throat, though there seemed to be nothing to clear, and said, "I was going to suggest you ride the storm out in my quarters. They are much more comfortable, and above the rough water line. Perhaps you . . ."

"Please," Malka said, rising, crimson with anger. "What you suggest is impossible. I am very uncomfortable in steerage, but not so much that I would sully my name and my reputation by . . . by . . ."

"Oh, my dear Miss Semel, my apologies! Perhaps I did not phrase myself correctly! I would not have insulted you intentionally, believe me. My only thought, since I will be spending most of the night hours on the bridge due to the anticipated storm, was that you would make use of the empty room. Forgive me if I was out of place."

"It is my turn to apologize, Captain. I did not understand. I am too quick to see evil where none exists, and this, I am sorry to say, is because I have seen so much of it."

He stood beside her at the railing and looked to the north where dark clouds began to cluster. Neither spoke. The waves slapped against the side, muted voices came from the distant play area, and these sounds were all that Malka seemed to hear.

"So you have seen much evil," Captain Potemkin said, his voice suddenly soft and quite sad. "What a shame. It is hoped that joy and goodness would be all that one so young would experience."

"Age has nothing to do with it, Captain. Perhaps it is more the result of circumstance, luck, fate, kismet, whatever your belief. Much too serious a discussion for, as you said, this lovely day. If you will excuse me . . ."

"I will not," he said, taking her arm. "We will stroll the deck and make all the men jealous!"

Malka was confused by his attentions. She thought she had been quite frank with him.

"I have been thinking about your journey," he said, nodding to a group of passengers, "and I have plotted the way for you. I am not the artist you are, judging from your embroidery, but for this I don't have to be. You will understand, I'm sure, when you see it."

"The way to Dawson City?"

"Well, not exactly. That you will find out once you cross the pass and reach the end, but I do know the best way to the pass from Seattle."

"I'm cold, Captain, and if you don't mind, I would like to sit down."

"By all means. Here, let us rest," he offered, swinging wide the doors of the salon. "I can show you the little map I made."

Sitting at a small table, he ordered two glasses of hot tea. He took out a folded paper from his jacket pocket. "You see, Miss Semel, the chief officer of this ship is quite concerned with the comfort, mental as well as physical, of his passengers. I hope this will illustrate that."

She dismissed his words, recognizing his thinly veiled attempt to scold her. She recalled the way he had bristled when she had first told him about having to eat unkosher food, taking the remark personally, as if he alone should have known and prepared for the Jewish passengers.

"Observe." He laid the piece of paper flat on the table, smoothed out the folds and pointed to a dot on the bottom of the picture.

"This is Seattle. You get there by train, a tedious trip, but also a good way to see the big country of America. When you arrive, you must buy a ticket on a boat to Skagvay."

"Skagvay?" Malka's pronunciation of the Indian word in Russian was clumsy, but the captain's had been no better. "Yes. That is in Alaska. You see," he pointed to the map, "this is the border of Alaska and Canada. At times, it is difficult to distinguish one country from the other. But you will soon learn, for they say the roughest conditions prevail on the American side, not the Canadian. Americans are crazy people. They talk loud, move fast, and know nothing of culture or the refinements of life. Perhaps the Canadians are better."

Malka could not comment. She had never met anyone but Russians, most of whom had been Jews. She wondered if he was right or making it all up to impress her. At any rate, his opinion could not diminish her excitement; soon she would be able to form her own.

"Now, the boat trip from Seattle to Skagvay is roughly eight hundred miles or three days. Not too bad, eh?"

"More time on a boat?" Malka muttered.

"Oh, a small boat . . . nothing like the *Nicolai*," Captain Potemkin said grandly, his arm sweeping wide to include all of his floating domain. "And the inland waters are calm. No, no, give it no more thought, Miss Semel."

"And when I get to Skagvay?"

"Ah, that is when the trip becomes interesting. Just a few miles to the beginning of the trail, pleasant enough, like a kibitka ride through the Khotin meadow."

The captain's allusion to a wagon ride was a surprise to Malka. Jacob had described the Chilkoot Pass as the most terrifying route to Dawson.

"I had heard quite the opposite, Captain."

"Yes, but this is not the pass, this is only the trail to the pass. And what you heard, no doubt, is accurate for the winter months. I would not," he protested, "lead you astray.

Here, take the map. I must go. Thank you for this charming interlude."

He bowed and walked quickly from the salon. She had offended him, that was clear, and she regretted it. But how else was she to come to an informed opinion without questioning him?

Life in the world outside the shtetl was more involved and more disturbing than she had been prepared for. People were different from those she had lived with all her life, and she was not adept at dealing with all their idiosyncrasies. The world was a vast place, and not patient or kind to those untrained in its tricky and unmapped courses. She wondered how long it would take her to learn the way. And how would she change? She placed the captain's paper in her bag and wandered outside. The sun had disappeared, leaving an angry sky thick with dark, rolling clouds. They were in for a storm, as the captain had said. Staying on deck would soon be impossible. She watched as sailors rounded up errant passengers and instructed them to return to their quarters. In a few minutes, she was told the same.

So, which is worse? To return to steerage and be sick as a dog, or stay on deck and be washed overboard? She laughed at something her father used to say at times like this: "Your health comes first . . . you can always hang yourself later."

The storm was unlike anything she had ever experienced so far, the fog so dense her hand held at arm's length was invisible. The roll of the water was more pronounced, but with less crashing and banging going on around her.

She was terribly sick again, and dizzy when she tried to stand. The room kept spinning even when she closed her eyes. Sleep was the only escape.

She had no idea how long she lay there, or how long the ship labored in the huge swells of the sea. The foghorn was a weird and dismal sound, repeating its two-note call over and over to warn away other ships, and she tried to drown it out with the pillow over her head.

Footsteps came and went by her bunk, prowling the darkened quarters, some slow and shuffling, others quick, in a hurry to reach the bathroom. When she opened her eyes, she could see a dim light coming through the round window, and she wondered if it was early morning or just before dark. But she could not summon the strength to look for herself or ask.

On the fourteenth day of the sea voyage, she awakened to the sound of excited voices and a rushing of the steerage passengers from the quarters to the stairs leading up to the deck.

Even though the ship still pitched about, everyone tried desperately to see something outside. Those still gray and wan with seasickness held tightly to others who pulled them along.

"What is it?" Malka asked a young boy passing her cot. He shook his head, not understanding her language.

"What is it?" she repeated to an older woman she knew to be from the Ukraine. "Where does everyone go?"

The woman paused, a toothless smile creasing her worn face, "America, outside is America! You must come and see!"

Malka had almost slept through one of the most exciting moments of the trip. Every one of her friends had confessed envy of her first glance of America, the rich, brave and free land they had heard about so long in story and fable. "Oh, what a thrill that will be! You must tell us all about it . . . the great statue in the harbor, the lady . . . with the lamp . . ."

They were confused, of course. The lady with the lamp was in New York harbor, and the *Nicolai* would be pulling into Baltimore. No chance there to see the famous landmark. But that was not important now. What mattered was not to miss the first sight of the great new country. Everyone was speaking at once, old women crying, young women holding their babies to their breasts and rocking back and forth. Sailors shouted to each other and heaved great coils of thick ropes over the side, and tugboats whistled as they guided the ship into port.

She stood barefoot and openmouthed. By the time the ship was secured at the pier Malka had pulled herself together, dressed, and packed her belongings. "Miss Semel, Miss Semel, over here, please." Captain Potemkin was gesturing to her. He stood near the stairs to the bridge; the corridor was sheltering her from the wind.

"Here," he said, whisking her into a cabin. "I have to say goodbye to my new friend, don't I?" His voice was friendly, with none of the mannerisms he had affected during the crossing.

"How thoughtful of you, Captain," she said, "and I must thank you for your kindness and excellent directions for my continued travel."

He nodded, and took something from his pocket. "Miss Semel, I wish you all the luck you deserve in your new adventure, but this is a very large and alien country, and I must do my best to make it easier for you." He pinned a kind of badge to her suit jacket, a square of paper about four by four on which four black letters were printed: **HIAS**.

"You see," he said, "we take good care of our passengers. This will identify you to one of your people in the Hebrew Immigrant Aid Society. Their officials have asked me to distribute them for quite a while and I must confess I never bothered with them. You see what a good influence you exert on me."

He smiled like a small boy caught in a mischievous prank.

"When ships arrive," he continued, "these people come to the pier to assist immigrants like you through the medical checkups, the eye exam, the questioning by officials as to their destination and work, and so on. Now, you must admit," he added, "no one could have had more excellent care. Is that not so?"

"You have indeed been very kind." She waited for the usual pinch, or kiss, or request for payment in return for his favor, but none came.

"Goodbye, Miss Semel, and good luck in your new life. Think kindly of Captain Potemkin once in a while, yes? And tell that new husband of yours he is a lucky man."

A representative of the group who spoke Yiddish met her at the port and guided her through the maze of disembarkation officials and regulations that otherwise would have detained her for days.

When questioned about her reasons for emigrating and the name of a responsible patron, it would have been easy to simply explain that she was meeting her fiancé, and this usually would have sufficed for her admittance. But Malka dared not admit she was to meet Jacob, for he was still a fugitive from Russia and the Czar and feared deportation.

She only told the HIAS man she had relatives in Canada and needed transportation to Seattle. He was an older man about her father's age, with a hump on his curved back. The cap he wore was embroidered with the letters of his organization, and every time he spoke of HIAS he pulled on the cap's brim for emphasis, as if the letters granted him all the authority and sanctions of the group.

He sped Malka through her medical tests and the dreaded eye exam by keeping up a constant stream of conversation in English with the medical official. It was annoying to this impatient man, and the ploy was successful; he finished with the young immigrant girl in minutes and pushed her along the line.

"You see," the HIAS man said gleefully, "he hates my

chatter, and well he should, for I spoke of the weather, how damp and rainy it is, and how it must cause his corns and bunions to ache."

"But how did you know he had corns and bunions?" Malka asked.

"His shoes!" the little man answered, laughing. "Anyone could see where the shoe leather has been cut open to make holes to relieve the pain. I'm a regular Sherlock Holmes!"

"Sher . . . ?"

"Never mind, I'll explain later. Here, get past this fellow and you can put Russia officially behind you."

He took her arm and led her to the final desk at the end of the line. The official glanced up and looked at Malka, the familiar glint appearing in his narrow eyes.

"Well, well, what have we here? As pretty a little matzo ball as I have laid eyes on in a long time." The words sounded harsh and lewd. "A bit scrawny, but that kind is more passionate, or so they say."

This was meant for the HIAS man, who obliged the official by winking.

There was more talk in the strange language Malka thought rough and discordant. If this was to be her new tongue, she began to despair of ever learning it. So many consonants, so little grace. But she could worry about it later, for the HIAS man led her out of the large building into the open air.

"So, now, Miss Semel, you are in America. How do you feel?"

Malka gave him a wide smile that hardly creased her pale face. Her eyes were bloodshot from lack of sleep, and if she told him how weak and dirty and nauseated she was, it would hurt his feelings.

"Of course I am happy to be here, sir, but I must confess to being very tired and hungry. And that, I fear, is making me grouchy."

"Ach, what a dumkopf I am! Of course you are hungry. The *Nicolai* did not provide a kosher buffet table, eh? I, too, have been a passenger in their infamous steerage. Have you eaten anything today?"

Malka shook her head.

He slapped his forehead with the palm of his hand, and said, "Oy, I'm prattling on and the little girl is starving! So, into my hands you must deliver yourself, and forgive me my thoughtlessness. You can always tell a fool by his long tongue!"

Later, after a bath and a lunch of simple but tasty kosher food at the HIAS home, Malka sat with her new friend, whom she now, at his insistence, addressed as Misha, and told him of her plans.

He listened, nodding once or twice. His eyes were gentle, and in spite of his deformity he gave her the impression of good health and high spirits.

From Misha she learned about the train to Chicago, and how she would have to change there for the train to Seattle. Although she still had money in her purse, his group paid her transportation to the west coast, her few rubles changed into dollars and cents to afford anything she might need along the way.

They assisted her in making sandwiches and packed a brown bag for raw vegetables and fruits. The train food would pose the same problems as the *Nicolai*, and she could not afford to lose any more weight. When the time came for her departure, Misha waited with her at the station. He kept up a steady stream of chatter, warning Malka of pickpockets and evil men who would try to take advantage of an immigrant girl. She listened to every word and assured him she would be careful.

She wore the same traveling suit in which she had left Khotin, although it was now scruffy and worn in spots, and had arranged her black hair in thick braids around her head. Her skin was clear and scrubbed, and her attitude was fresh and bursting with renewed energy.

She shook the HIAS man's hand. "Thank you, Misha, for your kindness, and HIAS's generosity. I will never forget. Perhaps some day I will be able to repay you."

"No need, my dear," he said, "we are doing what has to be done. After all, how can a Jew live without a windfall?" They both laughed, the bittersweet humor as familiar, as necessary, and as integral a part of their lives as food and water. Many days later, riding the train from Baltimore to Chicago, Malka would think of Misha, his misshapen body so grotesque at first glance, then eclipsed immediately by the sharpness of his mind, his humor, and the kindness he showed her.

If Malka wanted to see America before entering Canada, there was no more perfect way than the train ride from the east coast to the west. Long, tiring, dirty, with no way to sleep other than sitting up on the straight wicker bench night after endless night, it still afforded her a view of the vast country. By the time she arrived in Seattle, she had learned a few words of English, mostly from reading other passengers' newspapers and listening to them talk. She knew that Montana was two days long, and the Rocky Mountains were as high as the Russian Urals.

She was thrilled at the sight of cities like Chicago, and stared unbelieving at the miles and miles of farms and well-kept houses that seemed natural to this land. In Washington and Oregon the soaring beauty and majesty of its mountains brought a lump to her throat. But Jacob had assured her that Canada was equally beautiful, and glancing at Captain Potemkin's map, as she did often during the journey, she saw how close she was to her final destination.

After many days she arrived where the language was stranger than before.

Malka had seen so much since leaving her shtetl, her travels covering more ground than most people see in a lifetime, yet with each sight, each stretch of her head out of the window to see the engine pulling her train as it strained up and down the mountain grades, she felt the thrill of discovery.

It was as Misha had said when he bade her farewell: "*Sholom aleichem,* sweet girl, go with God, and look forward to your new life. Sure, it's a *schlepp,* but the only advantage to staying home is never wearing out your shoes!"

TWENTY-TWO

❧

"THIS BE NOTHIN', LITTLE LADY, NOTHIN' A' TALL, COMPARED to wintertime, no-sir-EE-sir! Wintertime, now that be sheer hell! Oh, pardon me, little lady, I be fergettin' my manners."

Malka shook her head. Her English was improving, but the words spoken by this stranger were another language altogether. And his dialect made it hopeless.

There were hundreds of stampeders in the group that had formed in the rowdy Alaskan town of Skagway. There were men and women from countries she had never heard of, exotic cultures she had never known existed. Some were grizzled veterans, like the one who had just spoken, but most were green and this journey, like hers, their first steps away from home.

She walked with them ankle-deep in the tidewater of the Dyea inlet, the gateway to the Chilkoot Pass. She was traveling with her packer and guide, a dour Chilkat Indian, who had packed stampeders for more than a year. She thought him insolent and grumpy, for he had hardly spoken once the trail had begun, his silence due either to a language problem or boredom with his routine job. But so far, it was the only sour note.

She had found him standing in front of an outfitters' store in Skagway. According to Jacob's direction, she had purchased her ton of supplies from the slick salesman, sure of himself as he told her, "These Indians hang around town, lady, just looking for someone to hire them. You won't have any trouble. Only don't argue price 'cause they've set their own and you got to pay it. Otherwise, you might as well forget the whole thing." He winked. "And a little girl like you can't carry all that over no pass."

She waited patiently with her huge pile of gear in front of the store, and watched for an Indian packer. But as the day wore on she grew apprehensive. There were Indians, just as the salesman said, but they passed her by, chuckling with each other and looking right through her. A strange race, she thought, not at all warlike as she had been warned, but certainly cheeky and unfriendly.

Finally, just before dark, a short, squat Indian, big-shouldered and grim, dressed in buckskin and wearing a large-brimmed, brown felt hat, stopped in front of her, looked her up and down, glanced at her pile of supplies, shrugged, and stuck a toothpick in his mouth.

"Chilkoot?" he asked.

"Uh . . . yes! Chilkoot, the Pass, yes?"

"How much?"

"How much? Uh . . ." Malka hesitated, her numbers still uncertain. She recalled the chart given her by the salesman, and pulled it from her purse.

"One ton," she announced, watching the Indian's face for any sign of rejection.

He looked puzzled. "One ton? Sure. But how much?"

"How much," Malka repeated, confused. "Oh! Yes." She again consulted her chart. "Um, ten cents for pound."

The Indian shook his head and worked his toothpick.

"Twelve," Malka said, against the salesman's advice. What did he know, anyway. One has to bargain. There is no other way. The Indian shook his head again.

"Fifteen. Last offer," Malka said, snapping her finger on the chart. "Take it or not."

The Indian chewed on the toothpick and surveyed her again. The expression on his face revealed nothing. This packer business had bred hard-nosed cupidity among his people. They alone had the key to the pass, the birthright jealously guarded and shrewdly bargained for, and their begrudging sufferance was all that allowed the stampeders to go through.

But as he studied the scrawny little white lady, his narrow eyes took in the different crowd strolling Skagway's main street: hard-eyed women with painted lips and spit curls, and men with guns, the holsters tight on their hips. He knew that at this late hour families had retreated into their homes, and the gold-seekers and their wives were settled for the night in rattletrap hotels. Small boys were now running through the muddy streets hawking lewd postcards and girlie shows in the next block.

The town had changed faces in the blink of an eye, and the Indian stared at Malka standing by her supplies, so young and small, like a newborn fawn far from mama and struggling in high-country snow. But he could also play her game.

"Twenty," he said, turning to go.

"Fifteen," Malka said, trembling, afraid now she was losing him.

The Indian spat out his toothpick and muttered something in his own language. Then he stuck out his right hand to Malka. "Deal," he said.

"Deal," she replied. They shook hands.

He produced a thick strap from within his shirt, wrapped it around his flat forehead, and, in only a few minutes, by using this strap as a tumpline to tow her gear, he had balanced a great part of it on his massive shoulders.

"Come," he said, and began walking.

"Wait! Supplies on ground . . . ?"

"Okay. I get them later. Come."

"But . . ." Malka hated to leave the brand new goods sitting on the store landing, but the Indian was far ahead, and she hurried to catch up. "Where do we go?" she cried.

"You sleep now. I take supplies. We start early in morning. Here, on this spot." He stood on a piece of high ground, away from the slimy green tidal ooze that crept like a parasite over the town's main street, and stared at his new client.

She stared back, but it was all show. Somewhere in the last ten minutes, Malka had lost control of the situation.

"All right," she said, trying to make herself tall and straight. The Indian was very short, but he looked down at least four inches to the top of her head. He grunted and walked away.

"Wait! What is your name? Your name?" she cried.

"Red Sky. Andrew Red Sky."

"All right, Andrew. My name . . ."

"You Missy. All I need. Missy."

He pointed to the vacancy sign in a rickety hotel and disappeared around a corner.

Malka was filled with misgivings. What had she done by letting this stranger walk away with her precious gear? He said he would be here, on this spot, in the morning. She had put her life in his hands when she hired him to see her safely over the Chilkoot. She had no choice but to trust him.

There were nearly three hundred men in the party crossing the Chilkoot. Big, small, old and young, some in brand new "duds," clothes the outfitters must have advertised as "What the well-dressed stampeder wears on the way to the gold fields!" Others wore motley combinations, no doubt hastily thrown together as they hurried to be one of the new millionaires. A few women were with husbands or small groups of female friends, their light chatter a contrast to the tough trail ahead.

The first few miles were easy, just as Captain Potemkin had promised: "No more than a kibitka ride through a pleasant Khotin meadow." They crossed several streams. The day was very warm, and when Malka took off her shoes, the water felt cool on her bare feet.

"No-sir-EE-sir," the old prospector continued, sloshing alongside Malka, "I heerd tell this is one rotten place to be in winter. Snow falls all the time, winds at the top howlin' like a banshee, ice underfoot so's you can't grip nothin'. No sir, lucky for us it's summer."

He looked over at Malka and smiled, his gaping mouth stripped of every last tooth. She gasped, and that pleased him. He thought her reaction proper for his grim narrative.

"Hush up, Pliney, don't be botherin' the girl none," his wife said sharply, giving her husband a poke in the back with her umbrella. She looked at Malka and grimaced. "He don't mean nothin' by all his talk. Just his way. Don't pay him no mind."

Malka shook her head. "No English," she said finally.

"No? Hmmph. D'ja hear that, Pliney? You been gabbin' up a blue streak and this little girl don' even know what yur sayin'. Ain't that a heap o' somethin'!"

"Aw, shut up, woman, jus' follow your feets and don' fall in this slop."

Everyone concentrated on the thin-crusted underbrush near the rapids, the rocks covered with moss, dangerous and slippery. Occasionally, when the high granite cliffs on both sides made the trail impassable, they had to wade back into the gravelly stream.

Although the terrain was new to her, Malka had no trouble with the water or the stones. She began to wonder why Jacob had pleaded so hard with her to avoid this way into

Dawson. The canyon was a lovely, shaded place on this warm May afternoon, and if the trail continued this smoothly, it would be a pleasant hike.

Soon, however, she noticed litter staining the landscape. A trunk sat upright in the shallow water, its lid propped open, revealing personal trinkets inside. Framed pictures spilled from the top tray, a pair of boots and fancy scarves underneath. She saw an iron stove, a complete set of pots and pans and a battered old doll thrown into the grove, and wondered why these cherished mementos had been dumped into the mud like garbage.

"I know what you're thinking," another woman said, falling in step with Malka. "My husband, that man up ahead in the green shirt, he told me not to bring anything extra, and now I see why. Look at all that stuff . . . poor devil."

"Yes. Why he do this?" Malka asked. The young woman shrugged her shoulders. "Who knows? Some people just don't listen. Kurt warned me. No cases. No trunks. Just canvas bags. No bigger than fifty inches long. See? Like mine."

Malka nodded and patted her own canvas bag. "Jacob say same words."

"Jacob? Your husband? Which one is he?"

"Oh . . . no, no husband." Malka smiled shyly. "We marry in Dawson."

"Oh, gee. Aren't you brave."

They had walked nearly five miles from the beginning of the trail when they approached a group of tents clustered around three or four scraggly buildings. One of the wooden huts housed a blacksmith's shop. From another, a sign reading "EATS" hung by one chain.

"Why, lookee here, Pliney," the old woman cried to her husband, "a restaurant, as I live and breathe! Here in the middle of nuthin'. Now that be downright grand."

Her husband laid down his heavy load on the coarse

grass. "Jest in time, too," he said, "a beer would go down nice and easy right about now."

The others sprawled on the ground, resting or eating from their bags. What Pliney's wife had called a restaurant was nothing but a sagging shack with a handmade table, some chairs that tilted alarmingly, and a warm pot of beans on the stove. But it also had a large keg of beer cooling in the running stream.

Malka turned to her Indian packer. "You like . . . ?" She gestured toward the drinkers.

The Indian took the coins she gave him, and bought two bottles of beer. They both sat on the bags drinking. He was pulling Malka's gear on a sledge by the tumpline he had used the day before. When they had started out, one of the men explained to her that the sledge would travel only to the pass entrance. After seeing her over safely, Red Sky would return, making several trips to bring the rest of her supplies through the pass into Canada.

His strength was amazing. Surely, she said, one man cannot carry so much weight. But the man laughed. "Hell, they make a darn fine living up here. Just look at him, he's hardly panting. Me, I feel like I been walking for days."

Impatient to continue after their beers, the Indians hoisted the loads and headed for the Dyea River canyon, a slim crevice fifty feet wide and about two miles long. It was the beginning of a dangerous and tricky course. Broken trees felled by high wind, large rocks fallen from the cliffs above, and great clumps of tangled roots blocked the way.

Suddenly, Malka and the others stumbled over the dead, bloated bodies of horses, lying where they had fallen from the high cliffs. There were dogs and donkeys and cattle. The count grew as they continued up the trail. Malka shivered with horror at the pieces and bones.

Swarms of mosquitoes attacked the climbers. Malka

brushed them away as fast as she could, but along with the mosquitoes came clouds of bulldog flies, biting hungrily at sweaty faces and necks until the air was filled with curses. Malka tied a scarf across her face, but the flies found their way in, and what the flies left, the mosquitoes quickly scavenged.

The footing was difficult; here and there a slippery log across a stream almost tumbled someone in. Waterfalls splashed down on the canyon walls in sprays of silver and crystal, watering the masses of flowers below. But the pack-laden men were too busy trying to keep their footing on the craggy path to notice anything else around them.

The gorge was now gloomy and dismal, its beauty lost in the shade of the steep walls. Malka felt uneasy for the first time since starting out. Her steps were tentative, and she edged closer to her Indian packer.

If he sensed her fear, he said nothing, but he did not move away. At one place, a particularly treacherous stretch of wet rocks and slush, she slipped and fought for balance, but he caught her arm before she could fall. Otherwise, he pretended ignorance of her anxiety.

When they reached a cool strip of woods at the end of the canyon trail, a place called Pleasant Camp, her mood lifted. Some of the group stopped here, but most chose to go on without resting. The Indian packers wanted to go on to Sheep Camp, a more comfortable site for the night.

Malka felt peculiar now, her legs heavy and stiff, her pulse fast, her breathing shallow. The grade was rising slowly, gravity pulling breath and strength from her slight figure. The Indian noticed and warned, "Go slow, breathe through nose, we go higher. Slow, slow."

Malka did as he said, breathing through her nose, slowing her pace, taking time to put one foot down, then the other, waiting, breathing deeply. When they finally reached Sheep Camp at the base of the mountains, Malka put down her knapsack and sat gratefully. She was bone tired, a mass of aches and pains from head to toe. And soaking wet. Her thin blouse stuck to her skin; perspiration trickled from her scalp into her eyes.

"You stay," the Indian said, dumping gear beside her, "Red Sky cut wood for fire."

She watched him take a sharp knife to the thin poplars that made up the deadfall around camp, his plump hands dexterous and quick, and idly wondered why he would build a fire on this hot, sticky day.

From the corner of her eye, Malka saw a huge man watching her. It was not the first time. Malka had noticed him before, in Skagway, behind her as she walked, in the outfitters' shop leaning against a glass showcase, in Pleasant Camp, watching, always watching.

She had paid no attention then. But it was beginning to annoy her. More than that, it was frightening. He was young, his cheeks fat and hairless. Standing almost two heads above her, he walked with a lumbering gait, shuffling his big feet, his long arms hanging to his knees. Malka thought of telling Red Sky about him, but decided she would sound silly and let it go.

Sheep Camp was surrounded by snow-capped peaks that loomed high and sharp-edged above her. The gap called Chilkoot was barely visible.

"You see pass?" Red Sky asked.

"It is far, no?"

"Not far. Four miles. But straight up."

For the first time, Malka saw Red Sky smile.

"Why is it called Sheep Camp?" she asked.

"Who else would climb like this?" Red Sky said, pointing to the slopes above them. "Man is crazy." He added more wood to the flames, then grinned at her. "Lady crazy, too."

With the setting sun, Malka realized Red Sky had built

the fire not only to cook supper, but because the night was suddenly cold.

The hovels in the camp were crammed together—tents, shacks, some leaning precariously, others so close they seemed to hold each other up.

Pliney's wife sat on her haunches next to Malka. "See that shack over yonder? I heard it has meals, like bacon and beans, for one dollar, and, get this . . . a woman for five dollars! Ain't that sumpn'? Five dollars . . . why if I'd a know'd that twenty years back when my Pliney and me wuz first hitched, I'd a made a fortune by now, and we wouldn't be trudgin' our asses off in this godforsaken place!"

She slapped her thighs and laughed out loud. Her words had sailed right over Malka's head, but not Red Sky's, and he frowned when the woman walked away.

They ate a crude supper, Malka finishing a whole can of beans from her supplies, the Indian digging into his precious bag of dried salmon and tea.

She had found a logical solution to the problem of starvation. After days of debating with her conscience during the second week of passage on the *Nicolai*, she made an uneasy but final peace with herself and ate the ship's food. In spite of her own tangled arguments, the answer was remarkably simple: The Holy One did not want her to starve. In fact, had He not commanded that one keep the body healthy and strong? And you cannot do that without food.

She promised to resume her kosher habits as soon as possible, not having the slightest idea when that would be. But she knew the words of the Talmud, "The earth is the Lord's, and the fullness thereof," and to Malka this meant all the earth and all the food. For now. She always made the proper benedictions, no matter how lean or miserable the plate before her, at least preserving for herself the nature of holiness. The impiety was unfortunate, but temporary.

She finished the can of beans and wondered if, given a choice, the martyrs at Masada would have done the same. The question had no answer. Perhaps fasting is easier in the absence of choice, but the disloyal thought increased her guilt. She dismissed it by concluding, regrettably, that she was not meant for martyrdom.

Dragging the spoon around the inside of the can to reach the last drop of beans, she smiled, then licked the spoon clean. If you do something wrong, her papa used to say, at least enjoy it.

TWENTY-THREE

❦

CIRCLING THE MOUNTAINTOP LIKE A HALO, THE EARLY morning fog kept the climbers waiting and fidgeting, anxious to get started. The sun finally broke through, burning away most of the fog, and the difficult trek up the steep incline began. As they broke camp, Malka asked Red Sky why some of the men were leaving supplies stashed along the trail.

"Nothing bad happen," he explained, "no man steal other man's cache. Is sacred."

"Oh? Never?"

Red Sky shrugged. "If man needs to take from cache, he repays later. That is way here. One time, a man took from cache and threw rest on ground. Animals come and make big mess. Man not repay cache."

"So, bad man goes free?" Malka asked.

"Owner find cache, is very angry and looks for man who not repay. Hang him, the owner say, but other men say take sled, but no dogs, send man outside over ice."

"And?"

"Nobody hear from thief. Never."

Malka grimaced.

"No. I say we have rules, like man must repay to cache. That way no man starve."

"Mm-hmm. You are right. Malka will learn."

"Yes, learn," Red Sky said sharply, "or die."

She washed in the icy stream, shivering from the cold as well as from the Indian's warning, then hurried into her jacket. The new traveling outfit would never be the same; its cuffs were dirty and unraveling, the skirt hem sagged with dried brown mud, and loose threads dangled from the precise button-holes she had sewn so meticulously only weeks before.

The climb was difficult, but she worried more about dishonoring Jacob if she arrived in Dawson City looking like a ragamuffin. Still, she was making this trip at Jacob's behest. If she looked seedy and disheveled, so be it.

She was very tired this morning. A sleeping bag on the cold dirt floor of a dilapidated shack was a lark the first time, but hateful after last night. Having no real bed since leaving Khotin, she thought even the filthy cot on the *Nicolai* would look good now. The pack horses, cut loose during the night, had kept her awake, roaming the camp, whinnying pitifully, stumbling blindly over ropes and gear. Toward dawn, more cries rent the thin air as the men rounded up the horses and were forced to shoot them because they were injured. The shots rang out and bounced like mournful cadence off the granite walls.

And there were other sounds, a strange gnashing and grinding, like the screws of the *Nicolai*, though the ship's sounds had been constant and rhythmic. These were fitful, like fragmented thunder high in the shrouded peaks. She wondered what they were, but there was no time to ask. . . .

As she followed Red Sky up the steeply rising trail, Malka struggled silently, the shale, still snow-covered in May, making every step a challenge. Sharp curves offered no solid footing, and the Indian led her in great circular arcs to avoid the huge boulders in the path.

Keeping her eyes straight ahead, she tried not to give in to the gnawing fear every time she looked down. At one point she slipped and fell, sprawling against the sharp riprap left by previous climbers. Her hands were skinned and a slight cut bled over one eye, but she was otherwise unhurt, and collected her pack while others passed her by, cursing her under their breath for the delay. Up ahead Red Sky saw what had happened, stepped out of line and walked back to see if she was hurt.

"No," she cried, "Go. Go!"

He turned to take his new place in the line while she summoned every ounce of strength to continue.

A few hours later, the path dipped slightly into a shallow bowl surrounded on three sides by the scree-covered mountains, and the line began breaking up as loads were tossed onto the ground.

"This here's where the gear is weighed by them fancy po-leece up yonder," Pliney said, showing off again.

"Hush up, you old coot," his wife scolded, "I'm sick of your flirtin'."

"Jealous? You? Hah!" Pliney winked at Malka. "Ain't that a kick? When I had teeth and hair, and everything else the good Lord provided, she wouldn't pee on me if I was on fire!"

Pliney's wife banged her umbrella on the old man's backside, then chased him up the path.

Malka shook her head. "How they have strength to fight after this climb?" she asked Red Sky. He took Malka's pack, adding it to his pile. "Pay no mind. People like them here to make other people laugh. Is good to laugh. Make climb easy."

The Indian pointed to a large, flat rock. "You sit there," he said sternly, "no more falling. Is more to climb up. And is hard." The warm sun eased her aching muscles, and Malka watched the Indian closely, learning from him as well as the others as he and the Mounties, "the fancy po-leece," weighed their gear. When she realized how far up they had climbed, her panic no longer embarrassed her. She was doing all right. One was entitled to a slip now and then in such a precarious place.

Perhaps her first impression of the Indian had been unfair. He was disagreeable, and his way incompatible with hers, but that was expected: he was Indian, not Russian. But he had his good points.

For one thing, he had agreed to the price; she learned later it was much lower than the going rate. And how could she reconcile his bad humor with the act of stepping out of his hard-won place in line to make sure she was unhurt? It had been the action of a charitable man.

She closed her eyes, resting her weary body in the warm sunlight, and an old adage flitted through her mind: a good friend costs nothing, but you pay plenty for an enemy. To fare well, she decided, there could be no better teacher than a friend here and there along the way.

She was brought sharply back to the present by the rumbles that had disturbed her last night's sleep. The disquieting sounds seemed to be above her, and she peered into the high, thin air.

"Look there," Red Sky said, pointing up, his voice hushed, "there is glacier, move all the time, shifting, make noise like thunder."

Malka gazed upward until she saw vast walls of shimmering blue ice. She caught her breath at this, thinking about the constant motion of the icy mass, melting, crumbling, freezing, creeping forward on its inexorable way over anything in its path. It was at once beautiful and frightening, and she wanted the time to watch the fantastic sight. But the line of people was climbing again, moving on and up, each footstep carefully placed in the ice-cliffs, fighting for balance, fingernails clawing for a hold on the unstable surface.

Before reclaiming their place in the line, Red Sky had taken a char stick from a cold fire and blackened Malka's cheekbones and eyelids. She knew better than to ask his purpose and suffered the small indignity in silence. Only when a few of the men nodded approvingly did she learn why he had marked her. "Smart fellow, that Indian," one man said. "He did that to help you see better when we crawl by that glacier."

"It looks blue from here, but just wait till you see it up close," another added. "The best thing is snow glasses to cut the bright sun, but those smudges will help some."

The black marks did cut down somewhat on the glare from the ice wall, but her eyes teared and struggled to stay open. She longed to see the ice up close, to touch it, to memorize the glorious shades of color glowing within its fissures. The glacier's face rose three hundred feet above her, its scintillating mass of colors shifting with the light: here sapphire blue, there a streak of turquoise, then blinding white in the wash of full sunlight. When dark clouds tumbled across the sun, the colors changed to delicate shades of mauve, pink and green, with murky glimmers of indigo that seemed to radiate from the glacier's deep core.

But the human line kept moving, the incline now steeper, almost thirty-five degrees straight up on sliding rock, and there was no time to stand and gape. The wind screamed like something wild, swirling the trail into a blinding mist of pulverized gravel. The footing shifted constantly, throwing everyone off balance. Bent under the weight of their packs, the climbers pushed and struggled against the elements and obstacles, crying out in frustration, cursing this malevolent monster called Chilkoot.

Suddenly, without warning, huge stone blocks began to tumble down on the moving chain. It was a rock slide, born in the peaks from loosening shale and sent hurtling through the air. Men toppled from the trail without uttering a cry and fell like rag dolls. Others threw themselves down, only to be crushed by falling debris.

When Malka heard the roar of rock, she tried to flatten out on the ground with her pack over her head. But there was no protection against this kind of rock slide. The heavy chunks of granite were encrusted with ice, their slickness contributed to a fast, deadly descent.

She suddenly felt herself lifted, carried not by the wind or rock but by strong arms to a shelter under an outcropping. She was terrified, unable to see, and offered no resistance when her rescuer placed his own body as a shield over hers. Screams echoed around her, wind-whipped back and forth over the face of the pass. She kept her eyes shut, fists clenched, every muscle straining under the protecting body.

Then, as quickly as it began, it was over. After a long, terrible silence, she heard the sobbing of the injured and dying men. She opened her eyes and began wriggling free. Red Sky slid off soundlessly, unconscious, his clothes torn, his long black hair matted with blood.

She quickly tore strips from her petticoat, wet them with water from her canteen and washed away most of the blood. Red Sky stirred and tried to speak, but Malka hushed him and finished bandaging his cuts. She could see men tending to the injured, while others bundled up the dead and placed them on sledges. They would be leaving their own caches behind, marked by poles or pieces of clothing, returning for them after bringing the bodies to Lake Bennett.

She was shaken by the sight and smell of death around her, and awed by her escape. It could scarcely be understood in light of the physical beauty she had seen only minutes before. She turned from the dead and willed herself to face what came next.

Then she saw him again. The huge, ugly man was standing a few feet away, staring at her, a line of spittle dribbling down his chin. He was following her. It was not her imagination. She was sure of it now.

Heart pounding, she turned away quickly. She decided it was time to alert Red Sky. But the Indian was in no shape for that now. She would ask his advice as soon as he felt better.

The sharp wind died down, and a hazy sun shone through the veil of mist on the peaks. Trembling with dread, Malka walked to the summit and looked back toward the beginning of the trail three thousand feet below.

Standing here at the top of the world, she felt terribly alone, alienated from everything she had ever known. There was no seductive Lorelei singing to her of the golden fortune waiting at the end of this hellish course. That siren's song was for the wild-eyed men as it trilled and teased with the promise of gold. She believed that Jacob Finesilver was not one of them, that a desperate need had brought him to the Klondike. One had to have lived in the Russian Pale that made all lesser demons seem trivial.

She pulled her shawl tighter and looked at the silent death around her. Are we fools or heroes? she asked herself. Either way, the answer gave little comfort.

Crossing into Canada, she caught her first sight of the Union Jack flying from the RCMP post. Two young Mounties, handsome in their scarlet tunics, breeches, and wide-brimmed hats, were writing the names of the immigrants in large notebooks.

"And you, Miss, your name?" one asked Malka.

So young and so neatly dressed, she thought. How do they manage that here in the middle of nowhere?

"Malka Semel," she replied. "S-E-M-E-L, yes?"

"Fine." The Mountie looked up from his writing at the pretty girl before him. "Where do you come, Miss Semel?"

"From Russia."

"But surely you can't be thinking of mining gold by yourself? Or . . ." An unpleasant thought crossed his mind. " . . . or are you planning to . . . to go into business?"

Puzzled, Malka turned to Red Sky. The Indian stepped forward, scowling under the bandages.

"Sir," he said, "this lady in my charge. She has one ton, like Mounties say, and she hire Red Sky to pack over pass to Dawson City. She break no law. This lady no make trouble, sir."

The Mountie smiled. "Red Sky, eh? Well, Red Sky, I hope your charge isn't planning to dance by the light of a red lantern, eh? Then you would both be in trouble."

Red Sky nodded curtly, muttered something Malka could not hear, and took her arm, leading her to the point in the path where three forks of the trail led over the pass, each one straight up.

"Now you say which way we go." He pointed to the left fork. "This way steep, lot of rocks and narrow ridge. On right is very long ravine trail, the center way very steep to mountain top."

He enjoyed his dramatic oration. She watched, fascinated, as he played out his part. "Left way dangerous. Right way used for dog team. Center is hard climb, but . . ."

Red Sky suddenly smiled, but Malka was learning to read that smile. Now comes little joke. "But . . . ?" she said, waiting.

" . . . but easier in winter!"

"Winter?"

"Yes. In winter, chop steps in snow, walk up steps to top. Now in summer, all the rock loose, dangerous, like slide."

"Well, we not wait for winter," Malka declared without hesitation, flashing a smile of her own, "we will go now in summer on center path . . . and hope for best."

TWENTY-FOUR

✧⊙✧

THE DESCENT FROM THE MOUNTAINTOP WAS A NIGHTMARE. Malka tripped and stumbled over rocks, and exposed roots snagged her skirts as she slipped perilously on loose gravel. When she finally lost her balance and fell flat on her face, she threw dignity to the wind, tucked her pack under her arms and slid down the rest of the way on her backside.

She sat dazed, dirty and exhausted, her knees and elbows skinned, limp with fatigue like a rag doll tossed in a corner, and stared in wonder at the thriving tent city sprawling around the edge of Lake Bennett. There must be no end, she thought, to this journey's wonders.

There were thousands of tents, all shapes and sizes, pup tents, army tents, hastily built lean-tos, and custom-made marvels with awnings. Brand new tents and old sad things torn by the wind and weather and patched with colorful calico and plaid, as if splashed willy-nilly with paint.

Although far from worldly wise, Malka concluded that the temporary town worked because everything necessary to it was there under canvas.

The beach was covered with tent hotels and barber shops, and hot baths and cold showers and a café. She counted chapels, sleeping cabins, bakeries, first-aid stations, casinos, saloons, mining agents and a post office. This commercial

enterprise under tents only proved to Malka that man's ingenuity, when motivated by the chance of wealth, was
unbounded. Was he as clever or as persevering, she wondered
uncharitably, when the goal was a cure for deadly disease or
feeding the poor?

She had asked herself why these people were doing what
they were doing. The gossip on the trail had answered that
question. With a worldwide depression, many of the gold-
seekers were unemployed. Finding gold seemed their only hope.

But the search was far from over. From Red Sky's patient
itinerary, Malka knew that here, where the mean trail ended,
there still remained hundreds of miles to navigate on the
Yukon River system river before reaching Dawson City. Like
everyone else she must buy, build or trade for a boat.

Every space on the shoreline was taken up by the boat
builders, the din of their labors steady and deafening.
Sawmills screeched, tall timber crashed and dog teams barked
as they ran over the sands. Boats were everywhere, strewn
over sand and water in differing stages of development.

Malka saw teepees of logs bundled together on end waiting to be claimed, and the bare ribs of half-finished hulls
looking like prehistoric skeletons. Prefabricated boats that
men had carried over the pass in boxes were being put
together like huge jigsaw puzzles. The scarlet-coated
Northwest Mounted Police moved calmly through this
rough-and-tumble, dispensing advice and black pitch for hull
numbers, and writing names in bulging log books. Every soul
in the convoy to Dawson had to be registered.

The completed vessels bobbed on the green surface of the
lake, a few taking on water and sinking slowly. One looked
so awkward, Malka had the image of a small boy hacking it
together with a pocket knife. The scene suggested the exotic
rites of some mad, uncivilized force, pursuing absurd means
to an even more absurd end. That she was a part of it could

be justified only by expedience, necessary until she reached Dawson. Otherwise, she told herself, she was just another inmate in the asylum.

She waited in her beach tent for Red Sky to finish bringing her supplies over the pass. On his return he bartered with the boatmakers for a sturdy scow that had two board seats and two sets of oars.

"Missy help Red Sky," he explained to Malka. "Rapids hard to sail."

This sudden show of faith in her surprised her. But she nodded. Please, she thought, don't let me give him reason to change his mind. The hard-won confidence was a heady victory, and she watched and copied him every moment they were together. The hours now were spent waiting for the river ice to thaw.

A raucous shout went up in camp one morning, and Malka and Red Sky ran to the shore along with hundreds of stampeders to see what had happened.

"The ice is out! The ice is out!" Pliney yelled, jumping up and down on the sand, waving his arms as if conducting the chorus of miners who were shouting with glee.

"Did'ja hear it? The boom? That was ice crackin'! Came from up river, that's for sure! So we can get goin'. Yes-sir-EE-sir! On to Dawson and GOLD! We's gonna be rich! We's gonna be rich!"

Puzzled, Malka stared at the river. There was no big flow of water, just a trickle compared to the huge white chunks of ice that were piling up along the shoreline. Nevertheless, everyone was cheering wildly. Some men linked arms and danced a merry jig, their spirits buoyed by the prospect of action at last. Others, veterans of the Canadian wilderness, walked slowly back to their tents.

"Why some happy and some sad?" Malka asked Red Sky.

The Indian shook his head. "These men know river. Ice

cracked some place, but will take more days, two, maybe three, to melt enough for boat to sail. We don't go yet."

As Red Sky predicted, the lake was unnavigable for two more days. Then, with only a few chunks of ice left bobbing in the smooth water, they pushed off shore early in the morning. Malka, seated facing Red Sky, her back to the bow end, was stiff with fright. She knew about the rapids. The packers had talked of little else, their horror stories vivid with details of the four sets of wild water on the way to Dawson City. About boats she knew nothing of bow, stern, or anything that lay between them, and though she would never admit it to Red Sky, deep water terrified her. She had never learned to swim, yet here she was, sitting in a homemade scow with a short, testy Indian in whose hands she had placed her life. She would watch him and learn what she needed to know.

She felt great pity for the men setting off too soon, who were later seen amid the wreckage of their boats downstream, forced to salvage gear, walk back to the tent city and start over again; and for the men whose poorly constructed boats foundered, their overloaded skiffs sinking beneath the muddy water. Some boats were running aground because their "skippers" had no experience. There was even one going backwards, the strong north wind pushing the men faster than they could row.

"How long to Dawson?" Malka shouted to Red Sky.

"Two week," he said, and resumed his long, easy strokes.

A crosswind blew as they sailed northward. Men in camp called it "the windy arm," pushing, lifting, whirling the boats down the lovely mountain lakes. As they swung by foothills of the jagged mountain ranges, Malka watched thousands of nesting martins in the surrounding cliffs. Spring flowers bloomed everywhere. The channels were thick with homing caribou, so close she could reach out and touch their velvety antlers. Sandbars in some of the lakes were speckled with sandpipers, plovers and snipe, and when the going was easy, Red Sky seemed more relaxed and friendly, and told her stories of the river.

"Yukon Indian word for great river," he said, as they drifted with the current. "River very long, all food come by river, all men and all animals. River so cold, if a man falls in, he never come out. Look"

Malka turned. Tiny houses like toys dotted the shoreline, one after the other, each with its own little fence.

"Graves," he explained, "under little houses are graves of Indians. The fence keeps animals out, gifts safe."

"What gifts?"

"Indians are buried with gifts for their spirits. Plate, cup, spoon all to help spirits eat." He treated Malka to one of his rare smiles and said, "Spirits of my people come to eat. Spirits of white people come to smell flowers."

Then they both heard the sound of rushing water, and Red Sky yelled, "Here come rapids! Take oar, stay on seat!"

He stood in the stern end, wielding his oar as a paddle. As sheets of spray poured over the boat, the river current suddenly accelerated, shooting the boat around a sharp bend just below the bluff. The roaring waters met them and tumbled the boat into the shallows as they tried desperately to avoid treacherous obstacles reaching out to snag the boat. Red Sky maneuvered through drifting logs and thrusting roots of dead trees, the bleached branches reminding Malka of giant hands straining to pull them under.

Red Sky skillfully avoided the jagged boulders looming out of the water, but the noise was deafening as they pitched into a seething crest of wild spray. The boat's nose seemed to falter in an eddy, the whirling force playing with the scow, throwing it down, then up, then down, over to one side and the other. The boat, unable to ride the waves, was at the mercy of the whirlpool. Struck dumb with fear, Malka was sure they were both going to be dumped into the rough water. Suddenly they shot out of Miles Canyon into the smooth water below.

"Oh! Oh!" Malka cried, slumping on the seat. "That scares me, I see pictures of my life before my eyes. Very scary. But we are safe now, yes?"

"Not yet," Red Sky muttered, "soon more rapids. Soon klikhas."

"Klik . . . ?"

"Klikhas. That mean bad, fast water. Here river is wide, but soon narrow and water rise, run fast. You will see."

Malka could hear the roar again, the same as at Miles Canyon, and looked to Red Sky for instruction. He gestured sharply that she stay at the oar.

Sheer black walls appeared on both sides of the water, making a chute of the canyon in which they moved. Small geysers erupted from the foam bubbling around the boat. Then they seemed to be free as the corridor bent sharply to the left. But even as she saw the whirlpool at least two hundred feet across on the inner side, they were caught, the churning whitecaps whirling them around and around like horses racing blindly on a circular track, and the scow was quickly inundated. In spite of their efforts to turn the nose into the stream and buck the whirlpool, the boat capsized, pitching Malka, Red Sky, and all the supplies into the wild water.

Down, down she went, her eyes open but unable to see anything but bubbles and white water. She was numbed instantly in the ice-cold river, and for a split second death grabbed her by the throat as she tumbled helplessly to the bottom.

Pushed like debris along the gravel and stones, frozen and out of breath, she fought back instinctively, too stubborn and angry with her own incompetence to give up. She struggled against the current and the depths, clawing, stretching and straining through the froth and silt to reach the surface. What seemed an eternity was only seconds until she broke through, coughing, spewing water, thrashing wildly to keep afloat.

She gulped at the precious air, holding it in, feeling her lungs expand. She heard Red Sky shout and looked around frantically. He was swimming for the boat twisting in the dizzying whirlpool. Then he caught it.

Without realizing it, Malka began to swim to shore, flailing her arms in imitation of Red Sky, turning her head to keep water out of her mouth and nose. Her diminutive size kept her on top of the waves, their force propelling her closer to the boat.

She heard Red Sky shout again as a large canvas bag swept by, and she reached out for it in a desperate grab. The drawstring caught in her fingers. Tugging with all her might, she pulled herself and the bag to shore.

But there was no real shore and little room to land on. The walls of the canyon were slimy with growth, and rocky outcropping tore at her wet clothes. Somehow she pulled in the bag, threw it on the land, and, with hardly a moment to regain her wind, slipped back into the murky depths, churning through the bubbles that hissed like soda water around her. She succeeded in dragging three more bags to shore before falling to the rocky ground, exhausted.

"Missy okay?"

Red Sky stood over her, dripping water and holding tight to the boat with one hand.

"Yes. Okay," Malka stammered, trying to sit up.

"No," the Indian said quickly, pushing her down, "you stay and rest. I dry sack in sun. No worry. Tight sack keep all dry."

"But . . . I help . . ."

"No. Sit in sun and dry, like sack." He turned abruptly and set about tying the scow to an overhanging tree. A few minutes later he had all the bags lined up and drying. Then he slumped against the tree's roots and slept. Near the end of the day, they repacked the boat and continued downstream.

They spoke little during the next few miles. The river that had almost claimed their lives in the whirling eddies of Whitehorse Rapids now flowed calmly and innocently, showing no sign of its darker, meaner side. Tall green spruce, white birch and slim cottonwoods patrolled the shore like a stalwart army, waving at the slim girl and her Indian packer as if no misfortune lurked anywhere among their peaceful ranks. Wildflowers bloomed in abundance, the mountainous land showing off its fertility with late spring blossoms in every color and variety. They drifted through streams choked with salmon and watched silently as two bears waddled down to the shore and scooped up fish in their paws.

Boats passed and people waved in friendly greeting. The *Lucky Star*, the *Pearl*, the *Four Leaf Clover*, *Dandy Dan*, the names emblazoned in black tar on each flimsy, overburdened craft. A junk floated by, and a catamaran, and an absurd houseboat with two dainty ladies aboard, the frilly sails fashioned from their petticoats fluttering a curious welcome in the breeze. In the midst of all this was a detective from Chicago chasing a murder suspect.

Hollow logs, packing boxes that floated, dugouts and skiffs, kayaks and sampans, the bizarre fleet sailed on the emerald-green water like children's crude toys. When they had reached Tagish Post earlier, the Mounted Police had registered four thousand boats. Malka learned later that three thousand more were counted before the end of summer.

She sat in the bow, her clothes dry but dirty and wrinkled, mud and leaves staining her skirt. Her shoes were drying on the seat board, stuffed with the ruined jacket of her traveling suit and a small bag of nuts.

It was close to midnight, but the sun still shone, giving them extra hours on the lake. They would make camp soon, as they had each night, Malka under netting in the tent, Red Sky preferring to stay outside, close and protective but preserving his solitude and privacy.

She thought this a good time to tell him about the spectre following her, his great lumping presence increasingly intolerable. But Red Sky had spotted a fresh campsite and turned the boat toward shore, and with the tasks of docking and making camp for the night, the spectre was forgotten.

Malka found it hard to fall asleep. The bright sky was unsettling. She could hear little paws pulling at the tent, quick panting breaths outside. The distant howl of wolves sent shivers up her spine. She listened for hours to the loons crying over the lake. When large animals crashed through the grove, she held her breath and prayed that whatever was out there would go away. It was comforting to know Red Sky was sitting on the bedroll outside the tent, calmly sharpening his long-bladed knife.

Lying awake in the sleeping bag, the crazy light still shining outside, she thought of her father, and her pupils, and the world she had left back in Khotin. Life there had been hard, and this now struck her as funny. If Khotin was no picnic, what was this? Ah, Malka, what stories you will tell your grandchildren some day, she thought and with this, she fell asleep.

But moments later, she was awakened. Her skin crawled. Someone or something had entered her canvas room. It was so close to her she could hear its breathing.

Because she was lying on the side away from the intruder, she pretended sleep, peering through the pale light. But it was senseless to stay like that, not knowing where or what it was. That might be prudent if the intruder was a hungry animal in search of food, but she felt too threatened to take the chance. She turned her head slowly. That was when he struck her, pinning her wrists against the ground, heaving his fat belly over her slim length, and panting foul breath in her face. Now she saw him clearly, the hulking monster who had been leering at her since Skagway. She writhed frantically beneath him, but he was too strong, too keen on getting what he wanted. She tried to scream, but her lungs were flattened under his weight, her feeble cries hushed.

Her nightshirt ripped across her chest, huge hands tore at her breasts, pinching her nipples. The sudden pain brought hot tears from her eyes, and she heard herself sobbing, choking as he tightened his grip around her throat.

"Shut up, little Jew lady," he hissed, "we don't need nobody to watch. Shut your mouth or I'll kill you first."

His face was a horror of pits and sores, oozing pustules and tunnels of embedded grime. Drool seeped from his twisted mouth. The rank smell of his body sickened her. He tore at her underwear, impatiently pulling the heavy cotton pants down her small hips. She locked her knees together, but he pushed his thick leg between them until her knees trembled and fell apart. His hands tightened around her neck and she gagged. Her wind cut off, and the spasms began deep in her throat.

Half fainting, Malka struggled to wrench herself free, but her actions inflamed his lust and he bore down harder.

"So you like it, little Jew lady? Then give it to me!" he cried, bucking his hips, thrusting his hardness against her naked body. She felt something jab between her thighs and she twisted, gyrating, straining every muscle to resist what seemed inevitable.

When his hands left her throat to grab at her breasts, she seized the moment to inhale deeply and screamed, "RED SKY!"

Her assailant cursed and slapped her viciously. The blow whipped her head against the cold ground. For a terrible moment, she was blind. There was no dark or light, no tent, no man, nothing.

Then like a mountain mist the darkness lifted and Malka saw Red Sky creep behind the man, his gleaming knife upraised, silently closer, his arm descending in a whistling arc. The blade penetrated the man's meaty back with a sickening thunk.

He made a horrid gurgling sound as he rolled off Malka's body, blood spurting from the wound. Red Sky sheathed his knife, picked up Malka in his arms, and carried her out of the tent, his face black with fury. A small crowd, alarmed by the screams, gathered outside and watched in stunned silence as Red Sky put Malka down on the grass and wiped away her tears.

"What the hell happened?" one man asked.

"Don't know," another said. "Something mighty bad, though, for that Injun to be so riled up."

One of the women, wringing her hands, walked up to Red Sky and whispered, "What can I do? Can I help?"

"Missy hurt," he said, "shirt torn. Can you fix?"

"Land's sakes," the woman cried, taking a good look at Malka. "What happened to the poor thing?"

She knelt and stroked Malka's head, dabbing at the blood and tears with her nightshirt. Then she looked at Red Sky. "You do this to her? Shame on you! Shame on you!"

The crowd murmured in a collective voice of outrage. One by one, they began moving threateningly toward Red Sky, their minds quickly made up.

"This red man needs a lesson!"

"Hangin's too good for him!"

"Well . . . there's a tree. Let's string him up!"

Red Sky was grabbed by two men and dragged to a clearing between the tents. Everyone cheered as a third man produced a rope and slung it over a low-hanging branch.

Someone brought a rock and placed it under the rope. Red Sky was lifted under the arms and forced to stand on the rock while curses were shouted and vile epithets echoed through the deep woods and rang across the river. The crowd surged into the clearing to watch the hanging, and throw stones and hunks of caked mud at the man who had defiled their white sister.

Yet even as they tightened the noose around Red Sky's neck, he said nothing. White men were deaf to an Indian's cries of innocence. He closed his eyes and prayed to the Great Spirit for a quick death. The yelling seemed fainter, the voices receding; he was glad of that. He did not want to hear those lies. A shout. Then a push off the rock. The rope pulled his neck, squeezed the muscle and sinew and skin; his legs thrashed in the air. He heard Missy shouting from a great distance.

"STOP!" Malka's tortured voice screamed, startling the crowd into silence. "Red Sky no hurt Malka!" She stumbled toward the clearing, clutching at shreds of linen to cover herself. "Red Sky good man! Save Malka's life . . . cut rope! CUT! NOW!"

A man pulled his knife, severed the rope and Red Sky dropped to the ground.

Malka rushed to him, yelling to the crowd, "Go and see the body lying in my tent. Man is in there."

The crowd surged to the tent, ripped open the flap,

"Lookee there," said one, "it's Ewald. Deader'n a door-nail!"

"Ewald?" cried another. "Why, that fool! What the hell he thinkin' of, to . . . ?"

The Chicago detective pushed them aside, kneeled over the body, felt for a pulse and turned to the crowd. "He's dead, all right. And from what I can see, it was a righteous killing."

He pushed the men out of the tent and said, "You all owe that Indian an apology." But they were unable to admit their mistake, and the detective spoke for them.

"Red Sky," he said to the Indian, "these people have a

strange sense of justice. They're good people, but too quick to act and too slow to think. If we're all going to finish this journey in peace, please accept this apology for their stupidity. Maybe it'll help to know they would have done the same to someone trying to hurt you."

Red Sky rubbed where the rope had bruised his neck, then said, "Red Sky has no bad feeling. No like to kill man, but take job very serious to pack Missy, keep Missy safe."

He walked to his sleeping bag outside Malka's tent, sat down, crossed his legs, and stared into space

"You can't go back in there, with that body and all," the woman said, "Why don't you spend the rest of the night with me. My man can sleep outside. "

Malka shook her head. "No, I stay with Red Sky." She sat down on the ground next to him and listened to the sounds of the awakening forest. When she trembled, he covered her with his blanket.

"Malka is now . . . broken goods?" she asked in a small voice.

"No. Missy still . . ." A faint blush crept under his brown skin. He shifted uncomfortably. "Devil-man not hurt Missy . . . that way. Red Sky kill man first."

"I feel shame," she said in a small voice. There were no words to describe the dirty hands that had mauled her. His image loomed in her mind like a demon from the bowels of hell and she feared it might never go away.

"Missy?"

"Yes?"

"You see devil-man before?"

"Yes."

"Why you not tell me?"

"I . . . I wanted to, but afraid you think Malka silly." Then she asked, "You were sitting outside tent. Why didn't you see him?"

"Devil-man come in back way, after I make my circle."
He explained his habit of walking around her tent many
times during the night to protect against just such attacks,
and against wild animals. He had completed his roundabout
only minutes before the attack.

"No use talking about it," she said.

"Don't think now. Evil is part of life. Trick is know one
from other. Missy will learn."

Malka nodded, her face squinched and resolute. But sobs
shook her body.

The Indian sat, impassive, his heart breaking for his
Missy. He could not comfort her. Braves stand alone. Women
tend babies. After a while he said, "You some smart lady. No
swim before rapids, right?" At her look of surprise, he said,
"Oh, Red Sky know things. Now Missy can swim. Yes? And
you learn fast. You help with boat and no sit like fancy pants
under umbrella. You strong, Missy. And you forget devil-
man so life goes on."

He nodded his head as if saying that's it, lady, now it's up
to you, Malka was touched by Red Sky's efforts to console
her. She wiped her face with the shirt and said, "Red Sky
friend of Malka forever, like Chinese believe when someone
saves life, that life belong to Chinaman. Red Sky now belong
to Malka."

"Missy no Chinaman," he said coolly. "Missy is brave
lady and save Red Sky from hanging. Now all is fair and
square. We even."

"Fair and square," she repeated, "we even."

TWENTY-FIVE

✁

SHORTLY BEFORE NOON, THEY SAILED INTO LAKE LEBARGE. The beauty was sudden and spectacular.

"Red Sky! Look! Water is blue like a jewel! And beach is white . . . like snow!"

He nodded, intent on getting through the upcoming Thirty-Mile River without mishap. He would leave the glory of the scenery to his client.

The sun caught the gleaming domes of mountains to the east, and Malka saw bluebells and lupins running in fields of violet across the cliffs. The perfume of wild roses floated on the hot breeze, and vines heavy with fruit ripened on the rocky, moss-covered shore.

She spotted camps on these shores with raggedy children sitting at smoky fires, and heard the words, "How muchee? How muchee?" ringing across the water.

"Who are they?" she asked Red Sky.

"Stick Indians. They smoke salmon, and want to buy or trade for whiskey. Pay them no mind. No more talk. Missy row. Red Sky rest."

The Indian put up his oar, lay back in the stern, pushed his wide-brimmed hat over his face and slept.

Neither one had mentioned last night's incident. Malka's face was bruised, but the marks were light and would fade.

Red Sky snoozed, still wearing the bloodstained shirt. She guessed he had his reasons.

She took over the oars, looking behind her as she rowed, basking in the stillness, the quiet broken only by the shouts from shore or boaters' greetings as they sailed by.

Looking down, Malka studied the rash of new freckles and sun blisters across her hands and wrists. She was grateful for the hat Red Sky had brought for her in his small bag that first day. It was made of woven reed, large-brimmed like his to keep the sun from her face, and tied securely under her chin.

The strong sun warmed her, and a light wind and the deep silence lulled her into a mechanical motion, pull, up, pull, up. A strong current slowly tugged at the boat, and Malka tightented her grip on the oars.

Idly gawking at the scenery, she had entered Thirty-Mile River, one of the most treacherous of the Yukon's twisting streams. The water was swift and clear and a miraculous blue. She could see half-submerged rocks ahead, leaping out at her from their white sprays.

She thought of waking Red Sky, but the boat was suddenly caught in one of the convoluted spins near the rocks. It twirled briefly in a circle, then zoomed out with the current into the calm of the Lewes River. Malka laughed. She had just pulled through a whirlpool with no damage to the boat. The victory made her feel cocky.

But when she looked behind her, the laugh stuck in her throat. The scow was heading straight for another set of rapids, the river's five fingers boiling between four huge boulders. She would have screamed, but her voice locked with fear. Holding the oars with stiff arms, she must have looked like a statue to the Mountie watching and guiding boats from shore.

"Stay to the right channel, Miss, stay to the right!" he yelled.

"Wha . . . what?"

The Mountie ran along with the boat and yelled again, "Stay to the right channel. You'll make it! Stay to the right!"

Quickly, Malka brought her left oar into play, dragging it in the churning water to swing the boat over to the right-hand side. She was almost to the rocks now, and angled the oars up to keep them from splintering.

Red Sky woke, his sharp eyes quickly taking in the situation. Planting his feet firmly on the boat floor, he gripped the sides and watched as they headed straight for the rocks, spinning around at the last minute to slide with the current into the clear water ahead.

Malka exhaled loudly. "Whew! That was good?"

"Good!" he answered.

"It is like test to Malka," she said, turning bright blue eyes to the Indian. Her long hair, freed from its braids weeks before, blew around her face in the high wind, black tendrils catching on her lashes and mouth. Freckles splashed across her small nose, her cheeks pink from the wind and sun.

"What is test?" Red Sky asked.

"You, and mountain pass, and boat, and this crazy ride up . . ."

"Down," he corrected.

" . . . down river. The Holy One must want Malka and Jacob together. Malka pass test, yes?"

He studied her, his Missy, looking pretty and petite and upright. Maybe there *was* hope for skinny white ladies. They were not all like flowers, crumbling with the first frost or hot sun.

"Missy pass test," he grudgingly agreed. "But no rest yet. More water. Then Dawson."

"Dawson!" Malka cried. "Can I believe it?"

He nodded. Then asked, "Why you go to Dawson? Missy look for gold?"

"Jacob is in Dawson. I will marry Jacob."

"You come all this way, climb mountains over pass, down lakes and rapids, to marry . . . Jacob?"

"There's more," she laughed. "I come from very far away in a big boat with many people. Then a train ride across America, a small boat to Alaska . . ."

"Stop!" Red Sky said. "It make me tired to hear Missy talk." He closed his eyes, thinking, then opened them. "This Jacob," he mumbled, straightening his big hat, "is lucky man."

Malka blushed at the unexpected compliment and stared at her bare feet. They, like the rest of her, were filthy, blistered, and bruised. Her clothes were in rags, she was a mass of bruises and sores, and she looked like a dirty bundle of laundry. Considering this, in the light of Red Sky's words, she wondered if Jacob would agree.

TWENTY-SIX

❦

JACOB WAS CERTAIN MALKA'S JOURNEY FROM KHOTIN had started around the beginning of April, but he could only guess at the date of her arrival in America, or the actual route she was taking to Dawson. And guesswork was no help in figuring time and distance. His best move was to prepare himself and Dawson for her arrival, the sooner the better.

He was shameless, nagging anyone who would listen and boring them with details and descriptions of his bride-to-be. He spoke of her endlessly to friends and strangers alike, from the gold fields to the beach. He alerted idle deckhands and the Northwest Mounties, those intrepid peacekeepers, who insisted that everyone entering and leaving Dawson sign in and out of the log book. He haunted the shipping companies, checking and rechecking schedules and procedures.

Recruiting volunteers from among the merchants, miners, barkeeps and dance hall girls, he showed them her picture, extracting promises from them that they watch for her among incoming passengers. They told him it was too early, the river was still solid ice, but Jacob insisted, reminding them over and over, never letting go of the subject until one of the men laughed and said Malka's face was now as familiar to him as his own mother's.

Not willing to chance missing her, Jacob took up his own

watch on the beach. By the end of May he was there every day. He roamed among the hundreds of tents erected by brand new "boom-towners," those men too green and too frightened to move from the safe haven of the riverfront. They formed a readymade corps of spotters, clinging together there and at the saloons.

Rabinowitz was right; these same men would soon turn around and go home, no richer, no wiser, but with a fortune's worth of adventure that would keep growing through the years like the story of the fish that got away. Until then, he told himself, they could watch for Malka.

When the commercial steamers and the strangely assorted fleet began arriving in Dawson, he prowled the shore day after day, beginning to look as odd and conspicuous as the boats. Because of Dingo's melting machine, many knew Jacob as "Almost Famous Jake." Almost famous, and almost worth a million dollars. But fame and fortune are all in the timing, and Jacob's was bad. The hydraulic mining companies moved into Dawson, and their huge pumps and water jets worked faster than fires or melting machines. Jacob had neither time nor money to fight the big companies with their huge financial backing. Nor was he a *schlemiel*. He did not land on his back and bruise his nose. He landed on his feet. He took out the patent in Dingo's name, had one machine built at the foundry in Dawson, and put his name as president of the company on the Klondike Melting Machine Company's official stationery. The beautiful bond paper and embossed envelopes were placed in a sealed box, along with the patent papers and a letter from Dingo's cousin who appeared out of nowhere. "happy to settle for fifty thousand dollars. After all, I'm not greedy!"

With all this behind him, Almost Famous Jake was just one of the guys, digging, panning, looking for the elusive mother lode, and waiting for Malka.

By the last day in May, he began to worry. "Take it easy, Jake," one man said. "One of these days she'll be here."

Jacob's eyes clouded with misgiving and he shook his head. "Think she could be lost?"

"Nah, Jake," the man said, lighting a hand-rolled cigarette, "not lost. If she's comin' by any of the regular ways, there'll be hundreds of people with her. She cain't get lost."

"What if she lies hurt somewhere, with no help? What if her boat sank? What if . . . "

"Seems to me you're jest askin' to worry," the old fellow scolded. "You can go on with your 'what ifs,' Jake, but that won't help none. Look," he said, putting an arm around Jacob's shoulder, which took some doing since he was a head shorter, "I'll be settin' right here on the beach. I know what she looks like by now. Believe me, that face is burned into my memory! And a lot of the other fellers too. We'll nab her when she gets here. Now go along and get to work. You don't want that pretty little thing to marry a pauper, do ya?"

The man was right, but the days passed slowly. Jacob worked his claim from early morning to evening, then swept and tidied the one-room house. He installed real glass in the windows and chinked fresh moss between the logs to keep out the rain. But time dragged, as if all the clocks in Dawson had stopped.

The fifth of June was a sultry, windless day on the beach, but by early evening a light breeze on shore brought some relief to the sweltering crowds. Jacob heard one of the steamers chugging slowly in from upriver. When it rounded the bend, he recognized the little *Bella*, the ship that had brought him to Dawson a year ago. His heart beat faster. She must be on this boat; the time was right, and the waiting could not go on forever.

He hurried to the dock and leaped onto the wooden pier, running along its length, scanning the crowd. The dapper

Mounties were everywhere, checking people and boats and gear, determined to keep order amidst the chaos. Jacob spied his spotters, his friends, neighbors, hundreds of arrivals, but no Malka.

With the *Bella* unloaded, he returned to the beach and searched among the faces as the smaller boats pulled in, some in clumps, but most straggling in one by one.

An old miner ambled over. "She weren't on the *Bella*."

"I guess not."

"The *Weare*'ll be comin' any day now; she may be on that. And there be others. A lot of us are lookin', Jake. There's Rufe, and Chester, Old Billy and the Clancy boys, and . . ."

Jacob smiled. "What would I do without friends?"

"What's a friend for? The good Lord put us on earth to look after one another. And that's jest what we're doin'." He spat and wiped his chin. "Y'know, you can check with the Mounties," he reminded Jacob. "They make lists of people comin' in over the Chilkoot. And duty lists, too. She could be on one of them."

Jacob shook his head. He had warned her not to take that route. But he had to do something. At the dock's police desk, he reminded the Mountie about Malka and asked if her name was on the new list.

"This is the latest one," the Mountie said, riffling through a sheaf of papers, "and it's from April. But if your girl left Russia around the first, she wouldn't have reached the pass by then. The new lists will come in next week. If you come back, we can check them again."

Where was she? Would he have to spend the rest of his life on this miserable beach, waiting?

It was not just the loneliness. He was impatient to share the beauty of this new country, the mountains and the lakes, the colors of fall, the kindness of his new friends. Waiting was the worst part of the whole matrimonial arrangement. During the months between Malka's acceptance of his proposal and her departure from Khotin, he thought he had shown remarkable patience. Now, with her arrival imminent, his frustration gnawed at his temper and disposition until both were fraying rapidly. So was Malka's as her destination grew close.

Soon after going through the Five Finger Rapids, Red Sky assured her Dawson City was only hours away. She tried to smooth the rumples in her scruffy clothes and remove the muddiest spots, but nothing would help return the outfit to its former grandeur, or even respectability.

She brushed her long hair, but when she began braiding it, Red Sky shook his head.

"What do you mean, 'no'?" she asked.

"No tie up hair. Jacob want woman with pretty long hair. Braid is for old lady."

"Indeed! And how does Red Sky know what Jacob wants?"

Ignoring her sharpness, he responded, "Red Sky is man. Jacob is man. Missy pretty with long hair. If Missy tie up hair, she look like old squaw with no man. Old squaw with no man no good!"

"I see," she said. "All right, I take advice of Red Sky. No braids, But," she said, grimacing, "what can I do with the rest of me?"

Red Sky took in his charge from top to toe, then began his slow smile.

"Oh. Here comes joke now?" Malka asked.

He shook his head. "No joke. Missy is fine. Trip from Skagway no happy dance around fire. No one think Missy should come to Dawson like queen! Red Sky say Missy wash her feet in river, put shoes on and smile. Then like queen!"

Malka could not help but be charmed by his logic. She

did smile, and trailed one foot at a time in the water, wiping them dry with a piece of gunny sacking. Turning modestly away from the Indian, she pulled on the heavy stockings, slipped her sore, blistered feet into her shoes, laced them up over the ankle and turned around.

"So!" Hands on her knees, elbows akimbo, she challenged him to criticize the result.

"Good," he said. "Missy fine. Ready for wedding." He picked up her oar, handed it over and said, "Now help row. Missy not queen yet!"

The afternoon was stifling, not a breeze, not a shady spot on the river to provide relief from the burning sun. The evening would be the same.

Nighthawks cried among the trees bordering the river, and Malka began to hum in imitation of the sound.

"Missy sing song?" Red Sky asked.

"Bird song. You like it?"

He nodded.

She felt a rush of affection for him. Perhaps it was the heat or the peace around them, or being together for almost two months. They would part in Dawson, and she still knew nothing about him.

"Where is home?" she asked Red Sky.

"Home is in Skagway now. Not always. If I say more, get in trouble."

"But why?"

"Not sure if I belong to Canada or USA. Indian camp not keep records. Mother dead. Father dead. Have no more family. It make big trouble if . . . how you say, cizzun . . . ship is question."

"I see. Red Sky has no papers, right?"

He nodded. "Why you ask, Missy?"

"I want to know my friend better. You go back to Skagvay after Dawson?"

He shook his head. "Not know yet. Maybe stay, look for gold like crazy white man."

Malka laughed. "Then who will Red Sky pay to pack over pass?"

He laughed too. "Old Indian saying: when chief use brave for work, chief is master. When brave use chief, is the end of world."

His smile faded. "No way Red Sky can win."

"Not true!" Malka protested. "All men can win, rich or poor. My people have old saying too: a man is what he is, not what he used to be."

Red Sky closed his eyes, apparently thinking over Malka's words. When he opened them he looked as if a big decision had been made. "Is strange, Missy saying sound like Indian. Maybe both our people the same."

"Maybe. Both believe in God."

"Mmm."

"And both wandering, looking for home."

"Yes," Red Sky said.

"And both can make good from bad, turn life around. Can have heaven or hell. But is for us to choose."

The boat drifted in silence. Red Sky let the oars dangle in the water, his face impassive, black eyes staring into space.

"Life is like walking on ice. Not know if you can until you try. You can fall and break your neck or . . ."

"Or skate across," Malka challenged. "Is up to you."

He dipped his oars into the water. "Red Sky row now."

So that's that, Malka thought. This strange, confusing man had allowed only the briefest glimpse into who he was, then slammed the door shut. But she had seen inside and found a man of strength and dignity in place of the grumpy, toothpick-chewing Indian remembered from the first day. A friend, true and heroic during the long, frightening days on the trail. How could she know anyone better than that?

If only she knew as much about Jacob. All she did know was written in his letters. Otherwise, Jacob Finesilver was unrevealed.

Her life would soon change drastically. She wondered how much, and in what ways, and how she would handle it. Would Jacob deny her the freedom of choice she had known with her father, the choice to read books, cook, work in the garden, use her own time in her own way rather than have it scheduled for her? Would he be an old-fashioned husband, the tyrant married to many of her friends? Would he expect her to work by his side all day, mining, shoveling, whatever it was he did to dig up gold? She had made a bargain, after all, and that might be part of it. But she also knew his expectations did not stop there.

This was the part that puzzled her. The physical aspects of marriage had rarely occurred to Malka before now, except in the briefest romantic daydreams. The actual procedure was undefined. Although her friends had promised to reveal everything after their weddings, they never had. Blushing and tearful, they stopped short of an accurate explanation, leaving her to wonder if the cause of their reticence was pain or pleasure. The vague ritual loomed before her as bewildering as ever.

She shook off the unsettling subject and turned her thoughts to life here in this unbelievable world. There was no way of guessing what it really offered. But that was half the fun of anticipation, she thought. The worst of it was the waiting. But that, along with this improbable journey, would soon end.

Her musings were interrupted by Red Sky's sudden cry. "Look! On bluff is Fort Selkirk."

Malka turned, seeing only some ruined red chimneys that nestled in the overgrowth above the river. "Where is the fort?"

"Gone. Nothing left. But big fort once. Indians raid, then burn down building." Red Sky patted his lips and gave out a bloodcurdling yell. "That is the war cry of fathers and grandfathers and many before that, but no one makes war now."

Malka grinned, "I am happy to hear that."

A short time later, the main body of the Yukon swept swiftly past the openings into the Stewart and Indian Rivers. Here the current was stronger, tugging and pushing the scow in different directions. Malka and Red Sky stabilized their course until they reached quieter water. Then she was able to gawk at the riot of flowers blooming on the hills, the shadowy forest shooting out flames of color, reds and salmon and dark pinks, tall thickets of blooms climbing as high as the trees. Moss growing along the banks looked orange in the eerie twilight, and a spark of iridescent blue flickered among the fireweed.

"Is big change in your great river," she said, "since we leave Lake Bennett, yes?"

"Yes."

"Before there is nice calm water, then whoosh! Big rapids dump boat into water."

"Maybe Missy has to go under," Red Sky observed, "hold hand of death before she know river."

"Maybe, but it has great power, this Yukon, and I have much re . . . how you say it? . . . re . . . ?"

"Respek," Red Sky said.

"Yes. I have much respek for Yukon. River is life to all this country." She held out her arms as if to say the world around them was now an intimate friend. Red Sky watched her, his eyes never leaving her face.

"I thank you, Red Sky, for all your help and care. And to teach me respek for Yukon."

"Red Sky say okay. Now Missy keep rowing."

She laughed. "You are worse than Pharaoh!"

She closed her eyes and thanked the Holy One, Praised Be He, for watching over her and her friend on this arduous journey. But stay with us, oh Lord, she added, the river may have more tricks up its sleeve.

The boat swung suddenly in a swift turn around the rocky bluff, and Malka saw the Klondike River thundering into the Yukon from the right. This was the sight Red Sky had told her to watch for, this and the mountain in back of the river, its front slope scooped out from an ancient slide.

Trembling with excitement, Malka saw the "city of gold" sprouting from the midst of the wilderness, so real, yet so alien she half expected everything to disappear in the shimmering heat. Where large buildings stood along the shore, others stretched back almost to the mountain. Tents, too, as at Lake Bennett, but hundreds more people, throngs moving in every direction.

One minute she had been in the wild country, the quiet so profound that bird calls shattered the stillness. Now suddenly she had entered a frenetic, boisterous world where the shouts of human voices mixed with the lowing of cattle, the neighing of horses and the bleat of frightened chickens. It was just like the scene at Lake Bennett, though on a larger scale.

She had arrived in Dawson City. A new road lay ahead, and it was Jacob now who would lead her along its uncertain paths.

He must be there somewhere on the beach. Surely he would come to meet the boat. But how would he know? And how was she to find him among those thousands of people? As if in a dream, Malka stepped from the scow into the cold water, searching for a man who looked the way Jacob had described himself: tall, black hair, blue eyes and red beard, though she could not remember if he wore it in summer or winter. But every man there on this beach matched that description.

Suddenly one man shouted, then another, and still another, until a dozen men came running toward the shore. "Malka?" one of the men asked. He was short, fat and elderly, almost her father's age. Her face crumbled with disappointment.

"Yes. I am Malka," she said.

"Is it Malka?" another man cried, joining the first. He was younger, but short and scrawny. She stared at him, her heart sinking.

"It's her, all right," the first man said, smiling.

More men surrounded her.

"Well, I'll be."

"She's purty as her pitcher."

"Hey, everybody," one yelled to the crowd, "she's here! Malka's here!"

Confused, Malka looked from one face to the other. One of the Mounties headed in her direction, smiling. Others pointed or stared or called to each other as they hurried toward her. But when the tall figure came running from across the beach, square-jawed, clean-shaven, his form moving gracefully at a full run in the sand, she knew it was Jacob. It was not even strange to her that she accepted the fact so quickly. This was the man to whom she had promised her life.

Stopping in front of her, his breath ragged, he said nothing for what seemed a long time. Then, finally, "Malka?" he asked.

"Yes, I am Malka," she answered in Yiddish. (*His eyes are bright blue, deep and gentle, happy, I think, to see me.*)

"Welcome to Dawson City, Malka. I am Jacob Finesilver." (*She is so much smaller than I expected, but Meyer warned me. I should have believed him.*)

"I am happy to be here at last." (*He is not wearing a beard. I am glad of that.*)

"You must have had a difficult journey." *(Her face is smudged with dirt, but her eyes are so blue and snapping with life.)*

"Yes, very difficult. But also very beautiful." *(He is so tall, I am getting a crick in my neck.)*

"We have much to talk about, Malka."

"Yes. I know." *(He is handsome, and his physique is large and muscular. Very romantic. . . .)*

A small group broke from the crowd and encircled them, laughing and chattering.

"You have so many friends," Malka said. "I am impressed with your popularity."

"Yes, I'm very lucky."

"It's as if the whole city of Dawson has come to greet me."

"I'm glad you're so well received," Jacob said. His tongue was beginning to stick to the roof of his mouth. He had never been so nervous, not even when facing down Cossacks on his flight from Khotin.

Red Sky stood silently by the boat, watching Malka and Jacob as they spoke together. Loath to interrupt them, he was also very tired and wanted to lie down.

"You did not come on the *Bella* from St. Michael as I suggested?" Jacob asked.

"No, the route over the pass was shorter, and I saved many miles that way."

"How did you know that? How did you learn of the pass?"

Malka blushed. "Captain Potemkin drew a map for me. He explained how many miles I would save and recommended the route in summer."

"Captain Potemkin?" Jaocb frowned. "Who is that?"

"The captain of the *Nicolai*. He was very kind."

She had not missed the flicker of jealousy in his eyes. Coolly, she said, "You are fortunate to have many friends,

Jacob. I'm sure they have made your life more pleasant here. I, too, am fortunate, for along the very difficult way from home, I found friends in unexpected places. I'm sure you are as happy for me as I am for you."

Her dazzling smile captivated him, and in spite of the dirt streaked across her forehead, the tattered clothes, the bruised and sunburned face, he thought her as pretty as Meyer had promised. And clever as well.

"We must see to your comfort, Malka," he said, "and then we can continue our discussion . . . to become better acquainted with each other."

"Yes, but first I must say goodbye to my friend."

She turned to Red Sky. "Jacob, this is Andrew Red Sky. He carried supplies for me over the mountain pass and brought me safely after many dangerous adventures to this place."

Jacob extended his hand, wondering how she and this Indian had traveled together all that way, day and night. But he shook Red Sky's hand and mumbled his gratitude in English.

"Missy is fine lady," Red Sky replied shyly.

"Glad to hear that," Jacob said, "may I pay you for . . . Missy?"

"All done. Indian say, no money, no work. White man say, no work, no money. Missy, Red Sky work it out."

Malka shook hands with Red Sky then, and with no thought for the crowds looking on, hugged him tightly.

"I will never forget you Red Sky," she said, "you save life of Malka for Jacob. This is not the end, for you are my best friend, always."

The Indian nodded solemnly, turned away and melted into the crowd.

Malka watched him until he was out of sight, then turned, waiting for Jacob to make the next move.

He arranged with friends to take care of the boat and Malka's gear, then turned to her with a smile. "So here you are. Tired and hungry, no doubt?" *(If she is so small, how will she have the strength to help me?)*

"Yes." *(If he knew how tired and hungry I am, he would send me back to Russia.)*

"Well, we shall be on our way to my little house then, to offer you a bath and a good hot supper, yes?"

Malka hesitated, cocked her head, struggling to express herself. But the words had to be said.

"I'm afraid, Jacob, that I can go nowhere with you until we are man and wife. Certainly not to your house. Although I'm most anxious to see where we shall be living. The agreement, after all, was . . ."

"Of course. Of course!" Jacob shook off his apparent stupidity and gave Malka a foolish grin. "We'll find the judge in town. Don't worry. He's a fine man, an American, a real judge. Will you agree to that?"

"There is no rabbi?" Malka whispered.

"Here?" Jacob laughed. "I fear not, Malka. This is the end of the world, after all! We do have a priest, however. And an Anglican minister. And two Protestant ministers. That should give you some idea of the Jewish population in Dawson, eh?"

"Only you?" Malka asked, surprised.

"Yes, and you, also, makes two. No, I am forgetting Mr. Rabinowitz from Seattle, and Mr. Levy from Boston. So that is four. Not quite enough for a *minyan.*"

"But could we have a *chupah?* At least a *chupah?*"

"I don't see why not," Jacob said, immediately regretting the rash promise. Finding a canopy at nine o'clock at night would not be easy. Was she willful? Demanding? What have I gotten myself into?

He took Malka's hand and guided her across the swampy,

tent-strewn sand to Front Street. He had not felt this way since leaving Khotin, half-frightened, half-confident, nervous but enthusiastic. His future with this woman was uncertain, yet it was like his long journey, full of promise.

Malka had trouble keeping up with his long strides. Finally she let go of his hand and stood back from him on the sidewalk.

"I'm tired, Jacob. I cannot walk so fast. Besides, I want to look around slowly and see the buildings and the town. You must point them out to me, tell me about them, perhaps introduce me to more of your friends. I've come a long way. It is only proper that I have a chance to observe my destination."

"Of course. Forgive me. I was anxious to find the judge."

"I'm sure," she said, trying not to appear headstrong or cranky, "he will be available an hour from now."

They continued walking, this time more slowly. Jacob pointed out the slide in the Midnight Dome, the assaying office, the doctor's house, stables, warehouses, all that they passed. But he was impatient.

I have waited so long to hold a soft woman in my arms. She is so tiny but quite curvaceous. I can almost see her lovely body under those torn, muddy clothes. And I will not apologize for these feelings. I only hope I will not be clumsy, that I do it right. I don't want her to hate me from our first hours together.

Malka listened to his descriptions, but her thoughts were elsewhere.

Why does he go so fast? Is he in such a hurry to get me to bed? Is this why men in far-off places send for wives? There must be other reasons, as he outlined in his letter. I prefer to think that way. And what is it that I do once we are married? I don't want to disappoint him. But I have feelings too. Will I be disappointed? This is so baffling. There must be more to marriage than what goes on in bed. I will sew for him some fine new shirts. And cook delicious meals. And keep the house tidy. That will satisfy him. What more could he want?

There was no little voice this time. It was silent. Malka had nothing to guide her except her own yearning and painful ignorance. She was frightened. God willing, they will live through this uncertainty and fear together.

TWENTY-SEVEN

⁂

JUDGE HENNEPIN'S HOUSE, WITH ITS GINGERBREAD TRIM and fancy carved porch railing, nestled behind the police station at the south end of town. Here in the cluttered parlor Malka and Jacob were married.

In this summer of '98, Hennepin was the only judge in Dawson. There had been three, but one had died of pneumonia and another had been invited to leave town after a scandal involving shares in a salted mine. Hennepin alone ruled the legal roost.

Now, in his hastily donned black suit and black string tie, he nodded to his wife seated at the organ. The wedding march wheezed forth from the ancient instrument, Mrs. Hennepin dabbing at her eyes between chords. Malka and Jacob held hands under the hastily contrived *chupah*, the canopy of cloth and wooden poles thrown together with the help of the Judge's children, who stood together as witnesses to the wedding, giggling and poking at each other.

Judge Hennepin had been reading his newspaper, dressed in pajamas and robe and sipping from a tumbler of whiskey when Jacob rang the bell. Not in the least annoyed by the request, short-notice marriages in Dawson occurring regularly, he quickly changed into his judge's robes, gathered together his wife and three children from the yard where they had been feeding chickens, and presided before the nervous couple.

"Judge, sir, Your Honor," Jacob said, "before you start service, I must say prayers."

The judge frowned. "Prayers? What prayers?"

"Jewish prayers, sir, tradition."

"How nice," his wife called from her organ seat.

"Quiet, Hattie. Prayers, eh? You people sure do things differently, don't you?"

"Differences make people interesting. If all of us cut out like cookies, world is dull place."

Malka looked at Jacob proudly, his retort to the Judge's slur accurate and thoughtful without being impolite. She admired him for that.

Judge Hennepin grunted. "You have a point, young man. Very well, say your prayers."

Jacob began to sing the benedictions—one honoring the religious aspect of the marriage, the next giving thanks to God for bestowing His image on human life and the blessing of marriage—and finished with prayers for his and Malka's happiness and for the restoration of Jerusalem.

Malka looked charming in her simple white cotton dress. The veil was donated by the judge's wife, who also insisted on picking a spray of white flowers from her garden for Malka's bouquet. They had washed and changed at the Yukon Hotel, Jacob paying for the room in advance. "But we will not stay here," Malka had protested.

"True, but we must prepare for our wedding," Jacob explained, "and you will not use my house—with which I agree," he added hastily. "Therefore, we'll bathe and change here. You first."

The warm bath refreshed Malka, bringing to her skin a radiance she had thought lost in the mountain pass. The mirror reassured her that the dress was perfect, fitting her well, although a bit low in front. She had lost so much weight the fabric sagged, and nothing could be done. It was not immodest, she finally told herself, it was stylish. It was also pretty, the swell of her bosom just visible at the edge of the lace. Soon she would be a woman. It was time she looked like one.

Jacob borrowed fresh clothes from the hotel's owner, a young man tall and slim like his Jewish friend and delighted to help the groom. The dark suit fit well, Jacob thought, hardly recognizing himself in the formal attire. He turned in the mirror, pleased that he looked so mature. The tie was a puzzle, and he had to call Malka to do it properly. She smiled, spreading the material until it lay neatly tied at his collar.

Jacob held her close. "Malka," he said softly, "you're very beautiful. I am . . . happy."

"I too, Jacob," she said. With his arms around her, Malka trembled, her legs suddenly weak. She felt a rush of warmth that wrapped her in a comforting cloak from her toes to her flaming cheeks, and she trembled with the strange new feeling.

"You're nervous," Jacob said, "I can feel it."

"No, not nervous, Jacob. I guess it's excitement that makes me tremble. I'm not sure. I have never been married before."

He laughed. "There will be many moments of trembling like this."

"You know this? How can you be so sure?"

"We're strangers to each other. Until we learn what to say or do as husband and wife, I think we will feel as we do now."

Jacob stepped back and gazed at Malka, unable to hide his longing. His eyes revealed the depth of his passion, intense and frighteningly seductive.

"We must go now," she said.

"Afraid, Malka?"

Without thinking, she answered, "Yes."

"Of me?"

"No . . . I mean . . . I don't know."

"We will be learning together. Does that help?"

Malka thought a moment, wondering if innocence was all that desirable. If he were experienced, she might not be so frightened. But then there would be comparisons. And her ignorance was against her.

"Jacob, please promise me you'll be patient. I . . . I know nothing about . . ."

"No more talk." Jacob took her hand. "First the wedding. What comes later is up to both of us. I will not, I promise you, act alone. Do you understand?"

Malka smiled. "Yes."

Jacob finished the prayers. The judge cleared his throat and began to read from his leather-bound book. The children giggled, and at last the judge declared the couple man and wife.

Jacob placed the glass, wrapped in a blue damask napkin, under his heel and smashed it. Mrs. Hennepin was so moved, she attacked the keyboard with renewed abandon, playing the music of the recessional until the glass knickknacks danced on the ornate shelves and the walls of the small house vibrated.

As Malka and Jacob raced down the front steps, the judge called, "Throw the flowers!" The white spray flew through the air and was caught by the youngest boy.

They entered the small cabin and Jacob stood aside to allow Malka her first glimpse of home.

"You built this? All by yourself? It's a wonderful cabin, Jacob. I'm truly impressed."

"Thank you. It's been my home for many months. I'm glad you approve."

Malka walked to the window and tried to touch the rays of the orange sun streaming through the new clear glass.

"It's beautiful, the sunshine, like a fire burning outside. But it will be that way all night, won't it?"

"It goes down for a few hours. But it never really grows dark," Jacob said.

Malka nodded. "I would like the dark better."

"I understand. I guess I would, too."

He sat on the chair, Malka on the edge of the bed, absently smoothing the material of her skirt.

"Your dress is so beautiful," Jacob said. "Did you make it?"

"Yes. I make all my clothes. And Papa's, too."

"Really? Well then, you shall have another client now."

"Yes."

Jacob undid his tie slowly, afraid of alarming his bride. In a businesslike tone, he said, "Tomorrow we will make arrangements to bring your supplies here. You needn't worry about them in Dawson. They're safe."

"I know."

"You know?"

"Yes. Red Sky told me."

"Red Sky? Ah, the Indian, yes. A nice fellow."

"He's my dearest friend. He . . . he saved me . . . for you . . . from . . ."

"Oh, the rapids. I've heard . . ."

"Not just the rapids, Jacob. More than that. A dirty man in the camp . . ."

"I know what happened, Malka," Jacob said quickly. "My friend who owns the hotel told me. The whole town knows by this time."

Malka blushed with shame. "Oh, Jacob, how terrible."

"No, no. On the contrary, it is not terrible at all. You are still . . . that is, everyone knows you weren't hurt, and they know how bravely the Indian defended you. He'll be very welcome in Dawson, if he chooses to stay."

Suddenly weary from the long trip, the wedding, the uncertainties, everything that had happened to Malka in the last few weeks overwhelmed her. Now that she no longer needed strength for the journey, her senses numbed and her body seemed to float away.

But there was Jacob, waiting patiently to claim his rights as a husband. How was she to grant them, tired and frightened, with no darkness in which to hide?

Jacob watched her face, the expression shifting, eyes cast downward, the deep blush of her cheeks turning to ashes.

"Malka, let's go to sleep. We're both tired and there is no rush to . . ."

"But you have the right . . ."

"I do not have the right," he said firmly, "to force myself on a woman who is exhausted from a journey that would kill a horse. No. I would not be much of a man if I did. We're married and we have our whole life ahead of us. In fact, we have nothing but time," he added with a smile.

Malka looked at her husband—his handsome face, the romantic physique she had dreamed of—but who was a stranger. Grateful for his kindness and understanding, she knew that another kind of man would have shown impatience and demanded his conjugal rights without a minute's thought. Yet their approaching intimacies and the pain and embarrassment she feared awaited her, was almost too much to bear.

"I cannot, in truth, promise you it will be different tomorrow, Jacob."

"What will be, will be," he said, hoping to quiet her fears. A wife as frightened as a jackrabbit would be no inspiration in the marriage bed. At the same time, he could not help asking himself, *what* will be?

The young woman sitting on his bed was a cherished addition in his life. If he acted rashly, letting loose his years of pent-up frustrations and desires, she would probably give in. But there was no pleasure in that thought.

He felt their only chance lay in sharing the same desire, and that was not possible yet. Just as he had endured the hardships of his long walk, spurred on by the goal waiting for him at its end, he could now endure Malka's virginal anxieties. The goal, after all, was more lasting than gold. He hoped his body would not betray him under the covers.

TWENTY-EIGHT

⊱⊱⊱

NOT A SOUL IN DAWSON SUSPECTED THE TRUTH ABOUT Jacob and Malka's marriage, or its battleground so alien to newly wedded bliss. Privacy in this otherwise wild and uncivilized part of the world was as respected as an open cabin or a cache dropped in the snow. Malka and Jacob were left to flounder alone in their uncertain alliance. Shy and increasingly nervous, they attempted to build a relationship which, under the usual system of courtship, would have existed before the wedding. They learned from anecdotes about each other's family and home life, shared laughter and trivia, found some views in common, others completely at odds. But they achieved only a friendly partnership, with Malka working at Jacob's side on his claim and tending the vegetable garden on the cabin roof. Jacob had stated that he would dig in the hard, sun-baked earth and gravel, and Malka would wash the gold. She agreed, after seeing Jacob straining with the shovel in the wretched heat. She learned quickly, after the first unforgettable sighting, to spot a golden flake or two in the muddy water of the cleanup sluice. The roof garden was more pleasure than work. Vegetables grew to enormous size with long hours of sunshine, and jars of preserved peas and spinach and cabbage soon filled the shed at the back of the house. They planted onions and flowers on the cabin's south side, and the night air was fragrant with sweet peas, canary vine and wild roses.

Jacob and Malka were together constantly. It was inevitable that each would eventually yearn to push out the small space, to make room for that elusive solitude now even more precious. That their friendship survived was a miracle.

But friendship is not marriage, and Jacob was losing patience with his reluctant bride. His clothes were clean and pressed, new shirts lay in the wardrobe trunk, curtains cut the sun's glare at the window, and the dirt floor was swept and clean. But during the rare moment alone, he resented his continuing celibacy. The peculiar situation was far too complex for the novice husband to resolve.

Each night as they prepared for bed, he watched Malka closely for any thaw in her remote reclusion, but saw none. The affectionate wife at other times became a different woman who slipped silently under the quilt at night, keeping well to her side of the bed.

Lying awake for hours, he tried to reconcile this Malka with the cheerful girl who worked so amiably by his side. These first weeks of what should have been a joyous experience for both were tearing him apart. If the marriage was not consummated, was he really married in the eyes of God?

His physical torment and unanswered questions, sacred and legal, plagued his nights. Even his days began to suffer. His concentration shattered in the hot sun, flew apart like gravel from his shovel, and the exhilaration of wresting gold from the parched land turned as dry as the earth itself.

Malka sensed his frustration, but something inside her shriveled each time she undressed for bed. Pain, humiliation, the embarrassment of nakedness, all the nebulous, unfounded fears built on each other like multiplying cells and destroyed any chance for intimacy.

"I appreciate your patience, Jacob," she said one night when both were unable to sleep. "My reluctance will not last forever, I promise you."

Hearing no answer, Malka peered through the dim light. She could see Jacob's eyes, open and staring, his mouth turned down in a grim line. "Are you angry?" she asked.

"No."

"But you look angry."

"I can't help how I look."

"I can't blame you if you are. I'm not keeping my part of our bargain."

He sat up. He wore only pajama bottoms in the hot nights, and his naked back gleamed in the pale light.

"You don't understand, do you, Malka? It isn't your part or my part of any bargain that's important. It's how you feel. And for that, I can only blame myself."

"But why?"

"If I have to explain, forget it."

"But it's not you . . . it's me." She shifted position, sat up against the pillows, and tried another tack. "Jacob, remember the event that happened to me on the trail to Dawson? That vile man who tried to . . . to . . . "

"Yes, yes," he said, trying to dismiss the terrible picture in his mind.

"I think that is what has happened to me. I mean, oh, this is so difficult. . . ."

"Go on, it is the only way, Malka."

"Yes. Well, he frightened me so badly that I am still reacting to him with you. Does that make sense?"

"Yes. It's very clever of you to realize this is so. Perhaps if we talk about it, we can put it right."

"Yes. We must talk it out."

"Now, Malka."

"Now?"

"Yes. Now."

"Very well. You see, Jacob, it was the first time I had ever seen a man . . . like that. . . ."

"Naked, you mean?"

"Yes."

"And it repulsed you?"

"In a way. He was so filthy, so disgusting, I cannot begin to describe him."

Jacob thought a moment. "Yes, but you must realize, all men are not like that. Even your Indian, Red Sky, while he is tough, he is also a kind, goodhearted, and a brave fellow, a hero, really. He saved you, and killed the terrible man. He is not disgusting or filthy."

Malka looked toward Jacob in the dark, repeating his words to herself. They made sense.

"You accept that, yes? But will it change anything?"

"I hope so, but did it ever occur to you that I may have some expectations too?"

He was surprised and said, "Explain, Malka."

"You're waiting for me to make the first move. And I won't do that. You stare at me every night, trying to determine if this is the right time, or if I am ready, or whether I will refuse you. I only become more self-conscious, more tense. This hardly sets the mood for, well, romance."

If Jacob was wounded or angered, his expression gave nothing away.

After a while he said, "I love you, Malka. I think from the first moment I saw you on the beach I have loved you. The way you looked, so small and so, so disreputable . . ."

Malka laughed, encouraging Jacob to continue.

"I was so proud of you, coming all that way with only the Indian to guide you. Your courage, that was what I admired so much. Here you are, scared, for which I don't blame you, too frightened to even undress in front of me. My God,

Malka, you climbed the bloody Chilkoot! Did you leave all that bravery on top of the pass?"

"That was different," she said. "I *had* to do it."

"Oh, and this you do not have to do?"

"It's pointless to talk any further, Jacob, I can see that."

"No, I don't agree. Talking can't hurt, and may clear things up for us." He took her hand. "Look, we hardly know each other. Oh, sure, I know your name, your home town, that your father is a butcher and that you taught children how to read and write. But do I know if you like cats or dogs, or whether you salt your food or what makes you angry or sad, or what makes you laugh?"

"But an arranged marriage precludes all that," Malka countered. "Most couples never meet until the wedding day."

"Yes," Jacob said, "and they somehow work it out, don't they? They have the wedding, and they go to bed. And like two blind kittens, they find their way to the milk."

Both were silent. Then she asked, "Had you ever thought about being with a woman before coming to Dawson?"

"Sometimes," he said without thinking, then looked sharply at her. "What do you mean, being with a woman? In friendship? In bed? What?"

"I used to dream, romantic dreams," Malka said hesitantly, "about kissing, hugging, that sort of thing. Do you understand?"

"Uh-huh."

"Is that so awful?"

"Not at all. In fact, you're one up on me."

"Oh?" she said, surprised. "That never occurred to you?"

He turned on his side. Her question made him uncomfortable. "Men don't think about things like that."

"Maybe that's why so many marriages don't really work," she said sharply. "Since when are certain thoughts masculine or feminine?"

"Since the beginning of time, I suppose."

"Nonsense! Boys can read but girls should cook? It's all nonsense!"

"Look, Malka, we're getting into an argument over something that has no bearing . . ."

"But it does! Why can't you see that? Why must you harp on . . . on . . ."

"Sex? Go on, say it," he snapped. "You won't be struck dead! It isn't a terrible thing. It's what happens between husband and wife, or should happen. You're a smart woman, you've been a teacher, you keep house, you know as much as I do about many things."

"And what do you know about sex?" Malka challenged.

"Nothing!" Jacob shot back. "I was hoping to learn with my wife!"

"Is that all you wanted from me?"

Jacob sat up and raked a hand through his damp hair. "I'm trying to explain, but you're not listening. I was lonely. Marriage seemed a sensible answer. No, sex is not all I wanted from you. It would mean nothing if I could not love you, too."

Jacob wondered if he had admitted too much. But she had wanted an honest discussion. Boldly, he said, "I admit I was hoping to hold a soft, willing woman in my arms. Is that unreasonable? If I only wanted a housekeeper, I could have hired one."

"Make up your mind, Jacob. One minute we're strangers, the next I am the cause of your disappointment. Can you blame me for being confused?"

He shrugged impatiently. "What did you think, Malka, when you agreed to this marriage? Did anyone ever tell you about the birds and the bees?"

She thought for a moment, so long a moment that Jacob wondered if she would answer at all. "No," she said, almost whispering. "Papa was too embarrassed, I guess. I asked friends, but they were no help at all. I admit to ignorance, Jacob, woeful ignorance."

"But there are women, Malka, who marry and beget children. They learn. Somehow they learn. Like I learned to live off the land and make fur clothes . . . and mine gold. By doing."

"You sound very logical," Malka said, polite now and careful of her words. "One can learn some things by doing. But this is different, don't you think? Then ask yourself why I care at all, why I lie awake night after night, so tense I feel like a wrapped mummy waiting for entombment. I would tell you it is because I can understand how denied you feel, and isn't that seeing it through your eyes?"

"All right. Your point of view seems to be one of wait and see . . . or, if I have to, I will . . . or maybe he'll forget about that unpleasant part of the marriage and we can live like brother and sister."

"That's not fair!" Malka protested.

"Fair! You think you know what fair is?"

A sudden wind dispelled some of the heat in the cabin. On the roof and on mounds of dry leaves outside a soft rain drummed, a welcome sound coming on the heels of the argument. It lasted a few minutes, then stopped abruptly. Now there was no breeze at all, and it seemed hotter than before.

"What do you want me to do, Jacob? Lie here and let you take me like an animal?"

"What would you think if I said yes?" he answered, leaning forward, his voice harsh.

"I would be sad. That is not the way . . ."

"How would you know the way!"

"I don't. I can only take my cue from you. And you don't give me one."

"For instance?"

Malka shook her head. "That I can't tell you. You must know it yourself."

"But I don't understand," Jacob protested. "If you expect something, or think I'm disappointing you, then you must explain."

She closed her eyes, lost in the extravagant fantasies she had always resorted to as a substitute for fact. If she tried now to define or interpret them for Jacob, they could come out so distorted, so garbled, he might never accept them. Or worse, he might laugh.

But she had painted herself into this corner and she had to find her way out. "Jacob, because of our circumstances, raised as we were in a religious household, never allowed to discuss what certainly must be the most delicate subject with someone more knowledgeable, we're in a bind. You cannot teach me, and I cannot teach you. The only way to overcome this obstacle, in my opinion, is to be patient and loving, and willing to bare our feelings of endearment, in whatever shape they take. A hand outstretched, a kiss in the morning, a kiss at night, a touch or an embrace . . ."

He looked at her sharply, his grimace of surprise unseen in the dark. "Is this my wife speaking? The woman who lies like a dead horse under the blanket, shaking with fright that I will come too near?" He sighed with exasperation. "I am the confused one now. Look at me, Malka, look at how stiff and full of pain my masculinity sits, waiting, hurting, crying with frustration! Or are you afraid to look? Afraid the sight of me might make you sick?"

He could hardly believe his own voice or the cruel, vulgar words that erupted from his mouth. What was happening to him? This woman was making him into something ugly and hateful, and he did not like himself at all.

"Enough of talking," he said, rising and moving to the door.

"Where are you going?" Malka cried.

"Out. For some air."

"But . . ."

"No buts. It's not working. Our marriage is a bad joke." She heard him pacing outside near the cabin. In difficult times, she thought, men pace and women cry, but tears were not helpful. Nor was anger or petulance.

She felt trapped under the weight of her ignorance. No matter what she said, it was wrong. No matter how much she explained, he did not understand. Nor did she.

This dilemma must have a solution and they must find it together. Otherwise, it would not be a solution at all, only surrender.

The next morning they walked to Dawson City for supplies and mail. The day was stifling; at seven in the morning, the sun was a ball of fire overhead. Not a breath of wind to stir a leaf or cool their flushed faces as they plodded the dirt path through the hills. Neither mentioned the previous night.

They reached Dawson around noon, hungry, grimy, and eager to sit down in a cool shady spot.

"Let's head for the river, Jacob," Malka urged, determined to establish a cheerful mood for the day. "At least we can wade in the water. I've never been so hot."

"A land of contrasts, yes?" Jacob took the path to the beach, helping Malka over the weedy hillock to Front Street's wooden sidewalk. "As hot as it is today, I've been through worse. On American Independence Day last year, the thermometer reached one hundred and three. In the shade!" He grimaced. "My first holiday in my new country, and all I could do was lie down and pant with my tongue hanging out like one of the sled dogs."

"Oh, my," Malka said, as she lingered in front of a fancy store and peered longingly into the display window at a mannequin dressed in the latest Paris gown. The wooden dummy stared back, its right hand holding a silk parasol trimmed in fringe.

"Look at this," Malka cried. "What does the sign say, Jacob?"

He studied the card next to the dummy. "**THE NEW LOOK—DIRECT FROM THE FAMOUS HOUSE OF** . . . I can't say the last word. It's a name starting with G . . . Gu . . . ee . . ." He stumbled over the French name and shrugged his shoulders.

"Guignol?" Malka asked. "Could it be Guignol?"

"I suppose. Do you know it?"

"Oo-la-la!" She shook her head and rolled her eyes. "The big French designer. I know it because of a picture in Papa's newspaper. Look, the silk is almost iridescent, and layered so beautifully down the front. The little black beads are called bugle beads . . . see how they edge the skirt and sleeves. Oh, what a dress!"

"Oy, what a price," he mumbled.

Studying the sign hanging over the board, he read, "**MADAME TREMBLAY'S.** The owner, I suppose. Are you surprised to find such elegance here in the wilderness?"

"Yes." They continued walking. "Which just proves," she said, "that some people here must have money to buy fine things, money earned from diligently mining the gold."

"Or a lucky poker game, or a good night's work at the casinos." Jacob steered her across the busy street, dodging wagons, dogs, small boys chasing a ball with sticks, and the usual crowd of lethargic strollers.

A wagon suddenly careened around the corner, the horses wild-eyed and frothing at the mouth, their reins loosely flopping on their backs. A young woman seated on the wagon seat screamed loudly and waved her hands in the air. Instantly Jacob, joined by three other men, ran alongside, yelling at the horses, attempting to reach the dangling reins.

One man slipped and fell, rolling in the dirt to escape being run over by the wheels. Jacob succeeded in catching one of the reins, but the horse bucked, throwing him off balance, and the rein fell from his grasp.

By this time more men had joined the rescue party, and together, pulling on the horses' manes and dragging their own feet in the dirt, they slowed the racing vehicle. Two men finally jumped on the horses' backs and brought them to a stop.

Jacob reached for the woman, held her slender waist and swung her to the ground.

"How can I thank you?" she cried breathlessly. "You've saved my life. And my horses. I'm sure we'd all be lying dead if not for your bravery and kindness."

Her lovely smile was lavished on all the men, and the tableau struck Malka as an ornamental illustration from a fairy tale book: the beautiful heroine thanking her courageous rescuers.

But she had to admit that the young woman, even smudged as she was with dirt and sweat, was breathtakingly beautiful. Her face was artfully made up; full lips bright red, the deep green of her eyes accented with shadow on the upper lids, her long lashes painted black and swept up almost to the penciled brows.

"Purty as a pitcher, ain't she?" said one of the men. He nudged Malka as he spoke, emphasizing his opinion with a rude gesture and leering smile. When Malka nodded, the man whispered, "And worth every cent, I heerd tell."

"What?"

"You know." The man winked and moved away.

While the exhausted horses were tended, women in the crowd turned their backs and walked with noses in the air from the scene, unwilling to lavish concern or care on the "fallen" woman. Jacob introduced her to Malka.

"Evelyn MacMillan," the woman said, smiling and extending her gloved hand. "Your husband is a treasure. So brave and fearless. You're very fortunate."

"Yes," Malka stammered, "I know. I am happy to meet you."

"You must come to my home and have tea with me. I would be honored to have you as my guests. Forgive the way I look, but that awful ride has spoiled my gown and dirtied my face." She laughed, a lovely sound that reminded Malka of milk bottles jingling in the back of a moving kibitka. She was more dazzled by her than the men were.

"I think you look wonderful," Malka said. Everyone laughed, but not in a genial way. Nevertheless, Evelyn smiled and threw kisses to them all.

"Bless you, friends, and thank you again."

As the crowd dispersed, Evelyn walked a little way with Jacob and Malka, pointing the way to her house one block from Front Street, between Queen and Princess Street. "Please come and visit me. It would be so nice to have friends." Something sad in the sound of her words caught Malka's attention.

"I am very proud of you, Jacob," Malka whispered, taking his hand. "To face those horses as you did, with no thought of yourself."

"I wasn't thinking," he acknowledged, "I did only what the others did. Nothing special. Let's eat lunch. I'm famished."

"Yes. But we will stop to have tea with Evelyn, won't we?"

He frowned. "We'll see."

They ate by the river, a shaded spot where Malka spread a cloth on which she paced the small basket of food. The tea in the canteen was laced with milk and sugar and a drop of honey added at the last minute. It tasted wonderful, and they drank slowly, allowing the cool liquid to slide down their dry throats.

"She is beautiful, isn't she, Jacob?"

"Mm-hmm."

"She looks about my age, don't you think?"

"About."

"She must be very rich to have her own house."

"Mm-hmm."

"Her clothes are so stylish and expensive-looking, and she drives her own wagon and horses. A real lady."

When Jacob did not answer, Malka looked up from slicing the cold chicken and frowned. "Is something the matter? Why do I get only hmphs and shmphs for answers?"

He was lying on the blanket with his back against a tree and looked up at Malka. "I'm eating. Hmphs and shmphs is all I can say when I'm eating."

She licked her fingers absently and shook her head. "No, there's something else, something you're not telling me. Am I right?"

"You don't have to know everything, do you?"

"Of course I do. Why shouldn't I?"

Jacob sat up, his eyes narrowed. "Because some things are better left unsaid."

"Why?"

"Because they might hurt someone. Malka, let's change the subject."

"That's not fair."

He started to say something, then stopped, paused, thought it over, and fell silent.

"Now I've done it, haven't I? Opened the wound. . . ." She began gathering the cups and cloth angrily, throwing everything into the basket and slamming down the lid.

He took his pipe from his pocket, filled it, then lit the tobacco, taking deep pulls until his head swam in the smoke.

"But what about Evelyn?"

"Evelyn?"

"Yes, Evelyn. You started to say . . ."

"Malka, for heavens sake. . . ."

"Why the mystery? She's a beautiful woman. So she wears a little makeup, so what?"

"Do you know any other woman who does that?"

"No."

"You cannot guess why?"

"Jacob . . . just tell me!"

"All right, ALL RIGHT!" He knocked the ash from his pipe and shoved it into a pocket. "Evelyn is a . . . a . . . *nafkeh*. That's right! A *kurveh*! A whore!"

Malka blinked with shock. "How do you know? Who told you? You didn't . . . ?"

"Of course not. But I know those who did. I wouldn't say something like that if I were unsure."

Malka's brain reeled. The truth sickened her, more so because of her attempt at friendship. But especially because the wounded look in her eyes did not seem like the look of a fallen woman.

"How can she do that?" she said, to herself more than to Jacob.

"That's not the point, Malka. She does do it, and it's not for us to ask why."

"It's not for us to judge, either." Malka felt a flurry of sympathy for women everywhere "Now I see why those ladies walked away. They were snubbing her."

"I suppose."

Here was Evelyn, giving herself to men who were strangers and getting paid for it, while she, who was legally married, could not even get close to Jacob. The whole thing was confusing. The only conclusion Malka could draw was that Evelyn was a sinner. She was beautiful and spirited, someone men admired and women envied. She remembered the age-old shibboleth about fallen women: never envy a sinner, for you know not what disaster awaits her.

If it was not envy Malka felt for Evelyn, it was close to it, counting as she was the teeth in someone else's mouth. But she herself was not toothless. And this was the part that rankled. Knowing about Evelyn, Malka felt like the dummy in the store window compared to the seductive young woman. She is whole and I am not, Malka thought. To go through life like a piece of wood is stupid and unnecessary. I must turn aside from my disastrous course and become a whole woman, not only for Jacob, but for myself. I have to grow up, accept the provisions of marriage and all its terms.

Malka felt ready to fight her ignorance and demons; the great weight that had pressed her down lifted and was gone. Wonderful. The only problem was how to begin.

TWENTY-NINE

 familiar symbol

EARLY ONE STEAMY MORNING IN JULY, FRANK NOVAK banged on the Finesilvers' cabin door. "What is it," Jacob asked, stumbling to the door. "Someone is sick?"

"No, nobody's sick. The *Bella* came in yesterday with cattle. And word is that if you can catch one of the animals, you can have it! Meat, Jacob! Fresh meat!"

Jacob dressed quickly and the two men, eager to be in on the windfall, ran to the dock. The ship's captain had just lowered the gangplank, and dozens of pigs, cows, chickens and bulls raced for freedom.

Suddenly men ran in all directions, following the animal they wanted or could reach. The frightened beasts lumbered along the beach, lowing and squawking and squealing. A few chickens tried to take wing but were easily caught. The pigs, distracted by the wet sand, wallowed in the glorious muddy bed and were soon snagged by their curly tails and carted away.

The cows and bulls posed a tougher problem. Their size alone made capture difficult. They ran vigorously up and down the sand, eluding the shouting men by veering off course or sitting down suddenly, offering no point of purchase to outstretched hands.

Ropes were brought and Jacob found himself stalking an angry black bull, twirling a rope high in the air as he aimed at the animal's horns. But the rope frightened the bull, and it lurched off down the beach. Jacob followed, hollering and cursing, falling in the water, determined to catch his prey. The bull was also determined not to be caught and zigzagged across the swamp in a maddening course, up, back, down, a blur of sweaty black steak on the hoof.

"Come on, you *momzer*," Jacob shouted, chasing after the brute, "come to papa! Come to papa!" The bull ran well ahead, kicking sand into Jacob's face, then turned suddenly and glared at his pursuer, eyes wide and mean.

Jacob bent low, twirled the rope and faced the animal with what he hoped was mastery and conquest. The bull snorted and pawed at the sand. It was then that the full impact of Jacob's miscalculations struck home.

The animal was enormous. It was also obviously enraged by the pursuit, every muscle tensed under its glistening black hide. By the time Jacob realized what this combination of size and rage might produce, it was too late.

The bull lowered his head, roared ominously, and pointed sharp horns directly at his tormentor, thick legs churning through the swampy sandbar as he rushed headlong for Jacob.

There was no place to hide. Men and animals were everywhere, blocking Jacob's escape. Even the river was no haven. Jacob dropped the rope and lay flat in the mud, hoping the bull would pass over him and give him time to run the other way. But the black beast charged, his head grazing the ground, and one of his sharp horns picked Jacob up by the seat of the pants and tossed him through the air.

Stunned, Jacob landed fifteen feet away on top of a chicken, the squawking bird suddenly dead under him. Before he could rally his defenses, the bull charged again. This time his aim was unerring. The sharp right horn plunged into Jacob's buttock and tore a vertical three-inch wound that began to bleed profusely.

Satisfied, the bull stood still, drooling and snorting with victory. He then shook himself off and sauntered away.

The men who had witnessed the goring crowded around Jacob. One of them came running through the circle and knelt beside him.

"Don't worry," he assured Jacob, "you'll be okay. Just lie still." His words were unnecessary; Jacob was mercifully unconscious.

"Here," the man hollered, "someone give me a shirt, towel, underwear, anything I can use to stop the bleeding."

He had already torn his own shirt from his back and was holding it tightly against the wound. More shirts were handed to him, one after the other, until the bleeding was finally stanched.

Fuzzy-eyed and disoriented, Jacob lay on his stomach on the hospital bed.

"Easy, Jacob," the man at his side said, "try not to move."

"What happened? Where am I?"

"You're in Father Judge's Hospital. Don't you remember? You were gored by a bull. Right smack in your *toches*!"

Jacob closed his eyes and saw the bull charging at him, the horns glinting in the sunlight. He grimaced.

"Now you remember?" the man said. "You're lucky, Jacob. A few inches more to the left, and you'd be singing soprano!"

Jacob groaned. "Some cowboy!" he mumbled. He stared at the man. "Who are you?"

"My name is Samuel Politzer. This same thing happened to my father once in the old country, but he lived to be eighty. I wish the same for you. Feeling better?" Politzer smiled, deepening lines in his ruddy, handsome face. He spoke with a pronounced accent.

"Polish?" Jacob asked.

"From Lublin. And you?"

They swapped experiences about their rough and difficult immigration. Politzer, two years older, had come alone, with forged papers and another man's identity, slipping into Canada as a Polish laborer. When he reached Dawson City, he took back his own name and hoped no one would find him out.

"So far, so good," he said, smoothing his handlebar mustache. "If I ever get into trouble, the truth will come out. I suppose it will hurt at first . . ."

"Like a thorn . . ." Jacob interjected.

"Like a thorn. But in the end, it will blossom like a rose. Yes? I see we had the same teachers."

"One teacher," Jacob corrected. "The Pale, right? Tell the truth and you ask for a beating!"

"Rest now, Jacob, I'll see you later."

"Listen, Samuel, my wife, Malka, I must get home. She'll worry. . . ."

"I'll tell her," Politzer said, turning to go, "about her husband the cowboy . . . and almost his last roundup!"

Malka had been asleep when Jacob left for Dawson, and had no idea where he had gone.

"Gored by a bull? A bull? Where is there a bull in Dawson? And where was he hurt? Is it bad? Can I see him?"

Samuel Politzer stood awkwardly, hating to speak of important things in a doorway.

"Oh, forgive me," Malka said, flustered. "Where are my manners? Please come in. I'll make you a glass of tea?"

"No, no thank you. But I will come in."

He sat on the edge of the chair and looked about the small cabin so comfortable, the feminine touch revealing a wife who enjoyed keeping house.

Malka studied him too, his long, blond hair, thick eyebrows growing in a wild tangle over brooding eyes, the mustache and the angle of his chin.

He assured Malka that Jacob was healthy except for the wound in his backside.

"Can I bring him home?"

"I'll borrow a carriage and bring him myself."

"You are very kind, Mr. Politzer."

"Samuel, please."

"How lucky for Jacob that you were there. But you did not enter into the game?"

"It was no game. The men were trying to secure fresh meat, a chance to stock up before the winter. You mustn't be too hard on him."

Malka shook her head. "It was foolish. And the meat is *trafe* anyway. What was he thinking?"

Politzer shifted uneasily. His bulk seemed to threaten the small wooden chair. Malka expected any moment to hear the legs splinter. "Trafe!" he said sharply. "That's no concern here, Malka, kosher or non-kosher. You haven't lived through a Dawson winter or you would know better."

Rebuked, Malka said, "So, you have a point, Samuel. But can this winter be worse than Khotin's? Cold is cold."

"Wait until next spring and then tell me that." He rose and extended his hand. "Nice to meet you, Malka. Jacob is surely in good hands with such a loving wife."

She blushed and shook his hand. "Again, thank you for your kindness. And please, come often to see us. Good friends are the best medicine, and hard to make here."

Politzer had few friends, and Malka's invitation was a lovely temptation.

THIRTY

⋞⊙⊙⊸

DOCTOR ABNER MCKANE WAS SEVENTY YEARS OLD, THE elder of the two doctors still practicing in Dawson. He was also the shorter, barely reaching five feet five. What he lacked in size he made up in gruffness, treating his patients like perverse children whose illnesses were deliberate and stupid. A grownup should know better than to get sick.

His one visit to the Finesilver cabin was to teach Malka how to dress Jacob's wound. It had to be done every day. "From now on," he announced, "don't bother me. Any damn fool thinks he can wrestle a bull doesn't need a doctor. He needs a new brain!"

With Jacob recuperating in bed, Malka tended the gardens. "The gold will wait," she said, trying to calm him. "It's been there for a million years. It can stay a few more weeks."

She brought him snacks and chattered about the weather and the vegetables, and changed the iodoform gauze on the wound. The first time after the doctor's visit, she hesitated, not because of the wound but because of its location. But it had to be done, embarrassing or not.

Jacob looked at Malka standing in a patch of sunlight by the bed, her skin almost transparent in the bright glow. She wore a white blouse, its high neck prim but alluring, the pleats of the black skirt flaring ever so slightly at the hip. She had braided her long hair into an intricate crown; a few tendrils, wilting from the heat, fell along her cheeks. He wanted to touch them.

She shifted the weight on her feet from one high-topped shoe to the other and nervously twisted the gold band on her right hand. "I must pull down your pants, Jacob," she said, trying to sound matter-of-fact.

He lay on his stomach and grinned. "Sorry, Malka, that it wasn't my knee or my arm. I should have told the bull . . ."

"Oh, come on, don't make it worse," she muttered. "So yours is the first backside I'll see. So what! Now cooperate. Help me."

Jacob assumed a serious expression and wiggled his hips. "Is this what you want?"

She laughed, then reached for his pajama pants at the waist and began tugging. "Do that some more. They're almost down."

Jacob closed his eyes and shivered at the touch of her soft hands, grateful he was on his stomach. His involuntary reaction went unobserved.

She lifted the stained dressing, noting that the shallow wound was clean and not as bad as she had expected. Her fingers holding the gauze trembled as she stared.

His body was firm, muscles tight, tensing under her hand. His legs were long and firm, the calves thick with ropes of muscle and ligament stretching up into the strong thighs. She pulled up his shirt around his neck and discovered the sprinkling of hair on his back and arms. He was tough and lean, no doubt from his long walk and the physical labor in the mine. It was her first look at his body, and heat rose in her cheeks. She quickly taped on the new dressing and turned away. Her confusion was not lost on Jacob.

"Malka?" he asked, "is my body so ugly that you must turn away?"

"Not ugly at all." She shivered slightly, a strange reaction in the stifling heat of the July day. "It is quite the opposite. You are . . . your . . ."

He let her struggle to express herself. He waited. And while he waited, he stroked her hand, his touch like a feather on her smooth skin.

It made her quiver. As her skin tingled with delight, a strange knot formed in the pit of her stomach. Her heart thudded against her chest, and she caught her breath. "What is this I feel, Jacob? Why am I floating?"

He elbowed himself closer and put his arms around her waist. "I am not you, so I don't know. What I *do* know is that I feel the same way, and I know why."

"Why?" she asked.

"Because," he said, nuzzling the skin at her neck, "you are my wife. My wife, Malka. That means . . ."

"I know," she whispered. "I know what that means."

"Do you?"

"Yes." Her voice broke and she held him tightly. "This is so strange for me, Jacob, but it's not unpleasant. In fact, it's a wonderful feeling . . . like drinking too much wine."

He bent her back on the bed until she was lying next to him and held her close. Her eyes, which minutes ago had concentrated solely on dressing the wound, were now half closed.

Burying his head on her soft breast, he inhaled the sweet fragrance of rosewater soap, but there was another slight aroma, puzzling, unfamiliar and arousing. He kissed her mouth, tentatively, without plan or routine as his guide. He moved like a man in a dream toward a destination that had eluded him, drifting further and further away. He was unprepared for Malka's sudden yielding, her taut body now limp in his arms.

"Malka?" he murmured. "Do you . . . can we . . . ?"

She touched her fingers to his mouth. "Sh, don't say anything, Jacob, just . . . just do that again."

He did, this time lingering on her lips. Passion rose in him, pounding at his temples and rushing to his toes like a summer rain down a mountainside. Far beyond where he could have stopped, he forgot the wound, the soreness of his muscles. He rolled on top of her, tearing at her clothes, urgency commanding him, shoving aside any gentle exploration or tenderness.

Malka's passion suddenly dissolved, leaving her struggling beneath him, tearing herself away with a choking cry, seething with humiliation and resentment.

"Stop!" she cried, tears sliding down her cheeks. "I cannot do this." She pulled herself to the head of the bed, huddled into a small ball and rocked back and forth, weeping.

Jacob turned his back.

She realized how angry he was. She mumbled something, moved closer to Jacob and reached for his hand.

He shook his head, indicating that he had not heard.

"I said, I have to try, in my own way, to figure this out. Please help me."

"I can do no more," he said miserably.

"But you must do more. Don't you see? When you kissed me, I melted. I was on fire. Believe me, Jacob, every drop of my blood was boiling through my veins. I found myself opening to you, burning with desire. That must be the answer. Because I turned again to ice when you . . . when you . . ."

He turned to her, curious. "I was too hasty," he said, "is that what you mean?"

"I think so. Believe it or not, but I am just as disappointed as you are."

Her words baffled him, forcing a reassessment, a search

into his own feelings, an understanding of turmoil and pain other than his own.

"I was so excited, Malka, so filled with desire that . . . I too was on fire, that's the only way I can explain it."

She listened intently. "Go on," she urged.

"You see, when that happens, I . . . I . . . my . . ." He pointed, embarrassed, to himself, and almost whispered, " . . . I become erect." He watched her face, expecting to see an expression of horror or disgust.

But her eyes focused on him, burning with curiosity, and followed every word and gesture. She was utterly engrossed. "Please, Jacob, continue."

He hesitated, watched her warily, drew a deep breath and plunged ahead. "Yes. Well, when the act has been completed, then I . . . it . . . I can resume my usual state."

"I thought there was a bone. . . ."

"No. No bone," he said, smothering a smile.

She relaxed against the wall but continued to stare at him. When he attempted to squirm into his shorts, she cried, "No. Please. Don't hide from me." Her cheeks burned with a bright flush, but she spoke quietly when she asked, "You love me, right?"

He smiled, "Right."

"Then I should be flattered?"

"Oh, yes."

She smiled, pleased. "Thank you, Jacob, for your explanation. I understand things better now."

"Wonderful."

"Will you be better soon?"

"I hope so."

He laughed suddenly and clambered over the bedclothes to embrace her. "You are not the kind of woman I expected."

"I'm sorry," she whispered.

"No, no, that's not what I mean." Jacob held her close. "You are not the only ignorant one in this virginal partnership, Malka. It seems we will have to teach each other."

"What could I possibly teach you?"

He murmured in her ear, "Why don't we find out?"

THIRTY-ONE

ॐ

SEPTEMBER'S COLD NORTH WIND RUSHED IN WITHOUT notice, cruelly tearing the gold and scarlet leaves from the trees, scattering them across the brown earth and out of sight. The canary vine covering the house had grown five inches every twenty-four hours during the summer, and some of the late asters stood seven feet high. But white frost now withered the foliage, pastel blooms fell to the hard ground as bedraggled litter, and the valley was thick with morning fog. Ice in the basin had to be heated on the stove before Jacob and Malka could wash. And the last of the vegetables made it to Malka's soup pot just in time.

A final series of mournful whistles blew from the last boat out of Dawson. With its exit, Jacob again warned Malka of the coming winter and their impending confinement.

"So soon? But it's only September."

"Yes, but it's different here. I remind you that the Arctic Circle is very close. I wasn't exaggerating in my letters."

"Strange," she said wistfully. It was Friday evening and the tempting fragrances of chicken soup and braided *challah* baking in the small oven filled the cozy cabin. Because the Bible spoke of love and closeness on the Sabbath, a fact Jacob had lost no time pointing out to Malka, she anticipated the early sunset and the pleasure they would share at bedtime.

Jacob had recovered quickly from the bull's goring, due in part to Malka's care, but it was the change in their relationship that had hastened his healing, and he credited Malka when the doctor pronounced his "idiot patient" recovered. But Jacob never explained what had really happened.

He did not tell the doctor how they had lost themselves in each other, spending days in passionate exploration and trial, learning from action and reaction, until those first awkward and unskilled moments were behind them forever. Now, because of their youth and sense of immortality, they foresaw a lifetime of fulfillment, and neither could remember the frustration and loneliness of life before marriage.

"It was the bull, Jacob," Malka said one night, "and we should be properly grateful."

"We are," Jacob replied, stroking her hair in the darkness. "We didn't eat him, did we?"

"He'll never know how much happiness he brought us."

"If I ever meet him again, I'll be sure to tell him."

Malka stirred the contents of the pot on the stove and hummed a melody.

"You're early with that music, aren't you?" Jacob asked, looking up from his book.

She nodded, pensive, and looked out the tiny window. "At home it's fall, with warm days and cool nights and sweaters that smell of camphor and cedar chips, and clothes to be mended for the High Holy Days. And then," she grinned, "it is usually too hot in the shul, and everyone itches and perspires in the new woolen finery."

"I remember," he said, "although it was rare when a Finesilver showed up in new clothes."

Malka peeked inside the pot and added salt. Lost in thought, she carelessly closed the latch on the oven and burned a finger. When Jacob rose to help, she protested that it was nothing and set the small table.

"When the sun is not visible in winter, how will we know when to light the Sabbath candles?"

"We'll make do, Malka. I have."

"Mm-hmm. And what of Succos? And what of Rosh Hashonah and Yom Kippur? And what of . . ."

"I know, I know," Jacob said. "I have wrestled with all those questions since leaving home. The only answer I can give you is that the Holy One needs us and wants us to survive. He must have wanted me to survive. Why else would I be here? That's why He allows for special circumstances. There is no sun, so decide for yourself when to light candles. There is no shul, so pray at home. There was no rabbi, and so we were married by a judge. I'm sure we have done no wrong."

"I wish I could be as sure as you."

"You could be, if you would accept what I say. After all, you told me about your compromise with the food aboard ship. That was logical. And acceptable."

"I thought so at the time. But I have misgivings, Jacob. Papa and I were very observant. This way it's hard for me."

"I understand. But life was hard in the Pale, too. There we had no chance at all. At least here, in this free country, we can work and save, and go as far as our strength and health will allow. That's why we left. He will not turn from us now."

Malka knew he spoke from his heart, and that the words made sense. Even so, she had qualms, feeling something was missing. She missed her father. They had never believed in photographs, so she had none of him to look at. It pained her now, for his face was becoming increasingly difficult to remember. She tried willing it into place, the kind face, the twinkle in his eye, wavy gray hair rising from the high forehead, distinguished and handsome. . . .

Tonight they had no wine, so Jacob sang *Kiddush* over a

tin cup of ice water. The cabin gleamed in the pallid wash of light from the Sabbath candles. During dinner Malka asked Jacob to tell her again about Dingo Malone and his first year in Dawson.

"Your letters only touched on it," she said, breaking off a piece of *challah* from the loaf. "Is that really why the man at the lumber mill called you 'Almost Famous Jake'?"

Jacob recounted the story of Dingo and his melting machine. He left out nothing, not even the sorry moments of self-doubt before the water had boiled and the machine had worked.

Malka listened soberly when he told of Dingo's death. "How sad that more men of the cloth do not share Father Judge's understanding and lack of prejudice."

"Maybe some do. After all, this is a big country with many religions. They would have to be careful, if only to get along with one another."

"But not many Jews. I wonder why."

"There aren't many of us anywhere, compared to Gentiles. And few up here. Perhaps there are more in the big cities."

"With shuls?" Malka asked hopefully.

"I can't say. Are you lonely, Malka?"

She thought a moment. "I don't think so. I miss my father, but that's only natural. As I told you, we were very close. And you and I are far too busy to be lonesome."

"I said lonely, not lonesome," Jacob corrected.

"I know what you said. Must you pick at my words?"

"Are you angry at me or is it something else that has you out of sorts?"

She wondered how he could read her every mood. Was she so transparent? Another fact of married life to file away with all the others.

"Is it really that bad, Jacob? The winter, I mean. Samuel said so, too, but I find it hard to believe."

"I told you the truth, it's bad, very bad. It seems to me that nature runs wild here in the north, doing everything on a grander, more extravagant scale. Wait until you see the huge herds of caribou migrating south, or hear the wolves howling at the moon on a bitterly cold night. Temperatures can drop from twenty-five above to fifty below in two days, and the Mounties ban all horses working outside when it drops to sixty below. Too cold for a horse, but men will scratch at the frozen earth or try to dig a mine shaft in that kind of weather. The frost will creep into the house and cover the nailheads and knobs."

He stopped when he saw the horrified expression on her face, and lightened his tone. "Of course, there is much beauty in the winter, like the northern lights on a frosty evening. Aurora borealis, it's called. They sweep over the sky like orange and red flames, always changing. You won't believe your eyes when you see them. And then there's the funny side of winter life." He reached for another piece of bread. "I was in town once during the first freeze and wandered to the riverfront to see if the river had iced over. There was some water still flowing, mostly cakes of ice bobbing along like drunken Cossacks, and then this old empty boat sailed by and jammed solid into a huge ice block, its flag still flying!"

Malka laughed and placed the Sabbath candles, still burning, on the shelf above the stove. Then she turned to Jacob, took a deep breath and plunged into the subject she knew would be controversial. She felt confined and longed to reach out for another life.

"I've been thinking, Jacob, and after talking with Mrs. Novak and a few of the ladies in town, I have the feeling we should move into Dawson."

"Leave here? But why?"

"I know it will be hard to leave this house. You've put a lot of work, a lot of yourself into it, and it shows. And it's near your claim. I'm aware of that. But you saw yourself how little yield we took these last weeks. Our poke will get us through until spring, but that's all."

She rushed her words together, fearful he would object and squelch her train of thought. It was important that Jacob understand how strongly she felt about staying this far from town with impassable roads and no one nearby to help.

"The doctor is in town, for one thing, if we ever get sick or hurt . . . and supplies, and. . ."

"And?" His eyes narrowed.

"At least we'll have people around us if we live in the city."

"It's not much of a city, Malka."

"I know. But it has houses and stores. It has a social life, I've heard about it, about the teas the women give, and the groups you can join. And we've seen the beautiful clothes in Madame Tremblay's windows. I've always dreamed of owning a ready-made dress."

"And?"

"What do you mean, 'and'?"

"Haven't you left out something? Or, rather, someone?"

"I don't understand."

"Sam Politzer. He lives in Dawson, right?"

Malka was puzzled.

"Are you saying it's because of Samuel that I want us to move to Dawson?" Malka asked. "Why, Jacob Finesilver, I believe you're jealous!" She laughed. "I'm glad you're jealous; that means you love me. But there's no reason to be jealous of Samuel. He's a friend to us both."

Jacob shook his head. "I guess I am jealous. It's a whole new feeling, and I'm not sure I like it. But the way he looks at you—I'm not blind, Malka. And the way he keeps telling me I'm so damn lucky. I know I'm lucky. I don't need him to tell me."

Malka suppressed a grin. "I'm glad you admit it."

"That doesn't mean I like it. A man like Samuel, brooding over my wife, imagining heaven knows what. It's unhealthy."

"That's not true!" Malka believed that Samuel Politzer was a good friend of theirs and nothing more. She knew that her perspective was not always accurate, that she tended to see what she wanted to see, sometimes missing the truth about people. She preferred to think of this as optimism, generosity of spirit, and not blind charity. But she was certain that what Jacob said was not the case with Samuel.

"You must stop this way of thinking," she scolded. "It will only lead to harsh words between us."

"Perhaps you're right. Pay no attention. This is my first marriage and I'm still learning."

"This is your last marriage, and so far you're doing just fine. So can we move?"

"That, as my Uncle Aaron would say, is another horse. We will talk further about such an important step. I'm not sure how I feel about it."

"So we'll talk," Malka soothed.

"Now?"

"Now!"

"All right! I don't like the idea," Jacob stated. "It would be expensive, difficult, and where would I get a wagon or a horse to move us? Do you know what that costs?"

"We have the money, Jacob. Right here in jars. Gold dust. We are not paupers."

"But we have to live on it. You yourself said . . ."

"I figured it out," she interrupted, determined not to be put off. "From its weight, and the going price per ounce, we have enough to buy food, medicine, and two bolts of cloth for the next eight months, with some left over to hire a horse and wagon."

"You figured that out?" he asked, aware that he was losing the argument. "All this figuring . . . without even consulting me first?"

"I had to have the facts before I could ask you."

He remembered one of his first impressions of her at the dock as clever, when she hadwon her point about his friends and the captain of the *Nicolai*. It was a trait he admired, and he had to smile. "Madame," he announced, "your wish is my command," and bowed from the waist.

Malka coquettishly waved an imaginary fan. "Of course it is!"

She's pretty and desirable and makes delicious *challah*, he thought, but his reasons for capitulating were important. The winter was becoming tedious to him. He was ready for a new adventure with Malka and hoped she would have the strength to get through it.

They moved before the first real snow, settling into the little house on the corner of Third and Queen streets, across from the Dawson Daily News. Malka had found it only a few weeks before. While Jacob worked in his tunnel, she had made the long trek into town. By the time she reached the foot of Midnight Dome that day, her feet and hands were blue with cold.

Dawson City lay between the Dome and the river, fourteen blocks running the width north to south, eight blocks from the eastern edge at the foot of the Dome to the riverfront. Front Street was almost all commercial, with shops, stores and warehouses side by side from one end to the other. To the east, homes, churches, the post office and government buildings were scattered throughout the small town.

Malka had promised Jacob they would not build. They would find a house they could afford or an abandoned house with enough basic structure that could be added to or remodeled. The winter was too close for them to start from scratch.

She found herself in Evelyn MacMillan's neighborhood.

Curious, numb with cold, she threw caution to the wind and rang the bell on her door, astonished at her boldness.

The musical chime within the house brought its owner to the door. "Hello, Malka," she said, "what a delightful surprise."

Inside the front parlor, Malka stood before the fireplace and held her hands to the flames. "I did not realize it was so cold. I would have worn mittens. These little cloth gloves are not worth anything."

Evelyn rang for the maid. "What brings you to the city?"

"I am the official house hunter, it seems. Jacob is not thrilled with the idea of moving and said it was up to me to find us a house." She sat on the couch and patted the satin pillows. "So pretty, I am almost afraid to muss them."

Evelyn laughed, that delightful sound Malka had heard before. "Couches are to be sat upon. Chairs, too. And sometimes, floors. Comfortable is the word I stress to my . . . friends. If not here, where?"

The maid, a tiny Japanese girl in a silk kimono, brought tea and cookies on a tray and left silently.

Malka's eyes widened. "A maid. How wonderful to have someone to help you."

"She just arrived," Evelyn explained. Malka was entranced as the girl poured tea into exquisite porcelain cups. Evelyn's gestures were so graceful, her clothes stylish. Her golden hair was piled on top of her head in great puffy curls caught with a studded comb that twinkled in the lamplight. Rings with real gems sparkled on her hands.

She sipped the tea and held her hands against the warmth of the cup. Everything in the room amazed Malka. Red satin drapes framed lace curtains at the windows. A piano stood in the corner, draped with an elaborately embroidered cloth. Brass wall sconces held tall, flickering candles, and oil lamps on many of the carved tables gave off a warm glow. Over the fireplace a huge mirror in an ornate gold frame reflected the costly furnishings.

Malka admired Evelyn not just for her beauty or her exquisite taste and sense of her own femininity. In spite of what she knew about Evelyn, she liked her because she was smart and loving, and neither she nor Malka cared that the other women in town disapproved. In each other they had found a friend, not easy to come by in this odd, unnatural environment.

"This is truly a fine house," Malka said, "I have never before seen so many beautiful things in one place."

"Thank you. I love to surround myself with beauty. It makes everything else seem worthwhile." Evelyn's candid words surprised Malka and she almost choked on her tea.

"Malka, honey, everyone knows who and what I am. Jacob must have told you. Especially after we had tea that day. I'm sure you didn't think I had mined gold for all this."

Malka set her cup on the tea wagon. "I knew, but still, your saying it, well . . ."

"Listen. If you can't be honest in this world, what's the sense? I earn my living on my back. I didn't plan it that way, believe me. I wasn't born a whore." She rose and walked to a small desk in the corner, where she thumbed through a photo album.

"Look, little Evelyn growing up in Winnipeg. My parents are Scots, versed in the Bible and hard work. There, my mother and my father. Nice people, kind, good-looking, cultured. They treated me well, and I will always love them."

"Yes, but then, why . . . ?" Malka could not phrase the question, but Evelyn understood and saved her further embarrassment.

"Fate, I guess. When I heard of the gold rush, I decided to try my luck. It wasn't so unusual for a woman to come here, although most came to dance in the saloons or . . . you know."

She rested the book on her lap and looked into the distance. "I was stupid. It seems the minute I landed in Dawson, every miner I met gave me a story. 'I'll give you half of my claim.' Or . . . 'Here, little girl, sign this and Bonanza lower ten is yours.' I believed them all. Maybe because I was only eighteen . . . dumb, my first time away from home. Parents can be too kind sometimes.

"Anyway, the men each had a price, and I paid it. Of course, they didn't give me anything . . . when I met one of the girls from Paradise Alley, she told me I was crazy to give it away. She was right. What's the difference, I was cold and hungry and had no place to sleep. Does that break your heart?"

Malka thumbed through pictures of a large white house, dogs, cats, children, a life in black and white that looked nothing like this woman at her side.

"So you lost," Malka said finally. "Life is made up of little defeats, testing us, how you say, daring us. Whether or not we stand ground or run away. Your story does not break my heart . . . you are still here."

Evelyn stared at Malka, who seemed pitifully young to be so philosophical, and probably the only female in town who had not turned her back.

"How old are you, Malka?"

"Eighteen."

"I'm twenty. But I look like your mother."

"Don't be silly. Go look in the mirror . . . you will see how wrong you are."

Evelyn stared at her reflection. Then she turned to Malka. "How old is your mother?"

"If she lived, she would be thirty-six."

"Oh, I'm sorry. I didn't know."

"Of course not. Evelyn, if you wash that paint off, you will be so pretty. Do you need to wear it?"

"Honey, advertising is the backbone of all business. Without it, no one knows what you do or what you have to offer. Say, how's that handsome husband of yours? Is he as wonderful as he looks?"

"He is."

"Will he be angry when you tell him you saw me?"

"Maybe, but that doesn't stop me."

"How can such a little person like you have so much . . . so much . . ."

At Malka's puzzled look, Evelyn laughed and rephrased the question. "Bravery. How'd you get so brave?"

Malka thought a moment, then pointed to a picture of the happy family seated in front of the big white house. "Let us just say that you did not need to be brave, but where I come from, I did."

The Japanese girl entered the room and began to remove the tea tray.

"Kyoko, please bring the decanter and two glasses. I won't need anything else. Until later."

The girl walked from the room. Her odd sandals, the toe in its white sock separated from the rest of the foot, made whispering sounds on the deep carpet.

"How can she walk in those shoes?" Malka asked.

Evelyn laughed and poured two little glasses of whiskey. "Here, drink up. To our friendship. You're the best thing that's happened to me since I moved here."

"I do not drink," Malka said apologetically.

"That's all right. It's never too late to start."

She tossed her head back and downed the liquid in one swallow. "See? It's easy. Go ahead."

Malka did the same as Evelyn, but immediately began coughing and choking. "This is terrible," she croaked hoarsely, tears spilling down her flaming cheeks.

"I know," Evelyn laughed, "but you get used to it. And it

feels good after a while. Here," she said, filling both glasses. "Down the hatch."

"Down the hatch." Malka drank again, but this time in small sips. After two or three, she smacked her lips and wondered how it had suddenly turned so warm.

"By the way," Evelyn said, again filling the glasses, "there's a little house for sale down the street. I know the people. They left on the last boat out. Asked me to sell it for them. Interested?"

Malka's brain whirled with the room, her thoughts scattered and disorganized. She blinked her eyes, hoping Evelyn's face would come into focus again. "Who? What housh?"

"Uh-oh. You're drunk, Malka."

"So I am."

The two women laughed. Oh, Malka thought, it felt so good to laugh, so good to have nothing to do, no dishes, no cleaning, no dinner to . . . dinner! She sat up swiftly

"I must go, Evelyn, and I have not found a housh. Jacob will be so . . . oh!" She dropped her spinning head in her hands and moaned.

"C'mon, Malka honey, I'll help you to the basin. This damn oriental rug isn't paid for yet."

When Malka returned late in the evening, Jacob was pacing the floor. The small cabin reeked with smoke. He kissed Malka and looked at her in surprise. "You've been drinking."

"Sh," said Malka, putting a finger to his lips, "don't tell anyone." She giggled. "But the walk back wasn't as long as going there, I'll tell you that."

"Where have you been? And where did you get a drink?"

"That's not important," she protested, flinging her coat and hat on the bed. "I found us a house. A nice house. Two rooms, two rooms, Jacob! And that's just the first floor. On the second floor there are two more rooms, big ones, with many windows. And there's a big stove and pots . . . the people left in a hurry, and we can get it cheap."

"Malka, I asked you where you found a drink."

"Evelyn's house. I was frozen stiff and went there to ask for hot tea. But Jacob, whiskey's better. It lasts longer. Why didn't you tell me?"

"The same reason I couldn't tell you about making love; some things you have to learn for yourself."

"I make so many discoveries lately, about things so new and so . . . complicated."

"There's nothing complicated about whiskey, Malka," he said sternly. "If you drink enough, you get drunk."

Malka lay down on the bed, one arm covering her eyes. "Why is it that so many good things in life carry such a high price?"

"Not all of them," Jacob said, dropping down on the bed next to her.

"She has a maid, Jacob, a maid! A little Japanese girl who . . ."

"She's breaking her in," he mumbled.

"She seemed to know what to do, brought tea and anything else we might need to . . ."

"Not as a maid."

"Oh."

How innocent she is, he thought. He kissed her. And then, lest his happiness tempt the evil eye, he prayed against misfortune.

After they settled into their new house, Malka discovered to her great delight that Red Sky was in Dawson. They ran into each other at the Dawson post office, and after their greetings he told her his packing days were over. With one of his rare smiles, he added that if Missy and Jacob could stand to live in crazy place like Dawson, so could he. Besides, his wife Dove was from nearby Moosehide, knew the area and had family there. "Soon be baby. And baby need family. House full of people make home."

His words brought tears to Malka's eyes. With her father so far away, family seemed so out of reach. Nathan's letters, one of which she had just received, were all she had of him now.

After that first meeting, Dove and Red Sky spent much of their time reminiscing about the trail. The only sour note was Red Sky's lack of work. He was more than willing to take on any job but always came up against prejudice.

"I wish I could help," Jacob said one night as they sat around the dinner table. "I know about prejudice. It's all bad. Americans and Canadians have troubles with their own natives, so it rubs off on you. But it's no excuse."

He offered to ask friends if they could use an extra hand at their claims or in their stores. But in the days following, Jacob's work started at dawn and ended long after sunset, and he spent little time thinking about anything else.

He did not know how profoundly Red Sky would affect his life.

THIRTY-TWO

✎❦✎

"YOU THINK IT'S ALL GONE?" MALKA CRIED, INCREDULOUS. "There's no more gold in the ground? But that's impossible, isn't it? I mean, the gold has been here forever. It can't just run out."

"Yes it can," Jacob said, shaking his head. "This wasn't the mother lode, you know."

They were seated on the dirt crown of Jacob's claim, twenty feet above King Solomon's Dome, their mood as sunless and cold as the March day. They had been feverishly digging into the frozen earth and gravel for a week, and had nothing to show for their efforts except enough gold dust to cover the bottom of a Mason jar.

Jacob picked up a handful of dirt and let it sift slowly through his fingers. "I'm not surprised, Malka. This is just the beginning of the backbreaking work. Don't forget, it's twenty *above* the dome. Any bench land claim above or below the original discovery site is going to peter out sooner or later. With us, it was sooner."

"But you said yourself that the creek flowing down from the Dome is thirty miles long," Malka protested. "We haven't given it enough time. There's the whole summer before us."

"But we don't own that land along the creek," Jacob said,

becoming impatient, "only twenty feet. And that's above the creek. Forget it, Malka, we're not going to be millionaires."

"All right. So what do we do? Give up? Look, the men down there are working. And all along the tributary. We saw them as we came up. Besides, shaking a fist at fate doesn't do any good."

The clouds swirled high in the restless spring sky, casting cold shadows on the landscape. The sudden darkness brought a chill wind. Malka shivered and sat close to Jacob.

It made no sense that the gold should be running out. Only yesterday she had heard in town that nuggets had been found near Indian Creek. Jacob had called it "luck, pure luck" and dismissed the story with a shrug. Now he was ready to throw everything away.

"Where is your spirit?" Malka admonished him. "All that energy and ambition to find this mine in the first place."

"It's still there. But facts have to be faced. Digging up bucket after bucket of dead dirt won't prove anything."

"You're so certain it's dead!"

"Listen to me. I've thought about this all winter. The way it looked last year should have warned me, but I kept hoping, just like you. We can't waste any more time. It won't make any difference, Malka. Face it. We could work and scratch at this without making much more than the barest living, unless we find another El Dorado or Bonanza Creek. And that's unlikely. It could be years before the hard work would end."

He was right. His troubled eyes revealed the seriousness of their situation.

"Just another week?" she asked.

"And another after that, and another and another. It will always be the same. And we have to eat."

"I still can't believe it."

"I can," he said grimly. "I've seen veins go dry and men

turn away defeated and suddenly old. I won't let that happen to me. I'm not ready to quit living yet."

She looked at him quizzically. "Go on, Jacob," she said. "You have something else to say, right?"

"Sometimes you read me so quickly, it's frightening." He smiled. "Good thing I have only pure and innocent thoughts. Look, I like people, and I like the world of business and commerce. The lifeblood of Dawson is the general store. Without it, all of us would starve. To say nothing of the supplies, wood, tools, bits and pieces of metal and stone to make other tools or fix something, medicines and clothing. We could make a good living with a store. It seems a proper move to me, but I want your opinion, too."

Malka did not react at first. She was surprised, for she had never thought he would move so far from the gold or give up the mine after all he had been through. Another creek, perhaps, or renting a claim from someone wanting to go home. But this?

He read her look of confusion as dismay, and quickly added, "Of course, I would hope you would work at my side, in the store, I mean."

"Me?"

"Yes. You're good in mathematics and good with people. You have the knack of easy conversation and making them feel welcome. Too welcome, sometimes."

"Oh, come on, Jacob, you know as well as I it's for the rare treat of a good home-cooked meal that Samuel comes to our house so often. And good conversation with you. The way you two argue . . ."

"About the store," he interrupted testily, "what do you think?"

She stared at him for a moment, knowing exactly how she felt and what she would say, but not wanting to appear too enthusiastic too soon. Yet he looked so earnest and hopeful of a positive response, she could not bear to leave him hanging.

"You will no doubt be surprised at my answer, but here it is, Jacob." She smiled. "I think it's a wonderful idea. Not because the work will be easier; it will be just as hard, really, only in a different way."

Rising from the ground, she walked slowly around the hillock. "Neither of us knows about stock, or what Mr. Rabinowitz calls markups, or buying low and selling for profit. But we could learn, I'm sure. Samuel knows about meat. He could help there. And I know about making clothes, so I could run the dry goods department. . . ."

"You're not just saying this to make me feel better, are you?" Jacob asked.

"Of course not! If I didn't like it, I'd say so, you know that. We have never minced our words, have we?"

"No." Jacob smiled. "In fact, sometimes I think you're too honest with me."

"That's the way it should be! And I'm being honest now. A store is a great idea. If there *is* room for one more in Dawson. Have you studied that? Can a town of twenty-five thousand support another store?"

"I think so. Murray Fowler is selling out and moving home to Kansas. And the Emporium has always been too rich for most miners. The AC Company can use some competition."

"Yes, but . . ."

"But what?"

"You yourself said people were leaving. The veins are drying up in other creeks. What if . . ."

"They still have to eat," Jacob muttered.

"True."

"And they'll still get sick."

"Yes."

"And those whose claims are still producing will continue needing supplies. The town won't empty out in one season. And another thing," he went on, eagerness in his eyes, "I can put Red Sky to work. I know that has to mean something to you."

"Well then, go ahead."

"Go ahead?"

Malka laughed. "Yes, go ahead. You'll need a loan, but the banks will help with that. And Samuel says . . ."

"Samuel . . . SAMUEL!" Jacob yelped.

"Oh stop, Jacob. Yes, Samuel. Of course Samuel. He's friends with the owner of the Dawson City Bank and Trust Company, he's smart with finance, and if he ever strikes gold, he'll be the first to offer to subsidize us."

"If he ever strikes gold, the Messiah will come!"

Malka snapped, "I hope you're right. We could use the Messiah right now."

"So it's all right with you? You won't mind the work? Or the lean times until the store is on its feet?"

"Yes, no, and maybe. In that order." Malka grinned and followed Jacob down the hill.

Her guess about Samuel Politzer was correct. His friend in the Dawson bank found the Finesilvers worthy of a sizable loan, and the Bonanza Market opened on First Avenue between Princess and Harper Streets on the first day of June the following summer. Jacob had sent to Skagway for initial supplies, and he and Malka and Red Sky sorted the stock and set up shelving along the walls. Jacob ordered again, this time from Seattle and St. Michael, dealing directly with suppliers, painstakingly detailing every item of food and gear. Malka worked out prices on everything from tinned biscuits to heavy parkas, candles to telephone wire, bolts of cloth to twenty different sizes of nails. She figured the cost, the margin of profit, when to have a sale and when to stand firm. She even hung a small sign in the window that read: **PLEASE DO NOT DISCUSS PRICES. WHAT IT SAYS IS WHAT IT COSTS.** Jacob knew the women of Dawson would trust Malka, and that the men would find her charming. Although he fussed publicly about that, he admitted to himself that he counted on it and probably would not have succeeded without it.

But the success they both hoped for did not happen. They never seemed to have a full register, and the books were disappointing. One night, counting the receipts, Jacob exploded.

"What is the matter?" he cried, scattering papers on the floor. "What are we doing wrong? Why is this not working?" He pounded his fist on the counter.

Malka rolled down the shade on the door, turned the **CLOSED** sign to face the outside, and blew out the lamps in the front of the store. She walked to the rear slowly, working out her reply.

"Are you asking me a question? By that I mean are you just angry, or do you want an answer?"

"Of course I want an answer," he boomed, waving the pages of accounts in the air.

"Well then, sit, put those pages down so we can study them, and I'll tell you what the matter is."

"Oh, so now you're a *maven* in finance, eh?"

"I don't know how expert I am, but I do have eyes and a brain, and it's so obvious, a child could figure it out."

The pain of their impending failure was bad enough, but being insulted was intolerable. Jacob barked out angry words and flailed his arms helplessly.

Malka sat him down on a stool and seated herself beside him. Picking up the pages, she tracked the items with the point of a pencil as she spoke. "June thirteenth," she began, "thirty-four dollars and sixteen cents. Jacob Rowell. Credit. June fourteenth. Fourteen dollars and sixty-three cents. Abe

Valeska. Credit. June sixteenth, sixty-four dollars, Avery Baldwin. Credit."

Every time Malka came to the word credit, her voice rose. "June seventeenth, twelve dollars and ten cents, Jim Beacher. Credit. June twentieth, forty-seven dollars and fifteen cents, Mrs. Gertrude Thorne. Credit. June twenty-first . . ."

"She has five children . . ."

" . . . twenty-first," Malka continued, "nine dollars and forty-six cents, Tobias Price. Credit."

"He has been sick with tuber . . . tu . . ."

"Tuberculosis."

"Yes. And unable to work. You can't expect a man to . . ."

"June . . ."

"Enough. I get the point. So I'm a *schlemiel.*"

"You are *not* a schlemiel!" Malka protested, "You're a generous man who cares about people. You are also a merchant who puts honor above profit."

"I am also a schlemiel," Jacob said, shaking his head. "The total of all those credits would add up to a nice cash flow, right?"

"Right. It is never wrong, Jacob, to be generous with those less fortunate than we are. But too many credits is just not good business."

"You are right, as usual. I will stop giving credit."

"But if someone is down on his luck . . ."

"No. No more. This is a business. Like any other."

"Right."

"You can't pay suppliers with credit slips."

"Correct."

"From now on, pay up, or don't buy."

"Now you've got it."

Jacob swiveled swiftly around on his stool and braked his spin by grabbing the counter. "I knew if we talked rationally about this I'd find the answer."

"Of course."

Jacob beamed. He pointed to the account book. "It's all there in black and white."

"There it is."

"A little nudge of the brain, some calm reason, and I have it."

"You have it."

"The key to our success."

She smiled. "The very key."

July fourth was celebrated in Dawson not only as both Independence Day and Canada's Dominion Day, but also as the day Samuel Politzer made one of the biggest strikes in Klondike history. When the news reached town, Yukon River steamer whistles blew, crowds streamed to the claims office, and a proud Samuel, filthy with mud and covered with white dust, posed by the canvas bags containing the fortune he had brought in.

"Hard work and determination," he said, puffing on his big cigar, "and knowing where to dig!"

"What are you going to do with all the money?" someone asked.

"Spend it," Samuel yelled. "Wine, women, and song. Yes sir. . . ."

"Come to my place, Sammy boy," a little woman called out, the diamond in her front tooth sparkling in the flash of camera lights.

"You bet, Gertie," Samuel answered, "the first one on my list."

"Diamond Tooth Gertie, the first on his list?" Malka whispered to Jacob, referring to the biggest gambling casino in town. "He doesn't even know how to play cards."

"He knows how to drink, Malka, and the girls are pretty."

Malka made a face but soon was hugging Samuel and yelling with the rest of the crowd.

The commander of the police post in Dawson escorted Samuel and hangers-on to the bank where his bags of dust and nuggets were deposited for the night. The crowd wanted a special celebration, but because of the holiday they made do with drinks on the house at the Aurora saloon.

The next night Dawson put on a party that was big even by that town's standards. The Palace Theatre, an exquisite little Victorian building built by Arizona Charlie Meadows, presented a special show in honor of Samuel's strike. Everyone who could walk or crawl was in the audience.

Years later Malka would retell the story of that night to her enraptured grandchildren, complete with every gaudy detail of the women's clothes, the half-naked dancers, the men inside and out on the street shooting off firecrackers and dancing madly with each other. Dawson, after its few years of gold hysteria, had begun to wind down, and this strike gave the city its last chance to whoop it up again. Not long afterwards, Samuel sat in the Finesilvers' parlor and wondered what he would do with the fortune he had amassed.

"Of course, my family in Poland, if there is any family left," he said, "will come into a lot of money. I only hope they actually get it, you know, if the officials don't steal it first."

"We've got to think of a way," Jacob said, "something clever. Maybe hiding it in a bundle of dirty clothes. They wouldn't want to paw through that."

Malka interrupted, "Surely you're not thinking of sending it all home. You have a life here now in Canada. You could build a fine house, settle down and marry, and have children to carry on your name."

"No, my dear Malka, no wife, no children. There's no one here for me. But a house, maybe. I've been thinking a lot about something you said not long ago. About the difficulties in bringing Jacob's family here, plus the poor remnants of all the Jewish families in the Pale. Maybe that's why I've been working so hard, to find the means to do it. Because that's where this fortune of mine is going."

"Samuel, that's very ambitious," Malka said, "but do you think it's possible?"

"Anything is possible with money. This is a big, wonderful country. If Dawson City is any example, there must be a huge, mixed population in its big cities. In that way, it's like America. They have opened their land to the rest of the world. If we can believe what we hear about its size, then millions of refugees could come in and hardly make a difference."

The three talked into the night about relocating Jews from Eastern Europe and plans that would have to be made to keep the work going. The project was daunting, but it gave Samuel a new purpose in his life and a newfound optimism. And the time was right for Jacob to arrange his family's immigration to Canada. Perhaps this would make up for his flight from Khotin and the misery it had probably inflicted on them. But he also had a selfish reaction that he kept to himself: because of Samuel's new riches and plans for the future, he would have less time to brood over Malka. The subject was closed.

THIRTY-THREE

⚜

ON THE TENTH DAY OF AUGUST MALKA FAINTED IN THE store. Red Sky had been stacking tins of chipped beef and he ran to her, cradling her in his arms, imploring one of the ladies to run for the doctor. When Jacob came home from the buying trip to Skagway, she told him she was pregnant.

He became her shadow, following her, fetching, carrying, and watching every move she made. "Don't reach, I'll get it. Here, sit, you shouldn't be standing so long."

"Jacob, for heaven's sake, don't nag so. I'm not a china doll. I won't break. If you keep this up for nine months, we'll both be crazy."

"Eight months," Jacob mused, "next March. Do you realize I could be on a buying trip to Skagway then? What if I'm not here? What will you do? I can't go. We won't have any supplies. . . ."

"Nonsense. Red Sky is here, and the doctor, and Dove. Nothing will happen while you're gone. And if it does, I'm well taken care of."

"But what if the doctor's busy, or sick, or delivering another baby, or . . ."

"You're a real worrier, but I'll make you a promise. The baby will be fine, I will be fine, and there is absolutely nothing to it."

"Don't say that, Malka. You don't want to tempt the evil eye."

"If that's the case, I can't make preparations for the baby. Evil spirits would see me, right? So what do I do?"

"Don't make fun," Jacob scolded, but only half-heartedly.

Malka laughed. "Oh, all right. When someone asks me what I'm knitting, I'll tell them it's for the cat."

"We don't have a cat."

"We'll get one."

December first was snowy and bitterly cold. Malka awoke with a bad cold. Although she fought Jacob to stay "at her post," she lost the argument.

"You can't wait on people with a runny nose," he scolded before leaving the house that morning. "No one wants your germs. Besides," he added, hugging her, "I don't want this cold to get worse. And there's the baby to think of. No. You are staying home. Pamper yourself, Malka, stay in bed. Read and sleep and get well."

She grumbled but knew he was right. "Won't you miss me?" she asked wistfully as Jacob prepared to leave.

He kissed her on the cheek. "I hope I'm too busy to miss you."

When she crept into bed, pulled up the quilt and tried to sleep, she remembered tonight was *Erev Rosh Hashonah*, the night before the Jewish New Year, the first of the High Holy Days. She thought of her father again, and how he must be shining his shoes and mending tears in his clothes, the ones he would wear to *shul*.

For the second year in a row, the prospect of no shul, no services, and no cantor singing the heavenly prayers brought tears to her eyes and blocked her nose even more. How can this be, she thought, after all my years of faithful prayer?

Should I do as Jacob says and accommodate myself to the situation?

She could see him saying that, lecturing her like a father to a child, saying do as I do. He did try to help her over the rough times, the Sabbath nights with no sunset, the lack of wine, the lack of ritual. Of course he was right, but there was just so much accommodating one could do. After that, it was pure deprivation. She was certain she had lost her birthright, the gift of the Torah from God, the joy of prayer in her own house of worship, no matter how old and crumbling it was.

Nonsense, said her little voice.

What do you mean, nonsense? What do you know about it?

Plenty. I've been there, remember? Anyway, you haven't lost anything. The Torah is still yours, the word of the Lord and the Talmud, and all the holidays and rituals. You're just temporarily not observing, that's all.

Then you should know how hard this is for me.

So where is it written that life should be easy?

Once in a while, it wouldn't hurt.

Ah, would that it were, what I know is it cannot be.

What is that supposed to mean?

If things don't get better they'll get worse.

You're making fun of me.

I'm trying to show you the truth.

And I'm trying to understand.

Then stop whining, Malka. You can pray at home.

It's not the same.

No, but He will still hear you.

How can you be sure?

It's easy, Malka. It is said that any spot on which a man raises his eyes to heaven is holy. Believe me, He knows where you are and what you are doing with your life. Besides, He knows there's no shul in Dawson. He's not unreasonable.

Am I?

Yes.

And when Jacob goes to work on *Yom Kippur*, the holiest day of the year, will He be reasonable then?

I . . . I'm not sure.

Oh. Now you're not sure.

Are you, Malka?

No. Yes. He cannot go. We cannot go. We must not . . . oh, oh . . .

She turned her face into the pillow and wept.

Jacob walked to the store on Front Street, fretting about Malka's cold, her flush of fever, the unusual hoarseness in her voice. He would close the store at lunchtime to look in on her.

At noon he left Red Sky alone to handle customers and went home. He found Malka sleeping, pinned a note to the pillow, kissed her damp forehead and returned to the store. What he heard there did not please him.

"I ain't lettin' no Injun handle my food!" the man yelled, standing redfaced among the barrels. His attitude was menacing, one hand on a sheathed hunting knife at his belt. Red Sky, rigid with anger behind the counter, looked vulnerable, no match for the hulking customer. Jacob knew otherwise.

"Just a minute there," Jacob boomed, "I will have no violence in my store!"

"Then get rid of the Injun!" the man blurted.

"Red Sky works for me. If you don't like it, *you* can leave."

"Fine! And you and the Injun can go to hell!"

The man stalked angrily from the store and slammed the front door, jangling the string of bells against the glass.

"Jacob lose customer," Red Sky said, his face wet with perspiration. "Bad for business."

"To hell with that kind of customer," Jacob said, shrugging angrily out of his jacket and donning a white apron. "This town has enough bigots. If he and his ilk don't like shopping here, it's no loss to me."

Red Sky said nothing and resumed his stacking chores. The afternoon was busy with shoppers, the women gossiping in small groups by the stove. It was a comfortable place to linger. A small table with cups for tea and two chairs was in front of the stove, inviting and welcome. It had been Malka's notion that sitting and looking around at leisure would result in extra sales.

Today the customers seemed edgy. News of the quarrel had traveled quickly. One woman took Jacob aside. "You think that's a good idea, Jake? Fighting over that Indian? A lot of folks don't like them."

"Why do you suppose that is, Mrs. Nye?"

"Oh, you know, they're dirty, and they drink. And that one'll probably steal you blind behind your back."

"Is that right?" Jacob said innocently. "Now where did you hear that?"

Mrs. Nye pursed her lips and folded her arms on her billowing bosom. "Everyone knows that, Jake. And you know it, too. The best thing for you to do, if you want to keep your business, is to get rid of him."

Jacob was outraged but remained civil. "I do not know such things, Mrs. Nye. What I do know is that this Indian is a brave and loyal man. He saved Malka's life more than once on the trail to Dawson, and for that I shall always be in his debt. He is completely honorable, a hard worker, and he does *not* steal, nor does he drink on the job. He is clean and neat. An employer could not ask for more. Now, if you will excuse me, I must get back to work."

Mrs. Nye huffed her way out, followed by her irate friends. Red Sky removed his apron, put on his hat and made for the door.

"Where are you going?" Jacob shouted.

"No can stay. Too much trouble for you."

"The hell you say! Come back here. I'm the boss in this store, not them. If I say you work, you work."

"Jacob good man, but . . ."

"Then put on your apron and finish with those turnips. After that, I need you to help with the meat. And not another word about this. Understood?"

Red Sky cocked his head, thought over what Jacob had said, and read the fire in his resolute blue eyes. He removed his hat, put the apron back on and began sorting the turnips.

For the rest of the day Jacob knew this scene was only the beginning of trouble. There would be more, for it seemed that since man had first stood upright he had needed to look down on someone, to blame some lower caste for his misfortune.

Here, this land's own natives were subjected to the same abuse, and Jacob had tried to fight back for his friend with words. If necessary, he would use any weapon at his command. He hoped it would not come to that.

That night he expected Malka to declare herself ready to return to work and to try and convince him over dinner. When she said nothing about it, he was puzzled. But not for long. "Jacob," she said, curling up in his arms under the heavy quilt, "tomorrow is Rosh Hashonah."

"I know."

"In my father's last letter, he felt the need to remind me. Perhaps he anticipated my lapses, my non-observance, but I must tell you I'm filled with guilt."

"From what you've told me about him, I doubt very much if he had that in mind. He only meant to wish you and me a happy new year."

"Maybe, but it gnaws at me all the same. I've been thinking . . ."

"That means trouble."

"What I mean is, I was thinking about the Holy Days, and I thought maybe you should stay home. Wait, listen to me before you say no. If you stay home, we could recite prayers and sing a few songs. . . ."

"Malka, do you realize what that would mean? How much we would lose? How we would be depriving our customers, many of whom plan their shopping on certain days?"

"There are other stores in Dawson."

"That's just the point. Those other stores would be taking our business."

"For one day."

"Not necessarily. What if they liked the others better and . . . ?"

"They won't. Not after shopping at the Bonanza. They know us now, and know we have better merchandise."

"You're counting on loyalty, eh?"

"Yes."

The incident at the store with Red Sky was on Jacob's tongue, but he kept silent. Malka would hear of it sooner or later.

She sat up in bed and said firmly, "You argue that the Holy One will understand if we ignore the Holy Days, but I have come to the conclusion that He is available even to us living here in '*alle schvartz yoren!*' Furthermore . . ."

"Malka!" Jacob warned, his face flushed with annoyance and guilt. "Of course He is available. Even here, in all the black years, as you put it. Which means we can pray to Him without losing a penny."

"No," she said quietly. "That is not what it means. It means as long as He is in our hearts, He will hear us. But we must do what is right. And you know it."

"I know no such thing." He stomped out of the bedroom. But Malka was determined. She followed him into the parlor. "What happens," she said, "when Easter and Christmas fall on days during the week?"

"I know where you're going with that question, and it has no relevance."

"Of course it does. They are both religious holidays for the Christians, which means most of Dawson's people."

"You want me to admit they close up shop then, eh?"

"It's the truth."

"Do you have any idea how many Jews there are in town?"

"A handful."

"Correct."

"But Jacob, that's not a reason. Don't you think they wonder about us, the Christians, I mean? They can see we don't have horns. But all the other lies they've been told must surface once in a while. The Jews who use little boys as sacrifices in the temples, or squirrel away their money and cheat the poor, or . . ."

Jacob peered out of the frosted windows at the accumulation of snow outside the house. "If you worry about that sort of crap, excuse me, Malka, you are wasting your time."

"It exists."

"Sure. And will go on existing as long as they stay angry at us for 'rejecting' Christ."

"Maybe you and I, in our own way, could change that."

"Nonsense!"

"Maybe," she went on, ignoring his anger, "by keeping our faith even here, and it *is* 'all the black years' and you know it, it would show them we are at least sincere."

"I'm very tired, Malka, and this argument is leading us nowhere."

She was hurt and exasperated. With her cold in full bloom, she dabbed constantly at her nose and eyes. Her cheeks were pale and her head was full of cotton.

Nonetheless, she continued, "Jacob, you are a brave man with great resolve. You walked from Russia to Alaska, fought off hunger and cold, outwitted the police and survived the Arctic cold. You taught yourself a new language and learned to mine for gold. For all of that, I give you the credit you deserve. But you are a stubborn and arrogant man. Perhaps that is why you succeeded, but it's time you learned to bend with the wind. If you cannot bend a little, we will never be able to resolve our differences, and I am going back to bed." She turned on her heel and walked away quickly, closing the bedroom door with a strong thump.

Jacob was surprised at Malka's vehemence and shocked by her last words. He had never thought of himself as stubborn. As for arrogant, how could she say such a thing? A strong word for someone like Gittel Finesilver's eldest son, who had become head of a household as a young boy and always did his share of the work, never once raising his voice or disobeying. The more he thought about it, the more confused he became. Where did this strong feeling of hers come from? Why hadn't she brought it up before? To wait until Erev Rosh Hashonah and then spring it on him . . . that he should close the store.

Women, Jacob thought wearily, with their unpredictable moods, their overweening sentiments, their relentless optimism. How does a man cope with it? How does a husband convince such a wife that you don't change the world with warm cookies and fair play?

Grumbling to himself, he entered the bedroom, undressed and eased himself into bed. But he was too upset to sleep. Everything Malka had said disturbed his conscience and forced him to rethink the situation. It was almost morning when he finally made his decision and slept.

The Bonanza was closed for Rosh Hashonah, surprising the regular patrons, who wondered if the Finesilvers were ill or had suffered a death in the family. When Jacob opened the store two days later, some asked him outright about his absence. Jacob told them the truth, prepared for criticism. Their reaction was unexpected. Old Mrs. Swain summed it up for the majority of the Bonanza's friends when she said, "Of course you stayed home on your religious holiday. Don't the town shut up tight as a drum for Christmas? If your religion says do something, you do it."

Ten days later, on the eve of Yom Kippur, the holiest of Jewish holidays, Jacob, without a word from Malka, placed the sign in the window reading **"CLOSED TOMORROW"** and went home, righteous and content.

THIRTY-FOUR

⌒◯◯⌒

When Malka had recovered from her cold and returned to the store a week later, she saw how much Red Sky had done. He had reorganized the produce into one section and the hardware along the back wall. He had left the fabrics and sewing notions where she had placed them, but had moved the dress forms into one window, draping the headless wire frames with bolts of bright gingham.

"Dove's idea," he said modestly when Malka complimented him. "Dove like to make windows pretty and that bring in ladies to shop."

"Tell Dove that we like her idea very much. Better yet, bring Dove in so I can tell her myself."

"Thank you, Missy, but Dove is big with child now and waddles like fat duck. Baby come any time."

Malka made him promise to let her know when Dove had the baby and if they could help. He and Dove knew few people and were too shy to make friends easily. Although Red Sky still smarted from the hostility shown him on his first day at work, he held no grudges and hoped he and Dove could stay in Dawson and live in peace.

Their home was a small shack on the west edge of town abutting the lower rise of the Midnight Dome. The area was a shabby one where drifters or those down on their luck, as well as a few poor Indian families, were moving in. Some were from other tribes near the small towns north of Dawson. None, Red Sky intimated, had sought them out, preferring to keep to themselves. Indians, he knew, were seen at their best only when far from the white man.

Jacob's boast that the town would welcome Red Sky because of his heroism on the Chilkoot trail did not come true. More Dawsonites accepted the Indian, but not enough to make his life easy or pleasant.

"But," he said to Malka, "working for Jacob make up for everything." A few weeks later, at the end of the Sabbath, as Jacob was lighting the lamps and preparing for the *Havdallah* service, there was a banging on the front door. A distraught Red Sky stood on the stoop.

"Jacob, Missy, come quick. Dove—Dove—"

Jacob grabbed their coats and boots, and for some reason the *Havdallah* candle, stick and all.

When they rushed into Red Sky's shack, Dove was lying on a cot by the stove, sweating profusely, her face contorted with pain.

"Don't stand there like statues," Malka said to both men. "Jacob, boil big pots of water on the stove. Red Sky, gather up rags, old clothes, cloth of any kind. Put some in the pot to boil and bring me the rest. And newspapers. I heard they are sterile. Then fetch Dr. Nadler from the hospital. Go!"

Red Sky brought her the rags, clothes and newspapers, and hurried from the house. With Jacob tending the pots on the stove, Malka pulled off the covers and raised Dove's nightshirt. Gently, she pressed the palm of her hand on the swollen belly. Please, oh Holy One, she prayed silently, let the head be down, I do not know how to turn it.

"The contractions are coming faster now," she said to Jacob. "Go get more water. Quickly!"

"Missy," Dove whispered, catching at Malka's dress, "the baby . . . it hurts so much."

"I know, I know, but you are a brave woman. This will be over soon, and you will have a beautiful child to show for the pain."

"How soon?"

Malka wiped Dove's face with a clean rag and held her hand. "I don't know, Dove. Just hold on."

Although she seemed composed, Malka was frightened for both Dove and the baby. She had never delivered a child, never seen one born, and her bravado was talk, not experience. She was acting on a strong desire to help and what she had heard growing up in Khotin.

The pains seemed to lessen, and Dove dozed.

"What's happening?" Jacob asked.

"I guess I don't know. The pains were so close, then they stopped. I pray nothing's wrong."

A scream suddenly pierced the silence. Malka dashed to the bed and saw the baby's head protruding from the birth canal.

"Push, Dove," she cried, "push with all your might! Jacob, bring clean towels. The baby's here!"

Dove's screams filled the little shack, but Malka was too busy to hear them. She reached down and cradled the tiny head in her hands. It was covered with black hair, wet and matted. As she held it, it suddenly popped free, followed by little wet shoulders, one at a time, then the trunk, and finally the legs and feet.

"Jacob, help me. Here's the cord coming, and all kinds of . . . quick."

Jacob took the baby from Malka, holding it in his huge hands like a piece of china.

"I need something to cut the cord with," Malka said.

"My pocketknife, but it must be washed. In my pocket."
He turned, still holding the baby, and Malka reached for the knife. She dropped it into the hot water, then wiped it quickly on the clean rag, and with one swipe cut the cord halfway between the baby and the afterbirth.

"It's not crying, Malka," Jacob whispered frantically, "it's not breathing. What should I do?"

"Hold her by the feet and slap her back. No, not timidly, give her a whack. Hard."

Nothing happened. The baby hung upside down, eyes closed, body limp, the skin taking on a faint blue cast. Jacob whacked her again and again, but the baby made no sound.

"Is the heart beating?" Malka whispered.

Jacob put his ear to the tiny chest but shook his head. "I can't tell."

"She's got to have air. Maybe if I blew into her mouth . . ."

Malka moved fast, laid clean cloths on the floor and placed the baby on her back. She leaned over, pried open the tiny mouth and then breathed hard into it, one, two, three breaths, four, five, six.

Nothing.

She looked up at Jacob standing helplessly, then leaned down and began the process again. Dove called feebly, "Baby? Is baby dead?"

As Malka blew again into the baby's mouth, there was a sudden gasp for breath, a wet gurgle, and the infant's tiny face scrunched with her first wail. Malka and Jacob hugged each other and cried with relief. When Jacob brought the screaming baby, wrapped in an old shirt, to her mother, he said to Dove, "Your daughter. Isn't she beautiful?"

Red Sky arrived a short time later with Dr. Nadler, who wondered why he had been summoned. "Well," he said, smiling, "I see the patients are doing fine."

He opened his medical bag and took out a scalpel. After

examining the baby and the severed cord, he said, "Neat. You do this?" He looked at Jacob.

"My wife. We couldn't wait . . . the baby couldn't wait . . . for the doctor."

"That happens frequently," the doctor said, snipping off another portion of cord and leaving a tiny stump on the baby's navel. "Otherwise man wouldn't have survived until doctors were invented. It's a fine girl, Dove, healthy and perfect."

Red Sky stared at the squalling infant and leaned over the bed to examine her further.

"Missy save baby," Dove whispered to him.

Red Sky took Malka's hand and said to Dove, "Don't talk about it. She start long story about China person and you never hear the end."

Malka smothered a smile, then watched as the doctor cleaned Dove and disposed of the afterbirth, filing away her new knowledge, just in case. At the same time, she told the doctor of the baby's breathing problem. "I hope I didn't do the wrong thing."

"You did right as could be, Mrs. Finesilver. If I'm not careful, you'll be putting me out of business."

As they walked back home, Jacob held tightly to Malka's hand, helping her through the snowdrifts and over the slippery spots. He was proud of Malka and of himself. Like so many other times in his life when it seemed everything was as good as it gets, Jacob silently recited his prayers, one after the other, hoping to ward off the evil eye.

THIRTY-FIVE

⊷⊙⊶

ON A BITTER COLD MORNING JUST BEFORE DAWN, AN urgent banging on the front door awakened Malka. She lit the bedside lamp, glanced quickly at Jacob, put on her robe and slippers and ran down the stairs. When she opened the front door, Dove was standing on the front steps.

"What is it? What has happened?" she asked. "Is it Red Sky or, heaven forbid, the baby?"

"No, no, Missy."

"Come in out of the cold. You look frozen."

Malka sat her by fireplace and threw another log on the glowing embers. "Warm yourself, then tell me why you are here in the dead of night."

The Indian woman's face was pale, her light brown skin tinged with blue beneath the pallor. She blew on her hands and spoke in her soft, singsong voice.

"Last night I take food to Samuel, for he ails from a sickness. I bring whole duck and mashed potato and try to feed him. But he burns with fever and cannot eat. I stay at Indian Creek for two hours . . . then he talks, how you say it . . . gibber-gabber. . . ."

"Delirious?" Malka prompted.

"Yes. He talks of his mother and worry over her. And Missy, over and over he says . . . Malka . . . Malka."

Malka stared in surprise. "My name?"

"Yes. So now baby is with Red Sky. I come to ask you, please see Samuel."

"Of course. Dove, you go home and get some rest. I will go immediately."

"No. I will wait for you. Country is hard to walk in high snow . . . Missy lose way."

Malka threw some first-aid supplies in a small backpack and dressed in the warmest clothes she could find: Jacob's long johns and trousers, heavy woolen shirt, two sweaters and fur parka, knee-high boots, mittens, scarf and hat. She left a note for Jacob, joined Dove, and together they set off on the fifteen-mile trek to Samuel's claim at Indian Creek.

The sun sat at eye level in the eastern sky when they reached Samuel's cabin. Dove lit a fire in the stove and set a kettle of water to boil. Malka went immediately to Samuel's bedside, her breath catching at the sight of her friend's condition.

Under the blanket, Samuel's large, muscular frame lay wasted and thin. His hands outside the cover were gray, the thick fingers lying still. His mouth, usually so occupied with unconstrained laughter or serious conversation, was pasty-lipped and hung open as he tried to catch his breath. His eyes were sunken and deeply shadowed, but he recognized Malka and tried to speak.

"I . . . I . . . so cold . . ."

"Hush," she whispered, "save your strength. We will talk later."

Dove brought weak tea in a mug and Malka tried to slip a few drops between his cracked lips. "Come on, Samuel, just a bit to warm you. You must try to drink it."

She bathed Samuel's face in warm water, murmuring words of encouragement as she worked.

Dove left early in the afternoon, promising to get word to

Jacob that Malka would stay with Samuel overnight. His fever raged, and whatever illness had struck him was now in full command of his shivering body. He could not be left alone.

Malka knew Jacob would be angry, but she had to chance that. Samuel was Jacob's friend, too, and she had no doubt he would do the same in a similar situation.

During the dark hours of the night Samuel called for Malka, saying her name over and over like a chant. The first few times she answered, running to see what he wanted. But she soon realized it was delirium, that he was only saying her name, not calling for her. His condition was frightening, and Malka was unsure if she was doing all the correct things.

She should have brought the doctor, but knew the man would not tramp all this way, even in good weather. When Samuel's fever seemed at its highest, Malka pulled off the covers and removed his underclothes. She paid no attention to his naked body other than to note its deterioration. The huge man was ravaged by illness, the ribcage bulging, the pelvis sharp and prominent under the slack skin, the dramatic loss of weight at once frightening and touching.

She was not a doctor. She did not even know why Samuel was sick or what disease he had contracted. And she knew nothing about medicines or methods of healing. She could only do what instinct prompted, and that was to try to bring the fever down. Wadding clean rags together, she soaked them in an alcohol solution and began bathing him, slowly and methodically, from head to toe.

At one point during the alcohol bath, he grabbed her arm and cried out, "They're coming! Quick! You must hide!"

"Who is coming, Samuel?"

"Mother is in the house. We must get her out or they will kill her!"

His hand gripped her arm, the sudden surge of strength

catching her off guard. "Stop it, Samuel," she said firmly, pulling free, "no one is coming. You are dreaming."

At the sound of her voice, Samuel's eyes seemed to focus. He stared at Malka and at his naked body under her fingers. "My God . . . what are you doing?"

"I'm bathing you with rubbing alcohol, Samuel Politzer, so don't get any fancy ideas!" Malka snapped. "You have a fever, and if I don't do this, you will die. Close your eyes if the sight is too painful. But don't make it more difficult than it already is."

Her scolding relaxed him, and when Malka resumed his bath Samuel closed his eyes and fell asleep. But his ravings kept on, some of it intelligible, most not. She heard the word, "mother," over and over, and snatches of pleading, although it was unclear what he pleaded for.

When she had finished, Malka dressed him in clean flannel pajamas and covered him with a light blanket. Then she pulled a chair over to the bed, settled herself into the cushions, and prepared for a long vigil.

"You are home, finally?" Jacob asked, as Malka let herself into the house. "Five days and five nights, I might add, that you have been away."

"I can count, too, Jacob," Malka replied, hanging her jacket on the hall tree. "I hope you missed me."

"How is Samuel?" he asked, ignoring her statement. "He must be better or you would not have returned."

"He is, as they say, out of the woods. His fever raged for days. I feared for his life at one point when his eyes rolled back in his head. I thought his heart had stopped beating."

Jacob frowned. "What was it?"

"I'm sure it was pneumonia. His chest rattled and the angel of death came and sat on the bed and laughed at the sound of his pitiful coughing."

"I see. And when do you hang out your shingle and give Dr. Nadler some competition?"

Malka stretched out on the sofa in the parlor and uttered a weary sigh. "I only say that because my mother died of it and that is how Papa used to describe her last hours."

Jacob, chastened by her words, turned to poke at the fireplace ashes, trying to re-ignite the kindling. When it flamed up, he said, "How did you find your way home in the dark?"

"Dove walked back with me."

"She was there, too?"

"No. She was, at the beginning, and she brought food one night, and when she came this afternoon, I told her I could leave. So she . . ."

Jacob had been stewing, simmering in anger like a pot on the fire. He suddenly whirled around and spoke his mind.

"You should not have done this, Malka. A pregnant, married woman, with responsibilities at home. The women are prattling like a flock of hens."

"So when did gossip suddenly make a coward of you?" she retorted. "What do we care what they say? And would it have been more seemly if I was a single woman? Or would that have been even more grist for their mill?"

"We will not discuss this."

"Oh, yes we will!" Malka sat up on the sofa, her cheeks ablaze. "I did what had to be done. Samuel was alone and dying. One does not leave a man alone to die. Especially a friend. What about Dingo Malone? You could not do that. And I have seen you nurse a goat back to health. Isn't Samuel more precious than a goat?"

Jacob stalked angrily upstairs. "We will talk about it tomorrow. I'm tired."

Malka ran to the foot of the stairs and yelled, "And what about me? I just walked fifteen miles in the snow and wind. Should I be dancing?"

Sleepless nights caring for Samuel and the long walk home suddenly sapped Malka's remaining strength. She clung to the newel post for support, but the wave of exhaustion swept over her like a dark shroud, and she dropped to the floor.

Sunlight poured into the bedroom window. From somewhere outside, Malka heard the sweet song of a bird. A wonderful way to awaken, she thought. The bird is real, I heard it. Can spring be far behind?

"Ah, you're awake." Jacob came into the room bearing a tray. "I've been bringing you breakfast for two days now, and it's time you ate it."

Malka stared at her husband, searching for the anger he had displayed such a short time ago. Could it have been two days?

"I slept all that time?" she asked.

"Like the dead. I poked you once to make sure you were still alive."

"Jacob . . ."

"Malka . . ."

She studied him, trying to assess his mood, whether or not he still harbored any anger toward her. But his smile seemed genuine, his concern real as he hovered over her.

"You seem yourself again," Jacob said, watching his wife eat the muffins and jam, refilling her glass with hot tea for the third time.

"This tastes heavenly. I don't think I knew how hungry I was. Thank you, Jacob. Sit here," she urged, moving over to make room on the edge of the bed.

"I must return to work. Red Sky is all alone in the store."

"Red Sky can handle everything, Jacob, and you know it. I think it's more important that we talk."

"What's to say?" he mumbled, sitting gingerly so as not to upset the tray.

"I cannot stand it when there are bad feelings between us," Malka said. "The last thing I remember is a pretty hateful scene, a jealous husband preferring not to understand why his wife acted in the only way she knew how."

"Mm-mm. Jealous, indeed, but I was helpless to fight it."

"You? Helpless? Tell me the world is flat, or that Jews are welcome in Minsk . . . but don't tell me you were helpless to fight anything!" Malka was not joking; her face was set, her eyes narrowed.

"Drink your tea. I refuse to heat all this up one more time."

"Jacob . . ."

"No, hear me out. If I can't get it said all in one piece, it will strangle me. I have suffered from a conflict of feelings since I found you gone last week. After Dove told me what happened, I was furious . . . and I was proud . . . all at the same time. Of course I am jealous of Samuel. He's handsome and tall . . ."

"So? You are ugly and short?"

" . . . and unmarried," he went on, ignoring her. "Malka, I'm not blind. It's obvious how Samuel feels about you."

When Malka vigorously shook her head, he blurted, "Then you are the one who is blind!" He rose angrily, upsetting the tray. But neither he nor Malka noticed. The argument seemed to be resuming at precisely the point where it had left off. It was all leading to a blind end, and Malka could not let that happen.

If only he could overcome those childish feelings, she thought, say what he thinks without feeling diminished as a man. What is the matter with men, anyway? Must they always act this way? As though no one is right but them? Even so, she knew it was up to her to put things right.

"I am sorry if I caused you concern, Jacob," she said, "but I had to help our friend. If I had not gone with Dove,

Samuel would be dead now. I guess it's better to be angry with me than to mourn at Samuel's funeral."

Jacob had had time to concoct an argument against all of Malka's assertions, but when the words formed on his lips, he found he could not speak them. What he found he wanted to say was something else entirely: "*I had a lot of time to think. And I finally realized that you are a dear, kind, compassionate woman, and I am the richer for it. I've acted like a fool, and I ask you to forgive me. . . .*"

Good words, honest and heartfelt, certain to break down the emotional impasse keeping them apart. But they too remained unspoken. Instead, Jacob nodded at his wife, mumbled something and walked out of the room.

Malka knew the anger was dissipated, that their lives would now go on as before. For Jacob. But for Malka, a little piece of her feeling for him crumbled. His stubborn streak, so admirable in times of crisis, was wearing her down.

But she had just made a startling discovery: she could be just as stubborn. And even more, she was learning how to use her stubbornness. Backed into a corner, Malka could fight just as hard as Jacob.

She picked up the tray, mopped at the spilled tea and sighed with resignation. Her righteousness was real, but she was convinced that marriage was a tenuous relationship, more dependent on the woman's attitudes and sensitivities than the man's. It was not fair. But neither were pogroms. One either hid in the barn or died.

And Malka was a survivor.

THIRTY-SIX

⌒⊙⌒

THERE WERE THREE SMALL BEDROOMS ON THE THIRD
floor of Evelyn MacMillan's house in which a lady of the
evening doled out her services to eager clients, services ren-
dered to match the clink of coins or the rustling of bills the
men placed atop the wooden chest of drawers.

On this cold late April night in the room furthest from the
stairway, Kitty Beebe, the newest, and at eighteen the
youngest of Evelyn's recruits, rested warily in the arms of Big
Jim Cusper. Kitty's eyes were wide open, her skin tingling with
bruises from the first rough coupling of the long night. Big Jim
Cusper had a notorious appetite, and one roll in the hay was
only the beginning for him. He rolled over and fondled Kitty's
backside, his breath sour with his cigar and rye whiskey when
he said sharply, "C'mon, honey, let's do it again."

"I need the money first," Kitty reminded him, her palm out.

"Don't be that way," Jim growled, pawing her roughly,
"you know I'm good for it."

"Evelyn says I have to charge for each—uh—you know."

"Yeah, all right. You'll get it. First let's have a nice kiss."

The more demanding Big Jim became, the more Kitty
pulled away. She was new to this game, but she was a quick
study. Coming over the Chilkoot last fall had been no picnic,
and she had toughed it out with help from a couple of stam-

peders who hoped she would remember and repay them with her kind of affection. The Klondike gold rush had offered the orphan from Seattle a chance to work and save enough money to live on for a long time when she went home.

She had found work at Evelyn MacMillan's house, the cleanest and best run brothel in town. She only had to know the rules.

"You'll learn," Evelyn had warned Kitty, "you'll get your fee each time they spurt. If you forget, or think I won't know the difference, you're through."

Kitty understood. With most customers, it was quick; a grab for her breasts, a lunge over her, a fast penetration, some heavy breathing and a friendly "Thank you, ma'am." She did not mind the sex. Sometimes she enjoyed the closeness with a man, so unlike her childhood, which had been lacking in any affection.

But with men like Big Jim, who took forever and wanted it all night long, Evelyn's words, "Cash before fun," echoed in her ears.

He was yanking her under his hungry body by her long red hair, and Kitty did not like that. "Stop it, Jim, let me go."

"I didn't pay for no back talk. Spread your legs again. Open up!"

"C'mon, Jim, give me a few minutes to wash and cool down a little. You know it gets awful warm up here in this little room."

"You sure you're just not tryin' to put me off? I been waitin' a long time for a juicy little tart like you, and I won't be pushed aside. Now," he said, his voice hissing through his teeth, his hands squeezing her knees until she thought she would scream, "like I said, spread your legs!"

Kitty's green eyes narrowed with anger. Why was he roughing her up like this? Her natural timidity melted and she reached out to push him away.

Surprised by her action, Big Jim lashed out with a huge hand, but Kitty ducked. His hand missed her head, swiping instead at the guttering oil lamp by the bed and knocking it to the wood floor. The bowl shattered and splashed kerosene everywhere. Flames shot up, licking at the wet fuel, dancing in an orange line of fire across the floor and up the satin bedsheets, jumping to the clothes on the open rack, the frilly curtains, the ceiling. The room was an inferno in a matter of seconds.

Evelyn's house was engulfed in flames that poured from every window, all things lacquered and festooned, feathery and lacy, fed the hungry blaze until nothing was left. Then the flames leapt to the next house and the next tavern, and the warehouses, and all the stores in its path that caught and crackled and lit up the sky.

Although it was April, the temperature was forty-two below zero, and the firemen worked in vain to chop ice from the Yukon River for water. It was useless, because the boilers for the hoses were cold. And their boilers were cold because the men had been on strike for better wages. After a disastrous fire the previous year, the town council had hemmed and hawed when asked to finance reels and hoses for the small company of firefighters, but they had raised the money. The new steam engines were stationed on the river ice and covered by double tents. These stood over large holes excavated in the ice down ten feet to flowing water. A man was supposed to be stationed at each engine to keep fire in the boilers at all times. But the men were on strike and no one was at the stations.

Without heat in the boilers, water froze before it could reach the nozzles, and the ice expanded and ripped the new hoses open. Bystanders and those in bucket brigades watched helplessly as Dawson City collapsed in a shower of explosions and flames. Those same buildings in which miners had lit their cigars with fifty-dollar bills or gambled away enough gold dust to buy equipment for three towns, were burned to the ground. The screams and yelling and crashing of falling buildings woke Malka and Jacob. They ran to the windows. Malka cried, "Jacob, look! Isn't that Evelyn's house? Come quickly, we've got to help."

He looked at Malka, pregnant, unsteady on her feet, and wondered how he could insist she stay home when all around them the danger was life-threatening. Their home could be next. Despite his misgivings, he agreed, and they threw on coats and boots and ran into the frigid night. But Jacob knew, as he watched each wooden structure collapse, there was no hope. The Bonanza Market was right in the fire's path.

While Jacob joined the men on the bucket line, Malka ran to Evelyn's house, screaming to the crowd, "Evelyn, Evelyn MacMillan. Is she out? Did she come out? Can you tell me where she is? Please! Someone!"

The steaming fog made it difficult to see anything as flames shot high into the air. Malka rushed through the conflagration, unmindful of the wood and glass exploding around her. She reached the flaming house only to be turned back by dense heat and smoke. A man, his face streaming with blackened sweat, took her roughly by the arm and steered her away.

"Let me go," Malka cried. "My friend is in there. Please!"

"There's nothing you can do, lady. Can't you see that? There ain't no house left, for Chrissake! And there ain't no friend of yours left, neither!"

"Oh, Lord of mercy, that cannot be true," Malka cried, freeing herself. She ran, stumbling and falling over the slick, snow-covered ground, searching among the faces in the crowd. Surely someone had seen Evelyn.

Those fortunate enough to escape the flames staggered under the weight of rescued treasure into the swampy land behind Front Street. Others frantically waved money in their fists as they shouted for help. Saloon owners overturned barrels of liquor in last-ditch attempts to save their buildings, but the whisky froze as it ran into the streets.

Malka wept with frustration and despair, darting back and forth like a spectre in the eerie orange light of the flames. Evelyn must have escaped, she must be there in the crowd somewhere. If only Malka could get closer, perhaps she could find her.

"Evelyn!" she screamed, but the noise of the fire and the crowd drowned out her voice. Her throat burned from the smoke, yet she edged back inside the fence, clawing her way up the walk, falling over huddled bodies so badly burned she could not tell men from women.

A roar of sound enveloped the scene as one of the dry wooden stores burst into flame. Malka stumbled backwards as shock waves from the noise and heat rolled over her. It was no use, no use at all. Evelyn was dead. The man had told the truth. Nothing could live through that fiery hell.

Suddenly she was bumped and thrown to the ground by screaming naked girls running from the brothels. Some of those folk standing nearby took off their coats to cover the terror-stricken women. Malka grabbed at one of them, crying, "Please, can you tell me? Evelyn, is she still inside?"

But the young woman could only sob hysterically, and Malka moved away. Another girl, her hair a smoky cluster of burned tufts, face black with smoke, ran to Malka and grabbed at her robe. "You're looking for Evelyn?"

"Yes! Can you tell me . . . ?"

"She's dead," the girl cried. "I fell over her body on the landing. All burned up, her dress still on fire, she was trying to pull Lola down the stairs, trying to save her. Oh, dear God!"

The girl was cradled in a man's arms and led from the scene. Malka turned away and wandered the street awash in a mass of slushy ice. As she reached the corner of Princess and Harper streets she stared numbly at the sight. The Bonanza Market, as well as the stores on both sides, was being devoured by billowing smoke. The intense heat held spectators back and discouraged their attempts to save anything inside.

Malka found Jacob, his shoulders sagging, watching their hard work and capital investment turn to ashes. Timbers crashed to the ground, glass sizzled and burst into millions of shards twisting and sparkling in the eerie light. From within the eye of the inferno, the wind spewed out a myriad of burning embers, popping and snapping like erupting firecrackers.

They stood in silence, illuminated by the fiery light reaching almost to the sky. The Bonanza, Malka thought, so much more than a store. Hours of work, careful stacking, buying the best to offer to the people of Dawson, shelves neat with bolts of gingham and voile and lace, and the treasured china teapot she had carried over the Chilkoot Pass. The finest meat and freshest fruit, the newest in tools, patterns and cloth from New York and Paris. It had rescued Red Sky from idleness, given him an independence and pride of work rarely enjoyed by his brothers, as well as the ability to provide a home for Dove and their baby. When the mine had dried up, the store had meant a new beginning for Jacob. He and Malka had forged a life for themselves in town, a life of prosperity and dignity no scratching for gold could have given them.

"We will rebuild, Jacob," Malka said.

"No," he said, his hoarse voice unsteady with sorrow, "it is over for us."

"I refuse to believe that. We started once. We can do it."

"Stop it!" Jacob cried. "You don't know what you're saying. We have lost everything!"

Malka took his smoke-blackened face between her hands. "No, not everything, Jacob. Evelyn lost everything. We still have our lives."

THIRTY-SEVEN

᠊ᠣᠥᠥ᠊

MALKA WAS RIGHT. WITH A NEW TEA TABLE GRACING THE front window, the Bonanza Market reopened for business on May first. Jacob expanded by buying bulls and pigs for slaughter and sale in Skagway and shipping them to Dawson City. The Bonanza was the only market in town offering fresh meat.

Once again the Dawson City Mercantile Bank lent Jacob the money, fully aware that the market's ample stock helped feed and supply most of the town through the brutal winters. But the interest on the mortgage was hefty. Unless the Finesilvers had a very good year, the result would be foreclosure.

"It was lucky the fire was in spring," Malka said one evening. They were tabulating the day's receipts at the tea table. Only one lantern was lit. The rest of the store receded into the shadows.

"Lucky? You call the fire lucky?" Jacob said, incredulous. "How can you say that?"

"Because, dear husband, if it had been in the fall, the river would have soon frozen, leaving us idle all winter with no hope and no money." Malka smiled confidently. "This way, we rebuilt and restocked before the river iced over. That's why I said we were lucky."

Jacob studied Malka's face in the lamplight. Such a pretty face, he thought. A sharp tongue, but smart. And loving. And strong. She was right. They were lucky.

"Mm-hmm," was all he said.

Malka closed the ledger and stretched her back. The low muscles had been aching more lately, making her tired and irritable, though she tried to hide it. After the dizzy spells and nausea of her first months of pregnancy had disappeared, she had begun to feel better. Helping Jacob rebuild the store had kept her busy and too involved to think about how she felt.

But his lengthy buying trips to Skagway left her alone for weeks at a time. Her legs and ankles swelled, but the doctor promised only four more weeks, and she could tolerate that.

She and Jacob would talk into the night about the plans they had for the baby, boy or girl. They had heated discussions about names. It was fine with Jacob if Malka named the first girl. Of course, if it was a boy, then he, as the father, would name him.

Malka wrote her father once a week. Nathan, for his part, had been almost as faithful. The only weeks he missed were those when he was too sick to hold the pen. But he did not tell her that. He blamed it on the weather, or a flurry of business at the butcher shop, or the nagging customers. Malka did not need to worry about her father, he said. But as for Jacob's mother, she never received half of Jacob's letters. The officials stole them, because he always included money. When she would ask for letters at the town hall, the Russians would wave her away.

"Nothing today, Jewish lady. Go home to your matzos and leave us alone. Your wonderful son should have thought of you before he ran off like a coward."

Perhaps twice a year, they would steal the money but give Gittel Finesilver a letter which she read to Velvel, Miriam,

Esther and Uncle Aaron. With half a year between letters, piecing it all together was difficult, but a little news was better than nothing.

On a bitter cold Friday morning in February, Malka doubled over with her first contraction. She was at home. Alone. Jacob had gone by dogsled to Yellow Knife for supplies, assured by Dr. Nadler the baby was not due for another week.

The baby had other ideas.

By the time Jacob returned from Yellow Knife, his new daughter was three days old and sleeping almost around the clock, awake only for her feedings. Samuel gave the baby a beautiful painted wooden cradle decorated with pink satin ribbons, which Malka had placed close enough to the bed so she could hear every sound from Mira, named for Jacob's sister.

"She's so small," Jacob said, "but she looks like you."

"You think so? I thought she looked more like you." Malka grinned. "Until you grew your beard, of course."

Mira's arrival seemed to be part of a grand plan put together by a saintly command and given life to enrich theirs. It was a dangerous belief, but her existence baffled, thrilled and delighted them. They doted on her, especially Jacob, who was fascinated by her tiny fingers and toes, her keen look whenever he nuzzled her nose to nose, the way she smiled when he came into the room and giggled when he tickled her tummy. Malka and Jacob shared the responsibility for diapers and walking the floor in the middle of the night, and Jacob took over the bottle washing and filling when Malka stopped nursing. Malka stayed home with Mira and hoped to now indulge in the social life of Dawson. A prosperous merchant's wife should be part of the scene. It was the custom for the women to select an afternoon or early evening in which they would be at home to preside over an open house with punch and small cakes and cookies, and to catch up on the latest news and gossip.

Many women knew Malka from the store, and she counted on their friendship to begin her series of teas. Although it was considered a snub to the hostess if one did not attend, Malka had never imagined this would happen to her. "Why, Jacob, why didn't they come?" she asked one evening as they were closing the store.

"Perhaps the word did not get around."

"No. They all knew. What should I have done, take the front page of the *Dawson Nugget* to advertise my tea party?"

"Don't fret, Malka, you can start again next week."

"I will. And if they don't show up then, to hell with them."

They did not come the following week either, and Malka, true to her word, shut her door permanently to the ladies of Dawson. At first she thought it was because she and Jacob were Jewish. But Jacob roared, "Not here! Not in this free land! Forget that, Malka, this is not the Pale."

He knew why the women had snubbed Malka. After weeks of watching the humiliation wear her down, he finally told her the truth.

"Promise not to get angry, Malka, but it's because of your friendship with Evelyn. They're furious with you, a respected member of the Dawson community, for having, you know, a shady lady for a friend."

"If you're right, I'm glad they didn't show up in my house. I'll never feel comfortable with any of them again."

"Don't blame them too much," Jacob soothed, "they do business with us, they're mostly from small towns in the States or Canada, and they don't tolerate what they don't understand."

"Fine. You and I are from a small town. Our shetl is about as small as a town can be. . . ."

"Don't try to figure it out, Malka. Just accept it. We won't be living here forever."

Malka tried to forget the ugly lesson taught her by the ladies of Dawson, for Jacob's sake. Their livelihood depended on good relations. She let it go at that. Still, it hurt not to be invited to the elaborate get-togethers at the governor's house. She longed to see the women dressed in rose panne velvet gowns and large hats that dripped with willow plumes. And the ornate silver services on lace-covered tea tables loaded with salted almonds and stuffed olives, homemade Turkish Delight and fudge and maple creams and pineapple sherbet.

They were also excluded from the dances at the Arctic Brotherhood Hall, where couples danced two-steps and schottisches and French minuets until dawn, fortified with huge bowls of salad, giant pots of baked beans, carved turkeys and a well-spiked punch bowl that never ran dry. All this because of Malka's friendship with the "wrong woman." It was a cruel lesson in peer pressure and censure not lost on Malka. Still, she spent happy days playing with Mira, and sewed beautiful little baby gowns and matching bonnets and quilts for the crib. The house shone from top to bottom with her loving care, dusting and cleaning and polishing. She loved cooking for Jacob, simple but delicious meals, especially on Shabbes eves: stews, thick soups and braided challahs with raisins. Jacob protested mildly, saying he was going to get fat, but he was still slim and handsome. And he loved her fussing over him.

The snubs by the women of the town gradually lost their sting. Malka knew what was right and what was not. No one had to show her the proper manners for table behavior, social graces or cordiality.

But she never forgot. If this was the worst they could do to her, so be it. That thought was comforting.

THIRTY-EIGHT

࿐

THE TYPHOID EPIDEMIC STRUCK DAWSON CITY WITH A terrible ferocity after a torrential all-night rain, the runoff spilling into both the Klondike and the Yukon Rivers, which already teemed with mud from the streets along with pieces of the wooden sidewalks. The disease spread with frightening speed. By nightfall it claimed thirty victims.

The hospital was filled to capacity, with beds overflowing into halls and passageways. No medicine seemed to affect the vicious organism, and those who sickened the quickest died the same way.

Little Mira, who almost never cried, now could not stop. For three days and nights she wailed. No cool cloths or warm milk could console the stricken baby. Malka sat by the cradle, rocking, singing, praying. Then, suddenly, without warning, Mira stopped crying. The quiet seized Malka's heart.

She screamed for Jacob to get the wagon, lifted Mira in her arms and stumbled down the stairs. Jacob flung open the stable door only to see the horse lying frozen to death in the straw. Bleak luck—Samuel had moved into town and was now their neighbor. Without losing a moment, and in snow up to his knees, Jacob struggled into the street and hollered at the top of his lungs, "SAMUEL! HEAR ME! HEAR ME!"

Samuel ran out of his house, immediately hitched up his wagon, and had Malka and Jacob on their way in minutes.

With her husband urging the horse onward, Malka sat on the wagon seat holding the bundled baby. "See, Mira," she murmured, "we're almost there. The doctor will help you, and . . ."

But she could see the baby changing color in front of her eyes. The beautiful skin turned darker and darker to a light shade of brown, then darker to gray, now black. The cotton bunting hardly moved over her chest. Malka knew. But she screamed, "Faster, Jacob, faster!"

When they reached the hospital, she jumped down from the wagon with Mira and ran, slipping through the snow. Jacob banged on the door until it was finally opened by one of the priests. "Mira, it is Mira," Malka cried frantically to the priest, "you must help her. She is so sick."

The priest took the baby, stared at her for a moment, then handed her to a nurse. "Mrs. Finesilver, surely you must know there is nothing we . . ."

"No! She only just got sick. In the afternoon she was fine. Please do something. You will make her well, I know."

Jacob turned from Malka and sat heavily on a chair. "Malka," he said hoarsely, "don't you know what Father Moore is saying? Mira is . . ."

"No. She is not," Malka cried aloud. "Please—"

But they knew. Malka and Jacob knew. They did not need the priest to tell them. Mira was gone, the child who would carry on their lives when they were no more. When the priest left them alone with their crushing sorrow, Malka closed her eyes and saw Mira's little face, her father beaming at his beautiful grandchild. Now he would never see her or hold her, touch the perfect little hands with the tiny half moons on each finger. Her anguish was so immense she could barely breathe, and she and Jacob could not comfort each other.

The next afternoon their friends gathered in the parlor,

trying to help. Red Sky and Dove made sandwiches, mostly to keep themselves busy but also to feed the people who grieved with them.

Jacob could not speak. Why, he wondered, almost like a child, why did I lose my precious baby? What could we have done? Oh God, how could you punish me so? The baby's expressive eyes, so full of curiosity, following his fingers when he waggled them in her face, little squeals when he tickled her with one of her stuffed animals . . . here for one minute, inexplicably gone the next, she had never had time to do anything but be adorable and sweet.

Malka sat surrounded by her friends, Samuel and Dove and Red Sky, even Cannibal Sam, who had walked all the way from Yellow Knife to pay his respects. Jacob marveled that Malka could even speak, for he was choked with tears.

Somehow the day finally ended. People drifted away, and Malka and Jacob were left alone with their sorrow. They held each other close and tried to talk of burial arrangements, how best to do this without a rabbi or a cemetery plot.

But the cemetery board ruled the next day that Mira was still contagious and could not be buried.

Malka hurried to the hospital for the priest's counsel. "Why has this happened to us? And what am I to do with my blessed child's body?"

The priest took her hand. "We do not question the Lord, Mrs. Finesilver, and you must not, either. He has a plan for everything."

"And is it part of His plan that Mira cannot be buried?"

The priest walked over to the stove, rubbed his hands in the warmth, and spoke without turning around. "Perhaps. At any rate, I, as operator of this hospital, can tell you that Baby Mira must not be buried in any cemetery. Because of the typhoid fever living in even a dead body, her tiny vessel must be cremated."

"No!" Malka rose swiftly from her seat. "We cannot do that. In our faith we . . ."

"My dear Mrs. Finesilver," the priest said, exasperated, "your faith and my faith have no rights in this case. When an epidemic as virulent as typhoid strikes a town of forty thousand people, one must put aside one's sensitivities, and yes, even faith, and do what is best for the many."

He took Malka's arm. "Please sit down, and we will discuss the details. God will not punish you. I will vouch for that."

It seemed to her that years of faithful observance were now being tested in every quarter of her life. Here she was, confiding in a Catholic priest, seeking out this man of an alien faith for comfort and guidance. Had the whole world going mad, or just her world? Would her life ever again have any spiritual meaning? She had never thought the time would come when expedience could replace tradition. Life had become a grim horror in this abysmal world of women against the hostile land, of men shuffling through town with no place to go and nothing to do, the eerie silence of winter creeks and brooding woods, and only the certainty that this wilderness stretched for thousands of unbroken miles in every direction.

Her little voice, silent since Mira's death, began to speak.
You are sad?

I'm not certain of anything any more.

Oh? You're going to question the Blessed One, Praised Be He?

I have to admit for the first time, my faith is shaken.

I can't listen to this. I'm going.

No! Please don't leave me. Tell me what to do. Life is so cruel.

You never felt that way before, even in the face of poverty and pogroms?

I never lost a child before.

You make a good point. . . .

Her voice could not console her. They decided to bury Mira's ashes with those of the valiant RCMPs who had died on duty and were laid to rest in a little cemetery near the Midnight Dome. Malka could take no more.

THIRTY-NINE

❦

"I'M LEAVING, JACOB. IF YOU WANT TO COME WITH ME, fine, but I'm going away from here, from Dawson, as far away as I can go."

Jacob sprawled in a chair by the fireplace. He listened to Malka but did not look at her. He stared at the floor, at the sagging wood strips badly warped and sloping toward the wall. He knew that every house, every building in Dawson sagged, built on the constantly shifting permafrost without the benefit of foundations high off the ground. It was just another fact to be filed away.

He looked up at her. "So go, Malka, if you have to."

"Go, Malka? That's all you have to say? "

"What do you want me to say? I can't go with you."

Malka's eyes were flat and hard with anger. "Why not?"

"The store, it's hardly paid for," he said grimly. "The debts are still outstanding. I am still an honorable man."

She shrugged. "You can sell it and probably get a good price for it. Look how successful it is. And with built-in help like Red Sky and Dove, someone here would be happy to snap it up."

There was no answer from Jacob for what seemed a long time. Malka tried to be patient. She knew Mira's death still weighed him down; her calm mien was mostly for her own sake. But her heart felt leaden, without feeling, without hope. Her pain was so searing she wondered how she could speak to Jacob. She felt old and shriveled in the grip of her despair.

Finally Jacob spoke, his voice so low she could barely hear him.

"No. Malka, I promised the bank I would stay in business to feed the population of Dawson City as long as I could. They are counting on the Bonanza for greens and fruit mostly, and now for fresh meat. We cannot let them down. Not them, nor the bank. A promise is a promise. I am nothing if not a man of my word."

Malka nodded without emotion, understanding but not agreeing. She moved to the small settee and sat, scrunched up, pale and worn. "You think I am unfeeling about Mira?" she asked.

Jacob closed his eyes. "Of course not. That is a silly question. You are angry at the ladies of Dawson, with good reason, and you're disappointed with the town in general. No mystery there. They are stupid and insensitive." He looked at Malka. "I guess I gave them too much credit."

"I feel so tired," she said. "So tired. And oh, how I miss my little baby. . . . She brought so much joy into our house. So much laughter and fulfillment. I cannot believe she is gone. Oh, Jacob, it's so unfair."

Jacob's face filled with fury. "Fair? What the hell is fair? Where did you get that stupid idea? You work and do your best and keep the laws and hope fate is not too unkind. We're no better than anyone else, Malka. No better and hopefully no worse." He shifted in the chair and rested his elbows on his knees, head down.

"Forgive my outburst. We are both suffering. The baby was a gift and now she is gone. The best thing for us to do is comfort each other as best we can. Don't go anywhere yet,

Malka, don't leave me. Give me time to mourn. I'll be all right."

She went to the door of the parlor and said in a small voice, "I'm not sure I can."

For the next few days Malka went through the routine chores during the day and lay awake, dry-eyed, all night. She knew she was being selfish, but she could not help herself. She had nothing to give to Jacob when her own needs were bottomless.

She longed to hear from her father, but the post could never get to Russia and back this fast. She needed him more than ever, his kindness, his burly arms around her to say, "*Malkeleh, everything will be all right. You'll have more children, and this misery will pass.*" She knew all this with her head, but emotions were all she was going on now and she could not feel these truths in her heart. Then her little voice, silent since Mira's death, began to speak.

You're feeling sad, right?

I am desolate. Can you help me?

I'm not sure. This one is very complicated.

Who do I turn to?

You know who.

No, I'm not certain of anything any more.

Oh? You're going to question the Blessed One, Praised Be He?

Yes. You know the blow my faith has suffered.

I can't listen to this. I'm going.

No! Please don't leave me. I am so alone.

Oh? I thought I saw a strapping young fellow in your bed last night.

Yes. But he is suffering too, so full of misery I feel a wall between us that I can't knock down. Tell me what to do.

I suppose I could tell you, but you don't always listen.

I will listen, I promise.

Be kind. Be patient. You need each other now more than ever. Stay off your high horse for once.

I can't bear it.

You will bear it.

How?

Think of your husband.

I think of him.

So go to him, comfort him. And you will see this will work to comfort you. Mira will always be in your heart. That will be your blessing.

You guarantee it?

Work on it. No worn-out clichés will help you now. This is no time to question your faith, for it will see you through this.

You can be so cruel.

Perhaps. But it is up to you now. You're the one in charge, the only one who can bring you both peace.

When Jacob left on a routine buying trip to Skagway a week before Christmas, Malka branched out in her own business venture of packing lunches for the Dawsonites, those still making long treks to their mine sites or living far from town. She liked the conviviality in the store with the miners, at times wondering why she could be kind and outgoing with them and not with Jacob. It was some kind of defect in her own person, she was certain, like her stubbornness with her father. Try as she might, she could not overcome it.

But she enjoyed the process of creating meals, even small ones, and different kinds of sandwiches—large and small, with lettuce or without, with meat or meatless, with a piece of fruit or tomato. She invented a sauce that would keep the meal moist and tasty, and homemade cookies and small cakes that gave the box lunch personality and her own unique touch. As much as Jacob was an entrepreneur, so was Malka in her own right. Both contributed to the family income, and work gave their lives an extra dimension.

It was during this time Malka discovered she was pregnant again.

"Don't worry, my dear," said Dr. Nadler, "you'll be fine over the winter. Just don't get frisky on the icy footpaths or stay outside in the cold for too long. I know you're small, but you're also strong. You'll have a healthy baby by next August."

His little speech made Malka feel better. Nothing to worry about, he said. Nothing at all. Except that she was alone when Jacob was gone on his business trips.

By the time he hitched up the dog team, sledded out of Dawson, bought the supplies and sledded home, his trips to Skagway usually lasted two to three weeks. But this latest trip lasted far too long. Malka tore off the pages of January, then half of February. By the end of the month she was frantic. With no word about Jacob from others coming into town, she began to check daily with the Mounties who kept a log on all visitors entering or leaving Dawson City.

"Don't worry, Missy," Red Sky urged, "Jacob strong and know rough country. And if not home soon, Red Sky go look."

Grateful for his encouraging words, Malka tended to business until two weeks into February. Then she lost patience and informed Red Sky, Dove, the RCMP command post, and anyone else who would listen that she was going to look for her husband.

"Madame, that is impossible," the officer informed her. "You cannot negotiate the paths or ice in the dead of winter, nor are you skilled enough with the dogsled to make a long trip like that. I'm afraid I must keep you here."

Always an admirer of the Mounties, Malka now decided

this man was an arrogant, unfeeling dandy. How dare he be so flip with her when she needed their help so desperately?

"Don't you understand?" she asked, furious. "My husband must be injured or ill and I am helpless to know anything about it. I cannot sit and wait for the bad news. Please help me."

The Mountie explained that he was alone right now due to an unfortunate situation in the Upper Yukon gold fields and could not leave his post. "The other two officers will be returning in a week or so, and then I can go look for Mr. Finesilver."

Malka swallowed hard, thanked him, said she must make other arrangements and went back to the store. The following day Red Sky took the sled and dog team to Yellow Knife and recruited Cannibal Sam in his efforts to find Jacob. The big Indian immediately agreed to join Red Sky in the search. Red Sky had confidence in Sam, for he was not only a fine hunter and trapper and an expert on the trails, but he knew intimately the stopoff points for men adrift in the deep woods. With Red Sky's skills to augment Sam's, they were an ideal search team.

Several men in town met the two hunters at dawn at the base of Midnight Dome with extra rations and supplies. Extra fur skins were piled on the sled in case Jacob was hurt, and long knives were donated by the hardware store to fight off unfriendly animals. With lanterns hanging on the sled handles, and steaming thermoses of coffee and hot soup in their packs, the two rescuers, with a great deal of yelling to both dogs, got underway.

Malka stood in the freezing cold, wrapped in a shawl and woolen cap, her breath steaming in the heavy air. Silently she prayed to the Holy One to spare Jacob's life and to reward these kind, generous men with a successful conclusion to their task. What else can go wrong, she asked herself bitterly.

Ah, but isn't Jacob suffering, too?

I suppose.

You suppose? He is devastated. How can you be so unfeeling?

Me? Unfeeling?

Yes, you, Malka. You think you are the only mourner here. You are thoughtless and inconsiderate.

But my heart . . .

Yes, I know, it is broken. But so is his.

Why must I keep everything bottled up inside of me? It's so hard for me to share my feelings lately.

It will become easier, in time.

I hope so. I'm very unhappy with myself.

That's why you cannot feel for him. First, dear Malka, you must feel for yourself.

Pulling the shawl tightly around her, and with her tears frozen on her cheeks, Malka went home.

FORTY

cↀↇↀ

Red Sky and Cannibal Sam kept hard on the trail to Skagway for three days and nights, alternating as driver and passenger every hour, resting the dogs at regular intervals and each other during the meager warmth of the daytime sun. Although it was fifty below zero, they ran much of the time behind the sled to lighten the load for the dogs, constantly fighting against chunk ice, deep drifts and a cruel, cutting wind. Snow beleaguered the run, often blinding the two men in wind-driven whiteouts that were intense and time-consuming. Just as suddenly as a blizzard struck, the snow would turn into a fine, constant fall. They barely spoke, intent only on the road ahead. During the day, they would pause periodically for water and a chew of dried salmon or beef, then feed the dogs frozen salmon and seal blubber and turn back again to the grim journey. They were well into the fourth day, the weak February sun hanging tenuously at the horizon, when Sam recognized a torn piece of flannel shirt fluttering on a tree branch. He yelled to Red Sky to halt the sled and ran out into the snow-packed meadow well off the sled track, sinking into the snow to his thighs. Retrieving the material, he turned it over in his hands and was sick at heart to see it caked with blood. He showed it to Red Sky, who made a grim face and shook his head decisively. "I hope it not belong to Jacob, but am sure now he wore this shirt when we count cans in store."

The two men lost no time in reflection. The bloody cloth made their quest more urgent, and they set off again, the dogs straining in their harnesses, first to the east, then back-tracking in the opposite direction until it was too dark to look further.

They camped overnight by a strong fire, fed the dogs and themselves, and, with few words between them, settled in for some needed sleep. In the dim winter light of the next morning, they tried again to pick up Jacob's trail. Then Sam remembered an old shack a mile or so to the west. "Crazy Sam," he cried, slapping his forehead, "how I forget Earl's old house? You remember, Red Sky? The log house at the bend in old road to Bennet's hill?"

They shouted to the dogs and were again off at a furious pace, anxious to see if Jacob had taken refuge in Earl Ludwig's rickety cabin. For years it had been one of the main points on the trail for lost or sick travelers seeking refuge, the original owner of the old log house having died without rel-atives to file a claim. It was the first of such cabins in the search area that Sam had remembered.

When they approached the cabin, there were no foot-prints or snowshoe prints in the deep snow—a bad sign. Because it had been snowing continuously since they left Dawson, they had high hopes for evidence that someone had crawled in here seeking sanctuary from the storm. Worse, they had heard wolves howling in the nights on the trail. Signs of bears were all around them in caves and undercrop-pings of big rocks. They dared not think about it.

"Jake!" Cannibal Sam yelled. "You there?" No answer. The silence filled the air around them as disquietingly as if thunder had roared through the hill. They walked in the deep snow to the door of the cabin, finding it unlocked, as it usually was. Not a sign of habitation, no wood in the fireplace, just a small pile of cold, dead ashes. The dirty cot was unmade, ragged scraps of linen hanging half off the sides. There was a small, half-filled bag of coffee, one filthy cup, and a frozen, almost empty tube of liniment on the wobbly shelf above the cold stove. Sam grunted in disappointment and gestured to Red Sky to leave the cabin. "Jake not here. We go."

The next two days were spent in more fruitless searching, from one log hovel to the next, all empty and cold. Sam and Red Sky struggled with the elements and their own misgivings, never losing the last shreds of hope, but finding little to build on. They wished for life signs of their friend, thinking, after one long and bitterly cold night, that even Jacob's dead body would have been more comforting than this terrible emptiness of not knowing.

"Death not so bad," Sam said, picking at his dried beef, "at least we know for sure, like they say, one way or other."

Red Sky said nothing, only threw more wood on the fire and shook his head. Both men looked into the flames, thinking private, anguished thoughts.

Red Sky thought of Missy, who had put her life in his hands and pushed her way across the treacherous pass. Stubborn but relentlessly optimistic, determined to learn everything . . . he wished he could feel some of her optimism now, with this hopeless task.

He shivered at the sound of wolves howling outside, their high-pitched wails almost muffled by the winds and driving snow, and threw more kindling on the fire. The evergreen needles crackled, their sweet smoke filling the small cabin with a pleasant, mind-numbing scent.

He lay back on his sleeping bag and let his thoughts wander back to his packing days on the pass. So many of those he had taken across had been hard- bitten men eager to get to the gold fields and make their fortunes. There were the novices too, the young city men afraid for their lives but unwilling to reveal that fear to an Indian. And the young women, planning to join their husbands in Dawson City, or desperate enough to consider embarking on a career of bar-keeping or prostitution, just to be sure of a meal once in a while. It was not up to him to judge. But he had judged his Missy from the very beginning, from the first moment they met outside the outfitters shop. Thin and small she was, and trying to act as if she knew how to bargain with someone like him, an old hand at the game. Because of her strange language, he had thought her unskilled and untutored. She had been a first-rate pest, nagging and nitpicking as an old squaw. But he had also thought her wise beyond her years in many ways, especially in dealing with him. How quickly she had learned on the trail, how smart she had been to keep silent and not ask foolish questions, but learn from those who knew what they were doing.

He saw the two of them drifting down the Yukon River, slowly pulling on the oars and talking about walking on ice. They had done it, all right, lived through the rapids and that crazy would-be rapist and those who would have hung Red Sky just because he was an Indian and they thought he *could* have done the deed. And when he met Jacob at the end of that trip, though he could not help liking him, and was happy that Missy would be in such good hands, he had been sad to let her go.

The next morning Red Sky and Sam set out at dawn, into the teeth of a twenty-mile-an-hour wind, the dogs yelping with the cold. They covered each dog with blankets against the wind and rubbed their faces free of ice. When the wind died down, they entered onto a meandering trail, one that must have been an old riverbed the way it twisted and turned, with earthen banks piled high on each side. The old bed was frozen over and thick with dead branches and twigs sticking out of the ice. The dogs were agile and wanted to leap over the sharp, jagged points without pausing, but the men were careful to lead them around the obstacles. They could not afford to lose the animals to sprained or torn feet.

After a while, the riverbed emptied into an expanse of frozen meadowland. There was no dwelling or any sign of life within miles, and the searchers sat dejectedly on the sled. The two Indians made a strange sight, one almost six feet seven, the other barely over five feet. But they were a resolute duo, perfect for this challenge.

"Where to now?" Sam asked. "We got no more salmon, only little beef, and two canteens of water left. You be one to say, Red Sky, Sam too tired to talk."

Heaving a great sigh, Red Sky turned to his companion. "You go home, Sam. Red Sky stay and look for Jacob."

"Aw," Sam said, throwing down his cap, "I knew you'd say that. You close to Jake, but me too. Jake my best white man friend." He turned to look Red Sky in the eye, and said with a smile, "You soft on Missy, right? Sam not blind."

For a moment, Red Sky was angry. Then he nodded. "Missy close to Red Sky's heart. We go through hard times together. She brave lady, and Jacob good man. Cannot look Missy in the eye if we not find him. Sam, you go back if you want. But I got to find Jacob."

"That good enough for Sam. We try this old mining road off the meadow, you remember it? Line shack use for way station there? Maybe bring us luck."

They raced the dogs again into the snowy woods, this time taking a completely different direction to a cabin about twenty miles south. Red Sky knew this cabin, had used it once himself when surprised by a heavy downpour. It was on the way to a small creek, long since dried up, where old sour-doughs had washed their gold pans before the winter. Now it was just another outpost in this barbarous weather, a haven in which to wait out storms or animals.

When the sled came within thirty or forty feet of the cabin, they made a terrible discovery. Blood was everywhere. The snow covering the path to the door was splotched with it, the door frame had the imprint of a bloody hand, from which a thick line of blood trickled down the front of the door. Blood had pooled on the front step and seeped onto the frozen ground beneath. When they rushed through the door, they spied bloody footprints stumbling into the cabin, and the floor by the bed was soaked with blood. The one-room cabin looked more like an abattoir than a haven for lost travelers.

And there on the bare cot was a mangled, bloody body, hands and legs limp and torn, bent at impossible angles, with shreds of skin hanging from the bones. Red Sky ran to the cot and turned the man over. He was covered with fresh blood, the wounds still oozing, the face almost unrecognizable.

"Sam," Red Sky said through gritted teeth, "this maybe Jacob. Maybe dead."

They turned the body. Red Sky put his ear to the man's chest. "Not much air come out. Give me mirror."

Sam handed him the small mirror from the emergency backpack, and Red Sky held it to the man's lips.

"Ah!" he cried, "see mist on mirror? This man alive. I think is Jacob. We fix wounds and wash off blood to see better."

While Sam built a fire in the stove and melted snow for wash water, Red Sky wet pieces of cloth from the pack and wiped blood from the ravaged face. "Now look," he cried, "face is clean, easy to see it is Jacob, but wounds very bad and deep. Look like bear claws did this. Big bear, too."

"And still out there," Sam said grimly, reaching for his long knife and slipping it through his belt. "You fix Jacob. I look for bear."

Two hours later, Cannibal Sam returned. Red Sky had cleaned Jacob as best he could, using warm water heated on the stove and clean scraps of linen for bandages, but Jacob had not regained consciousness.

"You find bear?" he asked Sam.

"Nope. But I see tracks. And blood. And I think is not all Jacob's blood either. I think some is bear's. Look." He handed Red Sky something in his gloved hand. "This Jacob's knife. I remember from when we play cards. He always keep it by table for protection. See? Nice carving on handle."

Red Sky examined the knife and nodded. "Yes. Jacob's knife. And blood must be from bear. Jacob good at defending himself."

Sam came closer to the bed. "You think he live?" he asked.

"How Red Sky tell Missy if he dies? But not die, not long as Red Sky and Sam here, and you find us food to eat. Anyway, man at saloon give us four bottles of strong beer before we leave," Red Sky added, with a grim chuckle. "Now is a good time to drink it. So we stay here fine. When Jacob good to travel, we go home."

Sam nodded and left the cabin to look for something to shoot for supper. When he was gone, Red Sky washed Jacob's wounds and again talked to him in a low voice. "No sir, Jacob, you not make Red Sky tell Missy you dead. Red Sky rather be kicked by ten mules and dropped on head in river before he tell her news like that. You lucky man, Jacob, and me lucky, too, you betcha."

Grimly cheerful, he kept up his running commentary, trying to jog Jacob's brain into consciousness while treating the awful wounds. The bear's claws had come frighteningly close to Jacob's eyes, missing them by millimeters while tearing off pieces of his scalp, face and eyebrows. One of his arms was broken and hung limply in the shredded shirt sleeve. Red Sky fashioned a makeshift sling and pulled it tight to Jacob's body to immobilize the arm.

"You are one lucky white man," Red Sky muttered, "one lucky son-of-bitch."

Sam came in later with two rabbits and a squirrel, and they cooked the animals on sticks in the fireplace, eating in relative silence, each man aware of the fickleness of fate, knowing the man lying on the bloody bed might just as easily have been one of them. Maybe the Indians knew the lay of the land better than Jacob, or the habits and capriciously malevolent nature of hibernating bears. But they also knew Jacob had learned his lessons about the Klondike, had lived among all manner and kind of predatory animals and knew as much as they did about dogsledding in the deep winter. Luck, that's all it was. And almost as bad as luck could get.

"We sleep now," Sam said, laying out his sleeping bag on the floor by the fire. "Tomorrow, we see if Jake better." He put a hand on Red Sky's shoulder. "No worry now," Red Sky said, "Jacob too tough to die." But he kept watch as Sam unwound his long frame on the quilted bag and fell immediately asleep.

The next morning, they packed up and made for Dawson City, stopping only to fill the canteens with chunks of ice for water and to give Jacob small bites of bread. They did not sleep, preferring to travel by the light from the moon and stars. When they arrived in Dawson City, they headed straight for Father Judge's hospital. Red Sky jumped off the sled as they passed the Bonanza Market, running in to tell Malka, "We find him! Come and see!"

Later, after the doctor had set Jacob's arm and some of the smaller broken bones, and the nurse had bathed and stitched the awful wounds, Malka sat on his bed and held his hand tightly.

"Thank God," she whispered over and over, "The Holy One, Praised Be He, has saved you."

Jacob nodded. "Yes, but Red Sky and Sam deserve the credit, Malka."

"I know, but hush now," she said, "we will talk later. You must sleep."

Townspeople drifted in, wanting to see for themselves the well-liked merchant who had been snatched from death by the two intrepid Indians. If Indians could act in such a civilized way, they said, maybe there was hope for all of them. Or, some thought cynically, maybe it was all in the hope of a reward.

The hospital corridors were jammed with well-wishers and gawkers, most of the town happy to have Jacob home. With the storekeeper back among the living, they were sure to keep receiving their fresh meats and vegetables.

Two of the nurses tried to shoo everyone away, but finally gave up. It was like having a celebrity in their midst.

When Malka and Jacob were finally alone, Jacob said hoarsely, "The bear, Malka, the bear," repeating the fearful words over and over.

She put a finger to her lips. "Don't try to talk. And don't think about the bear now."

"But I must tell you," Jacob protested, trying to sit up despite the clumsy cast on his arm. "He was so big, so huge, like a building . . . like the warehouse on the riverfront, big and ugly, and mean as a Cossack, and covered with snow and mud. I must have interrupted his sleep. . . . He was raging mad, roaring at me, his eyes mean and yellow, and he smelled. . . . He stank to high heaven! I have never smelled anything so bad in my whole life. His breath . . . !" Jacob shuddered and turned to the wall.

When the doctor determined that the bones would heal straight and the wounds were not infected, Jacob was allowed to go home. It was a slow recuperation, but he had been in good shape before this last trip to Skagway, due to all the sledding trips he had made over the years to stock the market. Once the healing began, it proceeded quickly.

Malka's pregnancy went well. The doctor assured her there were no hitches or complications, and she finally heard from her father. He wrote that he was feeling good as new, the ladies in the balcony of the synagogue were still crazy about him, offering to cook and clean his house, "since his precious Malka had deserted him so cruelly." His shop was thriving, business so good he could soon be a rich man. She laughed, wondering which of these lies was the biggest.

A few days later Jacob came home early to talk to her. She recognized at once his expression, one he used when trying to seem calm. "Malka, sit down and listen. I have been talking to the merchants in Skagway about your wish to leave Dawson City, asking them to keep their ears open for another place to live and work."

Startled, Malka said, "Go on, Jacob."

"Well, I just heard about a wonderful opportunity in Winnipeg! No, no, don't say anything yet. Just hear me out. It's a store in a big city, with a nice two-story house next door. It's a clothing store, but it holds no mystery for me. A store is a store, right? I could learn about the business in no time, and this is a real city, Malka, no bears!"

He talked excitedly, hoping Malka would share his enthusiasm. This store was in western Canada, the bread basket of this wonderful big country, and with what they would get from the sale of the Bonanza, they could start over. "Say yes, Malka, please, I cannot do this without you."

Oh, yes you can, she thought to herself, you are a born adventurer, a pilgrim to the gold fields and a rover of strange lands. You can do anything you set your mind to. I know it, the whole town knows it.

Still, somewhat dismayed, she said finally, "But we've worked so hard, how can we leave it all behind? The years in the gold fields, shoveling and digging, hoping to strike it rich. What about the gold, Jacob? You wanted it so badly to help bring out your family. There won't be another chance. You never found your gold."

Jacob took Malka's face in his hands and drew her close. "I am going to bring my family here. It is already in the works. But ah, Malka, my beloved wife, don't you realize I have found my gold, more gold than any man has a right to? It was here all the time—on the beach, in the vegetable garden in the store—it could have jumped up and bitten me on the nose! No man ever lived as lucky as I am. With God's help, my dearest Malka, I have found my gold."

The End

ও৩৬৩৯

EPILOGUE

༄

THE BIG HOUSE OVERLOOKING WINNIPEG'S RED RIVER was unnaturally quiet, accustomed as it was to children playing within its huge rooms, boisterous parties in the spacious dining room, the bustle of life in a large family under its orange tiled roof. Now it stood, hushed, the children, except for one, gone their separate ways, only its master and mistress living within its sheltering walls.

Where does it go, the time? wondered the old woman, sitting on the small couch outside the master suite. How did I grow so old so soon?

She turned to her granddaughter standing near. "Leah, ask the nurse if I can go in to see Grandpa. Ask her."

Leah sat next to Malka, took her tiny hand in her own and spoke gently. "Grandma, I cannot go in the room, you know that. That nurse is a monster, but she's a good nurse. She'll come out soon. Just be patient."

Leah Finesilver was understating her opinion of the witch in white, but that was her way, especially with her grandmother. It was difficult for the old woman to accept her husband's illness. He had never been sick. After fifty years together, the loss of her beloved Jake was going to be devastating.

Malka smiled at her granddaughter's choice of words. Leah was so much like Malka's father, the straight nose, strong chin, eyes that looked at the world with candor and curiosity. All her children were handsome, she thought.

Malka finished rolling her cigarette, pulled the string on the bag of Bull Durham with her teeth, and licked the paper around the cigarette to seal it. She lit the end with a kitchen match, blowing clouds of smoke that floated to the ceiling of the sunlit hall, around the paneled hallway, the rich brown wood glossy from years of wax and care. Pictures hung on satin ropes from the carved moldings, oils on canvas of ships and landscapes, portraits of their children, and pink and red peonies in a white vase. Her favorite was Cannibal Sam's painting of the Midnight Dome, the view as she had seen it that first day. Dawson City. And Jacob waiting on the shore. She never tired of looking at it.

Dawson City, 1899. Wild, boisterous, growing on swampland between two rivers like a tenacious weed that prospers where nothing else will grow, blessed by fortune and home to anyone willing to endure the hardships of getting there and working the gold fields. How she and Jacob had worked, hope guiding their hands, need calling forth every ounce of energy they could summon.

Malka thought, now I am old and bent, with shadows and recollections for company. And Jacob will die.

The nurse appeared in the open double doors of the master suite and summoned Leah.

"The old man is dead," she said.

"Dead? But Grandma wanted to see him. Why didn't you call her in?" "He was unconscious. He wouldn't have heard her."

"That was not for you to decide," Leah snapped.

"It's what I do in most cases," the nurse said.

"This was not most cases." Leah walked back to the bench, trembling with anger. She sat next to her grandmother. "He's gone, Grandma. Grandpa Jake is gone."

"I know."

Leah's expression almost made Malka laugh.

"Oh, dear Leah, don't look so shocked. When you have been together as long as Jacob and me, you know these things."

Leah put her arms around Malka and hugged her.

"I'm so sorry, I'm so sorry."

"Yes. Of course you are. Now I am going in to say good-bye. No," she said, as Leah rose with her, "Both of you stay here. What I have to say to Grandpa Jake is only for him to hear." Malka smiled impishly. "Very private words, Leah, you understand."

Jacob was lying so still under the sheet. Malka caught her breath and closed her eyes, and said the *Kaddish*. When she finished, she pulled the sheet down from his face and looked at Jacob for the last time.

"Oh, Jacob," she said, "we had a good life. Weren't we lucky, Jacob? To find each other among all the men and women in the wide world? I loved you with all my heart. So tall and handsome you were, your blue eyes looking through me that day we finally met. A little jealous of Red Sky, eh? Oh, I knew. You didn't fool me. And I was pleased, did you know that?"

She gave a little laugh. Fumbling for Jacob's hand under the sheet, she held it, stroking it, the odd hand with the missing little finger.

"Now that was a story," she told him, "and I'll tell you something . . . I could hardly believe it! But our lives were like that. Unbelievable. We did things no one does anymore. It's a different world. I'm not sure it's better, but it *is* different."

She closed her eyes. Tears streamed down her wrinkled face. Without letting go of his hand, she sat for a long time, sometimes in silence, sometimes crooning a little melody, rocking back and forth.

"I love you, Jacob, I love you," she said. "I love you."

Wedding Picture of Jacob and Malka

ACKNOWLEDGEMENTS

I WOULD LIKE TO THANK MY HUSBAND, ARMAND, AND my family, whose support and faith in me never wavered. I also appreciate the help from the dedicated scholars in the Yukon Archives in White Horse, Canada.